**Praise for the novels of *New York Times*
bestselling author Lynn Kurland**

One Magic Moment

"Stepping into one of Lynn Kurland's time-travel novels is definitely one magic moment in itself . . ."　　—*All About Romance*

"A sweet, tenderhearted time-travel romance . . . Lynn Kurland makes you want to find one of those infamous gateways to the past and find your very own knight in shining armor!"
　　　　　　　　　　　　　　　　　　—*Joyfully Reviewed*

"A story on an epic scale with humor and clever dialogue . . . Kurland has written another time-travel marvel where the reader will be just as enchanted by the hero as the heroine is . . . Perfect for those looking for a happily ever after."　　—*RT Book Reviews*

One Enchanted Evening

"Kurland presents another triumphant romance . . . Readers unfamiliar with her works will have great joy and ease in following the story . . . and longtime readers will exult in having more familial pieces fall into place."　　　　　　　　　—*Fresh Fiction*

"A perfect blend of medieval intrigue and time-travel romance. I was totally enthralled from the beginning to the end."
　　　　　　　　　　　　　　　　　—*Once Upon a Romance*

"Woven with magic, handsome heroes, lovely heroines, oodles of fun, and plenty of romance . . . a typical Lynn Kurland book—beautifully written with an enchanting, entertaining, and just plain wonderful story line."　　　—*Romance Reviews Today*

continued . . .

Till There Was You

"Expertly mixes past with present to prove that love endures all things and outlasts almost everything, including time itself. With an eye to detail and deliciously vivid imagery, this paranormal tale of matchmaking comes fully to life . . . Spellbinding and lovely, this is one story readers won't want to miss."
—*Romance Reader at Heart*

"A fantastic story that will delight both readers who are familiar with the families and those who aren't."
—*Romance Reviews Today* (Perfect 10 Award)

"An amusing time-travel romance starring a terrific, fully developed hero whose good intentions, present and past, are devastated by love . . . fast-paced." —*Midwest Book Review*

With Every Breath

"As always, [Kurland] delivers a delightful read!"
—*RT Book Reviews* (4 stars)

"Kurland is a skilled enchantress . . . *With Every Breath* is breathtaking in its magnificent scope, a true invitation to the delights of romance." —*Night Owl Reviews*

When I Fall in Love

"Kurland infuses her polished writing with a deliciously dry wit, and her latest time-travel love story is sweetly romantic and thoroughly satisfying." —*Booklist*

"The continuation of a wonderful series, this story can also be read alone. It's an extremely good book." —*Affaire de Coeur*

Much Ado in the Moonlight

"A pure delight." —*Huntress Book Reviews*

"A consummate storyteller . . . [Kurland] will keep the reader on the edge of their seat, unable to put the book down until the very last word." —*ParaNormal Romance*

Dreams of Stardust

"Kurland weaves another fabulous read with just the right amounts of laughter, romance, and fantasy." —*Affaire de Coeur*

"Kurland crafts some of the most ingenious time-travel romances readers can find . . . wonderfully clever and completely enchanting." —*RT Book Reviews*

A Garden in the Rain

"Kurland laces her exquisitely romantic, utterly bewitching blend of contemporary romance and time travel with a delectable touch of tart wit, leaving readers savoring every word of this superbly written romance." —*Booklist*

"Kurland is clearly one of romance's finest writers—she consistently delivers the kind of stories readers dream about. Don't miss this one." —*The Oakland Press*

From This Moment On

"A disarming blend of romance, suspense, and heartwarming humor, this book is romantic comedy at its best." —*Publishers Weekly*

"A deftly plotted delight, seasoned with a wonderfully wry sense of humor and graced with endearing, unforgettable characters." —*Booklist*

My Heart Stood Still

"Written with poetic grace and a wickedly subtle sense of humor . . . romance with characters readers will come to care about and a love story they will cherish." —*Booklist*

If I Had You

"A passionate story filled with danger, intrigue, and sparkling dialogue." —*Rendezvous*

continued . . .

The More I See You

"The superlative Ms. Kurland once again wows her readers with her formidable talent as she weaves a tale of enchantment that blends history with spellbinding passion and impressive characterization, not to mention a magnificent plot." —*Rendezvous*

Another Chance to Dream

"Kurland creates a special romance between a memorable knight and his lady." —*Publishers Weekly*

The Very Thought of You

"A masterpiece . . . this fabulous tale will enchant anyone who reads it." —*Painted Rock Reviews*

This Is All I Ask

"Both powerful and sensitive . . . a wonderfully rich and rewarding book." —Susan Wiggs

ALL FOR YOU

LYNN KURLAND

JOVE BOOKS, NEW YORK

THE BERKLEY PUBLISHING GROUP
Published by the Penguin Group
Penguin Group (USA) Inc.
375 Hudson Street, New York, New York 10014, USA

Penguin Group (Canada), 90 Eglinton Avenue East, Suite 700, Toronto, Ontario M4P 2Y3, Canada
(a division of Pearson Penguin Canada Inc.) • Penguin Books Ltd., 80 Strand, London WC2R 0RL,
England • Penguin Group Ireland, 25 St. Stephen's Green, Dublin 2, Ireland (a division of Penguin
Books Ltd.) • Penguin Group (Australia), 250 Camberwell Road, Camberwell, Victoria 3124, Australia
(a division of Pearson Australia Group Pty. Ltd.) • Penguin Books India Pvt. Ltd., 11 Community
Centre, Panchsheel Park, New Delhi—110 017, India • Penguin Group (NZ), 67 Apollo Drive,
Rosedale, Auckland 0632, New Zealand (a division of Pearson New Zealand Ltd.) • Penguin Books
(South Africa) (Pty.) Ltd., 24 Sturdee Avenue, Rosebank, Johannesburg 2196, South Africa

Penguin Books Ltd., Registered Offices: 80 Strand, London WC2R 0RL, England

This is a work of fiction. Names, characters, places, and incidents either are the product of the author's
imagination or are used fictitiously, and any resemblance to actual persons, living or dead, business
establishments, events, or locales is entirely coincidental. The publisher does not have control over
and does not have any responsibility for author or third-party websites or their content.

ALL FOR YOU

A Jove Book / published by arrangement with Kurland Book Productions, Inc.

PUBLISHING HISTORY
Jove mass-market edition / May 2012

Copyright © 2012 by Kurland Book Productions, Inc.
Cover art by Jim Griffin.
Cover handlettering by Ron Zinn.
Cover design by George Long.

All rights reserved.
No part of this book may be reproduced, scanned, or distributed in any printed or
electronic form without permission. Please do not participate in or encourage piracy of
copyrighted materials in violation of the author's rights. Purchase only authorized editions.
For information, address: The Berkley Publishing Group,
a division of Penguin Group (USA) Inc.,
375 Hudson Street, New York, New York 10014.

ISBN: 978-0-515-15065-0

JOVE®
Jove Books are published by The Berkley Publishing Group,
a division of Penguin Group (USA) Inc.,
375 Hudson Street, New York, New York 10014.
JOVE® is a registered trademark of Penguin Group (USA) Inc.
The "J" design is a trademark of Penguin Group (USA) Inc.

PRINTED IN THE UNITED STATES OF AMERICA

10 9 8 7 6 5 4 3 2 1

If you purchased this book without a cover, you should be aware that this book is
stolen property. It was reported as "unsold and destroyed" to the publisher, and neither the
author nor the publisher has received any payment for this "stripped book."

ALWAYS LEARNING   PEARSON

ALL FOR YOU

Chapter 1

If life were a set of scales, Peaches Alexander could safely say that Fate had just dumped a load of bricks on the opposite balance.

She didn't like the feeling of being flung off the proverbial pan and not so much into the fire but up into the air without a clue as to where she would land. She liked being in control of her life, having her ducks in a row, her shoes organized by color, her spices waiting obediently in the cabinet, secure in their alphabetical sorting. This business of having events spiral out of control without her permission was just not in her plans.

She scowled. Very well, so she'd been needing a bit of a change. She had known for quite a while that she was just marking time and not using her gifts. But having Fate tinkering with things to this extent, well, this was not at all to her liking.

She stood in the courtyard of her sister's castle and looked around, frowning and wishing there was somewhere she could hide until she'd figured out how she was going to get out of her current mess. She had already gone for a run that morning, but that had felt less like clearing her head and more like scampering away from her problems. No, she needed something constructive to do with her hands so her mind could work on other more pressing problems.

She looked toward the gatehouse and saw her salvation. She walked across the finely laid stone and winter-brittle grass and stopped in front of the door leading to her sister's prop room. Since it was really nothing more than a big closet—and she was used to organizing big closets—it would provide not only the hiding place she needed but a very welcome distraction. She didn't dare hope that while she was there she would manage to distract herself from Fate's handiwork that she held in her hand.

A very thick stack of faxes spelling the end of her life as she knew it.

She walked into the former guardroom and had to pause for a moment and admire. That she was standing in what centuries before would have been a rather fragrant haunt of the front-gate guards was actually rather amazing. It was all due to her twin sister, who had decided to come to Cambridge to study, then remained in England long enough to find herself the owner of a castle boasting a guardroom turned into a prop room for the use of guests that wanted to pretend they were going back in time and thought dressing the part might help the process.

Peaches had her own thoughts on the notion of pretending to travel through time and what sorts of *accoutrements* might be necessary, but she supposed it would be wise to just let those thoughts continue on into the realm of the ridiculous where they belonged.

She glanced at the faxes in her hand, then set them down on a trunk near the door. She knew what they said; reading them again would only get her stirred up. There was plenty to keep her busy, most notably in that long rack of men's costumes she'd almost finished arranging before she had decamped for France to leave her sister and her new husband a bit of privacy. She was happy to see that everything was where it should have been.

Well, everything but the notable exception of a medieval-style tabard bearing a black lion rampant who looked down his nose superciliously from a turquoise blue eye.

Peaches scowled as she returned the feisty lion to its rightful place. She knew who had worn *that* the last time around. That he had failed, in spite of his academic credentials and apparent ability to organize all sorts of interesting facts and tweed suit coats, to put it back where it went didn't surprise her in the least.

She continued to grumble about the inconsiderate nature of some people as she worked her way down the rack to the end. She looked at the various types of hats sitting on the shelf above her, turned away, then stopped and looked back. She reached and pulled down a Scottish cap with some sort of creature holding a bone in its mouth. She was certainly no expert in heraldry, but she was quite proficient in translating Latin thanks to a rather austere upbringing at her aunt Edna's. *Audentes Fortuna Juvat*.

Fortune favors the bold. Too bad she wasn't feeling particularly bold at the moment, in direct contrast to the McKinnon who had chosen that as his clan motto. She knew all the clan mottos because along with a copy of Burke's Peerage she had appropriated from Aunt Edna's vast library of obscure and dusty books, she had also memorized the contents of a very small tome on Scottish clans. Who would have thought any of it would come in handy—

A hanger squeaked.

Peaches froze, rolled her eyes, then blew out her breath and put her shoulders back. There was absolutely nothing odd about what she'd just heard because she was in a room full of hangers that could possibly have squeaked. The castle was drafty. In fact, she wasn't altogether sure she hadn't been talking to herself and that certainly would have set up enough moving hot air that a hanger could have—

The hanger squeaked again.

All right, now that was taking things too far. She wasn't above entertaining the thought of paranormal activity in her sister's castle for reasons she didn't care to examine too closely at the moment, but the thought of entertaining said activity *now* was anything but entertaining. She had important things to contemplate, solutions to come up with, her entire life that she was holding together with a very thin thread to gather up and wrap up a bit tighter before it completely exploded around her.

Unfortunately, she had the feeling she wasn't going to have a say in current events because the uncomfortable truth was that while Sedgwick might have been overlooked on a few Supernatural British Locales lists, she could personally verify that it was haunted.

By, for example, the red-haired, bekilted Scotsman standing ten feet from her with his hand on a hanger, apparently using quite a bit of energy to wiggle it—and the tabard draped over it—around. She didn't really want to have a little tête-à-tête with a ghost, but when in England . . .

"Is it heavy?" she asked, because it was the first thing that came to mind.

"Nay, but 'tis an Englishman's tabard," he said, breathing heavily. "I'm breathless with distaste."

She almost laughed, but then she realized just which Englishman's tabard the ghost was shaking and her amusement vanished abruptly. Even from where she stood, she could see that rearing lion of Artane eyeing her with disapproval. She pursed her lips.

"I can understand your feelings there," she said.

"'Tis a good family," the ghost said. "For Englishmen, that is." He looked at her and scrunched up his face. "Don't ye think?"

His purposeful look was profoundly unsettling. She would have preferred to believe he had simply taken hold of a random hanger, but the way he was hanging on to it as though his continued existence depended on it led her to believe the selection was a deliberate one.

"You do realize that's the de Piaget crest," she said, on the off chance he didn't.

The ghost looked at what he'd recently stopped shaking, then looked back at her. He blinked in surprise that wasn't at all innocent. "Why, lass, I believe it is."

"Why did you pick that one?" she demanded.

He shifted nervously. "Weel, ye see, lass, with ye being as yet unwed . . ." He peered at her from under bushy red eyebrows. "Do ye see?"

Peaches felt her mouth fall open. "Are you *matchmaking*?" she asked in astonishment.

"Shhh," he hissed frantically, doffing his cap and clutching it with his free hand. "What would the other shades think if they knew?"

"They would think I was the most sensible mortal they'd ever encountered because I'd told you I wouldn't be interested in anyone from that family if he were the last eligible bachelor on the planet."

The ghost blinked. "Are ye meaning young Stephen de Piaget?"

"That's the one," she said grimly. "I have no doubt that women all over the island are sighing in relief that he doesn't have a twin."

"To vex them with his handsomeness?" the ghost ventured.

Peaches suppressed a snort. "It isn't exactly his handsomeness he would be vexing them with, but maybe we should just not speculate on what that certain something might be."

The ghost wore a perplexed frown and his mouth worked silently, as if he repeated her words to attempt to unravel their meaning. Peaches would have given him a hand by enumerating for him the future Earl of Artane's numerous flaws, but she was interrupted by the sound of the door opening behind her. She turned and found her sister standing just inside the door, looking hesitant.

At least she wasn't looking terrified. Peaches glanced over her shoulder and saw the reason why. The ghost had disappeared, no doubt to spare his proprietress any undue distress. Peaches was happy to see him go, especially if it meant she didn't have to discuss the last de Piaget bachelor again. She walked over to her sister and realized with a start that Tess's face had a rather green tinge to it. Peaches reached out and put her hand on her sister's arm.

"What's wrong?" she asked in surprise. "Did something happen to you?"

Tess took a deep breath. "Unfortunately—but no, not to me or John."

Peaches frowned. She had just seen a ghost in a kilt. How much worse could it get than that? "I'm sure it can't be all that bad," she said easily.

"Oh, it could," Tess said. She took a deep breath. "I have a confession to make."

Peaches smiled. "What terrible thing did you do?"

Tess sat down on the trunk. She didn't seem to notice she had sat down on that rather thick stack of faxes. "It's a long story with an interesting ending."

"I can hardly wait to hear it."

"Well, it starts with you forgetting your cell phone when you went to France."

Peaches shrugged. "I left it behind on purpose." She had left her phone behind because when one was having a time-out from life, it was best to do it unplugged. Tess had had the holiday rental office's number for emergencies, which had seemed like more than enough accessibility.

Tess shifted uncomfortably. "Well, I didn't think your phone should go unanswered." She paused. "So I answered it."

Peaches resisted the urge to scratch her head. She knew her sister was gearing up to tell her something she obviously considered important, but she couldn't for the life of her figure out what that something might be. She didn't have a boyfriend to dump, or a landlord to appease, or rational clients to deal with. All she had was a collection of loonies who had apparently decided to jettison her *en masse* via the aforementioned faxes. None of that explained what had left Tess looking so green. She studied her sister for another moment or two, then frowned again. "Did you say something to a client?"

"I didn't say anything," Tess said quickly. Then she paused. "Well, I tried not to say anything."

Peaches sat down abruptly on the trunk, crunching the parts of the faxes her sister hadn't already done damage to. Things were getting clearer, but not more pleasant. "Who did you not say anything to?"

"Whom," Tess said miserably.

Peaches found it in her to glare. "*Whom* did you not say anything to?"

"Brandalyse Stevens."

Peaches felt the room begin to spin. She suddenly found herself with her head between her knees. That didn't help any, and it was exacerbated by Tess's unwillingness to let her up.

"I tried my best," Tess said, sounding rather faint herself, "I really did. But when she started in on your coming back to England and not being there to help her sort her thongs . . . well, I had to say something." Tess paused. "I suppose I probably shouldn't have started off by telling her she had a stupid name."

"Probably not," Peaches wheezed. So much for hoping all the communiqués she was sitting on were just a bad joke. "And?"

"I told her it was probably about time she learned to sort her own damn thongs." Tess began to pat her absently on the back. "And really, Peach, once I started, I couldn't seem to stop myself."

Peaches fumbled behind her for her sister's hand only because Tess was getting a little too enthusiastic in her patting. She thought she might have bruises soon. She sat up, waited until the stars cleared, then leaned her head carefully back against the stone and looked at her sister. It was difficult to believe that Tess had been the catalyst for the utter ruination of a very large part of her life, but it was very hard to deny.

"You couldn't stop yourself?"

Tess shook her head slowly.

"What else did you say?" she managed.

"I'm afraid I might have expressed an opinion or two on how many great guys Brandalyse has stolen from me—er, *you*, rather, because I was pretending to be you. That took a while."

Peaches closed her eyes briefly. "Great."

"I also might have insulted her blog."

"Did you criticize font or content?"

"I told her that her font was ugly and the pictures of all the interiors she'd designed were Photoshopped." Tess swallowed convulsively. "She asked me if that was it."

"And you told her no, that wasn't it, because she had the single worst highlight job you'd ever seen and that it really showed up on camera during every morning show she did." Peaches looked at her sister. "Is that about right?"

Tess's eyes widened. "How'd you know?"

Peaches pulled the stack of papers from beneath herself and her sister, then handed the top one to Tess. On it was scrawled, *My roots don't show on camera, you stupid—*

Tess frowned. "Her language is rather salty."

"You should see the others."

"I'm not sure I want to." She looked at Peaches. "I'm so desperately sorry."

"So am I," Peaches said. "That I didn't get to hear it."

"I recorded it."

"Then what's there to complain about?" She thought about tossing all the faxes into the air in a defiant gesture of freedom, then thought better of it because the only thing that would accomplish would be leaving her a mess to clean up.

Tess took the faxes from her, then flipped through them. That took quite a while, but that was because Peaches had quite a long client list.

Had had, rather.

She leaned back against the cold stone wall of her sister's guardroom and contemplated her life. There were several truths to examine at present, and since she had quite a bit of time on her hands—that stack of faxes was rather thick, after all—she thought she would take advantage of it.

The thing was, she needed a change. She'd known for quite some time that she'd needed a change. She just hadn't expected that she would get the particular level of help she was getting at the moment to make that change.

Tess looked up. "Peach, these are all your clients—"

"I'll find new ones," Peaches said with a casualness she didn't feel. "No problem."

"I don't want to pry," Tess began slowly, "but—"

"I have plenty of money," Peaches said, hoping to cut Tess off before she asked for any details. Unfortunately, her sister was who she was and details were her specialty.

"How much is plenty?"

Peaches took a deep breath. "Almost three thousand dollars."

Tess blinked. "You mean almost thirty thousand."

"No," Peaches said, trying to sound cheerful but failing. "You know how I always tell people, *Never do business with friends*? Well, apparently there really is something to that."

"Peaches," Tess said, aghast. "What happened?"

"Oh, this and that," Peaches said. "A few bad investments in start-ups. The occasional dip into retirement funds to help out a friend in need." *Giving my PIN to a trusted guy friend who wasn't a husband.* "The usual."

Tess bowed her head for a moment or two, then looked at Peaches. "You'll stay here until you decide what to do, for as long as it takes."

"I can't," Peaches said miserably. "I thought my visa was a done deal, but I got a letter yesterday—"

"John knows a guy who knows some guys," Tess interrupted her. "They'll take care of it."

Peaches imagined they would. John did, after all, have some

particular immigration issues that would have definitely required the services of a guy.

"I'm going back to the house now," Tess said, sounding suddenly very far away. "I'll go stir up some powdered grass drink for you."

Peaches looked at her sister. She was standing within reach, but somehow she sounded like she was in another world. She nodded, because she knew that was what she was supposed to do. What she wanted to do was burst into tears, but she knew that wouldn't accomplish anything. And she wasn't a crier; she was a gulper. If she had a nickel for every time she'd gulped, put her shoulders back, and soldiered on, she wouldn't have minded at all that she was holding on to a stack of faxes that spelled the end of her comfortable, balanced life in the States. The only client she had left was Roger Peabody, who only hired her to come clean out his office so she would be forced to look at the illustrated charts hanging on his walls detailing the benefits of her becoming his wife.

She looked again to find Tess gone. She wasn't sure when that had happened, which probably should have worried her. She couldn't even bring herself to look through the stack of faxes again. Anyone who believed Brandalyse Stevens probably wasn't really the client for her.

And perhaps, in the end, Fate was shoving her in the right direction.

She pushed herself to her feet, ignored the final twitch of hanger, then walked toward the door. It was open from where Tess had gone through it, which struck her as spooky for some reason. She would have paused to analyze why, but decided it was a bad idea. Maybe later, when she had gone at least twelve hours without seeing any sort of paranormal activity.

She walked through the barbican tunnel and stopped on the edge of Tess's courtyard. It was nothing out of the ordinary, that stopping. She had stopped either in the same place or near to it dozens of times before and spent an equal number of times looking at the courtyard in front of her.

Only during none of those dozens of times had she ever had the feeling of destiny come over her as it was coming over her now.

What if . . . what if she had the courage to acknowledge what it was she really wanted?

Audentes Fortuna Juvat.

The thought of it almost stole her breath. She stood on the edge of her sister's medieval courtyard, struggling to breathe normally, and realized that the time had come for her to make a decision.

Her dream, or more of her life spent putting that dream off.

It wasn't what she should have been thinking about given the fact that her life was lying in ruins around her. She should have been coming up with a life plan, not thinking about the residual effects left in her heart from too many of Aunt Edna's Barbara Cartland romances hidden behind dust jackets of Dostoyevsky and Voltaire. Of *course* she'd taken none of it truly seriously—

Not until one particular evening in spring when she'd been studying for the last finals of her undergrad career.

It had been a lovely night and she'd taken her notes out onto a bench near the quad in front of the library. A couple had been standing there in the middle of that space, bickering lightly about something, when the girl had turned and walked away. Peaches hadn't wanted to eavesdrop, but if they were willing to carry on their affairs in public, she hadn't supposed they cared who watched them.

The guy had run after the girl and caught her by the hand.

And time had slowed to a crawl.

Peaches had watched as he'd gone down on one knee. She had no idea what he'd said, but she'd watched him pull something out of his pocket and slip it on his girlfriend's finger. The girl had started to cry. And then her newly minted fiancé had taken her by the hand, pulled her into his arms, and begun to dance with her.

As if by magic, a violinist had appeared on the edge of that very pedestrian quad and begun to play a waltz.

The magic in the air had been palpable. Peaches had forgotten about her notes and simply stared, openmouthed, at the most romantic thing she had ever witnessed in the entirety of her life—in and out of a book.

The girl had looked around her in wonderment, then stared up at her fiancé with the same expression. "Why?" she had asked.

He had only shrugged with a slight smile. "It's all for you," he had said. "Isn't that reason enough?"

And Peaches had known then exactly what she had wanted: a man who would look at her, love her in spite of her flaws, then sink to one knee and ask her to spend the rest of her life with him.

The violin was, of course, optional.

She looked up into a rare clear winter sky and sighed. That sort of fairy tale had happened for her twin sister, who had walked away with a great guy and a castle. It had happened for her younger sister, who'd had a bit of dancing, a great guy, and a slightly older castle.

But it hadn't happened for her.

She wanted it to. And while she was wishing for the impossible, she decided she wanted the entire fairy tale. She wanted a guy to fall instantly in love with her, then cross through a sea of ultra-gorgeous would-be girlfriends and ask her to dance. And then after they'd danced, she wanted a wedding with a foofy cake and lots of food that probably couldn't be classified as healthy, an orchestra for their first dance, and then a carriage to climb into and ride off in with her prince to a fairy-tale castle that boasted running water and an Aga in the kitchen.

Peaches had to admit she wondered if she were crazy. Worse still, she didn't dare bounce the idea off Tess on the off chance that she was really losing it and Tess felt compelled—as she apparently had with Brandalyse Stevens—to tell her so.

"Excuse me, miss—"

Peaches whirled around to find a liveried servant standing there.

She felt her mouth fall open. All right, so he was just a delivery guy. He had on a tie and a cap and looked fairly official. She put her hand on the stone of Tess's castle wall to steady herself. It was obviously just something for Tess, but that didn't make her knees any less weak.

"Yes?"

"A delivery for Miss Peaches Alexander, care of the Lady of Sedgwick, Sedgwick Castle."

Peaches looked at the large white envelope he held out and felt something shudder to a halt. It might have been her heart, but she could still hear that pounding in her ears. It might have been a sonic boom above her head. It might have been Fate standing behind her shoving her really hard in the small of the back to get her to step forward.

She reached out with a shaking hand and took the envelope. As an afterthought, she patted herself for something to give the messenger, but found only a pair of breath mints and her cell phone. The younger man shook his head with a smile.

"I've been well paid, thanks."

She nodded and watched him walk away. She looked at the envelope, then flipped it over to look at the seal. It was tempting to hurry inside and dig out that book on English genealogy she'd put in her suitcase on a whim and see to whom the seal belonged. She decided that maybe the insides would reveal the same, so she very carefully lifted the wax up and opened the envelope. She pulled out a gilt-edged invitation and read.

Miss Peaches Alexander, you are hereby invited to a ball . . .

Peaches read the rest, realizing with a start that it was from David, the Duke of Kenneworth. The gorgeous, perfect, eminently available Duke of Kenneworth. She had just begun to hyperventilate when her phone rang. It continued to ring as she struggled to get it out of her pocket. She dropped it twice before she managed to answer it.

"Hello?"

"Peaches, it's Andrea."

Peaches blinked, trying to clear the fog from her brain. "Um—"

"Andrea Preston? David's cousin? Remember, we met at that house party at Payneswick earlier this month?"

"Oh, Andrea," Peaches managed faintly. "Of course."

"Did you get the invitation from David? I told you I was sure he would send it, judging by how he couldn't keep his eyes off you." She paused. "You remember, don't you?"

"Of course," Peaches managed, but at the moment she could hardly remember who Andrea was.

Actually, that wasn't true. She remembered Andrea and she most definitely remembered her cousin David. She might have remembered more, but she'd spent that Regency house party avoiding Stephen de Piaget and worrying that Tess was going to get herself killed before the weekend was over. She remembered sending Tess off back to Sedgwick and going to London with a trio of interior designers who had dragged her to a week's worth of parties with other designer types, which had convinced her that design was not her thing.

"He thought you were gorgeous, of course," Andrea said without a hint of envy. "That's why he wanted your address from me, so he could invite you to the house party next weekend. It's a silly Cinderella sort of thing, but I'm definitely going. The number of rich men who'll be there is vast, of course. Having David's sister there is a bit pants, but what can you do?"

Peaches agreed there was really nothing to be done about the absolute pantsitude of having David's sister there—a woman she most definitely couldn't remember—listened to Andrea continue to be excited for a moment or two, then managed to get off the phone with a promise to call back when the second communiqué arrived with all the details about the weekend itself.

Peaches carefully put her phone in her pocket, then looked out over the grassy courtyard and tried to identify the sensation she was experiencing.

It was a fluttering.

In the vicinity of her heart.

She was tempted to immediately list all the reasons it was ridiculous and then make another list of things she could do to bring herself back to reality, but for the first time in seven years, she took her sensible mental shoes and chucked them out the window. She would wear dangerously high heels, blow some money on a decent dress, and indulge herself in the fairy tale. Just for the weekend.

What could it hurt?

She held out her arms and spun, just twice, in the middle of the courtyard. She would have spun around more than that, but spinning made her dizzy so she thought it might be prudent to stop while she was still functional. She opened her eyes in unfortunately the exact spot where that Scottish ghost was loitering, just outside the prop room door. She quickly gathered her dignity, made him a brief wave, then turned and walked to the hall. She knew what sort of tabard he would be shaking at her and it wouldn't be a Kenneworth-inspired one.

At least she could reasonably expect that Stephen de Piaget wouldn't be at her fairy-tale weekend. She didn't know much about David Preston, but she had heard that he and Stephen weren't exactly on friendly terms. And why, when Stephen was only interested in musty old medieval texts?

She studiously ignored the fact that her sister Tess was also interested in musty old medieval texts but managed to stay insanely gorgeous and sexy.

Stephen probably not only went to sleep soothed by Gregorian chant, he no doubt donned tweed pajamas before he did so. He was not gorgeous, not charming, and he absolutely did not pad across any floor that had to endure him like a jaguar stalking its prey.

And she was not and had never, ever been interested in having any of his attentions.

She flipped her hair over her shoulder because it was a very symbolic way of putting him and his unattractive self behind her so she could move on to greener and more handsome prince-ish sorts of pastures.

Miss Peaches Alexander has been invited to a ball . . .

She could hardly believe it, but maybe dreams really did come true.

Chapter 2

Stephen de Piaget stood in the freezing drizzle, shaking with weariness, and wondered what in the hell had ever possessed him to get any closer to medieval mores than could be found in any number of lovely texts in the handcrafted bookcases in his office at Cambridge. He really should have left chivalry, swordplay, and the accompanying trappings of both safely in a book.

"Had enough, friend?"

Stephen looked at his sparring partner, the thoroughly evil and apparently indefatigable Ian MacLeod, and grimaced. "Not yet."

"Then hoist your feeble English sword, man, and let's have another go. I'll try not to leave you in tears today."

Stephen refrained from pointing out that it was a Claymore he was hoisting, which Ian well knew, not a feeble English sword. He also refused to acknowledge the rest of the taunt, for he never wept. He might have cursed a time or two in a gentlemanlike fashion, but tears? Never, not even when his younger brother Gideon—younger by a mere eleven months, as it happened—had blown cornering the entire UK telecommunications market.

"Thinking about what they'll put on your headstone?" Ian drawled.

"Skiing in the Alps, actually," Stephen lied politely. "And how unfortunate it is I'm only able to take time for a pair of trips each season instead of loitering there all year round to keep the old family seat visible."

Ian laughed. "You're a bloody snob. I can scarce believe I allow you through my gates. It must be the pleasure of humiliating an Englishman."

Stephen would have assured Ian that the pleasure of that most certainly wouldn't be his that day, but the truth was, he was facing a master at his craft and he wasn't completely certain Ian's words wouldn't be prophetic.

It turned out to be, he had to admit, a very long morning. Ian MacLeod had an inexhaustible supply of not only insults but skill, and he was apparently committed to trotting out both for Stephen's benefit. The only thing that kept Stephen from calling peace at least once—very well, several times—was pride. He was standing on Scottish soil, listening to an endless stream of Scottish battle dirges played by someone he couldn't see, and he was facing a Scot who from all indications hadn't learned his craft along with passing his O Levels. There was national pride to consider—along with his own, of course.

He felt, finally, that perhaps a small rest could be called, that he might be permitted to satisfy his curiosity. He rested the flat of his sword against his shoulder and frowned thoughtfully. "What is that recording?" he asked. "The Lone Piper at the Tattoo playing all his favorite tunes?"

Ian laughed. "'Tis no recording, my lad. That's Robert Mac-Leod."

"Who?"

Ian pointed to his right. "Our clan piper. In the olden days, of course."

Stephen shut his mouth when he realized it had been hanging open. After all, he knew he shouldn't have been surprised by anything he found on MacLeod soil.

He'd known Ian MacLeod and his cousins James and Patrick MacLeod for what was going on ten years now. He'd been a fairly brash young man in his twenties when he'd first headed north, extremely proud of his academic successes at Cambridge and looking for some way to expend a bit of energy. He'd heard rumors of some nutter in the Highlands who taught swordplay and felt compelled to investigate.

It had seemed strange to him then—and still did, actually—how many medieval activities a body could find to engage in with hardly any effort at all, but since that suited his purposes, he never complained. He had simply made an appointment with Ian MacLeod, hopped in his car and ventured north, then felt the hair on his arms stand up when he'd set foot on MacLeod soil.

He wasn't unaccustomed to dealing with intimidating people, but Ian MacLeod had been a different animal entirely. It wasn't merely that he'd looked as if he could have easily defended himself in any darkened alley, though that had been impressive in itself. Stephen hadn't been able to lay his finger on just what that something was until he'd walked out Ian's back door. Calling the space beyond that a garden hadn't done it any justice. If he hadn't known better at the time, he would have called it a rough Scottish interpretation of medieval lists.

That had been rather odd, truth be told.

Beyond that space had been an arena where no expense had been spared for the comfort and safety for what Stephen had immediately identified as very, very expensive Brazilian war horses. Those Lusitanos had been housed next to sturdy Highland mountain horses without any apparent worry over the dichotomy.

Stephen had realized two things that first day. The first, as he'd watched Ian MacLeod draw the six-foot Claymore from the scabbard on his back, was that he was profoundly out of his depth.

The second was there was no way in hell that MacLeod lad had learned his swordplay from a DVD.

"You're daydreaming, Stevie," Ian called cheerfully. "Or has Jamie's piper given you a start you can't recover from?"

Stephen realized he was standing in Ian's training field, simply staring off into the distance. Or, rather, staring at the Highlander—in full dress, no less—standing a hundred yards away with his kilt swaying with a wind that troubled nothing else. He suppressed a shiver, then turned to Ian. "We have paranormal oddities at Artane."

"Ah, but can they play the pipes like that?"

Stephen smiled briefly. "I'm afraid they can't. The ghosts in my father's hall just hide in alcoves and bellow 'boo' as the mood strikes."

Ian laughed. "I imagine they do, my friend." He resheathed his sword, then stretched his hands over his head until his knuckles popped. "Well, when shall we meet again?"

"Perhaps when my ego has recovered from this thrashing," Stephen said dryly.

Ian paused, then looked at him seriously. "'Twasn't a thrashing, Stephen. Not this time. Well," he added with a bit of a laugh, "not entirely. But for a lad who didn't have the benefit of either a father or an uncle to put a sword into his wee hands when he was a babe, you've done fairly well. Of course, you'll never best me, but no one does."

"Not even James MacLeod?"

"Jamie?" Ian asked with a snort. "Are you daft? He scarce remembers what end of his sword is the dangerous one, though with him both ends are perilous to his soft hands." He smiled smugly. "Nay, there is none to equal me."

Stephen rolled his eyes. "How does your lovely wife put up with you?"

"I keep her well supplied with wool, flowers, and my sweet attentions. And I change nappies. File that away in that poor brain of yours, my good Haulton, on the off chance you're ever fortunate enough to find yourself saddled with a mate."

"I will," Stephen promised, thanked Ian for his attentions on the field, then walked away before Ian made an offer for another round of torture.

He looked back over his shoulder once, just to see if the piper were still there. The man was watching him, which was extremely unsettling. Stephen watched as the man made him a low bow before he turned and vanished.

Stephen had to take a deeper breath than he might have otherwise, then walked swiftly back to the guesthouse Ian had added a pair of years earlier to the property for those brave enough to come for training. And whilst he walked, Stephen reviewed the things he couldn't help but admit were past disputing: Artane did have ghosts; Artane's ghosts were poorly behaved; and the rumors that Ian MacLeod had been born somewhere in the Middle Ages were absolutely true.

Actually, he'd heard all about Ian's past straight from the horse's mouth, though that wouldn't have mattered. All facts pointed to the truth of it.

He walked up to the door of the cottage, then realized he should have been paying more attention to his surroundings. He had been assaulted there more than once by another member of the clan MacLeod, partly because he was an Englishman cheeky enough to set foot on Scottish soil, but mostly because Ian wasn't the only person he came to Scotland to train with, if training it could be called.

There was no one there today, but he supposed he shouldn't have been surprised by that. He'd heard rumors that Patrick MacLeod, the survivalist instructor in Ian's school of medieval torments and Ian's own cousin, was off on holiday. Perhaps since Patrick wasn't about to rough him up, Stephen supposed he would do well to get himself back home before the sun set.

He showered, packed his gear, wrote Jane MacLeod a thank-you for the lovely dinners and conversation, then took everything out to his utilitarian Range Rover. He actually preferred his Mercedes for long trips, but it was a bit difficult to find a place in it to stash his Claymore. That, and it seemed as though Rovers were the beast of choice for English viscounts and Scottish lairds. No sense in causing any unwanted interest. He shut his gear in the boot, slid his Claymore into the especially constructed compartment in the roof that had taken some doing to have created, then turned.

And felt a brick connect with his nose.

Actually, it was only an elbow, and he knew that because his assaulter made some vile comment about the insult to his funny bone. Stephen would have made a comment about the blinding pain in his face he was currently enjoying, but he didn't have the breath for it.

The ensuing attack was vicious and relentless. Stephen would have been quite keen to merely stand to one side and watch whilst a clone of himself had to fight off a medieval clansman doing what he did best—which was using all kinds of moves that no medieval clansman could possibly have known.

Patrick MacLeod was evil. Stephen told him that a time or two, though perhaps not in such polite terms.

The first ten minutes of that fight were very dodgy only because he spent so much time spitting out the blood dripping down his face and trying to clear his eyes that were still smarting from the pain of what he was fairly sure was a broken nose. After that, things went better—if any sort of encounter with Patrick Mac-Leod could ever go well. All Stephen knew was that he managed to get his sword free from its hiding place so he at least had something in his hands to fight with. And he managed to use that sword for almost another ten minutes before Patrick kicked it out of his hands and left him backed up against his Rover with another, not-exactly-modern blade pressed uncomfortably against his throat.

Patrick tsk-tsked him.

"You'll have to wash that shirt now, I imagine."

"As well as explain the stain to my mother," Stephen said, forcing himself to take slow, even breaths in spite of how his lungs burned.

Patrick removed his sword and propped it up against his shoulder. He held out his hand—which was, fortunately, quite empty. Stephen dragged his sleeve across his face, then took Patrick's hand and shook it.

"Ian said you were on holiday."

"He lies," Patrick said mildly. "Never trust him."

"I won't make that mistake again," Stephen said with feeling. He started to walk away, then stopped and looked at Patrick. "I'm going to fetch my sword."

"I don't stab men in the back."

Well, there was that at least. Stephen retrieved his sword, replaced it from where he'd wrenched it free, then glanced at James MacLeod's younger brother. Patrick was smiling slightly.

"Ian said he didn't completely destroy you this weekend."

Stephen shrugged. "Perhaps."

"And you're still standing now," Patrick continued. "Bloodied, but unbowed."

"Are you daft?" Stephen said with a snort that made his eyes water. "I think you broke my damned nose."

"Stuff a pinch of knitbone up it."

Stephen rolled his eyes, went to rummage about in the garden in front of the cottage, then did as he'd been advised. He felt a complete arse, but at least he might escape a trip to the local surgery. Patrick stabbed his sword into the ground, walked over, and gave Stephen's nose a hearty pinch.

"Not broken, you woman."

Stephen laughed because it was all he could do. He could only hope he wouldn't choke to death from the blood he could now feel draining down the back of his throat. "You bastard."

"Nay, I'm not," Patrick said cheerfully, "but likely a handful of other things you should be clever enough to think up. Really, Haulton, this is an area in which you could use quite a bit of improvement. Your slurs are pitiful."

Stephen indulged him in a string of profanities that left Patrick's left eyebrow going up just the slightest bit.

Patrick retrieved his sword. "My ears are ringing."

"But unfortunately your mouth is still moving."

Patrick laughed and walked away. Stephen packed himself in his Rover, drove gratefully off MacLeod soil, and turned himself for home. He was going to be hard-pressed to get back to Cambridge in time for his Monday morning ten o'clock, but he'd been summoned to make an appearance at the family seat, and when duty called, he tended to answer. It was, after all, what an English gentleman of quality did without complaint.

Six hours later, he pulled to a stop in front of his father's gates. He had to let himself in and close the main gate behind him, but he did so again without complaint. It was well past supper and he certainly wouldn't have expected anyone to be waiting for him.

He parked in his accustomed spot, got out of the Rover, then had to pause and look up at the castle rising into the air in front of him. The lights were on the outer walls, of course, because that's what his father did to please those who might be driving through the village for a glimpse of eight hundred years of history tucked up there on that bluff. The keep itself was, Stephen had to admit, absolutely spectacular. It had taken buckets of money to keep it so, but that had never been an issue. His father had managed to thus far satisfy the Inland Revenue without selling anything. Stephen tried not to think about how that burden would eventually fall to him, but he had his hands full with his own titles and bits of land. He supposed when the time came, he would manage it.

Because he was the heir to Artane, and it was expected.

Not only expected, desired—and by him. He had loved Artane for as long as he could remember, been enormously proud of his heritage, and, thanks to his mother, been humbled that one day the care of all that heritage and stone would be his. He found himself smiling at the memories that just looking at the place stirred in him. How many times had he come charging out the front door of the keep itself as a boy, wooden sword in hand, prepared to defend his hall from imaginary foes and the odd tourist or two?

How many times had his father chased after him just as enthusiastically, bellowing threats of punishment for Stephen having picked the locks on glass cases to liberate various sharp objects in order to practice with them?

As time had gone on, he'd come to realize that that wasn't the sort of thing that the future earl of a very solvent, very visible castle was supposed to be doing, so he had pursued a more traditional path of academia.

In medieval studies, of course.

His parents thought, wrongly of course, that he'd put away those boyhood dreams of being a knight-errant. It was ridiculous, when one looked at it logically, for a man of his maturity and stature to be involved with sharp, pointy things. Then again, he was a fair horseman, so perhaps it was equally as silly to be taking his own very expensive jumpers and sending them flying over poles indiscrete distances off the ground.

He pushed away from his car and walked across the courtyard, then jogged up the steps to the front door. He steeled himself for comments from his parents over the condition of his shirt and where he'd been over the weekend. Perhaps he would tell them he'd been playing an especially vigorous game of cricket. He opened the door and found his mother standing in front of the fire.

"Stephen, darling, what's happened to the front of your shirt?"

Stephen sighed and shut the front door behind him.

D*inner* had been held for him along with the after-dinner conversation. After he'd made his way through both and assured his parents he had been behaving in a manner above reproach all weekend long, he gathered his gear from his car and took himself off to his bedroom. He set everything down, then noticed the envelope on the dresser. He flipped it over, then cursed at the sight of the seal on the back. Kenneworth, unfortunately, no doubt extending an invitation he knew already he would absolutely refuse for a variety of reasons he didn't care to examine at present.

He did unbend far enough, however, to allow himself to enjoy thoughts of David Preston enduring a few hours on Scottish soil, having the arrogance beaten out of him. He was rich, not overly ugly, and had a penchant for collecting gorgeous women and then tossing them aside when he was finished with them. If Stephen had had a sister, he wouldn't have allowed her within ten miles of the blighter. Why others in England didn't follow that same sensible plan, he didn't know.

He was tempted to just chuck the invite in the rubbish bin, but his curiosity got the better of him. He popped the seal and pulled the invitation out to read it. A house party, fancy ball dress, shooting, drinking, eating: the usual fare. Should he accept, it would require a tuxedo on his part. He wasn't sure why Kenneworth had included him, given the animosity that existed between their families. He wasn't even sure he could be trusted in a shooting party not to shoot his host when his host was David Preston.

And the thought of an entire weekend spent watching the man chasing some poor girl who hadn't the sense to see through his ploys was simply more than Stephen could take.

No, he wouldn't do it.

He leaned against the dresser and checked the texts he'd ignored earlier on his phone, then he sighed again. Messages from not one but all three of the women he was currently dating, telling him each assumed he would be accepting Kenneworth's invitation. The only positive thing about that was at least they knew he wasn't seeing any of them exclusively, which simplified things. They were also only interested in his title, which simplified things even more. His current income was more than sufficient for his own needs but not enough to keep any of the three in the style they would have liked to have become accustomed to. Why they continued to date him, he couldn't have said.

He tossed the invitation onto the dresser and went to put himself to bed. He knew he should have accepted the invitation, to put foolish rumors about family feuds to rest if nothing else, but he would be damned if he would. It would be easy enough to plead a deadline, go back to his office, and bury himself in as much medievalism as he could.

He looked up at the wooden canopy above his head for a moment with his hand on the lamp and frowned thoughtfully. His father, an unusually robust and hearty man, hadn't looked particularly well that evening, but perhaps that was from stress. He would have to quiz his mother at breakfast and see if there was something amiss. He had been coming home once a fortnight to see to things his father didn't want to give up but didn't have the energy to attend to properly, but perhaps it was time he increased his visits. After all, whilst Artane's library wasn't Cambridge's, it was extensive. And he wasn't past handing over a few tutoring duties if necessary.

Yes, he would forgo the delights of Kenneworth House and spend the following weekend at home.

It was the very least he could do.

Chapter 3

Peaches stood just outside the small train station near Sedgwick and took several deep, cleansing breaths. She reached for the first mantra that came to hand—which at the moment was *I will not kill my sister*—and wondered why it was that she just couldn't seem to say no to people she loved.

"It'll be okay," Tess said soothingly.

"Then *you* go do it!"

"I can't," Tess said, sounding far too reasonable for the current situation. "Terry Holmes is driving all the way down from Chevington to save me a trip there. And you know I can't be here and at Cambridge at the same time."

"Which is why you should have rescheduled the meeting that contained fewer people," Peaches said briskly, "which would have been, sister dear, the meeting with your Mr. Holmes."

Tess gave her a look that in another might have been called pleading. "This is really important to me," she said earnestly. "And I promise if you do this for me, I'll pay you back. Double."

"I'm not sure you can possibly pay me back for talking me into going to a stupid afternoon tea," Peaches groused. She shot Tess a look. "With academics, no less!"

"You'll be fine—"

"I vowed I would never do this again, if you remember."

"The details escape me," Tess said, frowning thoughtfully. "Are you sure you're not imagining things?"

"I am not," Peaches said. "The debacle happened during my junior year of high school, high school being a place you abandoned me to without a backward glance as you graduated early. You were at Aunt Edna's on break and promised both Bobby Rutledge and Gary Peters that you would go first to dinner, then to a stupid football game. Bobby offered Italian but you wanted French, so Gary won. I ended up wearing tomato sauce on my shirt all evening thanks to nerves over the possibility of running into you in the stands." She gritted her teeth. "I've never forgiven you for it."

"You shouldn't be holding on to these negative feelings," Tess said, one eyebrow raised. "I don't think it's healthy for you—"

"Shut up."

"And you didn't have to go, you know."

"I was hungry and Aunt Edna was making tongue sandwiches," Peaches muttered. "It had seemed at the time like the lesser of two evils."

"That's probably what turned you into a vegetarian."

"Aunt Edna is responsible, yes, and you're trying to distract me. Tell me again why it won't get out that you were happily lunching at home in your bunny slippers while being at Cambridge at the same time, wearing itchy nylons?"

"Nylons don't itch, which you would know if you wore them more often, and these are two entirely separate groups of people. They'll never cross paths."

Peaches suppressed the urge to swear at her.

"Why would I stake my entire academic reputation on you if this thing with Terry wasn't time critical?" Tess asked reasonably.

"You're a nut?"

Tess only laughed at her. "Go hop on that train. They're talking all about the psychology of medieval lords and ladies this afternoon. You can fake that."

Peaches glared at her. "You should be going not me— actually, your *husband* should be going. What do I know about the medieval mind-set?"

Tess looked at John. "Any advice for her? How do medieval men think?"

Peaches turned to look at John, who had come no doubt to help Tess in her nefarious goal of shoving an innocent unemployed former life coach in a direction she didn't want to go.

John shrugged. "Find the enemy, kill him, hurry home while the wine is still cold and the bread not burned."

Peaches scowled at him. "That's not useful."

"But it is accurate," he said with a smile. "And having seen both times myself, I'd say not much has changed. My task now is to protect my family, see them fed and clothed, and carve out a bit of time for the beauty of music and art. The only difference eight hundred years ago was that I didn't have a family and I was carrying a sword. I still grumbled about practicing the lute, still hated the itchy good clothes my mother put me in when I was a lad, and still happily put my feet up after a hard morning in the lists. Not much has changed but the amenities."

Peaches heaved a heavy sigh, then looked at her sister. "They'll still know I'm not you."

"Did you bring pantyhose?"

"Yes."

"Then they won't have a clue." Tess kissed her on the cheek. "Holly already has her couch made up for you."

Peaches might have protested a bit longer, but Tess had given her a good shove toward the train and the momentum wouldn't let her stop. She frowned at her sister over her shoulder, but found she couldn't keep it up for very long. The frowning, not the looking over her shoulder.

The truth was, Tess and John just looked so perfectly happy and perfectly normal, she never would have guessed when John had been born or how long and vociferously Tess had shunned all sorts of fairy tales. And there Tess now was, countess of her own castle, married to an earl of his own castle who happened to be a medieval knight who could hoist a sword in her defense if necessary or just punch someone in the nose if blades would have been considered impolite.

Tess was safe.

Peaches found herself swept up by such a wave of envy, she stumbled. Tess started forward, but Peaches shook her head quickly, smiled, then hoisted her bag and tromped off to look for the appropriate train track. Since there was only one, it was an easy find.

She didn't want John. She wasn't even sure she wanted a guy with a castle and a sword.

She just wanted her dream.

But if that guy, castle, and sword came with some sort of fairy-tale prelude, she supposed she wouldn't argue.

She got on her train, found a seat, and settled back for a long ride nor'nor'east. She'd had several decent nights' sleep with the invitation to the ball under her pillow and had fully resigned herself to the foolishness of pinning too many hopes on a single weekend. There was absolutely no way she would find anything special at Kenneworth House.

Her heart whispered differently.

She looked out the window to distract herself but found that watching the scenery go by was all too conducive to contemplating things she hadn't allowed herself to before.

Perhaps, in the end, it wasn't unhealthy to dream. Hadn't she just begun over the past few months to tell her clients—when she'd had clients, of course—to make a list of their most impossible, most cherished dreams because sometimes just the act of making that list was enough to change the direction of a life?

She was beginning to wonder if Fate was trying to tell her to change hers.

She sighed deeply, finding herself left with no choice but to examine that load of bricks that had been dumped on the other side of the scale. She did need a change. She'd been in the organizing business for seven years, since she graduated from college, and she had to admit that she'd almost had enough of people who couldn't limit themselves to touching a piece of paper only once.

And the thought of that terrified her.

It was the same sort of terror she'd felt at twenty when she'd been reaching for her bachelor of science diploma and accepted what she'd realized on the night she'd seen that couple waltzing around the quad, namely that she really didn't want to spend her life in a research lab. She'd faced the fact that while she had been content with the idea of helping people have a better life through the judicious use of pharmaceuticals, she had mostly just gone into science because it had been the hardest major she could see herself pursuing.

Funny how Aunt Edna had only remained silent after she had, still clutching her diploma, blurted out the truth.

A celebratory luncheon had been Aunt Edna's only comment. Her graduation gifts had been Peaches's acceptance letter into the Daughters of the American Revolution and an enormous book about the genealogies of Britain's most famous families.

Peaches had known there was a deeper meaning behind both gifts, but she'd had the distinct feeling that discovering that meaning would spell trouble for her. So she'd expressed the acceptable level of gratitude—it had been Aunt Edna, after all, who wasn't really her aunt but her great-aunt whose age one simply didn't discuss—then taken the first job she'd been able to find, which had been making smoothies in a little shop at Pike Place Market. She'd already been a vegetarian, which had helped, but she'd been convinced it was her patchouli-scented parents staggering accidentally into her interview that had gotten her the gig.

One of her regular clients had been, as it happened, Brandalyse Stevens. She'd first accepted a job as Brandi's raw-food chef, then found herself over the course of the ensuing six months not only uncooking but decluttering and organizing all of Brandi's closets and then the closets of Brandi's closest friends. That had blossomed into a business that while never enormous had at least given her the flexibility and cash to fly to England a couple of times a year and mooch off Tess.

She leaned her head back against the seat and sighed deeply. She supposed she could go on with her life as discoverer of intentions, dispenser of feng shui–ish advice, and all-around balancer of other people's lives, though heading back to Seattle to do that might be a little more difficult than it looked at first glance. She didn't have to dig through her backpack to find the fax that had been waiting for her that morning, the one from Roger Peabody telling her that her landlord had decided that since she hadn't been willing to sign another lease—why would she have when she hadn't been sure what Tess was doing?—he was going to re-rent her apartment. And that Roger had done her the favor of taking her meager belongings and storing them at his place.

The thought of his riffling through any of her things gave her the willies. In fact, it was enough to leave her thinking that everything she really needed, she had brought in her suitcase to England. The odds of her going back to Seattle were very slim, indeed.

Which left her where she was: homeless, fairly broke, and wishing something magical would happen.

She couldn't bring herself to hope that something might be found at David of Kenneworth's fancy dress ball.

It was four o'clock on the dot when she presented herself at the door of a surprisingly spacious semidetached house within walking distance of where she'd crashed with a friend of Tess's. She suppressed the urge to adjust her sensible business skirt—well, Tess's sensible business skirt, actually—and put on what she hoped was a respectable PhD's sort of smile when the door opened.

"Ah, Dr. Alexander," an older gentleman said, extending his hand. "So pleased you could come."

"Dr. Trotter-Smythe," Peaches said, almost without twitching. She had to bite her tongue to keep from saying, *I presume.* Because she was presuming. Tess had told her who was hosting, but the bulk of the guest list was peopled by academics Tess didn't know. Fortunately.

Dr. Trotter-Smythe beamed, then welcomed her into his salon that simply reeked of old money and pipe smoke.

Peaches ungritted her teeth. This was the very *last* time she did anything this stupid. If she hadn't felt so guilty about crashing Tess's first month as a newlywed . . .

She took a deep, steadying breath. Last time. Really.

"Let me introduce you to our guest of honor," Dr. Trotter-Smythe said, nodding in the direction of a tiny little woman who looked as if she'd been alive since the Middle Ages. "Dr. Plantagenet, and yes, the name is truly hers."

Peaches didn't doubt it. She approached Dame Medieval with the same enthusiasm she would have an audience with Bad King John and wondered if the woman would be surprised if she came down with a sudden attack of laryngitis.

Introductions were made, and Dr. Plantagenet looked at her assessingly.

"I've heard many good things about you, my dear," she said in a voice that sounded a bit like ancient rustling parchment. It matched the paper-thin state of her skin.

"How kind," Peaches managed. "I've been looking forward to meeting you as well." *And killing my sister as soon as possible afterward.*

Watery blue eyes assessed her a bit more. "Hmmm" was apparently the pithiest thing Dr. Plantagenet could manage at the moment. "Dr. Trotter-Smythe wants me to do a little presentation, but we'll have time I'm sure for a robust discussion afterward. I'll be interested in your thoughts on medieval mores."

Peaches imagined she would. And she imagined she herself would be suffering from a sudden onset of something more dire than laryngitis, which would require her to remove herself from the premises as quickly as possible.

So she could, as she had contemplated earlier, kill her sister.

She supposed people would notice if she rolled up her sleeves and took notes on her arms for future reference while Granny was talking, so she simply sat in a hard-backed chair and tried not to squirm. There was an enormous grandfather clock in the hall that made her jump every time it boomed out the quarter hour. She was beginning to feel like what she imagined a prisoner of the Tower must have felt each time he heard something heavy fall. Like a footstep outside his cell door. Or an axe on the green chopping the head off another miscreant.

Only her final meeting wasn't going to be with an axe, it was going to be with Dr. Plantagenet who would be quizzing her about her medieval opinions and finding she only had one, which was that she imagined that during medieval times the only ones going in for wheatgrass were the horses. What she wouldn't have given for a double shot of the same to see her through the rest of the afternoon.

Unfortunately, all she had to buoy up her courage was a plate of ladyfingers and some artificially sweetened lemonade. Her hands were shaking so badly, she was afraid she would spill her snack all over the faded but obviously expensive Aubusson carpet. She looked up to find Dr. Plantagenet starting across the room toward her, her eyes zeroing in on what Peaches could only hope was her sandwiches and not her, and knew there was nowhere to run. Tess's reputation was going to be ruined, she herself was probably going to be drawn and quartered, and then her opportunity to find her fairy tale at the Duke of Kenneworth's glittering ballroom was going to be ruin—

"Oh, I say, Trotter-Smythe," said a deep voice from behind her, "sorry to miss the notes. Ah, Tess, darling, I supposed you would . . . be . . ."

Peaches turned around in time to the winding down of the speech behind her until she was facing the speaker.

He was tall, dark-haired, and . . . she sighed. She could be nothing but honest. The man standing in front of her was absolutely gorgeous. Not only was he tall, as she had been forced to admit before, he was very finely built and had a killer smile she had fortunately never had used on her. He was currently looking at her from a pair of the most amazing gray eyes she had ever seen, eyes that widened so briefly she probably would have thought she'd imagined it if she hadn't known what was going through the possessor of those beautiful eyes' mind.

She wasn't Tess.

And Stephen de Piaget knew it.

Stephen made her a low bow, then straightened and smiled smoothly. "Dr. Alexander, I should say. Or perhaps Lady Sedgwick. So many titles and so well-deserved, wouldn't you say, Dr. Trotter-Smythe?"

"Oh, indeed," Dr. Trotter-Smythe agreed. "Very. So many accomplishments for one so young."

Peaches would have elbowed Dr. Trotter-Smythe to distract him before he launched into a discussion of Tess's accomplishments that *she* would have to elaborate on, but she was saved by the man becoming distracted by Stephen de Piaget's unwholesomely dazzling smile. Or it might have been the remains of a bruise on his nose. She could hardly believe it, but he looked as though he had recently been in a brawl.

She forced her eyes to remain open and not narrow as they so wanted to do, because despite the fact that Stephen was her archenemy, she was pretending to be her sister, and Tess was rather fond of him.

Peaches couldn't understand why. She'd heard from reliable sources that Stephen had helped Tess enormously during her academic career at Cambridge without hitting on her once. Peaches could only assume that was because the illustrious Viscount Haulton had already been busy with the harem of very rich, very beautiful socialites and celebrities he dated between bouts of insulting innocent life coaches from Seattle and teaching about pointy things he no doubt wouldn't have touched if his life had depended on it.

Not that there was anything wrong with being a college professor, especially of that ultra-sexy subject of medieval knights and their relentless chivalry. She just imagined the sharpest things Stephen came in contact with were either a harshly worded review or the business edge of his butter knife at dinner. If someone tried to mug her, he would probably give her a shove toward the mugger so he could dash off daintily and spare his fancy cashmere scarves a brush with grubby fingers.

Stephen removed her plate from her hand. She managed to smile politely instead of baring her teeth, but that took some doing.

"Let's find you a seat, shall we?" he asked politely. "You look a little flushed."

"It's the stockings," she muttered under her breath.

He only looked at her gravely, which made her want to squirm. Before she could protest, he had put her in a comfortable spot, deposited her drink and plate on the table at her elbow, and had sat down next to her—a very proper and discreet distance away—to no doubt monopolize any and all conversation that came her way.

She supposed that was something of a bonus. All she had to do was sit there and smile, but since that was probably how he liked his women, she was fitting right into his plans.

She felt an unwholesome tingle in her knees that she quickly identified as stress she immediately blamed on Tess. It had nothing to do with sitting next to a man whose face should have been outlawed, whose lovely posh consonants would have made her smile if they hadn't been coming out of *his* mouth, who seemed to draw people to him like flies.

He probably had a flyswatter hiding behind his back so he could whack them when least expected. He'd done it to her.

She didn't want to think about that particular moment of unpleasantness, but since he was there and she was trying to keep herself awake, she decided that perhaps it was best to get it all out of her system right then.

She'd met him in the midst of panic over losing Pippa some-where back in time. He had been an absolute rock, taking all pressure off Tess, being the perfect knight in trousers and tweed. She had to admit that even though she'd known he was way out of her league, she had . . . she sighed. The truth was, she'd de-veloped an immediate crush on him and spent the majority of her time in England alternately gaping at him and allowing him to figure prominently in her daydreams.

If he'd noticed, he hadn't said anything. He had treated her politely, but it had been a stiff sort of politeness, as if centuries of breeding hadn't allowed him to raise her hopes unnecessarily.

And then had come The Comment.

She'd been talking to a potential client at a Regency-style house party about her degree when Stephen had attempted a polite laugh and said, exactly, *Oh, I say, I thought organic was in reference to the manure you put in your garden.*

She'd been mortified. He hadn't even had the grace to look embarrassed as those around them had laughed heartily, then moved on to less smelly subjects. Stephen's face had shuttered. He had, when the crowd had dispersed, attempted a stiff apol-ogy, then been coldly polite to her ever since. She had been happy, on those unhappy occasions when she'd seen him since, to give him a wide berth.

Only now she was stuck.

She leaned back against the couch and let herself relax just the slightest bit only because she knew if she didn't, she would have a crushing headache. Unfortunately, that gave her nothing better to do than watch Stephen work the crowd.

How he managed to be so charming and such a jerk at the same time was a mystery. Granny was blushing. Other scholars were hanging on his every word. Peaches would have told him he was hogging the limelight, but then she realized he was somehow doing all the talking but giving credit to Tess for the research.

Peaches suppressed a frown. There was obviously something fishy going on.

He only looked at her once. He gave her a quick little smile that would have left her fanning herself if it hadn't come from him. Fortunately she was a woman with a steel spine and vast amounts of resistance to tweed-covered academics who thought nothing of tap-dancing in stompy boots over the hearts of innocent feng-shuiers.

It was a very uncomfortable three hours.

She was thrilled when Stephen announced that Dr. Alexander had another engagement to get to. Peaches accepted compliments with her best smile and didn't argue when Stephen managed to get them both out the front door without any catastrophes.

Peaches pulled her collar up to her ears and started out toward the sidewalk. "Thanks, Dr. de Piaget, for the rescue. See you around."

Stephen had very long legs and apparently knew how to use them. Peaches would have trotted down the street but she was in heels not her sensible Docs, so she had to walk carefully so she didn't fall on her face and ruin Tess's reputation.

"Miss Alexander—"

"I'm fine, thank you," she said politely. All right, so it had come out a bit crisply. He had made fun of her on that fateful night the month before, spent the rest of that particular evening flirting with three of his girlfriends, and now he expected her to be nice to him? "I'll tell Tess how you saved her this afternoon."

"Where are you staying?"

"None of your business."

"Holly's," he said with a sigh, taking her by the arm. "Come, I'll ferry you there."

Peaches ripped her arm away from his fingers so forcefully, she almost went sprawling. She regained her balance. "I think I've managed all twenty-eight years of my life without your help, thanks just the same."

He clasped his hands behind his back and just looked at her, silent and grave.

Peaches knew she was making a colossal idiot of herself, but honestly, she just couldn't help herself. She wasn't going to be a notch on his chivalry belt just so he could tell his group of nobility pals he'd been nice to some poor Yank.

She walked away, ignoring how slippery it was on the sidewalk and how cold her feet were getting in shoes that should have been limited to summer events.

She had stalked almost to Holly's before she realized someone was following her. A car, actually. A very expensive-looking, silver gray Mercedes that probably cost more than she would ever make in her lifetime.

Typical.

It waited until she was standing on the porch and had the door open before it drove off. Peaches decided that was probably for the best. She would go into Holly's, have a lukewarm shower, then put herself to bed and forget about a man who had saved her during a tea that could have been an absolute disaster, then followed her home to make sure she got there safely.

Obviously for his own perverse reasons, which she was sure included storing up amusing anecdotes to entertain his friends with.

She put her shoulders back and headed for the shower.

Her fairy tale awaited. The last thing she wanted was a titled, impossible, steak-eating jerk getting in the way.

Chapter 4

Stephen let himself into his flat, shrugged out of his overcoat, then tossed it and his keys onto the table in the entryway. He glanced at it and for some reason the sight brought him up short. It was an eighteenth-century card table sporting extensive inlay that featured none other than Czar Peter himself. It wasn't that which had startled him, it was that he had no idea where it had come from or when it had arrived. His grandmother had no doubt deposited it in his entryway. For all he knew, she had given him an extensive history of it at some point, but he imagined he had probably been too distracted by whatever paper he'd been working on at the time to pay attention. He would have to ask the details when next he was in London to have tea at her house.

He bypassed the kitchen and made his way into his study and flicked on a lamp. He started a fire, then sat down in a ridiculously comfortable chair and heaved an enormous sigh of relief.

And then he choked.

But that was probably because he had just noticed the three men standing on the other side of the hearth in a neat little row.

He didn't bother reaching for any of Patrick MacLeod's defense training. It was obvious to him by not only their somewhat vintage dress but their slight transparency that his visitors were not exactly of this world.

He regained his composure and bought himself a bit of time by studying his companions. He wasn't entirely sure he hadn't seen them before at Artane, but since he tended to avoid the paranormal, he couldn't have said for certain. The only thing he was sure of was that none of the three had ever jumped out of an alcove and yelled "boo" at him.

He realized with a start that he was starting to babble a bit, but really, who could blame him? He'd already been thoroughly knocked to his knees by an afternoon spent sitting next to Miss Peaches Alexander. Ghosts were the icing on the bun, as it were.

The man—er, ghost, rather—closest to the fire was a Highlander with a very big sword. Stephen felt fairly confident in making that assessment given that he'd spent the previous weekend fighting off just such a lad up north. Tartans hadn't had a set pattern or color until the eighteenth century—he congratulated himself on being able to produce that bit of trivia under such duress—so identifying that hoary-headed warrior by tartan alone was impossible. Fortunately for his own feeble powers of observation, there was an enormous MacLeod clan badge on the man's cap. Identification successful.

The man next to him was wearing the crest of the clan Mc-Kinnon on his cap as well as what Stephen recognized as the current-day plaid associated with that clan. He was ruddy-haired, ruddy-complected, and looked as if he were currently seeing red. Stephen wondered absently what he'd done to annoy the man—er, ghost, again, rather.

He wondered if he should stand up and offer a bow.

He considered that a bit longer as he looked at the third of the little group. Obviously of Elizabethan influence judging by his trousers and the enormous ruff around his neck. The ghost twitched his cloak back over his shoulders, which left Stephen blinking a little at the tabard the ghost wore: a black lion rampant with an aqua eye.

Part of his family crest, as it happened.

The man also looked a fair bit like what Stephen's father had looked like in his youth, rather more like Gideon, his brother, than he himself.

The de Piaget ghost cleared his throat in irritation.

Stephen pushed himself out of his chair, looked at the three, then made them a low bow.

"Stephen, Viscount Haulton and Baron Etham, at your service," he said politely.

The Elizabeth ghost looked at his companions and raised an eyebrow. "Me nevvy, don't you know. Look at them pretty manners. 'Tis in the blood."

The Scots didn't offer opinions.

Stephen cleared his throat politely. "If I could offer you seats, my lords—"

"No need, lad," said the ghost on the left who by his carriage showed himself to have no doubt been an important member of the clan MacLeod at some point. "We come with our own."

Stephen imagined they did. He waited until they'd conjured up chairs to suit themselves and plucked tankards of ale out of thin air before he dared resume his own seat. He reached for something innocuous to say.

"Isn't it a little late for Christmas ghosts?" he managed.

The de Piaget ghost dressed in his Elizabethan finery harrumphed. "Ye know, young Stephen, that 'twas *me* nocturnal visit to young Charles that gave him the idea for his tale full of do-gooding specters, but that isn't why we're here."

Stephen didn't dare speculate on why they *were* there. It was one thing to jump a little at ghosts lingering in his father's passageways, then suppress the urge to curse at their giggles; it was another thing entirely to host a trio of apparently very opinionated souls at his own hearth and attempt intelligent conversation. On his part, of course, not theirs. They didn't seem to be at all troubled by him.

The red-haired ghost sitting in the middle of the guests frowned at the Highlander on his right. "Ye know, Ambrose, I begin to wonder why we waste our time with these lads south of the border. Look at this one sitting there with his mouth gaping open. There's plenty of work to do on the proper side of the wall, I say. That young Derrick Cameron, perhaps—"

"We'll see to that in good time," the Macleod assured him. "This lad first, however. Perhaps introductions before we discuss business."

Stephen found himself pinned to the spot by a piercing stare.

"I am Ambrose MacLeod," the shade announced, "laird of the clan MacLeod during the glorious flowering of Elizabethan times. These are my compatriots, Hugh McKinnon and Fulbert de Piaget."

"Charmed," Stephen managed, nodding at the other Highlander and the Englishman who were helping themselves to what he could only assume was ale.

"And now to our business," Ambrose MacLeod said seriously.

Stephen remained silent. He was not a creator of fiction, so he couldn't imagine the trio facing him had come to inspire him to greater literary heights as they apparently had a certain penner of Victorian-era tales. He had to admit he was suddenly less than eager to find out, however, just why they had selected his study to haunt. Especially given that one of them was an ancestor. Of sorts.

Fulbert de Piaget smoothed his hand down over his tabard, then fluffed the lace ruff at his neck before he cleared his throat. "Now, you being me brother's son—"

"Son?" Stephen interrupted.

"Very well, his son's son's son's—" Fulbert frowned for a moment or two, then began to count on his fingers. "His son's son's son's—" He glared at Stephen. "Suffice it to say, yer me nevvy a time or two removed. I am the second son of my father, as it happens, and yer uncle. And as such, I feel a certain sense of responsibility for yer happiness."

Stephen blinked, then gaped.

Hugh McKinnon shot Ambrose MacLeod a knowing look, but said nothing. Stephen cleared his throat after a dodgy moment or two when he thought he might have to go look for a drink.

"I'm happy just as I am," he protested.

"But unwed," Laird MacLeod said pointedly. "We're here to remedy that."

"*I'm* here to remedy that," Fulbert said pointedly.

The McKinnon snorted. "What do either of ye know about this family? If ye'll remember, *I* was the one who arranged things the other two times."

Stephen watched the discussion grow rather warm and realized at some point that he was either losing his mind or that blow to his nose delivered by Patrick MacLeod had knocked something loose inside his head because he was currently watching two ghosts of a rather earlier-than-modern vintage go at each other, and he found all he could do was sit there and gape at them.

"I say," he protested at one point when swords were drawn. He was ignored.

Apparently Fulbert and the McKinnon had known each other for quite some time. Their insults were as finely honed as their swords though thankfully just as unable to draw blood. Stephen watched them fight in his den, using furniture and tables to launch themselves off and duck behind, and was very thankful they were ghosts.

Until what Fulbert de Piaget said had sunk in.

"Marriage?" he said incredulously.

Fulbert and Hugh stopped long enough to look at him. Fulbert pursed his lips in disgust.

"Of course, marriage. Why else would we be here?"

"Why, indeed," Stephen managed. He watched them turn back to their sport—and he used that term loosely—then realized the MacLeod wasn't joining in the fray. He rose unsteadily and went to put his backside to the fire where he could speak to the clan's chief privately. "Marriage?"

Ambrose MacLeod looked up at him from bright green eyes. "Well, aye, lad. It's about time, don't you think?"

Stephen didn't want to think. He had been having subtle and not-so-subtle hints about his lack of wife and heirs tossed at him for ten years now.

And to be completely honest, he was getting tired of dating, tired of trying to please his enormously discriminating granny who was demanding not only a titled bride but one who came with the cold, hard stuff as well. He had actually spent the previous summer looking at his life and thinking that perhaps it wasn't as satisfying as it should have been. It had occurred to him, much to his surprise, that he envied his younger brother his lovely wife and beautiful daughter.

And then he'd walked into Sedgwick Castle a pair of months earlier and laid his poor eyes on a woman who had, as they said across the Pond, knocked his socks off.

But he wasn't going to admit who that had been, not if his

life depended on it. Because she was absolutely unsuitable. His grandmother would have had an attack. Even his father might have raised an eyebrow. He needed a girl with a title and money to match, not a mouthy, linen-wearing, feng-shui spouting, tofu-eating—

"She doesn't eat tofu," Ambrose said mildly. "Too processed."

Stephen kept his mouth from falling open only because he had spent a lifetime being polite. "Whom are you talking about, my good man?"

"Mistress Peaches Alexander," Ambrose said in that mild tone that was all the more infuriating for serenity. "You recently fed her at your father's table, if memory serves."

"Which only added to my dislike of her," Stephen said, hardly able to believe he was talking about anything with a man who looked like he'd just stepped out of a seventeenth-century Scottish portrait. "I find her culinary judgment suspicious at best."

"There's more to life than steak."

"Ha," Stephen said, because it seemed like the proper thing to say. "First go the prime cuts of Angus beef, then bangers and mash, then steak and kidney pie. Then where are you left?"

"With unclogged arteries?"

"I'll take my chances, thank you just the same."

Ambrose rose and came to stand next to him, clasping his hands behind his back. "She's beautiful, which you cannot deny."

"She's a Yank."

"She has a generous heart."

"And an unfortunate lack of familiarity with the necessity of pressing one's clothes."

Ambrose looked at him in amusement. "You can admit you fancy her, you know."

"I don't," Stephen lied. He wasn't sure that had come out quite strongly enough, so he made another attempt. "I can hardly bear to be in the same room with her."

"Why not?"

Why not? Stephen hardly knew where to begin. Because even though he'd known her, if it could be called that based only on things Tess had said, for years yet never managed to encounter her despite her numerous visits to England, he hadn't expected to look at her, fresh-faced Yank that she was, and fall head over heels for her the moment he'd laid eyes on her. Because after the first hello, his usual smooth, suave conversation had completely deserted him and he'd been left with only an ever-increasing list of stupid things he'd said when he hadn't meant to.

Because when he was in the same room with her, he found himself turned immediately into a gawky, tongue-tied sixteen-year-old who was so gobsmacked by the goddess within reach that he consistently and thoroughly made an idiot of himself at every turn.

That afternoon had been an aberration in the course of their relationship. He'd managed to sit next to her on the sofa and keep his composure, but that had only been because he'd been concentrating so fully on making certain that everyone in the room thought Peaches was Tess. Once they'd been outside, he'd resumed his alter ego as a complete arse and things had proceeded as they usually did.

"Stephen?"

Stephen looked at Ambrose MacLeod. "Ah," he said, grasping for the thread of the stalled conversation, "I can't stand the woman because apart from her dietary delusions, she's a fixer, and I don't need to be fixed. She would organize everything from my socks to my files and leave me unable to find either."

"And that would be so terrible?" Ambrose asked.

Stephen would have answered, but the other ghosts there had ceased with their bellowing of threats and battle cries, put up their swords, and were now quaffing companionable mugs of ale. He steeled himself for the worst.

He wasn't disappointed.

Fulbert pulled up his chair and sat down with a contented sigh. "Now the true work's been done for the day, I'll turn me mind to yer wee problem, young Stephen."

Stephen decided resuming his seat was the wisest course of action. He managed to fall into it with a decent bit of grace, but that was, he was certain, sheer luck. "Good of you."

"Now," Fulbert said, pointing at Stephen with his mug and looking rather stern, "we understand there's a bit of hesitation about this fancy entertainment upcoming."

Stephen felt himself frowning. "Entertainment?"

"The ball," Hugh said wistfully, looking as if he might rather have wished to be going himself. "The fancy dress ball at Kenneworth House."

Fulbert shot Hugh a look. "'Tis hardly a house. More like a bleedin' palace, if you ask me, though tatty around the edges. I'm not sure how the young master affords it."

"He's always looking out for a rich gel to wed," Hugh said, stroking his chin thoughtfully with his free hand. "'Tis always the case, isn't it? A hall is a very hungry mistress."

"He'll have enough lassies with sires who have deep pockets to suit him," Fulbert said with a snort. He turned to Stephen. "But we're here to see to *your* future, nevvy."

"My future," Stephen said weakly. "There's nothing to see—"

The ale in Fulbert's mug splashed over the sides and landed silently on the floor where it disappeared. "Pull out that invitation from that young rogue from Kenneworth."

"What invitation—"

"The one in your gear!"

Stephen looked to Ambrose for aid, but the laird of the clan MacLeod had only resumed his seat and was watching the goings-on with an amused smile. Stephen sighed and supposed there was no use in arguing further. He reached over for his portfolio. The invitation was there, of course, burning a hole in the leather. He waved it wearily at Fulbert. "This one?"

"Send your acceptance over your wee mobile phone," Fulbert instructed. "Now, before it grows any later."

Stephen considered the three sitting across from him. He could say no, of course, because he was quite certain there was nothing they could do to him besides haunt him endlessly. Avoiding that, however, might be enough to induce him to suffer through a long weekend of rich food and deadly dull conversation. He pursed his lips and looked at Ambrose.

"Is there a reason you've chosen this event as your means of torturing me?"

Ambrose only smiled.

He turned to Hugh McKinnon. "Surely you're not interested in healing the breach, as it were, that lies between the Prestons and the de Piagets."

Hugh rolled his eyes. "Of course not. We've more important business here!"

Stephen suspected he knew just what that important business was. He looked reluctantly at Fulbert. "Is there someone there I'm supposed to meet?"

"Ye've already met her!" Fulbert exclaimed.

"I'm not sure I follow—"

"Mistress Peaches Alexander!"

Stephen frowned. It was one thing to be bellowed at in his own study by one of his ancestors. It was still that one thing to even be in his study *looking* at one of his ancestors. It was another thing entirely to be told by that same percher in his family tree that he was supposed to go to a fancy weekend party so he could become involved with a woman he couldn't bear to be in the same room with.

For all the reasons he'd gone over before.

"I'm busy," he said firmly.

"Unbusy yourself," Fulbert demanded.

"I—"

"Nay!"

"But—"

Fulbert stood and twitched aside his cloak to put his hand on his sword. "I'm prepared to prod ye there with me sword, nevvy."

Stephen looked at Hugh, who was looking equally fierce. Ambrose MacLeod, however, was just looking at him, smiling slightly. Stephen pursed his lips.

"Nothing to add, my laird?"

Ambrose lifted a shoulder briefly. "You know how things will proceed there, I imagine. It isn't as if you would leave any woman to David of Kenneworth's clutches now, is it? Not even, I imagine, a wheatgrass-drinking lass who turns your knees to mush."

"She doesn't turn my knees to mush."

"De Piaget men do not lie," Fulbert said sternly.

Stephen blew out his breath. It was preferable to throwing up his hands. An entire weekend spent trying to avoid being slandered by David Preston whilst keeping Peaches out of Preston's clutches. He exchanged another long, meaningful look with his uncle the appropriate number of generations removed, then sighed deeply. He pulled his phone out of his pocket and texted Kenneworth's social secretary. He set his phone down on the side table, then looked at Fulbert.

"Satisfied?"

"'Tis a start," Fulbert conceded. "We'll see how events proceed."

Stephen could hardly wait.

Because David Preston was a reprobate with no morals or scruples, his sister, Irene, had a list of men she intended to bag like helpless fowl—a list he himself headed, actually, to her brother's disgust—and Kenneworth House was large enough to accommodate all manner of paranormal participants.

He looked at his ghostly companions. "Tell me you aren't planning to come along."

Fulbert sat back down stiffly. "I daresay you won't know," he said ominously, "*unless* ye stray from the path we've laid out for ye."

Stephen sighed.

It was shaping up to be a fabulous weekend.

Chapter 5

Peaches was beginning to think she should have taken Tess up on the offer to use her little runabout to drive north. The weather was awful and growing worse by the moment. That would certainly have been less of an issue if she hadn't been out in it.

But taking Tess's car had been more charity than she'd been able to accept. Tess had been serious when she had insisted that Peaches crash at Sedgwick indefinitely because she had given Peaches her own set of keys to everything. That had been followed by the discovery of clothes suitable for a country house party, along with a ball gown with the tag still on. Peaches had tried to protest, but Tess had ignored her. By the time she'd dug through her things at Holly's only to find a wallet full of cash and a note telling her not to argue with its origin, she had given up fighting her sister.

The trip north had started out well enough. The train ride had been pleasant, so she'd had no complaints there. Her suitcase had wheels, making it easy enough to pull around behind her. Holly had fed her something that morning that had almost made it past the butterflies in her stomach.

Her first indication that Fate might be throwing a monkey wrench into the gears of her perfect fairy-tale weekend was getting off the train and realizing that the station was in the middle of a village that was at least ten miles from Kenneworth House.

She had assumed she would be able to get a taxi, or take a bus, or perhaps even find a chauffeur holding up a card with her name on it at the station. Unfortunately, all those methods of transportation seemed to have been otherwise engaged.

She'd managed to hitch a ride for the first five miles in a little wagon being pulled by a bicycle, a wagon that had apparently most recently transported ripe compost. She'd pulled her suitcase behind the cart that was being pulled behind the bicycle and hoped that no one important would drive by and notice her.

That had been about four miles ago based on her rate of trudging, which she figured left her a mile still before she reached any sort of shelter. It was only the thought of a hot shower and an equally hot fire that had kept her slogging through what had been freezing rain and had now just turned into a bitter chill that reminded her of being in a walk-in freezer. She'd never been in a walk-in freezer, but she had a good imagination and time on her hands, so she had no trouble making the comparison.

She pushed a lock of frozen hair out of her face, ignoring the faint crackling sound, and looked up to find a hint of Kenneworth House in front of her. It was shrouded in a very nasty fog, but the outline was still there, which was almost enough to leave her needing to take a brief seat on her suitcase to recover from her relief. She looked behind her to judge the condition of her suitcase, but saw that it was barely staving off the effects of the elements. It was definitely not up to the task of providing her any meaningful support.

She could only hope the blasted thing was waterproof. If it wasn't, her clothes were going to need some serious attention once she was in what she could only assume based on the invitation would be an embarrassingly opulent room.

She took another look around, just to see if the sleet that had begun a renewed assault on her was going to be moving past anytime soon, then jumped a little at the sight of lights coming up the road behind her.

Great. It was one thing to sneak in the kitchen door and make a dash for her room where she could lock the door, shower, then pull herself together before she made her grand entrance down the main staircase. It was another thing entirely to be seen in her bedraggled state by a party guest with a potentially very big mouth. She looked around herself quickly to see if there might be somewhere to hide, but unfortunately all that surrounded her were foggy acres of manicured grounds.

Dotted by topiaries, as it happened. Well, there was obviously only one thing to do, and she did it without hesitation. She leaped off the road and well into the verge, plopped her suitcase down flat on the soggy ground, then hopped up on it and struck a pose. It was foggy enough, surely, that she would just look like a toga-draped goddess atop a pedestal, shrouded by mystery and a few bird droppings.

She remained motionless as the car came closer. It wouldn't have been an exaggeration to say she prayed with great fervor that the owner of that automobile would be so overwhelmed by the sight of Kenneworth House rising up majestically in the distance that he would simply drive on and not be looking over onto the right of the road.

Alas, things were just not going her way.

Her mother would have told her it was karma dealing out just deserts for having traded her hummus and sprouts sandwiches to unsuspecting fifth graders for Twinkies and Ding Dongs. Peaches probably would have told any number of her clients the same thing.

But having karma gunning for her was another thing entirely.

The car slowed to stop. Peaches left her hands outstretched in a goddessy pose in hopes the driver would simply think he or she was seeing things and move right along.

The driver's side window began a slow, agonizing descent into its allotted space in the door. Peaches fully expected to see David, the Duke of Kenneworth, frowning thoughtfully at a statue none of his ancestors had put there.

Instead, the driver was revealed to be none other than Stephen de Piaget, vexer of innocent life organizers and chief tormenter of poor, helpless Yanks who were currently freezing their statuary off just north of the Yorkshire moors.

He frowned thoughtfully for a moment or two, then rolled his window back up.

Typical.

Peaches could hardly wait to see his taillights, but it occurred to her that if she did, that would mean that he was driving up the way to the manor, which meant he was going to be in the same space with her for the weekend.

Well, at least she wouldn't have to see him in the immediate future—

Or, maybe she would.

He had put on his flashers and gotten out of the car. She wanted to warn him that he was going to ruin his lovely dress shoes by tromping around in the slush, but she could only stand there, her arms outstretched and her mouth gaping open, as he walked across the greensward toward her.

And then he looked her straight in the eye.

She credited her breathlessness to the chill. Yes, that was it. It had nothing to do with his amazingly lovely eyes, or that face that had no doubt launched a thousand girlish fantasies, or the fact that he had just gently taken her hands and put her arms down. He took her elbow and helped her down off her suitcase. She went, because she was still coherent enough to realize that she wasn't doing her wardrobe any favors by standing on it.

She wrapped her arms around herself, because it seemed like the right thing to do. But when Stephen reached for her suitcase, she felt herself thawing enough to speak.

"What are you doing?" she croaked.

He didn't say anything, as usual. He simply carried her suitcase back to his car.

"But—" She pulled herself together and tromped through the slush after him. "I need that."

He ignored her, which was irritating in the extreme. She watched him put her suitcase in the boot of his car, then walk around to the passenger side and open the door. He said nothing, he merely gestured for her to get in.

She stopped on the driver's side of the car. "Look," she said, realizing that she was looking a nattily dressed gift horse in the mouth, but unable to stop herself, "you de Piaget men have this really annoying habit of bossing people around. My sisters may have to put up with it, but I'm not going to."

He looked at her evenly. "It is just a ride up the way, Miss Alexander."

She stuck her chin out. "I don't need a ride." Actually it had come out *I-I-I d-d-don't n-n-need a r-r-r-ide*, but she didn't suppose any of the topiaries were taking note of her chattering teeth. Professor de Piaget, however, was no doubt taking note of the same, to use against her at an inopportune moment.

He stared at her for another minute or two in silence, then shrugged and walked around the back of the car. She wanted to ask him bitterly if he was going to pull her suitcase out of his trunk and hand it back to her before he continued on his way, but she didn't have time before he was shrugging out of what have to have been an obscenely expensive overcoat.

He draped it around her shoulders, then walked back around the passenger side of his car. He didn't even glance her way before he simply got in.

Peaches frowned. She also pulled the coat around her with a gingerness its owner didn't deserve. It was cashmere, after all.

The driver's side door opened, making her jump back. She managed to find the only ankle-deep puddle in the area, apparently, but by landing in it instead of on her backside saved Stephen's coat and her trousers. She suppressed the urge to swear and bent down to peer into the car.

"What are you doing?" she asked.

Stephen leaned over and looked up at her. "You don't want to ride," he said, "so I thought you might rather drive."

Peaches thought she might have more success guiding the space shuttle than his car, but perhaps now was not the time to say as much. His very expensive Mercedes was beckoning to her with all the irresistible charms of a male Siren; she could feel the warmth pouring out of the door from where she stood. She took a step forward, then made a last grasp for the remaining vestiges of reason and good sense.

"I'll ruin your seats."

"They're leather. I daresay they were subjected to worse when they were still on the cow."

Peaches caught her breath. He had probably made steaks out of the rest of that cow—which she would think about later—but she had to admit he did have a point. She glanced up at the rapidly darkening sky and thought that perhaps she might do well to get out of the weather before she caught her death.

Her feet made a sucking sound as she pulled them free of the muck, though, which made her rethink her enthusiasm to fall into the Mercedes's seductive embrace. She put her hand on the door and the edge of the roof for support, then took another look at the immaculate insides of Stephen's car. They would be forever sullied if she put her muddy, sopping self inside. She leaned over again and looked at him.

"I could sit on the roof," she offered.

"Please, no."

"But—"

"Please, Miss Alexander," he said, sounding as if he had only one nerve left and she was getting on it, "just get in before we both spend the rest of this damned weekend sneezing."

Well, he didn't sound all that enthusiastic about her fairy-tale-in-the-making, but maybe his invitation hadn't been as nice as hers, or one of his girlfriends had let him know she wasn't going to be attending. For all she knew, the fare was going to be strictly vegetarian and Stephen was mourning the future lack of animal fats adorning his plate. What did she know about British nobility apart from her uncanny knowledge of their ranks thanks to Aunt Edna's eclectic choices in graduation gifts?

Stephen didn't sound particularly friendly, but, then again, she was about to give his cow a bath so perhaps she couldn't expect anything else. She took a deep breath, coughed, then turned and backed down onto the driver's seat. She looked at her feet still lingering outside the car in her ruined dress shoes. She wasn't sure what would do less damage, her shoes or her bare feet, but at least her naked toes were less mud-caked. She pulled her feet out of her shoes, winced at the pain, then leaned over and gathered her shoes up into her lap.

She tried not to drip all over everything, really she did.

She pulled the door shut and sighed in relief in spite of herself.

Stephen cleared his throat. "Shall we?"

Peaches looked at him quickly, but he was only watching her with that same grave expression he always watched her with, as if he just didn't know what to think of her. That was so different from how Tess always described him that Peaches wondered if he'd had a personality transplant when no one had been looking. Tess always claimed he was wonderful, not at all stuffy, the life of any academic party.

Peaches couldn't see it. Maybe he really let loose when discussing hose and tunics, but even during those first few days she'd known him when they'd been looking for Pippa, he'd been polite.

Gravely polite. As if he were biting his tongue for some reason.

She supposed the reasons could be many and most of them would have to do with some way she was failing to live up to his very proper, very noble expectations.

She rubbed her hands over her face, then shook her head. Her hair made a slight crunching sound, which she supposed was the ice breaking up. Well, best to get Stephen up to the door and herself out of his car before she defrosted on it. Then she could bid him a gravely polite *adieu* and be on her way to her happily ever after while he went off and did his nobility thing with other nobility guys.

And while he was doing that, she would get on with the rest of her life. Her clothes would dry out, she would thaw out, and she would spend the rest of the weekend living out her most secret fantasy. After all, she had all the ingredients: gorgeous clothes, palatial manor house, handsome duke who had hand-penned a little note tucked inside her invitation expressing his delight over the potential for seeing her. Things were looking up.

And while things were looking up, she wouldn't think about the fact that her sister Pippa had decided that the Middle Ages and a certain very handsome lord named Montgomery were more to her taste than the modern-day world with its constant noise, running water, and Wi-Fi connections, or that Tess had married Montgomery's medieval brother who had found modern-day England more to his taste than the medieval world with its blissful silences, long evenings with nothing to do but spin and weave, and nothing pulling the family apart but a good skirmish now and again.

Her own life, she was fairly sure, couldn't have been worse in either time period. She had no business, no reputation, and the contents of her underwear drawer no doubt being prominently displayed in a Plexiglas case on Roger Peabody's mantel.

Yes, the sooner she got on with Fate's plans for her, the better off she would be.

"Miss Alexander?"

She realized that she wasn't squirming in Seattle, she was rapidly thawing out in jolly old England in the car of a man who was probably counting the minutes until he could get her out onto some sort of tarmac.

"I'm fine," she said, straightening abruptly. "I'm fine, thank you."

She couldn't look at him, because he would still be wearing that polite expression that he no doubt used for all those he had to be polite to.

She found the clutch, took hold of the gearshift, and hoped for the best.

It was no mean feat to get that car up that very long driveway—especially with Stephen de Piaget sitting next to her, no doubt marking every drip on his coat and his former cow-turned-expensive-seats—but she managed it without killing the engine. It was not a very smooth ride, however.

She lurched to a stop in front of what looked like the front door, then fumbled around for the key until she figured out how to turn the engine off. She couldn't look at Stephen, and she didn't want to look at the liveried guy who was trotting down the stairs to get her door for her, so she closed her eyes and made a list.

Dry clothes, dry self, dry hair. Handsome duke, delicious food, an orchestra that played waltzes—

Her door opened, but only partway because an arm reached over her and caught the door before it could open more than a crack.

"Is there a less visible entrance to the hall?" Stephen asked in a low voice.

Peaches was just sure she would have blushed if she hadn't been so cold. Never mind that she'd been thinking the very same thing.

"Drips on the floor and all that," he added.

Bonks on the head and all that. She started to say something nasty, then reconsidered. Maybe she should give him the benefit of the doubt. It was entirely possible he was trying to save her pride by keeping her from looking like an idiot in front of all the nobility in the area.

"Don't want her squelching through the halls, do we?" he continued. "A bit of mess there, what?"

Peaches decided he shouldn't be given the benefit of the

doubt, he should be given a swift boot in the arse. She would have, if she hadn't been hesitating over the thought of her dirty foot on the seat of his clean trousers.

Well, apparently there was an entrance in the back for muddy squelchers, something she discovered five minutes later as she was limping through it. She was offered a towel to wipe her feet with, which she greatly appreciated. The servant who had escorted her and Stephen inside looked at her shoes she was carrying in consternation, as if he couldn't decide if he should offer a plastic bag or a garbage can for their containment.

A butler of some stripe or other appeared in front of them and looked them over. Or, rather, he looked Stephen over and immediately folded his very tall frame into a respectful bow.

"Viscount Haulton," he intoned. "We've been expecting you."

Stephen made polite conversation. Peaches was too busy dripping to attempt any of the same.

"And Miss Alexander, I presume," the man continued, one of his eyebrows raised practically into his hairline.

Peaches could only nod slightly. She didn't dare do anything else for fear of scattering droplets of things that might make the butler frown.

"Oh, Stephen, darling," a feminine voice said smoothly, "you finally found your way here."

"A bit of a slog," Stephen said, "but I'm here."

Peaches agreed with him. He was there. And unfortunately so was she. She leaned to her right to watch two women come sweeping down the final five feet of the hallway and stop to flutter in front of the hapless Viscount Haulton. She recognized one of them as David's cousin, Andrea. Andrea looked at her, blinked, then her mouth fell open.

"Peaches?" she asked incredulously.

"The very same," Peaches croaked, wishing she had remained amongst the nonjudgmental topiaries outside. "I was caught in the weather."

"Obviously," the other woman said icily. "And you seem to have brought a great deal of that weather inside with you."

"Oh, Irene, do be quiet," Andrea said, rolling her eyes. She reached for Peaches. "Let me take you to your room. This, by the way, is my cousin Irene. She's David's sister."

"Ah—" Peaches began, but found her input was not necessary. Andrea made arrangements for Peaches's suitcase to be brought inside, then dragged her off to points unknown.

She knew she should have memorized where she was going, but it was all she could do to keep up with Andrea's rapid-fire heels as they clicked across marble floors Peaches was enormously glad she hadn't had to polish that morning. She felt sorry for whoever was coming along behind her to see to it.

The floors became less lovely, though, as they progressed, and the art on the walls smaller and then nonexistent. Andrea finally stopped in front of a door in a hallway that had definitely seen better days.

"Here we are," Andrea said brightly. She opened the door and flicked on a single bulb that hung down from the ceiling. "Oh," she said, sounding slightly less enthusiastic. "Well, perhaps there's a lamp somewhere."

There was. Next to a bed that belonged in a school for girls directly inspired by a Charlotte Brontë novel. Peaches found that, as usual lately, her mouth was hanging open. She was so shocked by the absolute starkness of what she was looking at, she couldn't find anything at all to say.

"Not to worry," Andrea announced. "You won't be spending much time here anyway."

Well, there was that. Peaches tried to look on the bright side, but that side was lit by a harsh bulb that looked as if it belonged in a shabby little room where thugs were about to question the good guy about things he wasn't going to want to reveal.

"Thomas, this does seem a bit austere, doesn't it?"

"My apologies, Lady Andrea," said a voice from behind Peaches, "but we had a last-minute guest on the list and his rank demanded the accommodations intended for Miss Alexander."

"Who was that?" Andrea asked, looking surprised.

"The Viscount Haulton, of course."

Peaches looked over her shoulder to find a butler there herding a footman of some kind who was gingerly holding on to Peaches's suitcase and her shoes. She wasn't sure what she would die sooner of: mortification, fury, or frostbite. Given that she was starting to feel her toes again, perhaps the last one should have been removed from the list. Embarrassment, though, was vying for first place with the fury that was fast becoming a grim resignation. There was only one conclusion to come to.

Stephen de Piaget was trying to ruin her life.

"Oh, and here is Betty to attend you," Andrea said cheerfully. "David has obviously put thought into your comfort. Betty, let's have Miss Alexander's things unpacked, shall we? Then she will perhaps want to bathe."

Peaches couldn't even nod.

She was used to the sensation of being somewhere new and uncomfortable. She'd felt that way when she'd come to England the first time. She'd endured it numerous times in college while switching apartments and having to get to know an entirely new set of roommates. She had learned to manage the feeling very well thanks to a variety of experiences, but now it was as if she'd never dealt with it at all.

If she'd been a bawler, she would have sat down and bawled. Instead, she gulped. Several times. She continued to gulp as Betty put her sopping-wet suitcase on the end of the bed and began to pull equally sodden clothing from it.

"Oh," Andrea said, sounding slightly horrified. "Peaches, look at your gown."

Peaches did, then wished she hadn't. Her ball gown, which she shouldn't have packed in a suitcase anyway, was wrinkled beyond repair. Peaches wasn't entirely sure it wasn't wet as well.

"Never mind," Andrea said, sweeping the dress up into her arms, "I'll have it pressed. It will be as good as new." She blew Peaches a kiss and sailed out the door. "See you at supper later tonight!"

Supper. Peaches realized then that she hadn't eaten since breakfast, but considering how upset her stomach was at present, she wasn't sure that wasn't a good thing. She was tempted to just go to bed, but perhaps she should at least make an appearance. She watched the tail end of Andrea disappear around the corner, then turned slowly and looked at her maid, who was unpacking the rest of her clothing that showed quite clearly that her suitcase was not waterproof.

Betty pursed her lips.

Peaches couldn't have agreed more. She looked around her room hopefully for some sort of bathroom, but it was obvious none existed. She turned a hopeful glance on Betty.

"En suite facilities?" she asked.

Betty pointed toward the door. "Third door down the hallway. I'd make use of the loo quick, though, miss. There'll be quite a line before suppertime."

Peaches imagined there would be.

She experienced the renewed temptation to go to bed for the evening, but she was cold and filthy, so she put her shoulders back, took the completely inadequate towel she found on a rickety stool near the door, and headed for the loo.

Even Cinderella had gotten off to a rocky start, hadn't she?

Chapter 6

Stephen resisted the urge to peel Irene's fingers away from his arm only because he was a gentleman, but what he wanted to be doing was following Peaches to make certain she was treated properly. Given that such was impossible at present, he could only trust that David had put her somewhere close to his own suite of rooms. As long as Peaches had a decent lock on her door, she would be safe enough.

He continued to listen to Irene talk about things he didn't care about, which left him making all kinds of polite noises that he didn't mean. Fifteen very long minutes and a promise to sit with her during supper later, he was hastening through the kitchen and out the back door. His car was where he'd left it, making Kenneworth's staff nervous. A younger man was pacing restlessly and casting the occasional look at the house, as if he expected someone to come flying out the door to demand to know why the car hadn't already been put away.

Stephen trotted down the stairs to the courtyard and smiled reassuringly at him. "Where shall I take it?"

The young man came close to wringing his hands. "Oh, I'll see to it for you, my lord. It wouldn't do for you to see to it yourself."

Stephen smiled deprecatingly. "It wouldn't be the first time, but I appreciate the offer. You might want to put something down on the seat first. It was a bit of a soggy trip here."

"I'll see to it all, my lord," the lad said. He flashed Stephen a shy smile. "It would be an honor to see to your automobile, my lord. It deserves the best of care."

Stephen smiled to himself, made a mental note to see the lad rewarded properly for his pains, then handed his keys over without worry. He walked back into the house to find a servant waiting for him.

He followed the ancient footman through the house and up the carpeted stairs. The journey was accomplished without haste, which gave him ample opportunity to catalog what he was seeing. He had actually never been inside Kenneworth House. His father and David's father had been frostily polite to each other in public and rather pointedly rude in private, which had precluded any invitations being extended.

Stephen hadn't been inclined to bother much with David, though, which left him sadly failing to continue on the tradition of animosity. He'd heard from more than one source that there had been troubles going on between the families for generations, but he'd honestly never had an interest in finding out exactly what they concerned. Some offense given at some point, no doubt, leading to centuries of slurs being spoken in the privacy of libraries. It was nothing more than scores of other offenses dealt out over the centuries between other families.

Though as he glanced at portraits of Kenneworth ancestors staring down at him from their perches on the walls, he couldn't help but wonder which was the one who had either started or joined in the amusement. He paused at the top of the stairs and looked at the portrait of a man wearing rather medieval-looking garb.

"The first lord of Kenneworth," the servant intoned. "Hubert, my lord."

Stephen frowned at the portrait, because it seemed like the appropriate thing to do. For all he knew it had been that fool there to begin something he hadn't been able to finish.

He followed his hoary-headed guide down the long hallway, noted the rather threadbare patches here and there in the carpet, and wondered how it was David kept the lights on. He was rumored to be a gambler, but perhaps he was better at cards than he was at attending to his floors.

He was deposited inside a surprisingly opulent room. His personal valet rose immediately from his position by the fire, book in hand. Stephen smiled at the man who had been keeping him not only well dressed but organized for the better part of his life.

"Wodehouse?"

"A rather interesting time-travel romance, actually," Humphreys said, folding back the sedate dust jacket to reveal an obviously new paperback. "Mrs. Jane Fergusson gave it to me the last time I accompanied you to Scotland, but I haven't had the chance to give it the proper attention until this afternoon. It was written, I believe, by Laird MacLeod's wife, Elizabeth. One of her earlier works, it would seem."

"She has works?" Stephen asked in surprise.

"Apparently."

"Well, the winters in Scotland are long," Stephen offered.

"And their family tree is simply bursting with paranormal oddities," Humphreys said, straight-faced. "Unlike the de Piagets', of course."

Stephen flinched in spite of himself at the memory of a recent evening in his study, but Humphreys apparently didn't notice. Not that he would have been surprised. He'd had his share of encounters with boo-bellowing ghosties in the darkened hallways of Artane.

Humphreys set aside his book. "Your clothing is prepared, my lord. Shall you dress for supper now?"

What Stephen wanted to do was put his feet up and have a closer look at what his valet was reading, but obviously duty awaited. He thanked his man for his pains, then took himself off to the loo to wash off the evidence of his journey.

He put on what Humphreys had selected for him without comment. He supposed his own tastes had been molded over the years by what had been laid out for him, but Humphreys did have an excellent eye for clothes, so perhaps that had been a good thing.

He didn't, however, refuse a moment or two to simply sit by the fire and gather his thoughts as Humphreys tidied the chamber. He watched for a moment, then cleared his throat.

"I don't suppose," he began carefully, "that you would know where the other guests have been placed." He looked at his valet innocently. "Just to satisfy my curiosity, of course."

Humphreys walked over to the desk and produced a large sheaf of paper from under the blotter. He laid it down and looked at Stephen.

"Something like this, my lord?"

Stephen heaved himself out of the chair and crossed the room. There on the desk lay a schematic of Kenneworth House with names of guests penciled in where they had apparently been placed for the duration. Stephen shot Humphreys a look.

"I won't ask where you got this."

"That might be wise."

"Or why."

"Even wiser, my lord."

Stephen studied the map and was unsurprised to find himself staying in the room adjacent to Irene Preston's. What did surprise him, however, was to see that the three women who had texted him before the party to assure themselves that he would indeed be there with bells on were all in a tidy row to the south of his bedroom. He could only imagine the gauntlet he would be required to walk each night if he were to exit his chamber at an unfortunate hour.

He studied the map for another long moment, then frowned thoughtfully. "I don't see Miss Alexander listed here." He started to speak, then it occurred to him that perhaps David had assumed she would be staying with him.

It was surprising how quickly a blinding anger could overcome a man when he was least expecting it.

"I believe there was a last-minute shuffle," Humphreys said carefully.

Stephen looked at him sharply. "A last-minute shuffle?"

"So I understand."

"Why do I have the feeling I'm not going to like where this is going?"

Humphreys clasped his hands behind his back. "I have the feeling, my lord, that you're going to be highly displeased. I would have of course inserted myself into events to the extent I was able, but I feared to ruffle any Kenneworth feathers."

"Leaving the ruffling to me," Stephen said sourly.

"Your ability to obtain your desired ends with grace and diplomacy, my lord, is legendary."

Stephen laughed a little in spite of himself. "And I learned most of it from you, I daresay."

Humphreys only inclined his head modestly. "As you say, my lord."

"Do you think you could find out where Miss Alexander is staying without ruffling any feathers?"

"Of course, my lord."

"And I need you to do some investigating about another thing that puzzles me."

Humphreys did everything short of putting on a black bowler hat and drawing a monocle from his jacket pocket. He lifted his eyebrow inquiringly. "Investigating, my lord?"

"I'm curious about a certain guest," Stephen said, when he thought he could say it casually.

"Our Miss Alexander, I presume."

Stephen nodded. "I'm wondering who invited her," he said slowly and rather unwillingly. "It seems rather . . . unusual."

"Because she is an American?"

"That, and I wasn't aware she was so well acquainted with the Duke of Kenneworth as to merit his personal invitation."

"I believe he encountered her at Lord Payneswick's weekend earlier in the month. Rumor has it the duke was quite smitten."

Stephen didn't ask where Humphreys had heard that rumor and he didn't dare comment on what he thought of His Grace's amorous proclivities. He just knew hell would freeze over before he left Peaches alone with the snake.

Stephen looked at Humphreys. "I'm worried that I don't see her on this map."

"I understand completely, my lord."

"I'll leave you to unraveling the mystery of it, then."

"Have a pleasant evening, my lord."

"I will," Stephen assured him, though he imagined he wouldn't. It looked to him as if Peaches had been shuffled completely out of the house, though he couldn't imagine David would be pleased by that if luring her up to his bedroom was his goal.

Then again, David likely didn't concern himself with housekeeping matters. Neither did his mother, the dowager Duchess

of Kenneworth. She was a lovely woman, but made it her habit
to steer clear of her children. Stephen knew that only because
Raphaela Preston was a very good friend of his mother's, all
feuding aside. Stephen suspected that Irene had been the one
making the arrangements, which left him rather worried indeed.

But it wasn't as if he could go knocking on every door himself to see where Peaches was being housed. He would leave
that up to Humphreys and go make nice for the evening. At least
the evening was just the overture before the true opera began.
With any luck, he would find half the players hadn't yet arrived
and he wouldn't have to watch his own back so closely quite yet.

He found himself escorted downstairs by the same geriatric
guardian who had led him up those stairs, and the descent was
no more speedy than the ascent. Goggling over the ancestors
was his lot again, and he did it with enthusiasm, to tell his father
what he'd seen, if for no other reason. Lord Edward would have
been supremely satisfied to find that protruding ears and a snout
nose had run rampant in the family for generations. How David
had managed to avoid the full manifestation of either, Stephen
couldn't have said.

He was turned loose in a dining room that had been set up not
for supper but a buffet wholly inadequate to doing anything
more than making him wonder if Humphreys could find the pantry and pillage the contents later.

He spent a very unpleasant hour trying to balance a plate of
inedible hors d'oeuvres—David should most definitely replace
his chef—and negotiate the minefield that was his complicated
social life. Peaches hadn't arrived yet, which worried him, but
perhaps she had decided to take supper in her room. He wished
he could have joined her.

He wasn't sure he was equal to identifying all the players
gathered there, but he supposed he might as well identify the
hazards—especially the trio of girlfriends he was going to have
to manage. He decided to dispense with reminding himself of
their familial connections simply because those connections
didn't matter. The women were daughters of dukes, uniformly
well-heeled, and all very much enamored of the trappings of his
title and the glittering guests at his grandmother's regular soirees.

In him personally, he supposed, they were rather less interested, unless his Rolls and a few paparazzi were involved.

He considered the least dangerous of the lot first. Her name was Zoe, and she was dim enough that he suspected she had been at the dye bottle once too often and bleached not only her locks, but her brain as well. She loved his grandmother's parties and only pouted when he had other commitments. He wasn't sure she could even spell medieval, much less give any details about the time period.

Brittani, who sported stunning dark hair and an absolutely flawless face, possessed a personality that would have made vampires hike up their cloaks and tiptoe away whilst she remained peacefully and safely asleep. She especially loved his Rolls, trendy eateries in London, and his excellent seats in Drury Lane. She had read English Literature in college and could carry on a very interesting conversation when it suited her, which it rarely did. Stephen suspected that she would have agreed to marry him if he'd asked, but that would have required her to tell her Italian lover to set sail for other shores. Stephen had no fear that he would ever be standing before a priest with her.

The final woman in that trio of harpies was Victoria, who would have done her namesake proud. She didn't merely enjoy his preferred seating or taste in music or tickets to the opera, she carried on as if his lifestyle and the luxuries associated with it were her due. She was a dark blonde, he suspected, but he wasn't about to ask her the truth of it. He couldn't say any of his outings with her were enjoyable, but of the three, her pedigree pleased his grandmother the most so he endured her company to buy familial peace.

Really, he was going to have to put his foot down with the old woman at some point—and he wasn't talking about Victoria.

Things became quite a bit more dangerous when Irene spotted him and came to see how he fared. She was obviously a woman with a steel spine because she ignored Zoe and Brittani and simply smiled pleasantly at Victoria. If Stephen hadn't been more frightened of her than the other three combined, he might have admired her pluck.

She was very lovely in a pale-haired, fair-skinned, conservatively dressed way that he would have admired had it not been for the fact that he was rather too acquainted with a reputation that rather ruined the whole picture. She was, he had heard, particularly vicious to those whom she felt had slighted her and very vocal about ruining their reputations. Stephen didn't care for how often she seemed to find herself in the paper for this or that, but it wasn't for him to say how she conducted her affairs.

It was for him, however, to say how he conducted his own. Despite her numerous and not-very-subtle advances, he was not about to be entangled in her elegant and sophisticated tendrils.

"Enjoying yourself, Haulton?" she asked, gliding to a stop next to him.

"Immensely," he said politely. "It is a pleasure to see you in a setting that befits your beauty."

"Aren't you droll," she said with a bit of bite to her tone that made him unaccountably uneasy. "I don't see your bedraggled chauffeur here. Perhaps she's still drying out."

"Perhaps," Stephen said with a shrug. He had the distinct feeling he would be doing Peaches no favors by directing any of Irene's attention her way. She would garner enough of it, he imagined, if she found herself in David's company too often. "Lovely buffet you have here."

"Supper arrangements were changed without my knowledge," Irene said, "which unfortunately leaves you unable to enjoy my company at table. Perhaps tomorrow things will turn out differently."

He inclined his head. "It would be my pleasure to discuss the upcoming delights your brother has planned for the weekend with you first thing tomorrow over kippers and toast."

She only lifted a pale eyebrow before she turned and walked away. He didn't dare speculate on who had caught her attention, but he suspected it was Kenneworth's head butler, who was currently overseeing the buffet. Stephen hoped for his sake that he hadn't been the one to decide against a sit-down affair.

For himself, he was merely relieved to catch the eye of a passing servant and hand off his untouched plate. Four landmines in the room, and he'd only managed to avoid the worst of the lot—

"I'll keep you safe, if you like."

Stephen was certain he'd jumped, but perhaps he'd managed to hide his surprise better than he'd hoped. He looked next to him to find Andrea Preston standing there.

He stretched himself to come up with the connections that would have allowed Andrea to find herself running in Irene's lofty social circle without supervision, but apart from her being Irene's cousin, the best he could do was her being the youngest daughter of a very minor baron, the seventh, he thought, of some obscure village that consisted of a petrol station, a church turned into leisure center, and a cluster of very old row houses that abutted some extremely worn and poached fragments of an equally obscure and minor border keep.

Or something like that.

He had encountered her several times over the past handful of years, found her to be a polite and undemanding table companion, and rather more sensible than he would have supposed considering the friends she kept. He smiled politely.

"Do I need to be kept safe?" he asked.

She laughed lightly. "Oh, I think so. I've been watching the room."

"And how have you found the view?"

"Very nice," she said, "but I'm not the stag being hunted by every woman who possesses a pulse. And just so you don't worry, I don't include myself in that company."

"I believe I should be offended."

"Oh, no, you shouldn't," she said cheerfully. "You're too lofty for me."

Stephen smiled ruefully. "Oh, it's all rubbish, isn't it? But I'm sure you know that already."

She only shrugged and smiled before she turned with him to watch for any untoward stampedes. He found himself thinking kindly of her simply because she had been kind to Peaches.

It also might be useful to have another pair of eyes on the field of intrigue, especially a pair of eyes that wasn't looking his way. He leaned back against the wall and scanned the group of very well-dressed partygoers.

"Oh, my," Andrea breathed. "Oh, dear."

Stephen followed the general direction of her gaze, then closed his eyes briefly at the sight of the new addition to the room.

It was Peaches, looking rather worse for wear.

He wasn't sure where she had unearthed her clothes from, or why there hadn't been an iron to be found, but all signs pointed to an outfit that should have been consigned to the nearest rubbish bin.

He was rather disgusted with himself that his first thought was that she hadn't a clue how to dress properly for a social function. He attempted to redeem himself by latching on to his second thought, which was there had never been a woman more in need of a rescue. And given that no one else in the room was doing anything more than simply looking at her, he was obviously the one to execute the same.

Though he supposed he would be wise to do so silently.

There was no sense in adding to what he could see was going to be a rather miserable evening for her.

Chapter 7

Peaches could safely say she was not feeling like the belle of the ball at the moment.

In fact, she wasn't sure if she would have felt any more conspicuous if she'd arrived in her underwear. At least her underwear was dry and relatively unwrinkled. She certainly couldn't say the same about her clothes.

She *could* say that she wasn't convinced that her maid hadn't been plotting to ruin her evening. After she'd unthawed her extremities under some very lukewarm water in a loo that would have benefitted from a good scrubbing, she had returned to her room to find that Betty had unpacked all her things and distributed them around the room to dry, though in a rather haphazard fashion. The resemblance to her college dorm room had been slightly comforting, but seeing everything in its less-than-pristine state had left her choosing the least objectionable of what she had and hoping it would be good enough.

Obviously she had chosen amiss.

"Let me show you to the buffet, miss," said a voice at her side.

She looked to find a youngish maid there, looking at her with her eyes watering. Peaches wasn't sure if she was laughing or if the smell of wet wool sweater was overpowering the poor girl. Peaches was half tempted—actually, closer to 99 percent tempted—to turn and run away. Then she managed to identify in the sea of faces one that she recognized.

Stephen de Piaget, looking grave.

Perhaps that was the expression he wore when he was trying not to bray out a laugh about the faults and foibles of a woman he thought only intelligent enough to identify the ingredients going into her compost.

And if he was going to look at her that way, she absolutely wasn't going to give up.

Unfortunately, he was starting across the room toward her. Her only hope was to escape, and she decided her best avenue of escape was to go with the maid who was stifling without success her giggles. Hopefully some supper in her hand would give her courage to face the crowd.

Hobnobbing with nobility, she decided as she filled a plate that was wholly inadequate to supporting food while her trembling hand was carrying it, was just not her thing. She liked one-on-one encounters with people who liked her. She did *not* like being in a room full of people she didn't know, most of whom were looking at her as if she'd just come in from rolling around in the stables.

She stood at the buffet and gulped a time or two. Unfortunately the only thing that did was give her a good whiff of her sweater. She had to blink her eyes rapidly to keep them from tearing uncontrollably, but what else could she have done? Her only blouse had been hopelessly wrinkled and wearing an evening gown had seemed inappropriate. The sweater had been damp, but she hadn't realized it had been *that* fragrant. That said something about the state of her room, something she didn't want to think about. As for her current condition, it hadn't been as if she could have worn Stephen's overcoat, had it?

She looked in the mirror to see her doom coming toward her in three parts. David was laughing with guests as he moved toward her, but he was definitely on his way to talk to her. Andrea was currently engaged in conversation with Irene but looked to be trying to extricate herself from it to come Peaches's way. And, finally, there was Stephen de Piaget, inexorably working his way toward her while working the room at the same time. He looked like a jaguar, polished, lethal, and absolutely relentless. Women he stopped to speak to were left in various states of swoon. Men looked vaguely dissatisfied, as if they hadn't engaged in all the nobleman chitchat they'd desired.

He scared the hell out of her.

There, she had said it. He was snobby, tweedy, and absolutely undeterred, apparently, when he made up his mind about something. She pitied the poor books he was looking for in the library. She wouldn't have blamed them for hiding behind Tudor manuscripts just to escape his scrutiny.

She had no interest in what he would say to her, because she was certain it would have to do with her not having dressed suitably for the evening. She imagined it would also involve a long, tedious lecture on all reasons she didn't belong—actually, given that it was Stephen, it wouldn't be a long lecture. It would just be a look that would speak volumes.

Which was why she would avoid him like the plague.

Fortunately for her, Andrea reached her first. She looked at David's cousin warily, but was relieved to find Andrea seemed to be on her side.

"Oh, Peaches," Andrea said with a miserable smile, "it was a bit of a slog to get here, wasn't it?"

"Does it show?" Peaches asked lightly.

"You should have sent for something of mine," Andrea chided.

"I didn't think to," Peaches said, because that was true. She'd been too busy trying to regain the feeling in her hands and feet and wondering what in the hell she'd been going to do since she hadn't had anything dry to wear in public.

"Well, lovey, next time just trot down the hall—oh, except you aren't down the hall. No matter," she finished quickly. "Send your maid up later tonight for something to wear tomorrow if she hasn't already gone to bed by the time you get back to your room."

Peaches wasn't sure what Betty's nocturnal habits were, but she thought she could safely guarantee she herself would be indulging in an early night. If not, she would have no trouble kicking Betty's cot on her way to her room. Maybe the woman could be sent off on a mission of sartorial mercy.

"And here comes David," Andrea said. "I think he's been waiting for you."

Peaches resisted the urge to close her eyes and indulge in a little prayer, because someone might notice. Instead, she took a firmer grip on her plate and turned to find David Preston indeed coming toward her, entertaining souls along the way with his sparkling wit and no doubt vastly entertaining anecdotes about things Peaches was sure were just fascinating.

And she smelled like wet dog.

To his credit, David only wrinkled his nose once and so quickly that she hardly noticed. He frowned slightly.

"Get caught out in the wet, Peachy?"

She suppressed a wince, because the sound of that name was a bit like fingernails on the chalkboard, but then again, she was sure nothing could have made her happy at the moment. It didn't bother her at other times. Honestly.

She took a careful breath so she didn't make her eyes water and looked at him. "Yes," she said, doing her best to smile.

David continued to frown. "That's odd. Irene said she had sent someone to the station to pick you up. I'm sure of it."

Peaches didn't want to credit Irene with nefarious intentions, so she pushed aside a tiny, unpleasant thought about the fact that her clothes were damaged and she was making a bad first impression. Surely David's sister wasn't purposely malicious.

"Well, there was a mix-up somewhere," Andrea said with a shrug, "but we're all here now and mostly dry. Things could be much worse."

"Well," David began slowly.

"And isn't Peaches's sweater lovely?" Andrea continued. "And did you know she counts among her clients one of Seattle's most famous telly hosts?"

David continued to sniff despite Andrea's continued efforts to create a verbal résumé for her. Peaches was grateful for the thought, but she found it difficult to concentrate on what Andrea was saying. There was a smell that smelled even worse, if possible, than she did. She sniffed surreptitiously, then realized that the stench was coming from her plate. What next? Poison?

She looked for somewhere to deposit the goods, as it were, but couldn't find anywhere convenient to stash them. It wasn't possible that karma had a very long memory and those eleven-year-old kids she'd deprived of their Ding Dongs and Ho Hos had truly suffered, was it? And did retribution have to come while she was standing there in a damp wool sweater and wearing wool trousers that hadn't quite managed to be rid of the proof of their trip in the vegetable cart?

Apparently it did. She listened to Andrea and David discuss her in increasing detail, then watched in horror as other people came her way, people that made her wonder if she would actually manage to keep things on her plate. Stephen de Piaget was still working his way across the room toward her, still leaving swooning women and disappointed men trying to talk to him in his wake.

And then there was Irene Preston approaching in a more direct fashion and leaving those in her wake quivering in fear.

Peaches was beginning to think she'd made a terrible mistake. It was a fairy tale, all right, but not exactly the kind she'd been hoping for. She was horrendously uncomfortable, feeling terribly out of place, and now she had the twin terrors of Irene Preston and the Viscount Haulton to deal with.

Irene reached her first and her look of disdain was like a slap. "Interesting evening wear, Miss Alexander."

Peaches would be the first to admit she generally didn't much care what people thought of her. But somehow, now that she was out of her comfort zone and still smelling slightly like wet sheep, she cared very much.

"I thought we were sending a car for her," David said, looking at his sister sharply.

"Of course we were," Irene snapped at her brother. "Surely you don't think I would purposely put her out in the weather, do you? She probably sent it away so she would garner sympathy or something equally ridiculous. What do I know of how this person thinks? It's hardly my fault she hasn't a clue how to dress properly—"

Peaches found her plate leaving her hand. She jumped, terrified its contents were about to land on the floor, only to find that that dastardly Stephen de Piaget had poached it. Never mind that he had taken it out of her hands and simply set it on the buffet.

"Is that your *sweater* that smells so badly?" Irene asked incredulously.

Stephen took Peaches by the elbow. "If you'll excuse us, Miss Alexander needs to call her sister immediately."

Peaches looked at him in surprise. "What?"

"Sedgwick is on fire."

Peaches felt her knees buckle, but she was spared the indignity of landing on her less-than-pristine slacks by Stephen making excuses for her and pulling her through the crowd that had turned to look at her. She didn't want to credit them with smirking, but she didn't imagine it was Stephen they were snickering at. Being hauled out of dinner like a recalcitrant child was no doubt adding a great deal to the spectacle. She tried to pull her arm away from him, but he didn't seem inclined to release her.

"I can walk, you know," she said pointedly.

He said nothing. He simply continued to pull her along with him.

"Why did Tess call you and not me?"

He ignored her.

Peaches put up with it until they were out of the dining room and twenty feet down the hall before she pulled her arm away from him and glared at him.

"*Stop* herding me."

He simply looked at her. "You must be hungry."

She blinked. "What does that have to do with anything?"

"Nothing in particular."

She was obviously light-headed from having missed lunch. That was the only reason nothing that was happening at the moment made any sense. She focused on Stephen with difficulty. "Is Sedgwick on fire?"

"I haven't eaten, either," he said. "I imagine the edible food is still hiding in the pantry."

She rubbed her arms and wondered if she had just dropped into some sort of alternate reality. There was a man standing in front of her, an extremely handsome man dressed in a quite lovely sport coat, trousers, and burgundy tie. He didn't look as if he'd just lost his mind, but he was saying things that simply didn't make sense.

"Is my sister's hall on fire?" she asked again.

"No."

She felt her mouth fall open. "You pulled me out of that party with a *lie*?"

"Subterfuge," he corrected. "It comes in handy when the food at a buffet is inedible and the company intolerable."

The brittle laughter echoing down the hallway sent a renewed flush to her face. She had credited the last blush to the number of people in the room and still having her extremities warming up. Now, she had to admit, it had been more a blush of shame than anything else.

"They're very good people," Peaches said, trying to be polite. "High society, and all that."

"But the food was dreadful," he said, taking her by the elbow yet again. "And if we don't hurry, they'll fetch us and make us eat more of it."

"I don't want to be rude," she protested. "To Lord David."

"Trust me, he won't notice your absence. He has other things to keep him occupied."

It took her another twenty feet to realize what he'd said. And when she did, she felt as if she'd been kicked in the stomach. She managed to get her elbow away from him without undue fuss. It occurred to her that she didn't even have the energy to be angry with him for what he'd said because it was probably the truth.

Stephen cleared his throat. "I meant—"

"I'm tired," she said, her voice sounding far away and slightly tinny to her own ears. "I think I need to just go to bed, if you don't mind." She looked around herself, but all she could see were wallpapered walls decorated with mirrors that reflected just how unlovely she looked at the moment. "If I could just find my way—"

Stephen stepped between her and the largest mirror she couldn't seem to stop looking in, leaving her no choice but to look up at him. "I didn't have lunch," he said quietly, "and I imagine you didn't, either."

She was slightly unnerved by the kindness in his voice, but she decided to treat that as an aberration. He couldn't be trying to be nice to her. "I wonder if they'll let me have a glass of water before I retire?" she muttered.

Stephen didn't move; he only remained where he was, silent and very grave.

Peaches would have tried to get past him but she found her way blocked by a new butlerish sort of person who was dressed in clothes that looked as if he'd swiped them from a Regency-period piece set. He made Stephen a small bow.

"My lord," he said, then turned to her. "And Miss Alexander, of course. I have a meal prepared for you both."

Peaches felt her mouth fall open. "You do?"

The older man nodded. "His lordship doesn't much care for rich food, miss, and given his terrible temper, I do my best to humor him at all times."

Peaches retrieved her jaw from where it had descended. "Do you know each other?"

"Yes, miss," the man said. "I am Humphreys, Lord Stephen's gentleman's personal gentleman."

Peaches smiled in spite of herself. She thought it might have been the first time she'd smiled all day. "Are you, really?"

"I am," Humphreys said seriously. "Really. And as such, being familiar with his lordship's legendary unhappiness when he misses his usual fare, I have taken the liberty of providing what suits him. I hope, miss, that it will suit you as well."

She wanted to say that any meal that didn't include Irene Preston commenting on her wardrobe suited her just fine, but she didn't have the chance. She simply followed Stephen's keeper past the kitchen and along a hallway to a delightful little breakfast room.

An older woman was standing at the window, but she turned when they entered. Humphreys paused, then made the woman a bow before he turned and made introductions.

"Her Grace, Raphaela Preston, dowager Duchess of Kenneworth," he intoned, "may I present Miss Peaches Alexander. I believe, Your Grace, that you already know the Viscount Haulton."

"I believe I do," the duchess said, coming over to allow Stephen to kiss her hand. "I'm pleased you found these two, Humphreys. They look hungry."

Peaches found herself swept up into Raphaela Preston's cloud of perfume and exquisite manners and didn't have the energy or the desire to fight the trip.

Whoever had determined that supper down the way should be a buffet had obviously not dared tangle with the duchess and her desires for a decent meal. Peaches didn't pay much attention to what she ate past noting that it was hot, vegetarian, and delicious. Stephen's meal, from what she noticed of it, was much like hers with the addition of a few heartier side dishes that he plowed through with single-mindedness. Peaches looked at the duchess finally and smiled.

"Thank you, Your Grace."

The duchess waved her hand dismissively. "Call me Raphaela, darling. We don't stand on formality here in this little room."

Peaches was quite happy to discover that the duchess preferred private meals over lavish buffets and French over English. She was also enormously relieved that she had taken such pains to become fluent under Aunt Edna's Swiss-style finishing school tutelage. She was almost surprised to listen to Stephen take part now and again in the conversation in his own perfect French.

She had to close her eyes briefly. How could the man be so deliciously cultured yet such a cad at the same time?

"I see, my dear, that you have dressed very sensibly for a quiet evening after a long journey here."

"Ah, yes," Peaches managed, because it was the best she could do. She was acutely aware of her less-than-pristine attire. At least the worst of the wet sheep smell had been left behind in some location that wasn't her present one. "It has been a long day, Your Grace."

"Raphaela," the duchess said with a small smile, "though I've heard so much about you I think you might soon be calling me something more familiar than that. If my son has his way, of course. I wonder what Haulton has to say about that?"

Peaches looked at Stephen to find him watching the duchess with a bland expression. Whatever else could be said about the man, he would have made a formidable poker player.

"I believe, Your Grace," he said, "that on some subjects it is best to remain silent."

Peaches imagined it was and did her best not to scowl at Stephen. She could only imagine what he would say about David wishing to have anything of a romantic or fairy-tale nature to do with her.

Raphaela laughed and reached over to pat his hand. "Wisdom gained from many years treading carefully, no doubt. Now, Peaches darling, tell me of yourself. What brought you to England during such unpleasant weather?"

Peaches didn't dare look at Stephen as she spun a very elaborate tale about wanting to keep in touch with her twin sister, which easily led away from her own circumstances to a discussion of twins in general.

By the time she had warmed up sufficiently by the small fire in the delicate hearth, she was starting to feel less out of place. Raphaela Preston was a wonderful host, dinner had been marvelous, and the conversation delightful. Even Stephen had managed to keep his mouth shut.

She was almost to the point where she thought she could stop second-guessing her decision to come at all. She had a wonderful ball gown thanks to her sister's generosity. If she worked things right, she might manage to avoid tomorrow morning's shooting party and the accompanying humiliation of having to ride a horse. The afternoon would be more difficult, but maybe Raphaela had some intentions she needed help focusing, which would require Peaches to remain with her out of sight until supper. She could perhaps borrow something from Andrea for dinner, then spend the bulk of Saturday preparing for the ball.

And perhaps somewhere along the line, she might manage to pull together the slightly unraveled threads of her fairy tale.

She was in the kitchen, true, but she wasn't covered in soot. The lady of the house seemed to like her, not want to put her to work, and the eligible duke hadn't even had the chance to move past the unfortunate condition of her sweater to really get things zipping right along.

Now, if she could only manage to get rid of that enormous fly in the ointment sitting approximately three feet from her, sipping manfully at his tea, things might start really looking up.

Chapter 8

S tephen sat in the morning breakfast room with two beautiful women and the remains of an excellent supper, and was very grateful for both. He was fairly sure Peaches was no fonder of him than she had been before supper, but at least she was fed and out of the lion's den. For himself, he had been happy to simply sit back and listen to Peaches and Raphaela discuss everything from art to fashion to the deplorable lack of decent food north of Calais. He, being an Englishman, had been forced to defend his country's culinary roots, but he had been immediately overruled.

Raphaela wagged her finger at him. "You cannot deny the abysmal state of British cuisine, darling."

"Artane's chef is without peer," Stephen said mildly, "though I will admit that even yours has done himself proud tonight."

"And you would rather eat in London than in Paris?" she asked archly.

"I never said that," he conceded, "though I never said I wouldn't, either. I was merely trying to be politic and assure myself of a decent meal or two at your table over the remainder of the weekend."

Raphaela laughed lightly. "I promise not to have you poisoned, dastardly de Piaget spawn that you are. And before you are forced to sing the praises of my chef overmuch, we should perhaps see ourselves off to bed. I understand David has a morning of riding and hunting planned, and I wouldn't want you to miss any of your shots."

Stephen imagined she wouldn't. He smiled dryly, then rose to pull out Peaches's chair for her. She shot him a look of suspicion, as if she expected him to leave her sprawled on the floor. He simply looked away, because there was nothing he could say to change her mind about him, nor was there anything he should say in front of the lady of the house. He simply held Peaches's chair, then followed her and Raphaela from the morning room and into the hallway.

"Now, perhaps Stephen will escort us safely upstairs, then seek out his own accommodations. It wouldn't surprise me in the slightest to find David had put him in the cellar, though perhaps without the key to the wine room."

Stephen opened his mouth to engage in the required polite banter, but shut it at the look on Peaches's face. She was profoundly uncomfortable, though he couldn't account for it.

Unless that damned David Preston had actually had the cheek to put her *in* his room, in which case Stephen would most definitely be going to bed without delay so his shots in the morning wouldn't miss their mark.

Humphreys coughed discreetly. "It would be my honor to escort Miss Alexander to her room, Your Grace." He paused. "I took the liberty of memorizing where the guests were being housed, should the need for assistance arise."

Raphaela looked at Peaches. "Stephen doesn't deserve him."

Peaches only smiled, but it was a rather strained smile. Stephen didn't dare look at Humphreys, lest he reveal more than he cared to in his expression. Obviously investigations had been carried out. He had the feeling, based on Humphrey's tone, that he wasn't going to be happy with the results.

Her Grace was looking at Humphreys closely, as if she also sensed there was something going on she wouldn't care for. She slipped her arm through Peaches's and looked at Stephen's valet.

"I wasn't privy to that list you were able to memorize," Raphaela said, "so why don't we all escort Peaches to her room. To make sure she arrives safely."

"Oh, I think I can find it on my own," Peaches protested, looking even more uncomfortable, if possible, than before.

"Nonsense, darling," Raphaela said. "It's the least I can do to repay you for such delightful dinner conversation. We'll follow along after you, Humphreys." She looked over her shoulder. "You can be our bodyguard, Haulton, yes?"

Stephen had every intention of being that—and more—so he nodded without hesitation.

He walked behind the dowager Duchess of Kenneworth and that ethereal creature from across the Pond and felt somehow as if he were walking into a pitched battle. Peaches was stressed—he could see it in the set of her shoulders. He couldn't account for why until Humphreys paused well before the staircase that led to the bedrooms above. Humphreys said nothing, he simply turned and walked down a side hallway.

Stephen supposed it was only years of keeping on the mask that allowed him to continue bringing up the rear without expressing his thorough disgust at the direction they were heading. The duchess, as well, said nothing, but Stephen could see by the set of her jaw that she was becoming angrier by the footfall. His own ire only increased as they descended a serviceable but inelegant set of tightly curved stairs to the very basement of the hall.

He hoped, as an afterthought, that he managed to get through the weekend without taking David Preston outside and beating the bloody hell out of him.

He wondered, though, given David's appreciation for a beautiful woman, if someone else was responsible for putting Peaches in the lowliest of servants' quarters.

He came to a halt outside the room—and he used that term very loosely—that Peaches had been given and realized suddenly that his forearm had been taken in a grip that made him wince. And it was Raphaela Preston to do the gripping. He took the not-so-subtle hint and kept his bloody mouth shut.

"Well," she said finally, not looking at him as she released him, "there has been a mistake made, obviously."

Stephen watched Peaches smile and was faintly surprised to find it was a genuine smile.

"Your Grace, I'm perfectly comfortable and happy here. Out of the way and peaceful is just what I need."

"Well, it is out of the way," Stephen agreed, before he thought better of it.

Peaches shot him a murderous look, which he supposed he deserved. Given all the asinine things he'd said to her over the course of their non-relationship, she probably assumed he was happy to have her out of the way. That couldn't have been further from the truth, though he wasn't unhappy to have her out of David's reach and Irene's sights.

Obviously Humphreys was going to be doing more investigating into the housing of guests. Stephen was more than a little curious about who had been responsible for putting Peaches in a room that was one step up from a closet.

Peaches turned a happy smile on Raphaela as she opened the door. "It's actually quite cozy. And the maid I was given has done a . . . ah, a fabulous . . . job . . ."

Stephen looked over her head and closed his eyes briefly. It wasn't the Spartan nature of the hovel—and again, he used that word very loosely for it was far worse than a hovel—it was the fact that her maid was holding up a gown that was eminently suitable for a fancy dress ball.

Or had been at some point in the past.

It most certainly wasn't now. It was not only muddy but torn, as if someone had taken it outside and acquainted it repeatedly with rather sharp farm implements.

Raphaela slipped past Peaches, took the gown from the maid, and stepped back out of the room. She handed the gown without looking to Humphreys, who discreetly moved to stand out of Peaches's sights.

"This won't do," she said firmly. "I have several gowns that would suit you quite well. I'll have one altered to suit your height. As for this bedroom—"

Peaches looked at her, her eyes bright. "It is fine, Your Grace. Perfect, even."

Raphaela's lips tightened. "I would like to know how this came about."

"I believe," Humphreys said helpfully from his hiding place behind the door, "that Miss Alexander was displaced by the viscount Haulton. An unfortunate occurrence, of course."

Stephen would have elbowed his valet if he'd dared, but he didn't dare. Peaches didn't look surprised, which left him wondering who had told her the like already. He couldn't imagine that his response had been so tardy as to have displaced her, especially given that he had tendered it at the beginning of the week.

No, there was something else afoot here, something he fully intended to get to the bottom of.

"Are there no other rooms, then?" Raphaela asked Humphreys sharply. "Nothing more suitable?"

"I've been told everything is taken, Your Grace," Humphreys said politely. "I, of course, wouldn't presume to question your housekeeper about the arrangements she was asked to make."

Stephen looked at Peaches. He would have told her that it wasn't his idea, but he didn't imagine she would have listened to him, much less believed him. For the briefest of moments, she looked impossibly tired and discouraged, but then she put on a bright smile. She kissed Raphaela on the cheek suddenly, then stepped back into the room.

"Thank you for a lovely supper, Your Grace, and the escort here. If you don't mind, though, I think I'll go to bed."

"Of course, darling," Raphaela said with a smile. "I'll see you first thing."

The door closed. Stephen hadn't been able to look at Peaches's face as she did so, so he couldn't say what her expression had been but he could hazard a guess. He shot Humphreys a dark look, then offered Raphaela his arm. She took it without comment.

They walked in silence back to the main floor. She stopped him at the bottom of the grand staircase, considered, then looked up at him.

"To say anything now would be indiscreet," she said slowly.

He inclined his head slightly. "To reply would be equally indiscreet."

"Silence, then."

"As the situation demands, of course."

"You will see to what needs to be seen to, though, won't you?"

He knew without being told exactly what she meant. Moving Peaches was first, probably impossible, and second, definitely inadvisable. If there was someone in the house who had the boldness to house an invited guest in the worst of servants' quarters, there was no telling what else that someone might be will-ing to do. Stephen wasn't going to credit anyone from Kenneworth House with the stomach to perpetrate nefarious deeds, but he could certainly think of a rather caustic sister of the current lord who might take a bit of pleasure in the discom-fort of another.

There were also other things he would see to, things of a less life-changing but no less important nature.

He inclined his head slightly. "Of course, Your Grace."

Her expression didn't change. "You do realize, Stephen dar-ling, that my son will take credit for whatever you do. As long as it suits him, of course."

Stephen shrugged with a casualness he wasn't feeling at the moment. "Your son may have all of the credit he likes."

Raphaela smiled. "You are indeed your mother's son."

"And my father's."

"Which means that you have lovely manners, but no love for either my late husband or my son." She lifted her eyebrows briefly. "And I am not a Preston by birth, which leaves me with a bit of distance from their most pressing concerns."

Stephen smiled in spite of himself. "Are you preparing to tell me what those concerns might be, or am I left to rummage about the library in search of clues?"

"I think you might be shot if you do any rummaging, love, so I suggest you leave rumors and innuendo alone."

"I don't know," Stephen said thoughtfully. "Having a few details about what has gone on between our families over the years might reduce my loathing of the current duke."

Raphaela laughed again, a light, lovely sound that was re-freshingly free of anything but sunshine. "Stephen, darling, I don't think anything would reduce that, for I think he is pursuing something you want very much." She looked at him sideways. "Wouldn't you agree?"

"Sometimes things that are wanted don't want to be wanted."

"Is that so?"

"Yes, Your Grace, that is so."

She patted his arm. "You need sleep."

He had to agree that sleep might be the best thing for him. Better that than wondering just who in the hell it had been to insult Peaches so thoroughly.

She looked at the dress hanging over her arm, then at him. "I'll dispose of this, shall I?"

"I would appreciate it."

She nodded, bid him a final good night, then walked up the stairs. Stephen waited until she'd disappeared before he turned to Humphreys.

"You had to divulge details?" he grumbled.

"It was bound to be divulged eventually, my lord," Humphreys said reasonably. "I thought it best to come from you."

Stephen pursed his lips. "I believe she knew already, so you were right to confirm it." He looked about him, then back at his valet. "We're less likely to be eavesdropped on here, so let's make our plans. Where do you suggest we begin?"

"A new maid is critical," Humphreys said without hesitation. "The care of the gown is highly questionable."

"I'm not sure I want the details on that, if it's all the same to you."

"I won't seek them out. And I'll have my sister come stay with Miss Alexander for the weekend."

Stephen looked at him in surprise. He hadn't realized Humphreys had a sister, much less one who attended to more pedestrian affairs. "Is your sister a lady's maid?"

"In her current incarnation," Humphreys conceded. "She'll watch after Miss Alexander properly."

Stephen leaned against the newel post. That solved the first problem. "She'll need new clothes—"

"I have a list of dress shops in the area, my lord."

Of course he did. "And shoes?"

"Yes, my lord."

Stephen looked at his, well, to call him a valet was an insult. To label him merely a social secretary was to deny his other gifts. The man was a wonder.

"Humphreys, you never cease to amaze."

"I endeavor to perform satisfactorily, my lord."

"Too much Wodehouse, I think, tucked behind your romances."

Humphreys only smiled faintly. "One must have one's heroes, my lord, even if they are fictional."

"I'm quite sure Sir Pelham found corporeal inspiration somewhere," Stephen said dryly. "Very well, let's see if we can't determine sizes."

"If you would permit me, my lord, I think I can hazard a guess or two."

Stephen decided he would leave the man to it only because Humphreys had been minding him since he'd graduated Eton and a goodly part of his better instincts came from him. A widower with a large brood of grandchildren, he had been particularly adept at managing a headstrong young man. And Stephen didn't doubt Humphreys would manage to find Peaches outfits that fit.

"Any suggestions on a wardrobe," Stephen asked, "or haven't you gotten that far?"

Humphreys didn't hesitate. "Hunting clothes for tomorrow morning, then perhaps tailored trousers, a silk blouse, and cashmere for about the house in the afternoon. Dinner will be rather formal, so she'll want proper evening dress. A new gown for the ball is essential, though I'm still mulling the color."

"White," Stephen said without hesitation.

Humphreys looked startled. "But, my lord—"

"Do you have any ideas for design?"

Humphreys sighed a little. "I've already emailed you a selection, my lord. Choose your preferred gown and it will be delivered by Saturday afternoon."

Stephen imagined it would be. He nodded, then walked up the stairs with Humphreys. He considered quite a few things as he readied himself for bed, then paused and looked at his valet before he retired.

"I'm not comfortable leaving her alone."

"That has already been seen to, my lord."

Stephen knew he shouldn't have been surprised, but he was. "Here in the midst of enemy territory? How did you manage it?"

"An extremely hefty bribe to one of the less well-heeled but undeniably muscular footmen."

"And you trust this man?" Stephen asked incredulously.

"You are considering offering him employment, if he does his job well."

"How generous of me."

"He thought so," Humphreys said with a straight face. "He has dreams of the sea."

"How convenient I know someone with a castle on the coast."

"He agreed that was most fortuitous."

Stephen shook his head in wonder. He honestly didn't know how the man managed to always have the right answer or the perfect solution. He just knew he was damned grateful to have Humphreys on his side. David Preston, if he'd had any sense, would have been quite nervous to have Humphreys in his house.

And if the licentious Duke of Kenneworth knew what was good for him, he would keep his hands in his pockets and his sister on a leash.

Stephen bid his valet a good night, then turned off the light. The hunting wasn't starting overly early, but Stephen didn't want to be anything but alert. And at the moment, he was terribly tempted to see if he could spend the morning in the library, looking for interesting tidbits about the Preston family.

Though if the choice was between that and potentially getting shot by his host, he thought the latter might be the safer possibility.

Chapter 9

Peaches stood in the bathroom and shivered. It wasn't that the water hadn't been warm—well, it hadn't been but she hadn't expected anything else. She'd woken late and probably missed her window for a hot shower. She wasn't even troubled by the thought of having missed breakfast, which meant she would be shaking all the way to lunch unless she could find something to eat besides the soggy Kit Kat in her purse. No, it wasn't any of that.

It was that she was in completely over her head and had no idea how to get herself out of the swamp.

All right, so she'd been at a Regency house party earlier in the month and hobnobbed with all kinds of titled people. She had also been dressed in a costume so she blended in, she'd had her fury at Stephen de Piaget to keep her feeling warm and feisty, and she'd left half the attendees at that weekend no doubt mistaking her for her sister the countess. Deference had been the order of the day for that last bit alone.

Here, she was just Peaches Alexander, ill-dressed Yank, with only her charms to recommend her. And those charms were as soggy as her candy bar.

Feeling inferior wasn't her usual modus operandi. She frequently made very brutal assessments of her strengths and weaknesses so she could identify areas for improvement. A certain sort of clarity came with that kind of inventory taking, mostly because since she already knew where she was failing, having someone else pointing out her flaws held less sting than it might have otherwise.

Of course, she was accustomed to dealing with people who either liked her for herself or thought her useless based on her skills as a life coach. She wasn't at all used to being judged by the situation of her birth or her clothes.

The only thing that made her feel any better was knowing that if David Preston's friends had seen her parents, they would have gotten a collective and potentially quite fatal case of the vapors.

She pulled the tie of her robe more tightly around her and considered herself in the mirror. She thought her sister was stunning, though she could see nothing past ordinary in herself. Maybe if she slicked her hair back and wrestled it into something resembling a chignon, she might have passed for someone fit to be in the current house party.

She rolled her eyes and pulled herself together. She couldn't control what others thought of her; she could only control what she thought of herself. And while she wasn't a world-famous opera singer or Madame Curie, she was who she was and that was enough. She would borrow an iron, put her clothes back together as best she could, and go socialize.

Because her happily ever after wouldn't happen if she sat down in the mud and gave up.

She put her shoulders back and left the bathroom, shivering as she hurried down the stone of the hallway in her bare feet. It was a bit of a hike, as it happened, but she ignored that as well. She wasn't going to think about who had poached her room and how far it was for him from bed to bath. Maybe he would stub his toe and not get to go hunting that afternoon or trip over the piles of love notes from his feminine admirers and sprain his ankle, leaving him unable to trot onto the dance floor tomorrow.

With those happy thoughts to keep her warm, she walked briskly back to her room and threw open the door.

And came to a skidding halt.

There was a maid there, true, but it wasn't the girl from the day before. It was Aunt Edna . . . only slightly younger and more starched.

"Ah," Peaches began.

"I am Edwina," the woman announced crisply, rising from the stool she'd been sitting on, "and I am here to dress you."

Peaches managed to swallow. "Oh—"

"And see that all runs smoothly here in your quarters," Edwina continued, "which are now under my supervision."

Peaches nodded, because it seemed like the right thing to do.

"I understand there was trouble last night," Edwina said with a severe look, sounding extremely disappointed.

"My gown," Peaches began. "It had a little accident—"

"No matter," Edwina said dismissively. "We shall pull ourselves up by our bootstraps and soldier on. I'm not keen on excess, but I can see that in this house your old things were entirely unsuitable. A new wardrobe has therefore been provided."

Peaches followed the long arm and extended bony fingers to the hooks driven into the wall upon which hung exactly what Edwina had described.

A new wardrobe.

Peaches walked—no, she floated across the room to look at what was hanging there. There was a hook sporting riding gear with boots tucked discreetly against the wall underneath the breeches, another hook sporting something Audrey Hepburn would have relaxed in if she'd been at an English country house party, then a lovely dress that . . .

Peaches looked at Edwina. "Is that for the ball?"

Edwina drew herself up. "No, miss," she said, sounding appalled. "That is for supper tonight. It is hardly the sort of thing one wears to a formal ball."

"Oh," Peaches said quietly. "I thought—"

"Tomorrow will take care of itself, miss."

Peaches felt her way down onto the bed. That wasn't difficult because she'd been leaning against the wall and the bed was approximately three feet from any wall. "Of course."

"One can't expect miracles, Miss Alexander."

"Of course not." Peaches looked up at her maid. "Who did this?"

Edwina looked as if Peaches had asked her to hike up her

skirts and do the cancan. "I have been sworn to secrecy, miss, and to secrecy I will remain sworn."

"Not even a hint?"

"Not even a hint."

Peaches imagined she would have more success liberating a few bars of bullion from Fort Knox than getting the details out of Edwina. Besides, did it really matter who had taken pity on her and sent along a few things for Peaches to borrow for the weekend?

Or so she thought until she caught sight of the pile of tags in the wastebasket. She started to lean over to examine them more closely, but found herself thwarted by means of Edwina's foot placed strategically over the rim. Edwina clucked her tongue and frowned.

"Secrecy must be maintained."

Peaches gave up with a sigh.

Edwina rubbed her hands together purposefully. "I've sent for light refreshment for you, which should be arriving at any moment. You will want to dress for the hunt."

"I will?" Peaches squeaked. Her excuse for getting out of riding was racing off into the distance—which would be exactly what her horse would be doing in approximately half an hour. The truth was, her experience with horses was limited to trying not to shriek in terror when the nosey ones nosed her for carrots or apples or whatever it was they thought she might be carrying in her pockets. Actually climbing up on the back of one and trusting him not to scrape her off against the nearest immovable object wasn't anything she thought she could do anytime soon.

But before she knew it, she was dressed in breeches, a discreet shirt, and a hunting jacket. The boots fit, a miracle in and of itself. She couldn't bring herself to speculate on their cost and a casual look in Edwina's direction resulted in a slight shake of the head. No, no hints from that direction. Edwina was, as she had proclaimed earlier, an absolute vault when it came to secrecy. Peaches was left to admire her anonymous sartorial provider in silence.

Whoever he or she was, he or she had excellent taste.

She wondered if it might have been Raphaela, David's elegant mother, or perhaps Andrea, David's cousin.

But the thought that made her feel a bit weak in the knees was that it might have been David himself.

She refused to feel embarrassed that he, if it had been he, had felt the need to buy her anything. She would just be grateful and let the rest go.

She had breakfast and wondered if Stephen's butler had been hounding the chef again, for it was rather good. She then submitted to a thorough study by Edwina, found herself pronounced absolutely adequate, and was shown the door.

And she was on her own.

She left the servants' quarters, then walked along marble hallways, wondering when the house had been built and how many hunting and shooting parties had been held in it over the years. She could hear talking and laughter coming from a room to her right, so she started to open the door. It was pulled open for her by household staff, and she was left with no choice but to go right in.

All she could say was that at least she fit in. Everyone was wearing breeches and jackets and most were carrying heavier short coats. The men looked dashing and the women capable.

Why, then, did her gaze go immediately to Stephen de Piaget instead of lingering on David Preston as it should have?

She was going to have a stern talk with herself—maybe Edwina could help out with that later—but for the moment, she was going to casually ogle.

It could be said that the man had been born to wear tweed, but that would have completely ignored the absolute perfection that was the Viscount Haulton in riding breeches and a hunting jacket. She had admittedly been something of a Mr. Darcy groupie from the first time she'd met him between the pages of a dog-eared copy of *Pride and Prejudice*, but she could safely say that he had just been officially relegated to runner-up status.

What was it about a dark-haired, gorgeous, exceptionally fit man in tall boots that was so drool-inducing? Peaches grasped frantically for any shred of self-control and sanity. She didn't want an English gentleman, she wanted a raw-food guru. She didn't want elegant dress shirts and tan riding breeches, she wanted a beard and Birkenstocks. She didn't want a meat-eating, horse-riding, heartbreaking nobleman she had no hope of even dating much less forming an attachment with, she wanted a spinach-eating, smoothie-slurping, wheatgrass-juicing guy who wouldn't demand she produce patents of nobility when he picked her up to go find something vegetarian at the local pub.

And she especially didn't want an elegant gentleman when he was *that* elegant gentleman.

She looked frantically for David, who, as it happened, was coming to her rescue. She pasted on her most welcoming smile and took a few deep breaths to calm her racing heart. So last night hadn't gone all that well. Today was another day. She didn't smell like wet sheep, she'd had a decent breakfast, and her hair was completely thawed. Life was good.

And David was extremely good-looking, something she wasted no time in pointing out to herself. His blond hair had just the right number of highlights, his jacket stretched over just the right breadth of shoulders, his tall boots had just the right polish. Though he wasn't exactly tall and muscular, he looked just the right amount of fabulous in his breeches. In fact, just about everything about him was just right.

Not like that dark, brooding character standing over to the side, watching her from under his eyebrows and no doubt thinking critical thoughts about her.

She let David take her hand and was very happy that she didn't feel flushed or nervous or unsettled. Yes, *just* and *right* were going to be her watchwords for the weekend.

David brought Irene along, which put a bit of a damper on her happiness, but if she couldn't put up with a nasty potential-in-law or two, what sort of spine did she have?

"I was telling Irene," David said, tucking Peaches's hand into the crook of his elbow, "about your degree. It was something scientific, wasn't it?"

"Organic chemistry," Peaches agreed.

David laughed merrily. "I said it was something organic, but I thought at first you were talking about the compost for your garden."

Peaches laughed, because it would have been rude not to, but she had the grave misfortune of realizing that Stephen was standing within earshot. He had made that very same comment in just that same way, only then she hadn't laughed. She'd been utterly humiliated, then furious that he had been making fun of her. She stole a look at him now only to find him watching her steadily, without expression on his face.

Well, apart from his general broodiness, as if he couldn't stand to be where he was and couldn't wait to be somewhere else.

"I don't suppose that's something you just write off for from one of those agricultural universities you have in the States, is it?" David asked, a twinkle in his eye.

Peaches suppressed the urge to squirm. Would this deviation from his just-rightness ever end? She managed a smile. "No," she managed, "no, it isn't. I got my degree from Stanford."

"Well, that's in California," Irene said coolly. "No doubt you had ample opportunity to investigate all sorts of organic things there."

"I say, it looks like we should be heading out," David said, ignoring his sister. "Don't want to get caught out in the weather."

"The weather is already out there," Stephen said pointedly from behind them. "A bit foggy for a hunt, wouldn't you say?"

"Lest someone's shots go awry?" David asked politely. "Yes, which is why I've decided to call it a perfect day for a ride. Then we'll come in for hot drinks and a warm-up by the fire. I think it's a brilliant plan."

Peaches had several terms for the plan, but brilliant wasn't among them. But there was nothing to be gained by voicing an opinion, so she trotted along beside David, grateful to be away from both his sister and Stephen. Maybe those two would find themselves thrown together and their separate nastiness would cancel itself out and leave them both slightly bland but easily endured. Irene seemed to be happy enough to hang on Stephen's arm, so Peaches left her to it.

She kept up a steady stream of silent, confident self-talk until she found that the path had ended and she was facing her doom. It didn't look to be a very terrifying doom, but it was substantially bigger than she'd feared it might be.

"Diablo," David said, reaching out to pat the horse on the neck. "Perfect for you."

"Don't be an ass," Stephen said from just behind her. "Miss Alexander is a novice rider."

David only smiled. "And Diablo is a gentle horse." He handed Peaches the reins. "Up you go, love."

Stephen took the reins out of Peaches's hands. "Up she doesn't go, Your Grace," he said curtly. "That is too much horse for her."

"I think I'll be the judge—"

"And I think you won't," Stephen said, handing the reins to a groom.

Things didn't improve from there. Peaches wondered if the two men would soon come to blows, but apparently one did not slug one's host before lunch.

David finally swore and glared at Stephen. "Go look for a nag, then, and embarrass the girl. Here, Irene, you take Diablo and show His Lordship how gentle a lad he is."

Peaches watched David's sister take the reins and accept a leg up into the saddle. Diablo didn't buck David's sister off, but his front feet left the ground half a dozen times before Irene wrestled him into compliance. Peaches felt the sudden need to sit down. She was very grateful she wasn't currently trying to keep her seat on the back of that horse.

Stephen said nothing. He simply stood there with his hands clasped behind his back and watched David organize things. Peaches was tempted to dash back into the house and hide behind Edwina's very starched skirts before Stephen could say anything about other horses, but before she could, David turned and spoke to her. Angels didn't sing and the sun didn't break through the clouds, but close.

"What?" she said, looking at him.

"I said, lovely boots," he said easily.

"Yes, they are," she began, but he turned away before she could say anything else.

"Let's be off," he announced to the general assembly as he strode with just the right amount of jauntiness to his horse, an enormous thing with just the right amount of energy. "The others will catch up."

The company *en masse* started for their horses. Well, mostly *en masse*. Peaches noticed a trio of gals who didn't seem particularly eager to mount up and trot off. They were the same women who had glared at her the night before, though they'd cast an equal number of unhappy looks Irene's way so she'd thought little of them. It occurred to her, though, looking at them out in the sunlight, that she'd seen them before.

It had been at Payneswick, though they hadn't been in a group there. She had no idea who they were, but she could safely say she wasn't particularly interested in finding out.

"Let's go," Stephen said.

Peaches realized he was talking to her and considered taking umbrage at his bossiness, but she was too busy being towed toward the stables. She caught a gander of the small fight Irene was having with her horse and decided that whatever Stephen picked for her couldn't be worse than that hell beast. She wondered if the little cluster of women still dragging their feet were going to tear each other to shreds, then saw she needed have no fear. Once they seemed to reconcile themselves to the fact that she was the one walking with Stephen, a visible yet unspoken truce was struck and they turned as one to watch her.

She would have told them there was no need to be worried about her because she didn't even like their guy, but she didn't have a chance. She looked at Andrea, who was standing ten feet away, watching the whole thing with obvious amusement. She cast the only person she could reasonably call a friend a pleading look, but Andrea shook her head slowly. Peaches decided she could either face the Dawdling Debutantes or ignore them. So she ignored them.

She followed Stephen, but not too closely. Those gals had riding crops and she didn't want to meet the business end of them. She also didn't particularly want to get up on a horse, but she had the feeling she wasn't going to get out of it.

Stephen walked up and down four rows of stalls, soon joined by a man Peaches could only assume was the head groom. He was either intimidated by Stephen—and that she could understand—or he was seeing if Stephen had any clue what he was looking for. Stephen finally stopped, considered, then looked at the man.

"Miss Alexander has extremely limited experience on the back of a horse," he said.

"How do you know?" Peaches said, before she thought better of it. She thought refraining from adding *smarty-pants* showed extreme self-control.

Stephen looked at her and raised one of his eyebrows. Peaches wished desperately for somewhere to sit down—because the thought of getting on a horse was terrifying. Yes, that was it. It had absolutely nothing to do with the way Stephen had reached out and was gently stroking the nose of that beast in front of her, or that small smile he flashed that self-same creature.

The man was nicer to horses than he was to her. That was surely reason enough to want to slug him, wasn't it?

"I believe this lad here will suit her," Stephen was saying to the stable master, "but I will defer to your opinion, Andrews. Her Grace, the lady Raphaela, spoke very highly of your judgment."

Andrews looked as though Stephen had offered him the chance to go on a quest and be at the head of the procession. He seemed to be fighting a very pleased smile as he nodded. "Gunther is a perfect choice, my lord Haulton. He's a fine, old fellow, but always eager for a bit of exercise. I'll have him saddled immediately."

And immediately was just how fast he was saddled. Peaches found herself standing next to Stephen, shaking, as a saddle that looked wholly inadequate to giving her anywhere to sit was brought and applied to the back of a horse that had to have been a gazillion feet tall.

"He's big," Peaches said, her mouth dry. "Bigger than the other one."

"Aye, miss," Andrews said, looking at her seriously, "but he's the gentlest one here. He's schooled scores of riders without losing a one."

"Schooled *them*?" she squeaked.

The groom only winked at her and walked off to see to his charge. Peaches looked up at Stephen.

"How did you know to pick this one?"

"Nobility school."

She decided what made her want to punch him the hardest was that she was never quite sure when he was teasing and when he wasn't. She scowled at him. "Not galloping down the stairs of your father's hall on a stick horse, waving a sword over your head and bellowing like a banshee?"

"The de Piagets do not bellow," he said calmly. "We express our emotions in measured tones." He started to walk away, then looked over his shoulder. "And it wasn't a stick horse, it was a rocking horse named Dante that scraped my mother's floors to bits."

Before she could comment on that, she was swept up into intrigues and looks of alarm and disdain. And that was just her interactions with the horse.

"A leg up, miss?" the head groom asked.

Why not?

By the time she had bathed, dressed for dinner, then managed to choke most of it down, she had had it. Country house parties were just not for her. No matter how gentle her horse had been rumored to be, she'd been convinced the entire morning she was a heartbeat away from landing on her face. She had prayed she would simply survive the ride after which she would have gone straight to bed with visions of fairy tales still dancing in her head.

Only then she would have missed the current, singular experience of having the Duke of Kenneworth seat her next to him in a chair closest to the fire and flirt with her.

As he was currently doing.

She hadn't been born yesterday, so she knew he was hitting on her. And she had to admit she was utterly, completely, thoroughly flattered and all aflutter. He was just so . . . just right.

She glanced across the salon not because she needed to, but because she always wanted to know where Stephen was so she could avoid him. He, unlike David, was just wrong. That morning had been a perfect example of just how wrong he was.

He had gone out of his way to ride next to her, no doubt so he could mock her later when he had time to do a proper job of it. So what if he'd carried on a conversation that she could easily hear about his first lessons on the back of a horse, which he of course could hardly remember because he'd been at it so long? If he had bored those around him with a droning discussion of beginning-rider technique, apparently he just hadn't cared. No matter what his mother might have thought, *she* was convinced his manners definitely needed a polish.

Unlike David Preston who probably taught advanced studies in manners at Stephen de Piaget's nobility school.

"I'll be back in a flash, love," David said, smiling just for her as he rose. "Off to refill the glass, of course."

Peaches nodded and smiled, though she couldn't understand why his numerous servants couldn't have seen to his glass. Maybe he was trying to show her what an ordinary guy he was.

Unfortunately, that left his seat open. Irene Preston flopped down into it, grumbling loudly.

"All Haulton wants to talk about is his ridiculous charities," she snapped. "This is a bloody party, not a selection of potential donors."

"Language, Irene," Raphaela said mildly. "And I don't think Lord Stephen views your friends as potential donors. He's simply looking for something to add to the conversation besides his views on footballers and their scandals."

"Oh, Mother, you're so naive."

Peaches didn't think Raphaela was naive at all, but decided it was best not to offer her opinion. It was instructive enough to simply listen to the conversation around her and try to look as if she were interested.

Stephen? Charities? She could hardly believe it. She looked up into the mirror and saw David talking to Stephen, looking as if he were trying to talk him into something. Perhaps David had his own list of charities he contributed to. Stephen continued to say *no* in very calm, measured tones—he was a de Piaget, after all—which eventually left David saying something even she could see was very foul before he turned and stalked away.

She tried to concentrate on the ensuing discussion of Paris Fashion Week being carried on between Raphaela and Andrea, but she found that she was very distracted by the memory of the missing Duke of Kenneworth, who had flattered and flirted with her so deliciously that she was still feeling very weak in the knees. She patted her knees for good measure, just to be sure. Yes, very weak. In fact, it was probably for the best that she was still sitting just so she could recover. When it came to David Preston, it was best to stay put so her limbs weren't put under undue strain.

Not like that horrible heir to Artane and no doubt numerous other titles who didn't make her knees weak; he made her feet want to carry her off in another direction, quickly.

She was slightly surprised to find that others weren't making tracks for the door. As she watched Stephen in the mirror she had to admit, very grudgingly, that the man could certainly work

a room. She'd seen it the day before, but she had thought it was
a fluke.

She studied him a bit longer in the mirror and had to concede
that at least he didn't seem to be boring anyone with obscure
details about medieval battle strategies. David had given up on
him, but other men actually seemed to be talking to him about,
well, football from what she could hear.

The women, that trio of debutantes plus a fair number of
other guests, seemed to be keeping themselves from brawling to
get near him only out of respect for the antiques in the room.

"Dukes' daughters."

Peaches looked at Raphaela. "I beg your pardon, Your
Grace?"

"Those three glaring daggers at you are dukes' daughters,
chérie," Raphaela said, in French. "Perhaps we'll have a walk in
the garden tomorrow where I might tell you about their families."

"Or we could talk about compost."

Raphaela laughed lightly. "Are you not interested at all in
Lord Haulton?"

"Not at all."

"Are you interested in my son?"

"Who wouldn't be?" Peaches asked honestly. "He's perfect."

Raphaela only lifted one eyebrow briefly, then turned to Irene
and English again.

Peaches had no idea what to make of that exchange, so she
decided it would be wisest to make nothing of it at all.

She couldn't deny that she was rather glad when the evening
wound down and she was able to say good night. David was still
nowhere to be found, but Peaches saw several other men were
missing as well, so perhaps there had been some late-night football on the telly.

She was slightly surprised to have Raphaela walk her to her
room, with Stephen and his gentleman's personal gentleman following fifty feet behind them. Raphaela seemed not to notice as
she deposited Peaches in her room with a gracious good night
and retreated back up the way. Peaches wasn't sure what to
make of Stephen leaning against the wall, watching her instead
of his host's mother. Maybe he wanted his overcoat back.

She looked for it inside, but it was gone, perhaps returned to its owner. What was left, however, was Edwina sitting on her stool, quite obviously still in charge. Edwina rose majestically and gestured to one of the hooks.

"Something," she said gravely, "has arrived."

Peaches's first thought was that it was an eviction notice, but since there wasn't all that much to be evicted from, she wasn't going to stress over it. She watched as Edwina reached for a garment bag that was excessively long and excessively expensive-looking and thought she should probably just sit down.

So she sat down on the end of her bed and looked at her maid expectantly.

"Are you prepared, miss?"

Peaches thought about tossing off some remark that she hadn't seen a wheatgrass juicer in the kitchen so she was less prepared than she might otherwise have been, but the moment seemed to call for seriousness. She sat up straight and looked at Edwina.

"I think I am as prepared as I'll manage to be," she said honestly.

Edwina frowned, as if she'd just taken measure of the state of the queen's armada and found it not quite up to snuff, but good enough for the battle at hand. She reached for the zipper of the garment bag, then looked at Peaches.

"Your gown, miss."

Peaches gasped. It was better than fainting, which was her first inclination.

It looked as if her fairy tale might be coming true after all.

Chapter 10

Stephen was nervous.

He wasn't accustomed to being nervous. The fact of the matter was, he was too damned old to be nervous. His blood pressure might occasionally find itself elevated during a spirited argument over this medieval detail or that, and his pulse might race now and again when seeing one of his competing colleagues sneaking into the back of his lectures to steal his academic discoveries, but a simple case of nerves? Never.

Then again, he had never in his life had the dreams of a woman he was hopelessly fond of riding on his ability to send his valet off with a credit card to see her properly dressed. Even though being unsettled over the potential for sartorial disasters was ridiculous, he was unsettled nonetheless.

Because even though the goods had been delivered, there was still the possibility that the gown would be too long and the shoes too tight.

He suppressed the urge to rub his hands over his face and instead clasped them behind his back where they would be out of his way. That had the added benefit of rendering himself incapable of flinging either vintage dishes or modern fire irons at the indiscreet Duke of Kenneworth, who had spent the previous night gambling with funds he didn't have. Stephen was quite sure Kenneworth planned to spend the night lying in front of them gambling with something quite a bit more precious— namely Peaches Alexander's heart.

He wished he drank, for he would have indulged in a post-brunch double. Wasn't it enough that he was wringing his hands—figuratively, of course—over the possibility that shoes and a dress wouldn't suit? Did he also have to face the fact that he might be completely mad for a woman he wasn't quite sure he should like and definitely shouldn't love?

He watched Kenneworth walk around the room, attending to his hosting duties, and suppressed the urge to cross the room and plow his fist into the duke's face. The man was notorious for finding innocent lassies, wooing them into more than just dark-ened corners, then dropping them without troubling himself over the mess he'd left behind. If Stephen had had a sister, he would have forbid her any association with the lout. As it was, he did have a cousin or two who had had the misfortune of a brush with the man, but he'd nipped that in the bud.

Thinking about Kenneworth plying his trade on that innocent Yank had Stephen grinding his teeth, and not just because he knew what an absolute reprobate the duke was.

It was whom he was planning to ply his trade on, actually, that set Stephen's teeth on edge.

He looked away before he said or did something he would regret. Unfortunately, the next most interesting thing in the room happened to be his trio of on-again-off-again girlfriends who had apparently banded together to make his life hell. He at-tempted a polite smile and had hard stares in return.

Well, he perhaps had no one but himself to blame there. He'd brushed off the suggestions for walks, strolls, and ambles through either deserted hallways or wintery gardens with ex-cuses he couldn't quite remember but was sure amounted to, "have a bit of a headache, sorry."

He jumped a little when he realized Raphaela Preston had sidled up to him. Actually, the woman didn't sidle, she glided. The material point was, she was wearing an expression of seren-ity that he was sure boded very ill for his peace of mind.

"What?" he muttered grimly.

"Why, Haulton, your temper is ferocious tonight."

"Bad eggs for breakfast."

She laughed and slipped her hand into the crook of his elbow. "I have a few—how is it you would put it?—ah, yes, a few tidings for you, darling."

He could hardly wait.

"Your harem is plotting your demise," Raphaela said with the smirk of a cat who had just polished off an entire pitcher of cream and wouldn't be suffering injuries to its tum anytime soon. "They've been huddled together all day discussing their plans."

"Cut brake lines or ptomaine poisoning?" Stephen asked sourly.

"I believe they would prefer to see you drawn and quartered, but rumor has it they feared retribution from the authorities. I understand they've limited themselves to seeing you eviscerated in the press."

"A pity I never do anything controversial."

"They're planning on lying."

Stephen pursed his lips. "I hope they enjoy it."

She looked up at him in surprise, then laughed. "Yes, well, I'm sure they shall. Shall I tell you what else I know?"

"Is it possible to tell you to stop politely?"

"I don't think so," she said, politely. "Our sweet American was rather curious at the breakfast you couldn't seem to find your way to this morning about some additions to her bedroom. I told her I thought they might have been sent by my son." She blinked innocently. "What do you think?"

"That you are far too lovely and discreet to be called meddlesome," Stephen said, putting his hand over hers. "Unfortunately."

Raphaela looked at that son prowling around the room, looking particularly loathsome in his perfect evening wear. She studied him for quite some time in silence, then shook her head slowly.

"He should marry."

"He should," Stephen agreed. "The sooner, the better."

Raphaela looked up at him. "Does your mother say the same thing to you?"

"Often."

Raphaela studied him with the same searching look—he shifted in spite of himself—then went back to her contemplation of her son. "Miss Alexander is not for him."

"Because she doesn't have a title, or money, or pedigree?" Stephen asked lightly. "And haven't we had this conversation before?"

"If we haven't, we should have, and no, that isn't the reason. And I phrased it badly. I should have said, he is not for her."

Stephen remained silent—and to his mind it was wisely done.

"He will break her heart." Raphaela looked up at him. "But you wouldn't, would you?"

Stephen started to speak, then shut his mouth because there was nothing to be said. He took a deep breath. "Why do you like her?"

"Because she is charming and honest and laughs at an old woman's attempts at humor. And she speaks French very well. You should have her examine yours for flaws."

"That might take a while."

Raphaela smiled. "And so it might, which I doubt would trouble you. You're very welcome, Stephen darling, for the idea. Since you seem to be running short of ways to have her to yourself."

"She doesn't like me," he said with a sigh.

"What did you do?"

He laughed a little. "Why would you assume it's my fault?"

"Because, *cher*, you are a man," Raphaela said simply.

"I'm insulted."

"Not inspired?"

"I was taught from an early age to bite my tongue when so inspired."

"Your mother is my good friend, in spite of my late husband and hers who has no love for my son. I don't see enough of her. But I believe you and I were talking about something else entirely. What did you do to my darling Peaches to anger her so?"

Stephen sighed. "I draw breath in and let it out. Unfortunately, that letting out seems to be occasionally accompanied by words."

"Made an arse of yourself, did you?" she asked, her eyes twinkling.

"Repeatedly."

"Well, then why don't you apologize?" She shrugged. "That seems simple enough to me."

"For what purpose?" he asked very quietly. "There can be nothing between us."

She made a noise of impatience. "Stephen, you have spent too much time with your head buried in medieval texts. This is the twenty-first century and many things are allowed."

"You don't know my grandmother—"

"Do you worry she'll cut off your allowance if you wed where you prefer?" Raphaela asked lightly. "And yes, I know her very well, the old witch. She terrifies me, and I am not seeking her approval on my choice of spouse. I'm a little surprised you're allowing her to have an opinion on yours."

Stephen started to speak, but Raphaela shook her head.

"I understand what you face, for it is a part of my life I would rather do without. But we have our duties, don't we?" She turned back to her contemplation of her son. "His father indulged him too much and I wasn't strong enough to counter it. His elder brother would have made a better heir, of course, if he had lived . . ." She took a deep breath and smiled. "All behind us now, isn't it? The future beckons and David must wed. Not your lady, though. If Kenneworth is to be saved, it will take a very strong woman to manage him and the house, too. Money would help, of course, but I would prefer someone sensible to manage what we already have." She pulled her hand away and smiled. "I believe I'll put a stop to the champagne. It is much too early for that sort of thing."

Stephen watched her go and almost wished he hadn't heard that last bit. Perhaps his family wasn't perfect, but they worked hard and appreciated what they had. He had wondered, when he hadn't had anything better to do, about David Preston's lavish lifestyle and how he managed to afford it. He lived like a man who thought his ship was about to come in, a ship he had already seen out in the harbor and knew was near to docking.

And now to be faced with an evening spent watching that fool slobbering all over a girl without a penny to her name. Well, she might have had a bit, but Tess had intimated that morning when Stephen had called her to double-check sizes that Peaches had spent a decent amount of her savings on the gown that had been ruined.

He rubbed his hands over his face because it broke his train of thought. He wished he didn't know anything about David Preston, and wished he hadn't called Tess to find out details about Peaches that weren't any of his business.

Really, he was going to have to keep his mouth shut more often.

He leaned back against the wall and folded his arms over his chest. It kept his hands from reaching out and carrying him along with them as they made their way across the floor to strangle the current Duke of Kenneworth.

He could see why the man was attracted to Peaches. Who wouldn't be? But the truth of it was, David had absolutely no bloody idea who Peaches truly was. Her name, yes, and where she was from, but that was the extent of it.

For example, Kenneworth had no idea how profoundly kind Peaches could be. But Stephen did. She had had that kindness on display for him—before he made that stupid remark about organic earth. She had been gloriously wonderful with his uncle Kendrick's children and his brother Gideon's daughter. She had been lovely to his parents. And when Tess had gone on her little vacation to points unknown with John de Piaget, Peaches had stepped into her sister's shoes without hesitation and done what was necessary with grace and skill, and without complaint.

What wasn't to like about her?

The sticking point was, as he'd told Raphaela, that she didn't like him. Perhaps that was putting it mildly. She loathed him. It was a rather novel sensation, that. He'd never been shunned by a woman before. He had always done the "oh, so sorry, but I've an engagement" kind of thing to let them down easily. Peaches hadn't let him down; she'd given him the boot.

It was very unpleasant. After all, he was relatively rich, relatively young, and had a pair of titles. His father wasn't ancient, but Stephen had found himself taking on more and more of his father's public duties, which left him relatively responsible. His ancestral home had been used half a dozen times as a movie set and was just a minor slog over the dunes from the sea.

If that wasn't enough to impress a feisty, argumentative, impossible Yank, what would be?

He wasn't sure he wanted to know.

"Don't suppose you'd want to go for a walk in a wintry garden, would you?"

Stephen looked to his right to find Andrea Preston standing there, smiling an amused smile at him.

"Do I look like I need it?" he asked.

"You do look a little peaked," she agreed. "And so I thought a walk might be just the thing to bring the color back to your cheeks."

"You're too kind."

"My worst fault."

Stephen would have taken her up on her offer, but he made the mistake of turning and looking at the door.

He caught his breath.

Then he smiled.

White had been the right color. The woman standing there in the doorway looked like a princess. It helped, perhaps, that she was by far the most beautiful in the room, but he could honestly say that that wasn't it. It wasn't the dress, or her hair swept up off her shoulders, or her perfect face.

It was just Peaches Alexander, with her beauty shining through where all could see it.

Not even the sight of the Duke of Kenneworth trotting over to monopolize her was enough to sour his pleasure at just watching her.

She was escorted into the ballroom as if she had been royalty. Stephen was fairly certain he heard the grinding of teeth coming from various quarters, but he ignored it. He wasn't sure, but he suspected that even Andrea had deserted him for points unknown.

He wondered how it was he would ever get Peaches away from David to have even a single dance.

He imagined the evening would drag on endlessly. He would have been happy for that at another time, for it would have given him the chance to simply stand to the side and watch the absolute perfection that was Peaches Alexander, but at the moment he was too overcome by the desire to help David Preston meet with a crippling accident to concentrate on much else.

He tried to convince himself that he just wanted Peaches to be happy, but it occurred to him as he watched David signal the orchestra, then sweep Peaches into his arms, that he didn't want her just to be happy.

He wanted her to be his.

He'd suspected that all along, of course, but there was something about seeing her in another man's arms with her face aglow with happiness that forced him to face the truth. Indeed, it was almost enough to leave him looking for a place to sit down.

Instead, he simply found himself a handy sideboard topped with a few sturdy keepsakes and leaned against it. He put on his usual mask to hide his thoughts and gave himself over to deep thoughts.

He didn't know if she could learn to love him. He wasn't sure if she would be willing to take on the duties that would be required of her as the Countess of Artane when the time came. He wasn't even convinced she could live the rest of her life in England.

All he knew was that he wanted her, for scores of reasons he didn't dare consider at the moment.

He had another deep breath, then began to plan his strategy. He hadn't spent all that time in the bowels of various libraries across the world without having learned something about preparing a battle. He also hadn't endured innumerable defeats at Ian MacLeod's hands without finally learning a few less-than-gentlemanly tactics.

It was obvious the first step was to see if he couldn't convince her to set aside her animosity toward him. He would have preferred to have taken a bit more time to contemplate how that might best be accomplished, but the truth was, the battle was upon him and his foe was engaged in a waltzing offensive.

He would have to commandeer her dance card and cross out David's name at least once.

The night was young.

Chapter 11

Peaches looked at the grandfather clock standing against the wall and wondered, absently, if it were bolted to that wall or not. If not, she was slightly surprised to find it hadn't fallen over with all the dancing that had gone on that night.

It was eleven thirty.

All right, so she was used to all kinds of otherworldly sensations—and those weren't just the ones caused by whatever her parents had been smoking. She'd seen ghosts, had waves of history sweep over her at particular historical sites, known ahead of time things she shouldn't have been able to. But there was something else going on at present, something magical.

Something that felt a great deal like destiny.

"May I have this dance, Miss Alexander?"

Peaches was certain she had almost jumped out of her very lovely and surprisingly comfortable shoes. That was followed by the immediate desire to curse, which she suppressed because Aunt Edna had never sent her out the door without telling her to be a lady. She took a deep breath, silently told destiny to keep itself on ice, and decided she would get the polite thing to do over with and dance with that damned Viscount Haulton. She turned around and smiled. Politely.

"Of course," she said, with what she hoped was just the right touch of aloofness and dignity. After all, he'd made fun of her. It wouldn't do for him to think she'd forgotten it.

And then she made the mistake of touching his hand. That little zing that went up her arm and came close to frying her brain could have been ignored, but she made her second mistake immediately after, which was looking at him.

All right, so it was one thing to lust after him—or, rather, imagine what it would be like to lust after him if she liked him—while getting an eyeful of him in riding clothes. The very sad and unavoidable truth was, the man had been born to wear evening clothes.

She tried to look anywhere but at him, but that made dancing very difficult, so she gave up and gave in. She forced herself to concede that his tailor loved him to fit his tuxedo so well, and that whoever cut his hair had probably lingered over the job far longer than was polite. His dancing instructors—and she was quite sure he'd had a number of them in nobility school—hadn't shirked their duties, either. She found herself feeling rather more glad than she had felt dancing with David that she had taken so many semesters of ballroom dance in college. She made no misstep, but then again, neither did Stephen.

She glanced at the grandfather clock. Twenty minutes to midnight.

She couldn't hurry the dance along, but she didn't linger over polite chitchat with the future Earl of Artane, either. She thanked him politely and escaped while she still had her sanity and time enough to refresh her makeup.

She looked for David, who had been taken in hand, literally, eight minutes earlier by his sister and pulled away. She started to wave at him, but there was no need. He left Irene talking to thin air and immediately came over to her and offered her his arm.

"A walk in the garden?"

Why not? Her trip to the bathroom could wait. She walked with him across the ballroom, her heart aflutter.

Truly. Her heart was aflutter. She surreptitiously put a finger to her neck. Yes, her pulse was elevated. Surely it wasn't necessary to put a number on how much her pulse had increased, was it?

Her future was almost upon her. She could feel it.

The doors to the garden were open. Peaches felt as if she were walking out into a dream. Well, it was more like a very chilly hallucination, but she wasn't going to complain. Her fairy tale was about to be written.

The moon was full, the large porch free of snow and ice, and there was no one else to disturb what Peaches was convinced was her magical moment. David reached down and took her hand, then turned her to him and looked at her from perfectly acceptable blue eyes.

Not like those broody, clear gray eyes that looked like storm clouds.

"I know we haven't known each other very long," David began, interrupting her thoughts.

She happily left those disturbing thoughts behind and concentrated on the man in front of her. He was wonderful, wasn't he? And willing to overlook the fact that she was just an untitled, unemployed life coach? He wouldn't have brought her out for a private, magical moment in the garden otherwise.

Surely.

He released her hand and put his arms around her waist to pull her closer. Peaches held her breath, then closed her eyes to better savor the moment.

"Oh, I say," a male voice said brightly, "didn't know anyone was out here."

Peaches resisted the urge to swear. Would that man never cease to get in the way of her perfect life? If he wasn't insulting her, he was ruining moments that were none of his business to ruin. She glared at him, but he wasn't looking at her.

"A little chilly for a walk, isn't it?" Stephen continued, looking at David pointedly.

"Well, old man, we weren't exactly walking, were we?" David drawled. "And we'll be warm enough soon enough, I imagine."

"Your sister sent me to find you," Stephen said. "Being a gentleman, I accepted the charge."

Peaches felt David hesitate, then he released her and stepped back. He was obviously so unnerved by the interruption that he forgot to hold her hand.

"Being a gentleman as well," he said coldly, "I suppose I shall accept."

"I think that would be the polite thing to do."

"And I am always polite."

Stephen inclined his head. "So you are, Your Grace."

Peaches thought they should both be clunked over the head with whatever etiquette books they'd both memorized in nobility school. She found herself being towed back into the ballroom with rather less care than she'd been escorted out of it, but since she managed to glare at Stephen on her way by, she didn't mind. That necessity seen to, she graciously accepted David's apology for a conversation interrupted, resisted the urge to fan herself over his promise that he would find her the moment his sister was satisfied, then decided that the time to trot off to the bathroom had come.

She would have glared at Stephen again, but she didn't see him. His dastardly duty done, he had apparently slithered back into the hole he'd emerged from. She walked to the bathroom, realizing only as she walked into it that it belonged in a hotel. Maybe David and his family entertained more people than she was accustomed to and needed all that room for the hordes of women who no doubt flocked to Kenneworth House to have a go at its master. There was an outer sitting room sort of affair with a circular seat that looked like a life preserver. Past that and around a corner was the loo proper where she decamped while things looked to be empty.

The grandfather clock tolled a quarter to the hour.

She stood in front of the mirror and looked at herself carefully, wondering if anything was changing. She still looked just like herself, but she had another fifteen minutes to go before the magic went as well.

She had to admit that she had been dressed and groomed by a crew of professionals. She had managed to sneak brunch with Raphaela Preston again in the morning room, then retreat to her room for a luxurious nap followed by a rather lukewarm shower.

All right, so it had been just this side of cold, but she'd been excited enough about her dress and shoes that she'd managed to shiver through it as long as necessary.

And then she'd returned to her room and found herself in the midst of a makeover.

Her bed had been propped up against the wall to provide more floor space for the half-dozen beautifiers who had come to give her the royal treatment. She had been plucked and buffed and sprayed and polished with extreme care and many compliments on the raw materials she was providing. She had sipped delicate tea, partaken of a light, elegant supper, and rested before the final touches were put on her makeup and she was put into her dress.

Which, she had to admit, fit perfectly.

The shoes had fit no less perfectly, which surprised her. She had thought about it most of the afternoon and decided, finally, that it had been David to fork over his hard-earned sterling for the spa treatment and new wardrobe. Raphaela had only smiled when she'd hinted rather broadly that she suspected him of the same, which led her to believe her suspicions were dead-on.

She had to admit her makeup had worn well and her dress looked just as beautiful as it had earlier that evening. She was very grateful she'd been supplied with a small purse big enough for a little powder and a refreshing of her never-come-off lipstick. She hoped it would perform as advertised because she had every expectation that within moments she would be enjoying a midnight kiss.

The door opened around the corner, and the sound of voices floated in to serenade her with their dulcet tones.

"Well, of course I know she isn't anyone," a voice snapped. "You can tell that just by looking at her!"

"Then what are you worried about?" said a second voice soothingly. "It isn't as if she's trying to steal something that's yours."

"I could not possibly care less what sort of dalliances my brother David engages in. I do, however, care what other glances she's attracting."

Peaches closed her eyes briefly. That was Irene, obviously. She suspected the other voice belonged to Andrea.

"Viscount Haulton?"

"Yes, Andrea," Irene said crisply, "the Viscount Haulton, the heir to Artane, which is, if you hadn't noticed, a rather nice place."

"You don't like medieval artifacts."

"But I do like the man who has the ability to sell them and redecorate his home," Irene said, "which he will do ten minutes after we are wed. And the sooner I get that nobody out of the way, the faster that wedding will happen."

Peaches wanted to look around the corner and tell Irene that she didn't have to worry about anyone of an American persuasion wanting anything to do with the future Earl of Artane, but she didn't have the chance because Irene launched into a scathing attack on gold diggers in general and her in particular.

"But I think David likes her very much—"

Irene's laugh was like knives cutting through the air. "Don't be ridiculous, Andrea. He's toying with her."

"He arranged this house party for her," Andrea said firmly. "He told me so himself."

"Yes, darling, for a particular reason."

Andrea was silent for a moment or two. "I don't think I understand."

"Please, Andrea, don't be an idiot. He wanted an excuse to play cards with his friends and have his own private entertainment after that. She is here for the second reason alone."

"But David isn't like that—"

Irene laughed again, and it wasn't a pleasant laugh. "You don't know my brother. He's practically engaged, or didn't you know? To Phyllis Milbourne."

"Really? But she hasn't any title."

"But she does have what he wants, which is the ability to look the other way whilst he beds all the pretty girls in the northern hemisphere, and buckets of money."

"But Peaches—"

"Organizes socks," Irene said crisply, "has no money, and a face that will captivate him for all of forty-eight hours. You see, that's why he needs to marry a rich wife. Someone has to pay for his elaborate preparations to get women into his—"

"Shhhh!"

Peaches supposed Andrea might have said that because she had dropped her purse into the sink.

"There's someone else in here."

"I wonder who?" Irene said, sounding not in the least bit interested. "Let's see, shall we?"

Peaches wasn't sure if she were more humiliated that she'd had to listen to a private communication or that she'd had to listen to a private communication that involved details about her and her would-be boyfriend.

Details she just couldn't believe. David had been very kind to her, very attentive and generous. After all, he'd bought her what amounted to an entirely new wardrobe, hadn't he?

But to think that the only reason he had done so was so he could take advantage of her . . .

She eyed the only exit, which now lay beyond two exquisitely garbed, noble-by-birth women. Andrea was looking at her with miserable pity. Irene only looked at her coolly, as if she had actually enjoyed the pain she'd inflicted.

Peaches pushed past them, between them, without comment. Irene's laughter followed her from the bathroom and hung in the air until the closing of the door cut the thread.

She saw David standing at the end of the hallway and turned without thinking and walked the other way. Before she realized it, she was running, not walking. She had no idea where she was going, but *away* was good enough for the moment.

The only thing that struck her as odd as she fled out the door and down steps into the dark was how damned comfortable the shoes were she was wearing. Whatever else could be said about David Preston, it had to be said that the man knew how to pick out a pair of pumps.

Then again, perhaps he had done that sort of thing more than once.

She realized she had walked out onto the far end of the same porch she had been standing on earlier with David. She wasn't sure if she were more embarrassed that she'd been taken for a ride by David Preston or that she'd been seen making a fool out of herself by Stephen de Piaget. She who never cared what people thought of her, who had spent the past five years of her life telling people not to take themselves too seriously and get their lives in order and center themselves so the storms that would inevitably blow around them wouldn't touch them.

She started to cry, which was truly the final straw to an evening that had turned out to be less a fairy tale than a nightmare.

Damn it, she was going to ruin her makeup.

She heard a door open and saw more light spill out onto the porch, which propelled her forward.

The clock began to strike midnight.

She ran down the steps, grateful some enterprising soul had sanded them, and out into the garden that was remarkably free of snow and slush. She ran into what she quickly realized was a hedge maze. It wasn't particularly pleasant, actually, because the shadows that the hedges made peeking in and out of the fog that seemed to have suddenly sprung up were very unsettling.

And it had gone from being very cold to bone-chillingly bitter.

She wasn't sure when that had happened. Probably sometime about the same point where her desire to run away from everything that humiliated her had ebbed.

She came to a skidding halt, not for any more pressing reason than she had lost her shoe. She paused, then frowned. She hadn't been counting, of course, but it was odd how quickly that clock had gone through its twelve strokes.

Wasn't it?

And then Peaches realized something. She realized that particular something because she had a finely attuned woo-woo meter and the needle wasn't pegged, it had spun so hard into the red that it had left the meter entirely. She would have bent to look for it—figuratively of course—but she didn't dare.

Because she was standing on a time gate.

There was no point in examining why she knew that; she just did. It was rather surprising, however, to find such a thing loitering in the middle of David Preston's hedgerow maze. She wondered if he lost many visitors to it, or if most people just walked right over it without noticing it. Maybe it only opened its wretched portals to those who knew what to look for.

Maybe she was losing it and needed a brisk slap.

Well, she would deliver that to herself just as soon as she saw to business first, which was to hop off that particular spot of ground without delay.

Unfortunately, she had the distinct feeling her hopping had gone awry.

"Oooh, 'tis a faery!"

"Nay, a witch!"

"The queen o' the damned—"

Peaches turned around with a witty retort on her lips. After all, there was no sense in letting Kenneworth House's servants think they could get mouthy with one of the guests. She was just sure Irene wouldn't approve, and then the trio of servants who had commented on her sorry self would find themselves out . . . of . . . jobs . . . She looked up, then felt her mouth fall open.

The house was gone. All right, she would call it what it was. The bloody *palace* was gone. In its place was a hut. Well, it wasn't exactly a hut. If she'd been out in the Middle Ages looking for a quaint little place to crash in for the night, she would have found it perfectly acceptable. But when compared to the splendor that had been Kenneworth House, this was something else entirely.

It was a hovel.

And the unkempt, barely intelligible men standing in a little semicircle facing her were not wearing the standard uniform of David's footmen.

She made a very quick list of her options. She could scream, which was tempting; she could faint, which was even more tempting; or she could run. She considered the last, only she wasn't quite sure where she would run to. She backed up onto the gate and hopped up and down a time or two.

Nothing.

She swore, because it seemed like the right thing to do. She was left with her third resort, which was to run. Surely she would find another gate somewhere in the area. After all, England and Scotland were hotbeds of paranormal activity, especially of the specterish kind. And who could blame a shade? The climate was unreasonably lovely, what with all that rain and cloudiness and lovely winds caressing the trees.

Or perhaps they stayed for the history. There were castle stairs to come thumping down, old enemies to continue to vanquish, king and country to defend—as well as any number of lesser territories and families to uphold the honor of.

Then again, it might have been, she had to concede, continued irritation about the food. She was all for a lovely bed-and-breakfast or well-appointed hotel, but she had had the worst meals of her life in London.

She realized that the moon, which she hadn't noticed before, had come out in time to reveal her companions carrying a pointy thing each. She revisited the idea of running, but she only had one shoe left. Maybe the gate had rested long enough and would now carry her back to where she was supposed to be. She put aside her antipathy for everyone and everything at the future Kenneworth House and jumped forward onto the time gate.

She looked up, but no joy.

She decided that perhaps she just hadn't been firm enough, so she jumped a few more times. Her trio of companions seemed to find the sight rather alarming because they backed away, crossing themselves, spitting over their shoulders, and making all kinds of other hand motions she didn't recognize but imagined she wouldn't care to know the meaning of.

It took a while, but she eventually got tired of jumping. It wasn't that she wasn't in decent shape, it was just that she was in one high heel and a fancy ball gown, and she was slightly stressed.

She finally stopped and leaned over with her hands on her knees to try to catch her breath.

And that was the last thing she knew before blackness descended.

Chapter 12

Stephen stood in the middle of the ballroom and fidgeted. It wasn't that he was anxious to find someone to dance with, or that he was eager to go upstairs and take off his shoes that were pinching him with unusual vigor, or that he had watched Irene Preston and her cousin Andrea come back inside the ballroom in a suspicious manner.

He simply had the feeling something was wrong.

He walked out of the middle of the midnight revelers and positioned himself on the edge of the crowd so he could see who was there and what they were doing. He hadn't taken perfect note of who was in the party, but it hadn't been overly large, so he thought he could make a fair guess as to who was there and who was missing. Peaches Alexander was nowhere to be seen.

And for some reason, that made him very uneasy.

If David Preston had had his way, Peaches would have been right there with him, being pursued by him until she had given up and given in.

But she wasn't with him.

He knew David hadn't done anything to offend her only because he'd been watching the man for the past twenty minutes, since that moment when he had fortuitously stumbled out onto the porch and interrupted what he was certain would have been one of the worst attempts at romance perpetrated in at least a century.

But there were several women Stephen could bring to mind who would have been about mischief without thinking.

He watched as Irene Preston crossed the room and stopped in front of him. She seemed to expect deference, so he was happy to give it. Anything to find out what he wanted to know.

He inclined his head. "A lovely evening, isn't it, my lady?"

"Very, my lord."

"We seem to be missing one of the guests," Stephen said politely. "Miss Alexander."

"I haven't seen her."

"Haven't you?"

Irene seemed to be calculating something, but honesty apparently wasn't part of the equation. "Earlier, of course, but not recently."

Stephen looked at Andrea, who was standing five feet away, squirming. Well, those were obviously richer pastures, so he focused his attentions on her without hesitation.

"And you, Lady Andrea? Have you seen Miss Alexander?"

"How interested you are in a guest you didn't invite, Haulton," Irene said with a brittle laugh. "I imagine David can take care of her without any help from you."

"She was in the loo," Andrea said, then shut her mouth at the murderous look Irene threw her.

Stephen sent Andrea a look of thanks, then turned back to Irene. He inclined his head slightly. "I imagine David can take care of her perfectly well. I was only expressing a mild curiosity, nothing more. Perhaps you would care for something to drink, Lady Irene? Punch?"

Irene dragged her fingers down her throat in a gesture that was profoundly unsettling. "I do find that I'm parched. Andrea, go fetch us something."

"Allow me," Stephen said, then he turned to walk away before she could say anything else.

"Hurry," Irene called after him imperiously. "I am not finished with dancing for the evening."

Stephen couldn't have cared less what she was and was not

finished with for the evening. He walked along the edge of the company, making his way toward the refreshments. He found a liveried servant there and sent the man on a mission of mercy to keep Irene from dying of thirst. Duty done.

He managed to escape being caught by his trio of dukes' daughters only because some enterprising soul had announced the opening of very expensive champagne. He wasn't entirely sure that hadn't been the lady Raphaela's doing, and he was grateful for it.

He left the ballroom and looked for the nearest loo. Once that was identified, he looked at the various possible escape routes. If Peaches had been caught by Irene and her hapless disciple Andrea, then managed to escape the loo, where would she have gone? He considered for a moment or two, then followed his gut and chose the one that most expediently led away from the ballroom. He couldn't say he was much for hunches unless they led him to obscure historical details or alerted him to Patrick Mac-Leod standing behind him ready to clout him over the head with the hilt of a sword, but he had a feeling about the direction he was taking.

He walked out onto the patio, then stopped. He supposed Peaches could have taken any direction from there, either back into the house or toward the garages and stables, or even farther out into the garden. He shoved his hands into his pockets and stared up at the sky, wondering just what had happened since he'd seen her last.

He'd watched her leave the ballroom and assumed she was going to freshen up. He had also watched Irene and Andrea leave after her, though he hadn't imagined they'd been following her.

Now, he wasn't so sure.

It was possible, he supposed, that Irene had said something unpleasant to her. Andrea's guilty shifting was proof enough of that. But what would Peaches have done then? If she'd had any sense, she would have run back to her room, but perhaps she'd decided that taking a bit of air made more sense.

He looked down and wished absently for servants who were less diligent in keeping the walks free of snow and ice so he might have seen some footsteps.

He made a decision, then strode out into the garden, wishing the moon hadn't been obscured by clouds or that he'd had the good sense to bring a torch with him. There was a mini light on his keychain, but his keys were back in his bedroom being guarded ferociously by a romance-reading Humphreys. He would simply have to make do with less-than-adequate conditions.

He walked into the hedgerow maze, following it aimlessly until his eyes were adjusted to the darkness. He looked down, but there was nothing in the snow that spoke particularly to Peaches having traveled there recently. The entire bloody path was full of footsteps.

He continued to walk, shivering in spite of himself, until he had reached the center and could walk no farther. The hair on the back of his neck stood up, and he realized what lay one stride in front of him.

A time gate.

And next to it a single, elegant pump adorned with enough crystals to make it seem as if it were fashioned from glass.

He rubbed his face with two hands and indulged in an obscenity or two. Where had his calm, peaceful, unremarkable existence gone? Where were the days when the only specter he encountered was the odd ghost blowing down the back of his neck near the card catalog in the library? Why was it his generation that had been doomed to find itself facing all kinds of paranormal activity that his ancestors had managed to avoid?

He reached over and picked up the shoe—

"Trouble, Stephen?"

Stephen spun around, startled in spite of himself. Fortunately he had the good sense to keep the shoe fully hidden behind his back. "Lost my keys," he said blandly.

"Why would your keys find themselves out here?" David asked. "Seems an unlikely place for them."

"You know," Stephen said, stepping away from the time gate and leaving it safely behind him, "a garden is an unlikely place for many things, especially in the winter. I wonder that you brought Miss Alexander out in it given the chill."

"It was only to the porch and it wasn't for long," David drawled. "It would have been longer, of course, if we hadn't been so unpleasantly interrupted."

"Bad luck, old man," Stephen said with a shrug. "I'm sure you'll be more successful the next time."

"Exactly my plan," David said, looking at him with glittering eyes, "which is why I'm here. Did you bring Peachy out here?"

"No, I merely came myself for a bit of air."

"I thought you were looking for your keys."

"That, too," Stephen agreed. He smiled pleasantly. "Is there more supper inside, or is the party over?"

"I'm sure there's something left," David said shortly, "though perhaps less than if you hadn't been at table."

"I had many women to satisfy," Stephen said, shrugging. "Have to keep up the strength, of course."

David shot him a look of disgust, turned, and strode back to the house. Stephen followed him, slipping the shoe into the inside pocket of his jacket only because he didn't want David having any clue what he'd discovered. Of all things to find in Kenneworth's garden—a time gate?

He wondered if Peaches had known what she was stepping on, or if she had stepped on it, been carried off to points unknown, then realized her dilemma. She had as much experience with actually battling the insides of one as he did—which was exactly none.

He walked calmly after the Duke of Kenneworth, though he was having to fight the urge to run. He had absolutely no idea what to do short of simply jumping on the same spot Peaches had and hoping it would take him to the same place.

If it didn't, however, they were both lost.

"Coming back to the trough," Kenneworth asked, pausing just outside the doors to the ballroom, "or are you going straight to the kitchen to help yourself to the cooking sherry?"

"The latter, assuredly," Stephen said. He made Kenneworth a bow, then straightened. "If His Grace will excuse me?"

He waited until David had glared at him and stalked off inside before he turned and walked quickly to the door he'd come out of. He was going to go after Peaches, obviously, but there were things he had to put into place before he could. Such as, for instance, figuring out how the hell he was going to find her, then trying to wrap his mind around the fact that he was dealing with something as far-fetched as time traveling.

Perhaps he would do well to thumb through Lady Elizabeth MacLeod's latest offering to see how things truly worked.

He shook his head as he walked quickly down the hallway.

The things he had seen in the past several years . . . they would have turned his father gray overnight. Actually, those things *had* given his father gray hairs, especially those five lads and wee girl belonging to the Earl of Seakirk, who could have almost passed for Gideon's twin. And while Kendrick of Seakirk could have told him quite a few interesting tales, those weren't the details he needed. There was only one man belonging to his immediate—er, well, rather less than immediate, but certainly extended—family who could help him.

He ran up the steps to the upper floor and straight into a gaggle of noblewomen.

"Stephen!" was the word he was greeted with, spoken with various tones of reproach and disappointment.

He smiled pleasantly. "Zoe, Brittani, and Victoria, how lovely. Must dash, girls. Perhaps breakfast?"

Spluttering ensued. He made his escape rather daringly by hurrying straight through them and continuing on to his room before they could do anything more than express their disappointment in measured, ladylike tones.

He shut the door, locked it, then faced the first hurdle: Humphreys, who was apparently keeping himself awake by indulging in a good book.

Stephen quickly considered his present state of affairs. He had been taken over by Winston Humphreys upon his entrance to Eton in his thirteenth year. Stephen had looked on him as a second father of sorts, learned all manner of lessons from him ranging from how to properly tie a tie to how to pick a winner at any number of tracks running any number of horses. Along the way, Stephen had also found himself adopting Humphreys's strict moral code, his love of promptness and good manners, and his uncanny ability to smell a rat.

Humphreys knew, of course, about his activities in Scotland. He accompanied him there frequently, reputedly finding the society of Jane Fergusson and her brood to be a pleasant reminder of his own children raised before he took over the care of Stephen himself. If he had questions about exactly what Stephen was doing in Ian MacLeod's backyard, he had never asked them. If he found himself troubled by his encounters with Kendrick of Sedgwick, or Zachary Smith, who was married to Kendrick's rather blatantly medieval sister, or any number of other interesting individuals who managed to show their faces at Artane at various and sundry times, he never indicated it.

But Stephen wasn't sure what Humphreys would say to his actually taking part in any paranormal activities.

Humphreys rose and tucked his book under his arm. "My lord?"

Stephen pushed away from the door. "I have an emergency which requires absolute discretion and secrecy."

Humphreys didn't even so much as lift an eyebrow. "Of course, my lord."

"I am going to engage in a . . . paranormal oddity."

"Indeed, my lord."

Stephen shrugged out of his jacket on his way across the room, and Peaches's shoe fell out onto the floor. Stephen picked it up and handed it to Humphreys on his way over to the desk under the window where he'd left his mobile.

"And the other, my lord?" Humphreys asked without alarm.

"That's the question that needs to be answered." He found his phone, then looked at his valet, secretary, and keeper of several secrets. "I'm going to call Zachary Smith."

"The lady Elizabeth's brother," Humphreys noted, "the current Earl of Wyckham, and the husband of Mary de Piaget, sister of the Earl of Seakirk, daughter of—"

"Well, no need to get into that genealogy, is there?" Stephen said cutting him off before his eyebrows went up any farther. Just thinking about familial connections had apparently done what Peaches's shoe could not. "I'm going on a little trip."

"What shall I pack, my lord?"

Stephen considered quickly. "I think I'll wear riding clothes. I'll need my overcoat." He paused. "And a sword."

"A sword, Lord Stephen?"

"See what Kenneworth has hanging on his walls," Stephen said, looking up Zachary's personal mobile number. "I'll filch it later."

"Should it be sharp, my lord?"

"I wouldn't dare hope for it."

Humphreys only looked at him before he nodded, then made his way out of the room. Stephen waited until the door had closed behind him before he dialed. Zachary picked up on the second ring.

"The only reason I'm humoring you," he said, sounding rather weary, "is because I'm pacing the halls with the most beautiful baby ever born in my arms to keep her asleep."

"Would you ignore me otherwise?" Stephen asked politely.

Zachary laughed quietly. "Probably not. I'm always happy to offer a realistic perspective for your latest academic adventure, though I'm probably not the best one to ask. What's up tonight?"

"Peaches Alexander stepped through a time gate and I need to go fetch her."

Expletives accompanied a phone down to the ground. Stephen waited patiently whilst Zachary fumbled with a phone, a baby started howling and was taken by her mother, and equilibrium was restored.

"How long ago?"

Stephen gave him the details in as few words as possible, outlined his options for dressing the part, as it were, and asked his most pressing question.

"How do I know where she's gone?"

Zachary sighed. "That is the question. If I could get there soon enough, I could give you an idea of what the gate is doing, but I don't imagine you'll want to wait."

"I was hoping to go within the hour, but I don't dare until the house has gone to bed. I need to spread about some story of Peaches having gone home on her own. The last thing I need is David Preston poking his nose in this."

"I can't believe you're at his house at all," Zachary said with a bit of a laugh. "Following Peaches there?"

"In a roundabout way," Stephen agreed. "I was invited, if you can believe it."

"As were all your girlfriends, probably," Zachary said, "just to provide a bit of entertainment."

"How did you guess?"

"I read the odd gossip rag in Tesco now and again," Zachary said. "You rarely make the cover, but it doesn't take much digging to find the goods on your social life on about page six."

"The social life I would like to have is being interfered with by one-half of the relationship being slightly out of reach. Now, do you have any useful suggestions on how I might remedy that?"

"So, you're interested in Peaches Alexander now?"

"Zachary," Stephen warned.

Zachary only laughed. "I'm honestly not taking the situation lightly. I don't remember there being a gate near Kenneworth, but let me call Jamie and ask him what he knows. I'll text you a couple of suggestions for emergency exits, on the off chance the gate shuts behind you and won't open again."

"Which won't happen," Stephen said firmly.

"Hmmm" was the only reply.

Stephen suppressed the urge to curse. "Well? What else do I need to know about the gate?"

"Generally," Zachary said slowly, "you just think about where you want to go and *voilà*, you're there. It can sometimes be more useful to think about the person you're following if you don't have a clue where that person has gone. That's assuming that the gate is working smoothly."

"Assuming?" Stephen echoed.

"Well, you know the trouble we've had with the gate near Artane. Very unpredictable these days. I'm not sure that it won't eventually implode and destroy itself."

"I find myself surprised by how that thought disturbs me."

Zachary laughed. "I imagine my father-in-law Robin would say the same thing. It's too bad you've never had the chance to meet him. I think you would like him."

"Please, don't wish anything else on me," Stephen said grimly. "Make your call, if you would, then I would very much appreciate a contingency plan or two."

"I'd have a snack, if I were you," Zachary advised. "And take food with you."

"I'm not planning on being there long enough for a meal."

"Whatever you say," Zachary said, sounding amused. "I'll get back to you soon."

Stephen hung up, then stuffed the phone in his pocket. He was sure Humphreys would manage his investigations under the radar, as it were, but he would have to be a bit more visible for the moment. He would tell anyone who would listen that Peaches had been called away on an emergency, and he'd seen her sent off in a cab. He would then lay the groundwork for Humphreys being able to tell the party that he himself had been forced to leave before dawn for a very good reason he would leave to his valet to invent.

Because the very last thing he needed was Kenneworth sending out a search party for Peaches and having half the group disappear into the center of the garden as well. It was one thing for members of his family to engage in . . . well, the things they engaged in. It was another thing entirely to draw into their exclusive circle of adventurers those who might not be quite as discreet about the places they'd gone.

He retrieved his jacket, put it on, and left his room to set up his part of the subterfuge.

Chapter 13

Peaches was having a very bad dream.

She dreamed that she was lying on the ground, trussed up like a Christmas goose, listening to some marginally well-dressed man point at her in a threatening way. He was speaking French, but in spite of all her years of its study and her recent lovely conversations with Raphaela Preston, she couldn't understand a bloody word of it. It wasn't like those dreams where she found herself standing in a leotard alone on a coffee table where her thighs were just at the right height for everyone to get a perfect look at them. No, this was much more perilous—and apparently being conducted in a foreign language.

Her stomach growled and her haranguer stopped his diatribe and glared at her. He said something that she couldn't make out. Then one of the henchmen she hadn't noticed standing next to him came over and poked her with a stick.

It was then she realized that she wasn't dreaming.

"Ouch," she said, trying to move away from the stick. She realized very quickly that that wasn't possible because someone else was standing behind her with his foot on her side. He gave her a shove with that foot, which left her on her stomach with her face in the snow. She managed to lift her head well enough to breathe, then regretted it because it also allowed her the view of the man drawing his sword.

"But I'm a fairy," she blurted out in her best French.

It had worked for her younger sister Pippa. It was odd, though, how what worked for one sister didn't work for the other. The announcement that she wasn't just a nutter escaped from the local loony bin didn't seem to have impressed her new friends as much as she'd hoped it would. The conversation that ensued was agitated and unhappy. She managed to shift a little so she could at least see them as they were probably arguing about what would be the best way to put a fairy to death. Why hadn't she said she was a powerful witch who would cast a spell on them if they didn't back off right away?

She would have given anything for any number of household chemicals that she could have used to amaze and astonish, but she was fresh out of a basic chemistry kit. And it looked like she was fresh out of time to escape.

Mr. Swordwielder had obviously had enough of chatting with his friends over her fate. She would have complimented him on being a man of action, but he was holding on to that sword as if he meant to do business with it.

He started toward her.

She closed her eyes, seeing her life play before her in one long, slow-motion movie.

And then she heard the clang of sword against some other kind of metal. She would have thought maybe it was the guy's sword clanging against an as-yet-undetermined piece of armor worn by someone not her, but a quick glance upward revealed that his sword had come to rest abruptly against a rather fancy-looking ornamental-type sword.

That foofy-looking sword was currently being wielded by an absolute nutcase. She found that the ruffian foot resting in the middle of her back was suddenly no longer there thanks to a kick backward by her—well, she supposed he was her rescuer. He was at least standing with his back to her and seeing to her attacker. In her book, that made him a good guy.

She managed to roll over onto her side and then struggle to

her knees. Her hands were tied behind her back, which made that rather difficult, but she was in a fair bit of peril and that gave her an added bit of inspiration to get herself mobile.

It was only after her head cleared that things took a turn toward weird. And given who her parents were, she knew weird.

She sat back on her heels and watched the guy in front of her, who was dressed rather sportingly in riding clothes and a long, dark coat, continue to fight. All right, so she was fairly sure she wasn't dreaming; she wasn't at all sure she wasn't having a full-blown, broad-daylight sort of hallucination. Her rescuer was outnumbered by not only the head guy who had a sword and knew how to use it, but the three thugs she had seen earlier in Kenneworth's garden before she'd fainted. She was tempted to pat herself and see if anything untoward had happened to her while she was unconscious, but her hands were currently unavailable so she gave up on that idea.

She did, however, look behind her to see ruffian number four stirring. In fact, he stirred right up to his feet and began to swear.

"Hey," Peaches squeaked. "Hey."

She watched as her rescuer turned long enough to plow the hilt of his sword into the face of the guy behind her. The hilt was, as she had noted earlier, one of those fancy basket types adorned with all kinds of scrollwork and a few gems. One of the gems came off in Thug Number Four's forehead. He blinked, then fell backward and landed with a crash. He didn't move.

Peaches found herself hauled to her feet without ceremony. Her dress made a horrendous rending sound, but she noticed that less than she noticed the fact that she was no longer wearing her shoes. And then she realized something else.

Her rescuer was none other than Stephen de Piaget.

She swayed at that realization, partly because she hadn't expected to see him where he was and partly because he was displaying swordplay she hadn't imagined he possessed. Gone was that rather elegant Mr. Darcy type who knew his way around a library and no doubt had many similar well-dressed academic and nobleman friends. In his place was a Viking berserker who obviously knew how to use not only a sword, but also his fists and his feet.

If she'd had her hands free, she might have been tempted to put the back of her hand to her brow and indulge in a good, old-fashioned swoon.

And then it occurred to her just what she was seeing: Stephen de Piaget looking a great deal like one of those medieval de Piaget lads she knew. She frowned, but he didn't notice.

"Hey," she called.

He was apparently hard of hearing as well.

"Hey, you," she called, thinking that perhaps he hadn't realized she was talking to him.

"I'm a little busy right now," he threw over his shoulder.

"Where did you learn to do all that? I thought you couldn't do anything with a sword."

He ignored her a bit more. She actually couldn't blame him at present because the outnumbering was starting to look a little more serious than it had a few minutes earlier.

Stephen fought the leader of the group, who looked remarkably like a scruffy David Preston, for a moment or two, then punched him full in the face. Minor Thugs Two and Three were then completely disabled, but in their defense, they had likely never had modern riding boots hit them quite like that under the chin. She imagined they would awake from their dreamless slumbers to hurry off and tell anyone who would listen about the warlock who had bested them with his magical shoes.

She found Stephen stumbling back into her. More of her skirts pulled away from the bodice as she backed up.

"Are you going to answer my question now?" she asked. He was within earshot. There was no sense in not having a little conversation with him while she could. "You know, the one about why I thought you couldn't do anything with a sword?"

"Why would you think that?" he asked tightly, fending off the man who just had to be a Kenneworth progenitor.

"Because you weren't doing a very good job with Montgomery," she said.

"I lied," he said with a grunt, sending the first thug off to slumber thanks to a fist under his chin. That left him only the lord of Kenneworth to deal with.

"That doesn't make sense," she said. "Why didn't you admit to what you could do?"

"Because," he said, dragging his sleeve across his eyes, "my grandmother does not approve of unapproved activities."

"You have a grandmother?"

The look he shot her over his shoulder left her deciding that perhaps silence was golden. Well, it did for a bit until her curiosity got the better of her. It wasn't all that often that she saw Stephen de Piaget unplugged. He wasn't insulting her, she was slightly numb from the cold, and the time seemed to be right for a little light conversation.

"Are you saying your grandmother wouldn't approve of swordplay?"

"Yes," he said tightly.

"Where did you learn to do this?"

"From Ian MacLeod."

"Of course." She shook her head. "Everyone learns swordplay from Ian MacLeod."

"And if they don't, they should."

"What else doesn't your grandmother approve of?" she asked. "Things that don't involve tweed?"

"You know," he said, backing up and forcing her to back up a bit more, "you could make this easier if you'd stop yammering at me for just one minute."

"For just one?"

He looked at her in surprise, then he smiled before he turned back to his battle.

Peaches thought she might have to look for somewhere to sit down very soon. So he'd only smiled at her in a grave and polite way up until that moment. The smile he had just given her, that small little smile that seemed actually quite friendly, was something else entirely. She looked behind her, stepped over the man lying there and limped over to a tree. She had seen ropes worn through by rubbing them against the bark of a tree in movies. Given that she felt like she was on a set that should have been outlawed as cruel and unusual, she supposed there was no point in not giving a standard cinematic trick a try.

It was more difficult than it looked. That was, she supposed, because she was in a bit of a hurry, hoping that Stephen wouldn't get himself killed on the end of what looked like a very serviceable sword. His sword, however, looked rather wimpy.

"Is that your sword?" she called.

"Hell, no. And stop—"

"Yammering at you," she finished. "That was the last time, I promise."

He didn't bother to thank her, which she supposed his infamous granny would think was a display of bad manners, but she couldn't blame him. He had his hands full at the moment.

Her own hands, however, were free before she realized that she was rubbing her wrists alone against the bark. In her defense, she was rather distracted by listening to Stephen engage in conversation that sounded quite a bit like French but most definitely wasn't. It was that same medieval sort of Norman French that John spoke when he thought no one was listening.

Peaches leaned back against the tree and decided abruptly that if she had to be stuck in what she guessed was medieval England, it was best to be stuck there with Stephen de Piaget, medieval historian.

A medieval historian who could, it seemed, do more than just hand out Chaucerian reading assignments.

"What are you telling that guy?" she asked finally.

"That you're a wizard," Stephen threw over his shoulder. "Alchemize something, would you?"

"Like what?" she asked in surprise.

"I don't know, make something up! Something medieval."

"I already thought about that," she said defensively, "and having neither tie-dye nor organic compost to hand, I decided that I would have to rely on the old standby of being a fairy."

He shot her a dark look over his shoulder. "Well, then be the queen of the fairies, would you? You've the face for it."

She blinked. "Was that a compliment?"

"I think so," Stephen said, dredging up more skill from some well that Ian MacLeod had no doubt helped him dig.

Peaches found herself suddenly with her arms full of Stephen's coat that he'd shrugged out of.

"Put that on," was his only comment.

Well, she wasn't going to argue with that. She wrapped it around herself, tried not to enjoy too much the faint smell of whatever woodsy sort of cologne he had at some point worn while wearing it, and wished for shoes. She did the best she could with a pile of rotting leaves and suppressed a yawn as she waited for Stephen to finish up.

It occurred to her as time wore on that she could understand quite a bit of the conversation being carried on along with the sword fight.

"You're one of Artane's bastards, aren't you?" the lord of Kenneworth snarled.

Stephen didn't bother to respond.

"Why don't you answer?" the other man said in exasperation.

"Because you're not worth the breath," Stephen said calmly. "Whoever you are."

Well, that didn't go over well. Peaches wished she'd had pen and paper to write down a few of the things she'd heard. Tess would have wanted them for her collection of medieval slurs.

"Who am I?" Stephen's opponent said, dropping his sword for a moment. "You mean, you don't know?"

"Don't know, don't care," Stephen said with a shrug.

"I am Hubert of Kenneworth!" Hubert of Kenneworth shouted. "And my hall is every bit as fine as Robin of Artane's—"

Stephen laughed. "You can't be serious."

The current lord of Kenneworth was apparently very serious. He attacked with a renewed vigor that actually had Stephen backing up a pace or two.

And the unthinkable happened.

His sword broke off at the hilt.

Hubert of Kenneworth laughed. "That shows you—"

He stopped talking, and he stopped talking because he'd been treated to Stephen's fist in his mouth.

It didn't take long after that for him to be folding up like a cheap lawn chair. He smacked his head against a rock as he landed, and the sound was very loud in the stillness of the morning. Peaches would have asked Stephen if he was going to check to see if the first lord of Kenneworth was okay, but Stephen was apparently not interested in finding that out. He turned, took her by the hand, and pulled.

"Wait," she said, wincing as she stumbled after him. "I lost my shoe."

He blew his hair out of his eyes. "Where?"

"Well, if I knew where, it wouldn't be lost, would it?"

He looked at her, blinked, then smiled.

And the sun came out from wherever it had been hiding for the past twenty-eight years of her life.

She would have paused to admire all the things she had grudgingly admired about the perfection of his face and form, but she was too busy being pulled into his arms.

She didn't burst into tears because she wasn't a weeper. But she did gulp quite a bit as she clutched the back of his riding jacket. And she let herself enjoy a glorious, impossible, perfect moment in the arms of a man who was trembling slightly with something.

"Are you afraid?" she whispered.

"Freezing, rather."

"You can take back—"

"No," he said, rubbing her back with one hand, "I shan't. I brought the coat for you anyway."

She took a shaky breath. "You came for me?"

"Of course."

"How did you know where to come find me?"

"I'll tell you when we're safely away from wherever we are. And I believe your shoe is over there, though you might prefer the bedroom slippers I shoved into the pockets of that coat. Fortunately we don't have far to go." He released her far enough to look at her. "There's a gate in David's garden."

"I gathered as much."

"We'll talk about that later, too. Among other things," he added.

She wasn't sure what he meant by that, but she was thoroughly unnerved by the look he sent along with the words. It was a very serious look that she wasn't sure she liked the looks of.

"Will we?" she asked with an attempt at lightness as he released her completely to go fetch her shoe. "It was such a glorious night I'm not sure I'm equal to discussing it."

He shot her another look she couldn't quite decipher, so she didn't try. Perhaps he thought she wasn't good enough for David Preston. Maybe he thought she shouldn't be hobnobbing at any society parties.

Or maybe he was kneeling down to put slippers that were too big on her feet that were too frozen to care, and she just couldn't focus on whatever it was he had to say to her. If he would just stop touching her, she would be able to think clearly.

He rose, handed her the slightly worse-for-wear pump she'd managed to bring to medieval England with her, then looked around them and frowned at the damage he'd done to the locals. At least they were all still breathing, which she thought was a good thing. Stephen picked up the two halves of his broken sword, then looked at her.

"I could carry you back."

"It isn't far."

He nodded, then looked at the glorified lean-to that was Kenneworth House and frowned. "I think we should run, so we aren't seen. I would try to wait until tonight, but—"

"No, let's just go," she said with a shiver. She could last another fifteen minutes, but the thought of spending the entire day in medieval England was just a little more than she could take.

He took the hilt and the blade—which even she could see was as dull as a round rock—in one hand, then took her hand in his other. She ignored how pleasant that was and concentrated on keeping her almost useless feet going in the right direction. She glanced at the hut that was a bit closer than she was comfortable with and frowned.

"I didn't realize I'd gotten so far away from the house," she said slowly.

"The lord's helpers were trying to toss you back in the forest so the fairies would come claim you. Apparently you made quite an impression on them."

"What a great bunch of guys," she said happily.

He looked at her and smiled again, faintly. She decided right then that getting mixed up with the future Earl of Artane in any century would be extremely hazardous to her mental health. He looked remarkably like John de Piaget, but he was older, more serious, and somehow almost more gorgeous, if that were possible. When he smiled that little smile, she wanted to sit down—

"The first lord of Kenneworth, whom we just had the pleasure of encountering," he said, interrupting her thoughts, "thought you were certainly lovely enough to be a fairy, but he used his superior intellect to determine that you were merely a woman who was lost. He was offering quite politely to take you home and warm you up."

"I can only imagine," Peaches said faintly.

"I suggest you don't."

She continued on with him for another twenty paces before she cleared her throat. "It must run in the family."

"Lecherous tendencies?" Stephen asked politely.

"Yes."

He didn't answer. He only squeezed her hand slightly and continued along a path she couldn't see. She could tell, however, when they'd reached the appropriate patch of ground—and not just because the snow had been trampled quite thoroughly there.

Stephen stopped, glanced at the house, then looked down at the ground. He kept hold of her, dug around a bit with his toe, then swore. While he was doing that, she thought she might as well keep watch. She looked over at Kenneworth Hovel, then swore.

A lone horseman was galloping toward them.

Stephen cursed, but it was in French, so it added a certain cachet to the moment. He threw the hilt of the sword with surprising velocity right at the man's nose, then pulled the man off the horse as he reached down to strike at him with a pole. He caught the horse and swung up onto its back, then turned around and made straight for her. Peaches ripped more of her skirts as she made a grab for his arm and pulled herself up behind him. It was messy and undignified, but she supposed it was for the best.

"This might be their only horse," she pointed out as they galloped off.

"It might be," he agreed.

"You don't mind changing history?" she asked.

"Not when I don't like the alternative."

Which she supposed was her ending up being warmed up by the current lord of Kenneworth and Stephen meeting his end on any number of rustic blades. She thanked Stephen for his pains, had a grunt in return, and decided the best thing to do was just hold on and see what the rest of the day brought. She could only hope it included a return to a hot fire and something decent to eat.

Because landing in the past and having to stay there was just not for her. She didn't want to do the Cinderella thing with soot and ashes and unidentifiable meat products under sauce. She wanted to get back home where she could complain about British packaged food and American chocolate. She was cold, tired, and finding herself in the alarming position of having kind thoughts about the Viscount Haulton. Seeing him out of his school uniform had allowed her to see him in an entirely different light.

An entirely more favorable light.

She wondered absently if he were changing himself to suit the times, or if the man currently on display was who he was all the time. Maybe he was forced to hide everything he really was under tweed and proper manners.

"Warm enough for the moment?" he asked over his shoulder.

"Yes, thank you."

He patted her arm that was around his waist, then concentrated on getting them wherever it was he was taking them. She didn't dare ask.

She was simply glad it had been Stephen to come rescue her.

Chapter 14

Stephen watched a lad trot off into the distance on the horse he himself had pilfered the day before. It wasn't that he particularly wanted to walk any farther, it was that he thought it best to leave that lord of Kenneworth no reason to pursue them any longer. If nothing else, perhaps the return of the horse would distract those with less than altruistic thoughts of murder and mayhem.

Because the unfortunate truth was, they were only a dozen miles from Kenneworth House as it stood in either century and that was certainly close enough to be overtaken. Stephen hadn't minded exercising a few of his hard-won sword skills, but he hadn't had to kill anyone and preferred to keep it that way.

Though if it came down to the choice between the life of a medieval inhabitant of any station and Peaches, he knew the choice he would make.

That had surprised him, that rush that went through him at the thought of anyone harming her. He had to admit that he had watched the medieval expats in his family on the occasions that presented themselves, just to see how they were dealing with the modern world. In all the men, he had sensed an undercurrent that he hadn't understood at the time, but he most definitely understood now. Even though the skirmish that morning had lasted only half an hour at best, he knew he would never be the same again.

"Where now?"

He looked at Peaches standing in front of him, swathed in his coat, and wearing his slippers, shivering as if she were standing there in short sleeves. He honestly wasn't sure she wouldn't find herself with pneumonia in the end once they returned home.

If they could return home.

He realized as he stood there under a tree and shivered right along with her that he had gravely miscalculated the simple perils of the time period. He had intended, in spite of Zachary's warnings to the contrary, to simply go back, fetch Peaches, and be home within the hour. He'd shoved apples in his pockets, but nothing more substantial, and he hadn't prepared either of them for the weather. That didn't begin to address the fact that she looked like a princess and he looked like a Regency gentleman, which wasn't precisely current-day dress.

He was, he had to admit to himself, rather an idiot.

And the only other thing that he would tell anyone who would listen was never to have anything to do with Kenneworth or its environs. The gate had been stubborn when he'd tried to come through it and completely unresponsive when he'd tried to get himself and Peaches back to their proper time and place. Add that to the ridiculous lack of proper weaponry inside the hall itself, and it was no wonder none of the de Piagets had wanted anything to do with anyone of their ilk. The sheer frustration of navigating all of the craziness to be found there was enough to keep him away in the future.

He wondered if Peaches possibly felt the same way.

"Stephen?"

He smiled reflexively at the sound of his name from her before he managed to school his features into something less delighted-looking. "Yes?"

"You were saying?"

He pulled himself back to their present dilemma. The gate at Kenneworth hadn't worked, and the other rather close but reputedly fickle portal—again, close enough to Kenneworth that their influence was obviously being felt—had been likewise unresponsive to their pleas. That had left Stephen with no choice but to look farther afield, which was why he was where he hoped he was, namely within a quarter mile of a third possibility. Finding an inn in the area had been nothing short of a miracle.

"I believe there's an inn over there," he said, nodding in that direction. "I think we should take our chances with supper, then spend a few minutes in front of the fire before we make another attempt."

She nodded numbly, which he couldn't blame her for. He took her hand without thinking, then realized he didn't particularly want to let her go. She didn't seem completely opposed to the action, though, so he didn't make any mention of it. They were both under a fair bit of duress, so perhaps it was just the situation throwing them together that resulted in closeness.

Or it could have been that he was ruthlessly and without remorse taking advantage of the fact that she was too distracted to realize what he was doing. He was more than happy to hold her hand while she was otherwise distracted.

It was only as he was standing in front of the bar, getting ready to get them a meal, that he realized there was something standing in the way of feeding his lady and that something happened to be the fact that he had no funds.

He was, he would readily admit, not exactly at his best at the moment.

He was just putting his brain in gear to try to come up with some way to actually pay for food—and not curse himself for not having thought to bring anything to use in bartering—when his elbow was bumped.

"No need to pay," said a lad who was quite suddenly at his side. "Them young lords by the fire gave me coin for 'im and 'is lady. Meals and drinks."

Stephen wasn't sure what current-day protocol demanded, but he supposed a very brief thanks wasn't out of order. He could only hope he could manage it intelligently.

He nodded to the innkeeper, then walked over to where two men were sitting at a table closest to the fire. Stephen studied them as he walked, wishing he had spent a bit more time ignoring his professors during college and more time listening to the damned ghosts in his father's hall to determine what an authentic medieval Norman French accent should sound like.

He decided as he paused and inclined his head slightly that he was going to have to take Kendrick de Piaget out for a *very* expensive dinner the first chance he had. That he had even a slim hope of not sounding like a complete foreigner was only thanks to his uncle's mocking him endlessly in the garden about his French.

One of the men rose and held out a chair for Peaches, who hesitated, then shuffled over to sit in it. Stephen sat as well and tried to initiate a bit of polite conversation.

Their new friends didn't seem inclined to do anything but attend to their suppers.

Stephen examined his meal in a purely academic way, then decided that was unwise. He wasn't sure what they were about to eat, and he could only hope what they would wash it down with wouldn't kill them both. Their companions seemed to find nothing amiss with their suppers. They ate with enthusiasm, though they seemed to be careful to keep their faces hidden by the hoods of their cloaks. Stephen looked at Peaches, who only shrugged at him helplessly.

He cleared his throat, gearing up to broach some sort of innocuous topic, when one of the men banged his cup down on the table and whispered something to his companion. With a *good e'en to you both*, the two stood up and beat a hasty retreat through what Stephen could only assume were the kitchens. He might have been curious enough at another time to ask one of the other patrons what all the fuss had been about, but given his current time and place, he supposed it was just best to keep his mouth shut. He moved wooden trenchers and cups aside, wondering absently if anyone would notice if he simply poached a pair for his office, then took the seat next to Peaches.

"That was interesting," he murmured.

"I don't think we're through with interesting," Peaches managed. She slid a sheaf of paper toward him. "They left this behind. On purpose, I think."

He took it, unfolded it, then came close to dropping it in his surprise.

It was a map.

The inn was marked, then a trail leading to an X Zachary hadn't mentioned. Stephen hardly dared hope that X would lead him back to where he wanted to go, but he couldn't deny the sight of it was unusual. He looked at Peaches.

"What do you think?"

"They left us a small bag of coins as well," she said. "I think they knew us."

Stephen was about to make what he was sure would have been a pithy comment about his family connections stretching across the centuries, but he was interrupted by the arrival of someone inside the common room who skidded to a halt. Stephen couldn't see his face for the hood of his cloak, but it was quite obvious he was staring at them. For all he knew, it was someone from Kenneworth. He felt for Peaches's hand under the table.

"Can you flee?"

"Definitely," she said, sounding as nervous as he felt.

He waited until the man had turned aside to speak to the innkeeper before he pulled Peaches up with him and headed out the back door, tossing the bouncer there one of the coins that Peaches pressed into his hand. That pained him to give it up, but he hadn't had any choice. If giving up a potentially mint-condition medieval artifact meant the difference between freedom and death, he would choose the former.

They didn't make it as far as he would have liked. In fact, they didn't even make it to the stables where he would most certainly have poached the first semi-sound horse he could have and galloped off on it. The whisper of steel coming from a sheath behind him had him cursing fluently. He pushed Peaches in front of him, then turned, drawing the knife Patrick MacLeod had trained him never to be without from his boot as he did so.

His opponent looked at him, looked at his knife, then propped his sword up against his shoulder. "Surely you jest."

Stephen rapidly considered his options. He could throw his blade through his enemy's heart and flee. He could say nothing and do his best with a knife that was, at close range, completely inadequate to battling what he could see was a well-loved and very well-used sword. Or he could bluster.

He scratched his cheek with the hilt of his knife—the only part of the blade that wasn't honed to perilous sharpness. "I lost my sword this morning. One makes do when one must, don't you agree?"

The other man laughed, a sound that would have been reassuring at another time, but this was a time that was far from

Stephen's own and he wasn't reassured by anything at the moment. And then his foe pushed his hood back off his face.

Stephen felt his mouth fall open. Peaches gasped audibly.

The other man only lifted an eyebrow and looked at them both steadily. "Out for a stroll, are we?"

Stephen revised his idea to take Kendrick to supper and substituted instead a weekend away for Kendrick and his bride whilst he tended their children. That he could understand anything at all was certainly due to his uncle's help.

"Well," Stephen managed, "it seemed like a decent afternoon for it."

His opponent, a blond, rather older version of he himself, resheathed his sword. "I'm not sure your lady shares your enthusiasm. Perhaps I should help you get home before she freezes to death."

Stephen slipped the knife back down the side of his boot but didn't take his eyes off the man in front of him. "That is an interesting offer, my lord."

"Wyckham," the other man said casually. "Nicholas of Wyckham."

Stephen wasn't surprised. His uncle, several generations removed, of course.

"Who are you?" Nicholas of Wyckham asked politely.

"Stephen," Stephen said. "The Viscount Haulton, if you like."

"And Baron Etham," Peaches supplied, her teeth chattering. "If you want to be completely accurate."

Nicholas of Wyckham smiled at her. "Accuracy, Mistress Alexander, is always my most pressing concern." He tilted his head and studied her. "I am assuming you are who I think you are, unless you are my brother John's daughter and not his sister-in-law. I should think not, but it has been at least a score of years since I last saw the lady Tess at my hall." He shrugged. "Whoever you are, you gave me a bit of a start."

"I'm Peaches," she managed. "Tess's sister."

Nicholas nodded. "So you are."

Stephen had his arm around Peaches's shoulders, so he felt clearly the shiver that went through her. He looked at Nicholas in surprise. "But she and John were just at your hall last month."

"Were they?" Nicholas asked in surprise. He frowned at Stephen. "Something very strange is going on with the strands of time. How did you get here?"

"Through a gate at Kenneworth," Stephen admitted.

"Well, that explains it," Nicholas said with a snort. "They're far enough away that they don't vex me overmuch, but I can say with certainty that I've no love for any of their ilk. And their hall is no better than a kennel. I'm not surprised things went awry for you."

Stephen wasn't, either, but he saw no point in saying as much.

"I am here to meet two of my sons," Nicholas continued, "but they are notoriously late. I think we have a few moments for speech, but I'm not sure where would be the safest place. Let's try the stables, shall we?" He offered Peaches his arm. "How has your sister found the trial of being wed to my brother so far?"

"She's very happy," Peaches said with a smile.

"Remind him I vowed to come see to him if that ceases to be the case." He looked over his shoulder at Stephen. "Coming, Haulton?"

Stephen nodded and followed him.

Within minutes, he and Peaches were sitting on a pile of hay in a relatively warm part of the stable. Peaches hadn't argued with the blanket put over her legs and tucked under her feet, nor did she seem disinclined to put on the boots Nicholas purchased for her from an enterprising stable lad to take the place of Stephen's sodden bedroom slippers. Stephen put the boots on her feet, then sat down next to her and looked at his . . . He took a deep breath. His uncle, as it happened.

"Haulton is a lovely place," Nicholas remarked casually, rubbing his hands together and blowing on them. "One of my father's favorite estates, as it happens. Before he passed, my father insisted that Haulton always remain with the heir. Perhaps on the off chance that the heir tired of the family seat."

"Ah," Stephen managed.

"You might be surprised," Nicholas continued, "just how much you look like my father and brother, Robin." He shot Peaches a look. "Or he might not, eh, Mistress Peaches?"

Peaches smiled. "I don't think he would be."

"The current eldest son, is he?"

"The very same."

"How is the old pile of stones these days?" Nicholas asked.

Stephen realized Nicholas was asking him. "Glorious," he wheezed.

Nicholas winked at Peaches. "Aye, he is the eldest, isn't he? Though I daresay anyone who was born within those walls would love it as well. My brother John is the exception, I suppose."

"He loves it," Peaches said simply. "He simply loves my sister more."

Nicholas smiled. "I daresay that is the case. And as long as he is happy, I can't begrudge him his choices. I understand them, in a way. What do you think of Artane, Mistress Peaches?"

Stephen hardly dared look at her, but he couldn't resist at least a glance in her direction.

"It belongs in a dream," she said with a sigh Stephen couldn't quite decipher. "And Stephen is right about its condition. It is absolutely glorious."

"Then we should get you both back to it before you freeze out here in the wilderness." He looked at Stephen. "What have you tried to return home?"

"That useless gate at Kenneworth," Stephen said with a sigh, "then another very dodgy place near there. Zachary Smith gave me ideas for another place or two." He felt the map he'd been given burning a hole in his pocket, but he didn't suppose he should mention it. He had the feeling that if Nicholas's sons—if that's who they had been—had been in possession of such a thing, they had used it themselves.

He wasn't sure he wanted to think about what that might mean for any of them.

Nicholas pursed his lips. "I don't think you would ever make the gate at Kenneworth work for you. It is, as they say, a one-way ticket to the past. As for the others, Zachary would know from firsthand experience which ones were the most useful. Tell me what he told you and we'll discuss the quickest way home for you. I don't think your lady will manage too much more walking even if I find a cart to transport you as close as you dare come to your destination."

Stephen looked at Nicholas seriously. "Thank you, my lord."

Nicholas smiled. "What is family for, if not to aid you when you come to their time?"

Stephen wondered how much experience Nicholas had with just that sort of thing, but he didn't dare ask. He simply took one of Peaches's hands in his own, rubbed it gently to try to warm it, then turned to a discussion of things that belonged in a book of fiction.

It was several hours past sunset when Stephen stood on the side of the road with Peaches and listened to a cart rumble away, its very unsettled but well-paid driver apparently quite happy to leave them behind.

"Did you want to stay longer?"

Stephen started in surprise. "Stay longer?" he asked. He looked at her. "Whatever for?"

"For research purposes, I suppose." She paused, then took a deep breath. "I wouldn't mind."

He looked at her bedraggled self and shook his head. "I think even if we were suitably dressed and outfitted, we've made a long enough visit for now." He rubbed his hands together in a futile attempt to warm them. "I'm not sure I would want to stay longer than that. Certainly not in our current straits."

"Oh, I don't know," she said with a bit of a smile. "I'm sure you would dredge up a few useful somethings from all that research."

He shook his head. "I look too much like my ancestors to attain any sort of respectable position with a noble house, and I have no means of joining a guild even if they would let me in. And while I was looking for work, what would you do?"

"I'm not sure I want to think about that."

"Neither do I," he said seriously, "which is why we will trot home as quickly as we're able."

"Will we make it this time, do you think?"

"Nicholas seemed to think so."

She shivered. "That was weird."

"Very," he agreed.

She held out a bag. "He told me to give this to you. I guess you can add it to what the boys gave you."

Stephen felt it, then smiled to himself. "I imagine it's just the change from his pocket."

"He said something to that effect."

He had a final look around, then took her hand. "We'll examine it all after we've gotten home." He looked at the gate he could see shimmering ten feet in front of them. "Shall we?"

She nodded and followed him into the future.

Chapter 15

Peaches looked up at Kenneworth rising up in front of her, still shrouded in mist, but looking not nearly as friendly as it had however many days ago it had been when she'd first seen it. At the moment, she just couldn't remember how long it had been. It felt like forever.

She wasn't sure this was how the fairy tale was supposed to end.

"I believe we need a course change."

She looked up at Stephen de Piaget standing next to her. He was back to looking at her gravely. His terribly handsome face was covered in dirt that sweat had carved trails through, and he was looking a bit scruffy. But he had saved her life with a very blunt Kenneworth ceremonial sword and gotten her home. She couldn't ask for more than that.

"Course change?" she managed, her voice cracking on the words. "What sort?"

"Well," he said seriously, "I'm not sure how it would look if we were to waltz into Kenneworth's library dressed as we are, apologize for ruining his useless sword, and request baths."

Peaches managed to nod. "He wouldn't understand."

"He would call the police and have us committed," Stephen said with a snort. "And in my case, quite happily."

She didn't want to credit David with that kind of vindictiveness, but she was beginning to suspect she had misjudged quite a few things. She nodded, though it hurt her to do so. The next time she went to medieval England, she was going to run into better people at the beginning of her trip and make sure she had better shoes, though the slippers Stephen had brought her and the boots Nicholas had gotten for her had certainly saved her a raging case of frostbite.

She cleared her throat uncomfortably. "I have clothes in my room that I don't really want to leave behind." She couldn't bring herself to say that she wanted them because David had bought them. Not after everything Stephen had done for her.

"I'll have Humphreys fetch your clothes out for you, if that suits. As for the rest, I think we need a good cover story."

Peaches was too exhausted to offer an opinion. "Whatever you think best."

"Are you allowing me to herd you, Miss Alexander?"

She looked up at him quickly, but he was only watching her solemnly. "Yes, my lord Haulton, I am," she said, "especially if that herding includes being in a modern contraption where I don't have to use my feet any longer."

"That I think I can manage." He paused. "Shall I carry—"

"No," she said quickly. "I'm fine. It isn't that far."

Stephen didn't pick her up, but he did offer her his arm. She hardly hesitated before she took it, yawned, and walked with him across frozen ground, all the way to Kenneworth's garage.

A man sprang to his feet from where he'd been sitting in front of a small space heater. Polite words were halfway out of his mouth before his mouth caught up with what he was seeing. His mouth was already half open, but it fell fully open and stayed there.

"Ah," he wheezed.

"Got lost on the moors," Stephen said smoothly. "It's amazing the adventures you can have this time of year."

The man gurgled.

Stephen smiled pleasantly. "If you'll fetch me my keys, my good man, we'll be on our way."

Keys were fetched, and nothing more was said. Peaches

didn't dare look at the servant who was still gaping at them as if they'd just walked out of his worst nightmare.

"But, you look . . . unwell," the man protested.

"Not to worry," Stephen said easily. "Let me tell you what happened and ease your mind."

Peaches was happy to listen to Stephen invent a very interesting story about Miss Alexander having suffered a blow to the head that had rendered her temporarily disoriented. He himself had been out for a walk before he'd proceeded with his plans to leave early the day before and been lucky enough to stumble upon her. He had considered courses of action and decided that it was best to get her as quickly as possible to his father's personal physician. Given that Artane wasn't unreachable in good time, they would make for his father's hall and would the man be so good as to report the same to His Grace?

The man nodded weakly and signaled for a helper to come open the bay doors for Stephen. He made Stephen a shaky bow then departed on his mission to inform any concerned parties of the return of Lord Haulton and his maiden in distress.

Peaches wondered, absently, how easily David had been talked out of worrying about her. She didn't think she could ask Stephen for the complete set of details. One thing was certain: if Irene had anything to say about it, no search party had been sent out.

She limped with Stephen over to his Mercedes, watched him open the door, then hesitated. She looked inside, then at him.

"I'm not sure I can ruin this side of your car, too."

"We'll send it out to be cleaned later," he said with a weary smile. "And it is just a car, Miss Alexander."

She realized then that he'd never called her by her given name. She supposed the moment for asking him if he ever intended to was not the present moment. She looked inside his car one last time, considered the condition of his coat, then sighed. Her alternatives were either walking to Sedgwick or going inside to beg a ride. She turned and backed into the seat, then leaned over to look at boots that belonged in a museum.

Stephen squatted down in front of her and studied her feet for a moment or two in silence. He looked up at her. "I think I should take them off."

"Only if you have a bag to stash them in," she managed.

"Think of all that medieval dirt caked on them. For all you know, there might be some sort of artifact hiding in it."

"You, Miss Alexander," he said seriously, "just might make a formidable scholar of all things medieval."

"Actually, I'm just afraid of what is left of my feet. I'm not sure I want them touching your car's carpet."

He came as close to smiling as he had since they'd returned to their proper time. "Somehow, I doubt that. Let's see if we can pull, gently."

She didn't holler, she didn't gulp, but she felt tears begin to run down her cheeks. It wasn't so much that her feet hurt her as it was that she was so happy to know that her future footwear choices weren't going to be limited to worn, smelly boots. Well, that and she was extraordinarily glad she was back in her proper place in time. She was never, *ever* going to step on another gate through time.

Stephen unearthed a tissue from the glove box and handed it to her. She was busy wiping her face as he tucked a blanket around her legs and feet after she'd shifted to put herself fully into his car. She was fairly sure the thing was cashmere and found it in her to wonder if the man had any other favorites amongst finely knitted fabrics. Tweaking him about it, though, was completely beyond her.

He buckled her in, then shut her door.

Peaches started to shiver, which she supposed was a good thing. A moment later Stephen climbed into his side of the car and closed the door. He dug a cell phone out of the glove box in front of her, though he didn't use it. He simply turned the car on and drove out into the courtyard. Peaches could see the back door of the house opening, but Stephen didn't stop to find out who was coming to see them. He wasted no time in speeding away from the house, something she agreed with completely. She had smelled rather strongly of wet sheep the last time she'd made a grand entrance at Kenneworth House, but that was nothing compared to what she smelled like at present.

Stephen's phone rang, making her jump. He glanced at the number but didn't take the call. Peaches looked at him with a frown.

"Do I dare ask?"

"Irene," he said briefly. "She'll keep. But I'd best ring Humphreys before he's assaulted by questions he won't know how to answer."

"Have you got answers for him?" she asked in surprise.

He shot her a look. "He has a vague idea of my evening's activities, but I don't care to be more specific than I have to, which means I'm going to be inventing a few things as I go. Please don't let that be a permanent blot on my character."

She waved him on to his subterfuge, which he engaged in the moment they hit the main road and he found a place to pull over.

He very briefly discussed with his valet the situation and the necessity of collecting both his and Miss Alexander's things and dismissing Miss Edwina. She closed her eyes and realized that it was becoming far too easy to rely on him to take care of things and worry later about—

Her thoughts ground to a halt.

Dismissing Miss Edwina?

She waited until he'd pulled back on the road and they'd driven for a bit before she dared look at him. Fortunately, she couldn't see him too clearly, which made it easier for her to think. She contemplated what she could say, if anything, about his very brief conversation with his valet.

If Humphreys had provided her with Edwina the Stern, was it possible that Humphreys had provided her with other things at Stephen's direction?

Such as a new wardrobe?

She was beginning to think she had been a complete and utter idiot.

Stephen yawned. "I think I should stop for petrol and something to feed us—" He blinked. "What is it?"

She opened her mouth, then shut it. She didn't want to know. The thought that Stephen de Piaget, the man she had loved to loathe, had been the one to spend his hard-earned sterling on clothes so she wouldn't look like a country bumpkin . . .

Well, it was almost more than she could take in.

He fished out another tissue and started to use it on her. He stopped with his hand approximately an inch from her face, looked at her seriously, then held the tissue out.

"I think your feet must pain you."

It was more her conscience that was paining her, but she

didn't think she could admit as much. She gulped a time or two instead.

"Do you—" She had to take a deep breath. "Do you want me to go inside and get food?"

"I think the ball gown and overcoat might be too conspicuous," he said seriously.

"Well, we are in the country," she managed. "I guess riding boots wouldn't look too strange."

"Not at this time of night, at least," he said wryly. "We'll stop the first chance that presents itself." He paused. "Are you unwell?"

No, just feeling like an idiot. Of course, she couldn't say that without talking about all kinds of things she didn't want to talk about. She limited herself to shaking her head, which seemed to be enough for him.

She closed her eyes, but that made the world spin uncomfortably, so she resigned herself to merely wishing she could close her eyes.

The first chance for food presented itself sooner than she dared hope. She watched Stephen buy gas and snacks, noted that no one inside seemed to find his gear out of the ordinary, then waited a bit more until she was holding a hot cup of tea and they were back on the road. She cleared her throat.

"Thank you," she managed.

He glanced at her. "The tea is that good?"

"I wasn't talking about the tea," she said. "I meant the other business."

He frowned, then realization apparently dawned. "Oh, that. It was nothing, really."

Peaches supposed there was no time like the present to offer a full complement of apologies, if she was going to do it at all.

"It was something to me," she said, shifting a little so she could look at him. "You saved my life. Thank you."

He shrugged. "My pleasure."

She paused. "I'm afraid I wasn't very gracious about it at the time."

He didn't look at her. "You needn't like me, Miss Alexander." He shot her a brief glance. "I can be something of an arse from time to time."

"Can you?" she mused. "I wonder."

"You probably shouldn't."

Well, that wasn't exactly a warming of relations, but she supposed she might as well press on while she had the chance.

"You were very kind to me and Tess before Christmas," she said quickly, before she lost her courage. "I repaid you poorly."

"Did you?"

She was starting to wonder if she shouldn't just keep her mouth shut, but she had just had a brush with death and getting stuff off her chest seemed like the right thing to do.

"You were, I think, teasing me once," she said. "At that little party—"

"I know the one."

She took a deep breath. "I took it personally, and I don't think I should have." She paused. "I apologize."

He said nothing. She waited, but he still said nothing. Maybe he wasn't good at accepting apologies, or he thought she was crazy, or he just didn't care what she thought.

Maybe he hadn't been teasing her, and he really thought she was a flake.

She waited for what she was sure was at least half an eternity before she cleared her throat and changed the subject.

"Where are we going?"

He put them on the motorway, but he still didn't look at her. She was almost to the point where she was back to thinking she ought to just punch him and be done with it when he spoke.

"I think I can get us to Cambridge without falling asleep and causing an incident," he said wearily, "though I fear Sedgwick is beyond me tonight." He shot her a brief look. "I think it imprudent to go to Artane, unfortunately, regardless of what I said earlier to the garage lad."

"Because your parents wouldn't approve?" she asked lightly.

"They think my interest in swords is limited to admiring them as they loiter behind glass cases."

"I wasn't talking about the swords, actually," she said, striving to maintain a casual tone. "I was thinking they wouldn't approve of your being out late at night with a woman dressed in a lovely but rather soiled ball gown."

He shook his head. "My parents are far past the point where they question my activities or the company I keep, but that isn't my reason for avoiding the hall. I think it best we simply go to my flat and avoid discussion. Humphreys will bring your things in the morning." He glanced at her then. "You'll be perfectly safe."

She shifted so she could look at him by the faint light of his dashboard. She supposed of all the things she would ever think about him, thinking that he would be anything but a perfect gentleman would never have crossed her mind. She was actually more worried about his reputation than anything else, though she supposed he was, as he said, an adult. If he felt uncomfortable about her sleeping over at his house, he could drop her off at a hotel.

But she found she couldn't say any of that. All she could do was watch him as unobtrusively as possible and wonder how it was they had gotten so far off on the wrong foot. And their recent bonding in medieval England aside, she wasn't sure he was interested in changing that. Seeing her thawed, yes. Putting her back on a train to Sedgwick, definitely.

But not anything else, surely.

So she spent the trip drinking tea, ignoring the pain of her hands and feet thawing, and watching Stephen keep himself awake. He changed radio stations, opened the window now and again, and otherwise simply soldiered on. Still, it was pushing three on the car's clock before he pulled into the driveway of a semi-detached house near Cambridge's colleges. He shut the car off but left his hands on the steering wheel for quite some time.

Peaches almost wondered if he'd fallen asleep, but he looked at her at just the moment before she opened her mouth.

"You make me nervous."

She blinked, wondering if she were dreaming. "What?"

"I have difficulties saying the right thing," he said slowly. He glanced at her briefly. "To you."

She shook her head, because she was just sure she was hearing things. "What in the world are you talking about?"

He only looked at her, longer this time, as if he strove to memorize what she looked like, then he shook his head, pulled the keys out of the ignition, and opened the driver's side door.

"Wait for me."

"Arf."

"That's *baa*, Miss Alexander. *Baa*."

Peaches watched him go and then found herself smiling. She

thought she might understand just a bit how he could have so many women chasing him.

Oh, who was she kidding? Women would chase him just for his face and his body alone. The title probably was a bonus and most of them probably had absolutely no appreciation for his very dry sense of humor or his abundant charm.

Her door was opened. Stephen looked at her, then started a bit.

"Are you feeling suddenly unwell?"

She opened her mouth to tell him she was just being overwhelmed by kind thoughts about him, then decided silence was the better part of valor. She shut her mouth, shook her head, then wondered if her legs were equal to holding her up. Stephen unbuckled her, then slipped his arms around her back and under her knees.

Peaches squawked.

He stopped. "Something wrong?"

"You can't carry me."

"I think I can, actually."

"I mean, you *shouldn't* carry me," she said. "What will the neighbors think?"

"The neighbors are dreaming sweet dreams without care, but they'll stop if you protest all the way into the house."

She barely missed elbowing him in the nose as she put her arm around his neck, and she managed to shut the door without shutting him in it.

"I'm sturdier than I look," she offered. "Really."

He only carried her to his front porch without comment—or any huffing and puffing. He managed to get the door unlocked and open without dropping her. He set her on her feet, then pushed the switch to turn on the lights.

Peaches caught her breath in spite of herself. She felt as if she'd walked back in time a hundred years. No, maybe not that long. The décor was early 1950s British professor, and it was spectacular.

"Wow," she managed.

He sighed. "Overdone, I know, but my grandmother keeps foisting her damned antiques off on me. I'd prefer a decent lamp and a comfortable chair by the fire, but she thinks if I'm going to pretend to be a scholar, I might as well not embarrass the family by doddering about in a tatty bathrobe."

Peaches smiled. "I like her taste."

"She will be enormously gratified to hear it. Let's look at your feet, then you'll decide if you want a shower or a bath. The second bedroom has neither, I fear, but you can have your choice of what lies in other places."

"I'm not sure I want to move from here," Peaches said honestly. "I don't want to leave a trail on your floors."

He shook his head. "The floors don't matter. Here, sit on the stairs."

She sat, then looked at her feet as he squatted down and pulled her skirts out of the way. Her toes weren't frostbitten, miraculously, and didn't look all that much worse for the wear. Just filthy.

Stephen looked up at her. "Shower or bath?"

"Shower," she said gratefully. "Tell me you have one of those endlessly heating things so I can stand in there for the rest of the night."

"I do," he said, rising. "If you'll wait but a minute, I'll fetch you a robe."

She waited and almost fell asleep as she did so. She accepted a robe and a towel, managed to get herself into the shower and wash off all the medieval grime, then get herself somewhat dressed for company.

Stephen had warmed up some sort of broth she didn't dare ask the source of. She ate what he gave her without question and ignored the fact that her imaginary bearded raw-food guru would have been appalled by the distinctly bovine bouquet. Stephen helped her to the bottom of the stairs, then stopped.

"The guest room is up and to the left," he said. "Use whatever you find there that suits you."

"I don't know how to begin to thank you," she said, with feeling.

He was back to solemn and grave. "Truly, Miss Alexander, there is no need."

It would have taken three steps. Three normal, easy, doable steps to be in his arms. She'd been there once, in the past, for approximately sixty seconds. She wondered how he felt about that. She wondered how he would feel if she took those three steps at present and put her arms around him.

She settled for something less taxing. "You could call me Peaches, you know."

He went very still. She saw him do it. She also thought he might have been on the verge of reaching out to pull her into his arms.

But he didn't. He simply took her hand, then made a low bow over it. Then he straightened and merely looked at her.

Peaches supposed that was answer enough. She turned and trudged up the stairs. She put her hand out to open the guest room door.

"Good night, Peaches," came the quiet words from below.

She smiled. "Good night, Stephen."

She heard his firm footsteps carry him off into the depths of the downstairs, no doubt so he could enjoy his own endless shower. She walked into the bedroom, turned on the light long enough to find the bed, then put herself between the sheets, robe and all.

If an ordinary bed wasn't absolute heaven after endless hours in medieval England, she didn't know what was.

Good night, Peaches.

She fell asleep smiling.

Chapter 16

S*tephen* walked up the street, wondering if he'd lost his mind. It was possible, of course. Time travel was uncharted territory for him. He supposed he might have made a second call to Zachary Smith to ask him a few more pointed questions. Given the number of times Zachary had apparently traveled through the centuries, he would certainly know.

Yes, perhaps the strain of lingering in a time not his own had affected him adversely. He considered that quite seriously as he let himself in his front door. It was exceptionally strange how one minute a man could be living a very normal, unremarkable life, then the next find himself completely out of his element.

Take what he was holding in his hands, for example. He walked into his kitchen and set his burdens down on the table: green drink of some species and scones made from whole grains. He looked at them suspiciously. It occurred to him that he might well enjoy the cardboard carrier it had all come in more than the goods themselves, but the long-haired, rather earthy lad at the juice bar had assured him that both the scones and the drinks would be delicious.

Perhaps it would be well to whip up a few eggs to mitigate any possible ill effects.

By the time he had a plate full of eggs scrambled with some lovely sausage, Peaches had emerged from another shower. He was yet again unaccountably nervous, which he found to be quite possibly the most ridiculous occurrence of his life, but there it was. He cleared his throat. It was all he could do not to shift from one foot to the other.

"Green drink," he said, gesturing toward what he'd put at her plate. "And scones that are rumored to be healthier than ordinary scones, but you'll have to be the judge."

She sank down into her chair, then looked up at him in surprise. "Green drink?"

"I didn't make it myself, if that eases your mind any."

She smiled.

And he was lost yet again.

He sat down without delay, because it seemed the wisest course of action. He made a production of arranging silverware and examining his own cup of green juice. It looked absolutely disgusting and smelled remarkably like horse breath after the horse in question had spent the day chewing down a pasture, but he had faced sterner tests than this and survived. If imbibing things of this nature was what was required to impress the woman sitting across from him, then imbibe them he would.

"You're having some as well?"

She sounded absolutely delighted, which he knew should have given him pause, but perhaps she had nothing more nefarious in mind than good wishes for his health. He attempted a smile, but was afraid it had come out as a grimace.

"Yes, accompanied by real food I sautéed in half a cup of butter," he admitted. "I wouldn't want to overwhelm myself right off."

She sipped, then sighed in pleasure. "It's delicious. I'll have yours if it doesn't agree with you."

He sipped. It was rather tasty if one could ignore the color, which resembled pond scum, and the aftertaste, which left him fully believing he'd just clipped the lawn with his teeth. He considered its immediate effects on his tum, then slid the cup across the table. Better safe than sorry. "All yours."

"After what you've eaten—or not eaten—in a vacation locale we won't mention?"

"I'm still trying to recover," he said, tucking happily into his eggs. "This will make great strides in erasing the unsettling culinary memories."

Silence fell. He looked at her finally to find her merely toying with her scone. She was watching him.

"What is it?" he asked, finally giving in to shifting uncomfortably. He never shifted. It was testament enough of the week he'd had that he did it without hesitation.

"I was just wondering."

He set his fork down and looked at her. "About what?" he asked uneasily.

"About our little adventure. About what you were thinking about, well, things." She looked at him. "It seemed as though we had reached a—"

"Stephen, where *are* you?"

Stephen flinched at the sound of a voice he absolutely didn't want to hear at the moment. He didn't even have the chance to tell Peaches that he wanted nothing to do with anyone else besides her before into his kitchen walked none other than Lady Victoria Andrews, daughter of the Duke of Stow. She was trailed by Humphreys, his gentleman's personal gentleman, who was frowning slightly. With Humphreys, this indicated great distress. Stephen understood completely.

Victoria came to a screeching halt. She looked at Stephen, then at Peaches in his bathrobe, then at him again.

"*Well,*" she said, imbuing the word with so many layers of meaning Stephen was certain it would take him half the morning to sort through them all.

"Good morning, Victoria," Stephen said with a sigh.

Things went rapidly downhill from there. It wasn't, as it happened, that Stephen had slept with Victoria. If he was notorious in some circles for his dedication with several types of swords, he was equally notorious with the rest of his social sphere for being discreet to the point of monkishness.

None of that seemed to matter to Victoria at present. Stephen could tell she was gearing up to give him the tongue-lashing of his life, so he excused himself and led her out of the kitchen. Humphreys had the good sense to at least shut the kitchen door, though Stephen wondered how much ire that would stifle. Victoria seemed perfectly content to shriek at him right there in the hallway.

He started to tell her that he and Peaches were just friends—unfortunately—but before he could, she had stomped into his sitting room. He followed her, on the off chance she might do damage to something, and watched her look for the first-edition James Joyce she'd given him for Christmas the year before. She pulled it off the shelf and flung it into the roaring fire he'd started for Peaches before he'd gone off to look for breakfast.

He watched it burn for a minute or two, then looked at her. "Brilliantly done, Victoria. It takes a certain sort of woman to have so little respect for the marvels of the written word."

She slapped him smartly across the face, then flounced out of his house.

He watched her go, then rubbed his cheek thoughtfully. He had no desire to date her and hadn't for some time. It had just been easier to keep up appearances than try to break off a non-relationship with her for no good reason.

And then it occurred to him that he had left the woman he *was* very interested in sitting in his kitchen in his bathrobe.

He strode back into the kitchen, but she wasn't there. He heard the distinct sound of his Range Rover roaring off into the distance and sighed. He considered where any sort of communication might have been left. Peaches wasn't the sort of woman to carve a message into any of his antiques, which meant a note if he were fortunate. He ran up the stairs and found what he was looking for on Peaches's nicely made bed.

Thank you for the clothes, Lord Haulton. I'll put a check in the mail for them as soon as I'm home.

A thrill of alarm ran through him. Home? Was she heading to Seattle?

He went to find his mobile and dialed Tess without hesitation.

"Stephen," she said, sounding relieved, "tell me Peaches is with you. I've been trying to reach her since Saturday night. How did the ball go?"

"It was . . . interesting," he managed.

Tess was silent for a moment or two. "Why do I have the feeling that things went on I should know about?"

"Probably because you're a twin," he said with a deep sigh. "And yes, Peaches is well. I think we are both happy to be away from Kenneworth." He paused. "We had a bit of an adventure."

Tess was silent for a very long minute. "What kind of adventure, Stephen?"

"Oh, the usual kind that seems to happen with alarming regularity in this family. I'll tell you all about it when next we meet. I'm actually calling to find out if your sister's rung you."

"Let me understand this," Tess said slowly. "You had an adventure with my sister away from Kenneworth House, but now she's not with you?"

"That sums it up quite nicely, rather," he agreed.

"Is there something you want to tell me, my lord Haulton?"

"I'm sure Peaches will tell you all you want to hear," he said, "but what I want to hear is if she's rung you or not."

"She hasn't—wait. Don't hang up."

He hadn't planned to. He waited for long enough, however, that he tired of pacing in the hallway and wound up sitting in his chair in front of his fire. He watched Joyce continue to blacken and curl and almost fell asleep. He realized that only because he dropped his phone in surprise when Tess came back on the line. At least she wasn't shouting at him.

"She's on her way to Sedgwick."

Stephen considered. "Did you tell her I called?"

"Are you kidding?" Tess laughed briefly. "I am not about to get embroiled in the raging inferno that is your relationship with my sister. She said your keeper was driving her to the station and that she would be home this afternoon." Tess paused. "I don't suppose it's safe to ask why you aren't driving her home."

"Victoria of Stow walked in and found your sister wearing my bathrobe at my kitchen table."

"Well, that answers that."

"I haven't slept with her, Tess."

"Victoria or Peaches?"

"Either."

"Thank you, Stephen," Tess said dryly. "That peek into your personal life has been very illuminating."

He dragged his hand through his hair. "Sorry. Last glimpse, I promise. I'm not exactly myself. It was a bit of a journey, actually. I'm not sure I'm fully recovered."

"I can hardly wait to hear all about your trip. Coming south anytime soon?"

"As soon as I can find my keys."

Tess was silent for so long, he began to grow a little nervous. "What is it?" he asked.

"Far be it from me to give advice," she began slowly.

"Ha," he said with a snort. "Why this new reticence? You've never been shy about expressing your opinions before."

"That's because you were dating bimbos and I was worried about you in a very maternal sort of way. Now I'm worried about both you and my sister and I'm again trying not to get obliterated by the cross fire."

"Your sister and I are very calm, rational, coolheaded individuals—and you may certainly stop laughing now," he said stiffly.

She was still laughing when she hung up on him. He pursed his lips and shoved his mobile into his pocket. He walked into his den, poked at his first-edition Joyce that was still feeding a cheery blaze, then sat down in the chair in front of the hearth and contemplated his life.

Humphreys had deserted him, of course, having taken Peaches to the station. He was all alone with his thoughts and the last vestiges of Victoria's cloying perfume. He was tempted to dig in his desk for that enormous box of cigars someone he couldn't remember had given him an indeterminate number of years ago, but he didn't smoke and it seemed a shame to break the seal.

He stalked into the kitchen, fetched his pan of eggs from the sink, and went back to his study to wave it around a bit and leave a more healthful smell in the place. He put the pan down on the floor and began to pace in front of his fire.

He could, he supposed, go on as he always did, dating expensive, titled women and shunning his responsibility to wed and produce an heir. He could do the other thing he always did, which was trot over to the college and bury himself in the library. He could, if he was feeling particularly fanciful, give Peaches a call in a fortnight and see if she might be willing to go on a casual, noncommittal date or two with him.

Or he could snatch up his keys, hop in his Mercedes, and see if he couldn't beat the bloody train to Sedgwick at which point he would drop to his knees right there on the platform and beg her to be his, heirs and titles and money be damned.

He banked the fire and was halfway out the front door when he ran bodily into Humphreys.

"Is she off?" he demanded.

Humphreys smoothed his hand over his hair. "Yes, my lord, I saw her on the train myself—"

"Move. I've business with her before she drops the portcullis." He ran into Humphreys's hand.

"Not, my lord, before you've seen to your ten o'clock."

Stephen frowned fiercely. "My what?"

"Your lecture, my lord. At ten o'clock. I believe you'll still arrive on time if you allow me to hand you your portfolio."

Stephen clapped a hand to his forehead. "That bloody class."

"I wouldn't presume to pass judgment on what sort of class, my lord, but a class it indeed is. Shall I have the car ready and your suitcase packed for a journey afterward?"

"Definitely."

"She is quite charming, if I might venture an opinion."

"You might, and you might also remind yourself the next time a fresh-faced Yank talks you into using my automobile to take her out of my reach that you are in my employ, not hers."

Humphreys only lifted an eyebrow. "As you say, my lord."

Stephen pursed his lips. At least there was no need to prepare for his class. Fortunately he was teaching on medieval life in general and since he'd just had a big helping of that, he felt capable of going on ahead without notes.

Going on ahead with his life was a different tale entirely, but he would see to that as soon as he was finished at school.

He accepted an overcoat and his portfolio from his butler, then checked to make sure he was wearing trousers and not jeans—it spoke eloquently to his long weekend that he wasn't sure which it was—then started off toward the lecture hall. He pulled his mobile back out of his pocket and tried the main number at Sedgwick. No sense in not alerting them to his intentions so he wouldn't be forced to sleep in the stables.

"Sedgwick Castle," a male voice drawled, "tours and lectures for those so inclined, swords and supper for those who already know too much about the time period, and proper beatings for those tampering with the hearts of sisters-in-law."

Stephen pursed his lips. "Do you have any *useful* things down there in that mediocre pile of stones you call home?"

"Why don't you bring your soft-handed self down here and find out?"

"I have class. You know, that working thing that keeps food on the table and petrol in my Mercedes."

John de Piaget made a sound of derision. "Spare me your pitiful mewlings about your bank account. I understand you were off without supervision in the wilds over the weekend."

"Yes, and that was just at Kenneworth. You'd be surprised what we found in medieval England."

"I imagine I wouldn't," John said.

Stephen was amazed how clearly a smirk could float over a wireless connection. "I'll tell you about my pleasant conversation with your brother Nicholas later, when it's convenient for me."

John was silent for a long moment. "Very well, you win this round. What do you need?"

"Hospitality."

"I think you need more than that," John said dryly. "Perhaps a wooing idea or two, since it's obvious you're unschooled in the ways of women. Have you ever had your nose out of a book, Stephen?"

"I'm not sure I've been dating women," Stephen said with a sigh. "Harpies, perhaps, which has led me to more bouts of reading than you'd care to hear about."

"Then perhaps you should come for a visit."

"I was hoping for an invitation."

"Bring a sword."

"I will." He hesitated. "I should say that I'm fairly sure she doesn't like me."

"She wasn't using your name preceded by curses when she called. I'd say that's promising."

"She's numb from our recent journey."

"I would suggest, then, that you take advantage of that and woo her whilst she's almost senseless."

"You wouldn't do that," Stephen said with a smile.

"Nay, but I'm not you, am I? My charms are adequate to the task whilst yours . . ." He sighed heavily. "I think your only hope is to wear her down from the sheer obnoxiousness of your presence. Whilst she's off having a lie-down to recover from the nausea, we can work out something else."

Stephen pursed his lips. "Are we related?"

John laughed. "To my continued surprise."

"I don't need any more points on my license," Stephen continued, "so it may be this afternoon before I can manage to get there."

John paused. "And the rest of your week?"

"Nothing until Friday."

"Then take my advice and come tomorrow morning."

"Are you daft?" Stephen said incredulously. "The next thing I know, she'll have driven herself to the airport!"

"She is a runner," John agreed, "but chasing her will only drive her farther away. Come tomorrow—and still bring your sword. Perhaps you can hope for a bit of sympathy from her after I've left you on the ground, writhing in pain."

Stephen could only hope he would make a better showing than that, but he knew where John had come from. He sighed deeply. "She's had a difficult weekend," he said. "Take care of her, would you?"

"Why, Stephen my lad, I think you might be fond of the gel."

Stephen swore at him, then hung up before he said something he would be repaid for in what served as Sedgwick's lists. He would teach his class, take care of whatever else he needed to see to for the next handful of days whilst he was still awake, then lock his door and put himself to bed early so he could get an even earlier start.

And if John de Piaget was willing to give him a wooing idea or two, he wasn't going to shun them.

They couldn't be any worse than what he would come up with himself.

Chapter 17

Peaches stood by the fire in her sister's kitchen and looked at the cup of tea she'd brewed and left sitting on the table. She was cold, which she shouldn't have been. She'd already been for a run and taken the hottest shower possible, but neither had done anything for her.

Maybe that was just the aftereffects of having spent a brisk almost twenty-four hours in medieval England. She still felt a little like sitting down until she stopped shaking. She'd tried to put herself back into some sort of routine, but walking through Tess's castle gates the afternoon before had been unsettling. Waking up to an authentic-looking canopy over her head had only added to the sensation. She'd been all right on her run, except for the fact that after she'd watched her feet for three miles, then turned around and come back the way she'd gone, still watching her feet, then looked up to see Sedgwick rising up in the distance. Very medieval. Very not what she was used to.

All of which left her ignoring very vigorously the thing that was really eating at her while standing in her sister's kitchen, warming her backside against a raging fire, and wondering just what in the world she was supposed to do now.

Her list of options was not encouraging. She could go back to Seattle and try to resurrect her business. Brandalyse might have looked good on camera and known everyone who was anyone in town, but that could be overcome with enough effort, couldn't it? She could create a new list of better, more disorganized clients, couldn't she? Three thousand dollars that wasn't quite three thousand any longer was enough to survive on while she got a temporary job in a juice bar, wasn't it?

She wasn't sure she had any other choices. After all, it wasn't as if she could stay in England indefinitely, mooching off her sister and her husband until they got thoroughly sick of her and kicked her out. She would eventually have to go back to Seattle and try to put her life together.

The only saving grace was that she was indeed not in medieval England where her opportunities for gainful employment would have been limited to food service, farming, or perhaps more unsavory trades.

She looked up as Tess strolled into the kitchen looking happier than anyone had the right to be. Sadly enough, Tess deserved every moment of happiness she was enjoying, so Peaches couldn't begrudge her any of it. She did, however, look at her with a scowl, because she was having that kind of day so far.

Tess only lifted her eyebrows briefly and put a kettle on for tea. She dug out a thermos, a couple of mugs, and a small picnic hamper. Peaches watched her, assuming that perhaps she and John were off for a romantic brunch. Tess poured tea into a teapot to allow it to steep for a bit, then sat down at the worktable.

"Good run?"

"Lovely," Peaches said politely. "And your morning so far?"

"Spectacular," Tess said. She folded her hands together and rested her chin on top of them. "What are you doing? If you don't mind my asking, of course."

Peaches knew her sister wasn't asking about her current occupation of trying to keep herself warm. She had to take a deep breath. "I don't know."

"What do you *want* to do?"

"Have a successful career, fulfill my potential, think about having a relationship in ten years or so—"

"Get serious," Tess said with a smile. "What do you really want?"

Peaches found that she was physically incapable of saying what she really wanted because it was so ridiculous. And it involved a man whom she couldn't have even if she wanted him, which she was fairly sure she didn't. She sighed deeply.

"I want a vacation."

"You just had one."

Peaches shot her sister a look. "I want one in a place with running water."

Tess looked at her seriously. "I'm sorry you were there alone."

"I wasn't alone for very long," Peaches said. "Stephen came as quickly as he could."

"He takes his chivalry very seriously," Tess said, "though I imagine his lofty ideals aren't the only reason he went after you."

Peaches shook her head. "He was very kind to me, but that's the extent of his feelings for me. I'm sure of it."

Tess nodded and seemed to have nothing more to say about it. Peaches didn't blame her. It wasn't as though there was anything *to* say. Stephen was not for her and she was not for him. The sooner she came to grips with that, the happier she would be.

Besides, she didn't like him. He was bossy, serious, and had far too many girlfriends with bad manners popping in to see him at odd hours. She was looking for someone who would be content to let her walk all over him. Really.

She looked at Tess. "What should I do? With my life, I mean."

"Oh, no, you don't," Tess said with an uncomfortable laugh. "I'm not the dispenser of advice. That's your job. If you were you giving advice to someone in your situation, what would you tell them?"

"Not to make any snap decisions, but rather lay out all the options and examine each carefully and with love," Peaches said dutifully.

"Well, then there you go." Tess poured the tea into the thermos and packed up the picnic basket with all kinds of goodies. "Let's go avoid making any snap decisions. And go examine stuff with love."

"You and me?" Peaches asked.

"You and I," Tess said pleasantly, "and yes, we should go enjoy the morning. It's very nice outside."

"It's freezing," Peaches said, "which doesn't begin to address the idea that you want us to go have fun with John as third wheel."

"John won't be a third wheel," Tess said, putting her coat on. "He has his hands full. This picnic stuff is just for us. We're spectating this morning."

"Spectating what?"

"Whom," Tess corrected.

"Spectating whom, then," Peaches said, suppressing the urge to throw up her hands in frustration.

"John and his friend. They're in the lists, working out."

Peaches put her coat on because Tess shoved it at her. "Who is his friend?"

Tess looked at her in amusement. "Wouldn't you like to know?"

Peaches felt suddenly as though she might like to sit down. "Don't mess with me, Tess. My chi is way out of balance right now. *Whom* are we spectating?"

Tess took the basket in one hand and Peaches in the other. "Stephen."

"Stephen de Piaget?"

"The very same."

Peaches closed her eyes and took several deep, calming breaths. So Stephen had come to Sedgwick. The man had car keys and was old enough to drive. He was free to go wherever he wanted to.

Besides, he had probably come to discuss his recent adventures with John. If he happened to have brought his sword with him, who was she to quibble? It had nothing to do with her. She could go out to the lists with Tess, watch the goings-on dispassionately, then come inside and have a very lovely, leisurely supper no matter who else was at the table.

She took in a deep, cleansing breath, repeated a soothing mantra, then opened her eyes and looked at her sister.

"I would have thought he had class," she said.

"He had class yesterday, which was why he wasn't here for supper last night. Today is a different story."

"He must have been very eager to see John."

"Oh, yes, I'm sure that's the reason," Tess agreed.

Peaches ignored the way that sent her pulse spiking. "Doesn't Dr. de Piaget teach more than one day a week?"

"Apparently not," Tess said without so much as a hint of a smirk. "And if you're curious—though it's obvious by the way you keep repeating your serenity mantras out loud and not realizing that you're doing so—Stephen has been here for well over an hour. I'm surprised you didn't see him as you were running away from the castle earlier."

"I was watching the ground," Peaches said, with another handful of deep breaths.

"We should go see what's left of your friend. They've been out there for quite a while."

"John might be surprised. All that business of Stephen's not being able to hold his own with Montgomery was fake. He's been training with Ian MacLeod for I don't know how long. Too long, probably."

"I'm not worried."

"You shouldn't be, but I am," Peaches said, finding her mouth very dry all of the sudden. She looked at her sister and tried not to panic. "Why is he here?"

"I believe John invited him for lunch."

"Why was John talking to him in the first place?"

"He called," Tess said easily. "Yesterday, which I'm not sure I told you. Right after the very lovely Victoria of Stow threw a very expensive first-edition Joyce into his fire, which bothered him somewhat, and he realized you had gone. Apparently, you left your brush in his bathroom."

Peaches shot Tess a look. "I didn't have a brush, though I did use his bathroom. I was just borrowing the shower."

Tess looked at her in amusement. "Peaches, you're an adult—"

"And I was just borrowing his shower. One of his girlfriends showed up while I was still in his bathrobe because I didn't have anything but a filthy ball gown to put back on and didn't realize Humphreys had brought me my clothes. Victoria of Stow can believe what she wants. You have to believe that I was just borrowing Stephen's shower."

"It's best to wait until marriage," Tess said solemnly.

"Is it?"

"It is."

Peaches rolled her eyes. "I'm not quite sure why we're talking about that because—" She blew out her breath. "I wonder if I can get a flight out of here this morning."

"To where?" Tess asked seriously.

"To retrieve my underwear from their place of honor on Roger Peabody's mantel, that's where."

Tess stopped and put down her burden, then put her arms around Peaches. She hugged her tightly for a moment or two, then released her only far enough to put her hands on her shoulders. "Stay."

"I'm afraid to," Peaches whispered.

"You might like him."

"I'm not planning my life around a man."

"Why not?"

"Because I have things to do," Peaches said, pulling away. "Important things to get together."

"Well, while you're making a plan to get all those important things back together, why don't you stay?" Tess asked reasonably. "The castle's big enough for all of us. You figure out what you want to do, and while you're figuring that out, you can see Stephen when he's down this way doing research."

"Research on what?"

"On you."

Peaches would have shoved her sister, but she'd given that up when she was five. She scowled at her instead. "Don't push this where it doesn't want to go. I've just recently forgiven him for being a jerk—"

"He wasn't a jerk. He was tongue-tied."

"Did he tell you that?"

"Peach, I've known Stephen de Piaget for almost eight years. The man is a verbal Niagara Falls. It's impossible to shut him up."

"He hardly says anything to me."

"That's because you scare him."

"Why?"

"Because he likes you."

"Why?" Peaches asked miserably.

"Are you kidding?" Tess said with a laugh. "Have you looked at yourself lately?"

"Is that it?" Peaches managed. "He's only interested in outsides?"

"Oh, no, you don't," Tess said, taking her by the arm and pulling her out of the solar. "I'm not going to make a lengthy list of your considerable assets."

"But I can't *do* anything—"

Tess stopped so suddenly, she almost pulled Peaches off her feet. She looked at her seriously. "You listen to me, Peaches Alexander, before I go all Aunt Edna on you. Your gifts are numerous, your brainpower staggering, and your possibilities limited only by your courage. But if you want to know the single most amazing thing about you—which is going to make you impossible to live with—it is that when you talk to someone, the rest of the world falls away and the person so blessed by your attention feels like the most important person in the world. And if you think that's a small thing, think again."

Peaches found herself towed across the floor again. "I don't have a title."

"Maybe he doesn't want to marry you."

"I'm not going to be h-h-his," Peaches spluttered. "Well, whatever it is, I'm not going to be his version of it. I don't even like him!"

"Liar."

Peaches couldn't refute that, so she shut her mouth and followed her sister across the courtyard and out to the lists.

"Watch out for the rock."

Peaches looked down to find herself standing far too close to the flat stone that marked the time gate at the end of Tess's bridge. She looked at her sister. "I think I want to stay here."

"In England?"

"No, in the castle. Back in the kitchen."

"Why?"

Peaches took a deep breath. "Because I'm afraid."

"Afraid to see Stephen or leave Stephen?"

Peaches blew her bangs out of her eyes.

Tess patted her. "I wouldn't worry. You don't like him anyway, remember?"

Peaches supposed it would be a poor thank-you for Tess's hospitality to push her into her moat, so she merely scowled at her again and followed her out to what served as the lists.

She sat down on a log and looked around at anything besides what was going on in front of her. She studied the flat clouds above her head, the muddy lists, the forest of bare trees that surrounded the castle at a discreet distance.

But the ring of swords was relentlessly distracting.

She finally sighed deeply and gave in. And wished immediately that she hadn't.

She hadn't thought to ask Stephen how old he was, mid-thirties perhaps, though there was no difference between him and John when it came to energy or grace. John had the benefit of a lifetime of training, but he didn't seem to be taking it all that easy on Stephen.

She gave up watching her brother-in-law and gave in to the impulse to just watch a man who was nothing at all like she'd originally thought him to be. He might have had his collection of diplomas on the wall and his certificates from nobility school, and while that might have been a good representation of who he was, it wasn't all he was.

He had bought her a ball gown to make her feel beautiful, endured her snarls at him, watched her drool openly over David Preston. He had hoisted a second-rate sword in her defense, ignored the ruination of the insides of a very expensive car, and taken her to his house where she would be comfortable and safe.

He had bought her green drink, simply because he'd known she would like it.

But he was also the future Earl of Artane, the current Viscount Haulton and Baron Etham, and a full-fledged professor at Cambridge who had earned his posh office not because of his father's money or influence but by virtue of his own hard work.

She wondered why he wasn't married.

She wondered why she couldn't escape the thought that that was maybe a good thing.

Tess leaned close. "You don't like him."

Peaches had to take a deep breath before she could answer. "Nope."

"He's not your type."

"Absolutely not."

"I understand he enjoys a good filet mignon from time to time."

"Barbaric," Peaches murmured.

"He's gorgeous, though, isn't he?"

"Y—" Peaches shut her mouth around the word and glared at her sister. "Stop that."

"I like to see where your thoughts are leading you."

"You're a busybody."

Tess only smiled pleasantly and went back to watching her husband. Peaches fought with herself for several minutes, minutes during which swords clanged and medieval verbs were conjugated and corrected, then gave in and leaned close to her sister.

"He has girlfriends. Three of them."

"Two, now," Tess corrected. "And he doesn't like them."

"Then why does he date them?"

"It keeps Granny off his back."

Peaches looked into the mirror of her own eyes. "He would never, ever want to marry someone like me," she said in a miserable whisper.

Tess looked at her as seriously as she ever had during all their years of serious conversations. "Why don't you, my dearest Peaches, let him be the judge of that?"

Peaches threw her arms around her sister, hugged her until Tess squeaked, then jumped up and ran away.

She didn't want anyone to see her seriously consider bursting into tears.

By the time the afternoon was over, she was a wreck. Stephen was his normal self . . . only he wasn't. He was gravely polite to her, though she could now see that it wasn't disinterest that made him so, it was solicitousness. He laughed with John over things about the modern day that amused them both, switched gears easily to grill Tess on her meeting with Terry Holmes, then seamlessly continued discussions in medieval Norman French.

He did glance her way briefly during that last bit, one of his eyebrows raised.

She waved him on to his pleasures, trying not to feel flattered that he'd been interested enough in her comfort level with that version of the language that he would think to ask. He was the product of good breeding and the beneficiary of a mother who had obviously taught him good manners, nothing more.

Nothing that meant anything out of the ordinary for her.

She managed to convince herself of that all the way until he asked her politely if she wouldn't walk him to his car.

She went, because Tess pushed her out the door.

And honestly, by that point it would have been rude to turn and run the other way, so she put her shoulders back, reminded herself she was a grown-up, and walked with him through the courtyard. She was extremely grateful to be in jeans, a warm sweater, and boots instead of one high heel and a Cinderella dress.

He paused at the end of the drawbridge, eyed the marker there, and moved to the other side of the bridge. Peaches looked at him in surprise.

"Why are we stopping?"

"It's cold," he said with a shrug, "and I wanted to make sure you got back inside safely."

She looked at him and frowned. "Then why did we come out here?"

"Because I wanted to ask you something."

She didn't dare speculate on what that something might be, so she simply looked at him, mute and terrified.

"Are you going back to Seattle?"

The question was abrupt enough to startle her. She blinked, then took a deep breath. "I don't know."

He chewed on his words for a moment or two. "Tess mentioned something in passing about a bit of a blip in your business, but I didn't ask the details."

"Blip," Peaches echoed. "You could call it that."

"What would you call it, then?"

"Complete destruction. She told my biggest client to shove off. That client took the rest of them with her."

He studied her in silence for several very long moments, which made her extremely nervous. "That must have been unpleasant."

"Oh, I don't know," Peaches said, aiming for lightness but fearing she had only managed to sound as panicked as she felt. "A booming business is highly overrated. Besides, it was just sorting socks."

Stephen leaned against the iron railing and looked at her thoughtfully. "Well, I suspect it wasn't just that, but I don't know enough about it to comment." He paused. "I'm wondering, though, if you might be willing to take a day or two for a charitable mission before you go back to rebuilding your empire."

"Not if that mission requires any time traveling," she said with a shiver, "and just know I feel as weird saying that as it sounds."

Stephen smiled faintly. "Nothing so perilous." He paused, then jammed his hands into the pockets of his jacket. "I have something that needs to be done, and I was wondering if you might be willing to lend a hand."

"Do you need your socks sorted?"

He smiled very briefly.

The sight about knocked her flat.

"Nothing so lofty, I fear. I was thinking more along the lines of help with research. I was thinking that given your background—"

"In organic substances?" she asked, that time managing a bit of lightness.

Stephen looked at her seriously. It was a different expression from his usual gravely polite one. She wasn't sure if that made it better or worse, but it was definitely different.

"I was trying to find something to say that evening," he said quietly, "and succeeded only in offending you." He took a deep breath, then let it out slowly. "I would pay you, of course, for the aid with my research."

"What do you need researched?"

"Oh," he began slowly, "just things."

"Sounds pressing."

"One must publish often," he said. "That sort of thing."

She wasn't sure she would get anything done for him. She wasn't sure she could sit inside his office and read. Maybe she could hide in the library and send him her notes via courier pigeon. She looked at him frankly.

"I have visa issues," she said, "but John's working on it. He knows a guy."

"I imagine he knows several."

"Don't look at me," she said, holding up her hands. "He's *your* uncle."

"So it would seem." He looked at her. "And your answer?"

"Can I think about it?" she asked.

He nodded slowly. "Of course." He stepped up on the bridge, looked at her, then extended his elbow. "I'll walk you back."

She looked at him in surprise. "Wasn't I walking you?"

"That was just an excuse to have you alone," he said seriously. "Let's go, love, before you catch your death."

Love. She had listened to John call Tess that dozens of times and smiled every single time. Having a de Piaget lad use that term on her was slightly more knee-weakening than she'd thought it would be. She took Stephen's proffered arm, because it seemed like the best way to get herself back inside the gates while remaining on her feet.

She found herself soon deposited on the front steps, then turned and watched him walk down the three steps to the courtyard. He paused and looked up at her.

"I meant to give you this earlier."

She wrapped her arms around herself. "Give me what?"

He pulled a shoe out of the inside of his jacket.

It was the mate to the glass slipper she'd completely trashed in medieval England. She took the pristine shoe, then looked at him, mute.

He smiled gravely. "I thought you might want it."

And then he turned and walked away before she could say anything. She clutched the shoe and watched him walk back across the courtyard. He paused at the barbican, turned, and held up his hand briefly.

She waved back, because it made more sense than running after him and flinging herself into his arms.

"Go inside, Peaches," came words that floated back over his shoulder as he started across the bridge.

Peaches went inside and shut the door behind her. Work for him? As a research assistant?

It was insane. She would have a ringside seat for all his trysts with his girlfriends, get to watch him prepare for all his society functions, see him living in a world that suited him so perfectly and he managed so well.

Well, she would just give herself a good night's rest to regain her good sense, then she would tell him no.

"Did he give you a *shoe*?" John asked as she walked across the great hall.

"Yes," she said shortly.

"Well, it could have been worse," Tess offered. "It could have been a ring."

Peaches glared at them both and trotted toward the stairs, ignoring their giggles. She wasn't going to chuck her shoe at them, though they certainly deserved it.

A good night's rest, then a resounding no.

It was the only thing she could do.

Chapter 18

Stephen sat in a chair in front of the fire in his office and tried to concentrate. That task was made substantially more difficult by the addition not of three ghosts, but one very mortal, very beautiful woman sitting across from him, plowing through Regency research items.

He wondered if he should have been surprised Peaches had been willing to help him. She had spent most of the day before at Sedgwick ignoring him. Well, perhaps that wasn't completely accurate. She hadn't been rude to him. She had simply said only the bare minimum and found other things to look at. He had actually been stunned early that morning when she'd texted him one word.

Yes.

He would have happily accepted that answer to any number of questions, but he decided he would be wise to take things a step at a time. So he'd sent an innocuous reply and promised to meet her at his office after lunch.

Lunch had come and gone, and he'd begun to wonder if perhaps he was making a serious mistake. After all, his schedule was rather lighter than usual that semester, leaving him more time than he would have normally had to simply sit in his office and read. Inviting Peaches to sit there with him was self-torture of the worst kind. It would have been easier, perhaps, if he'd had lectures or tutoring to keep him busy. Anything to keep him in some other location.

And then she'd arrived, grave and serious. She had walked into his office in clothes he had purchased for her to wear at Kenneworth, clothes he was certain she had chosen because she would have thought they were conservative enough for the locale, and he had been forced to clutch the door to keep himself from falling to his knees and begging her to put him out of his misery and marry him that very day.

"I'm confused."

So, heaven help him, was he. He grasped for his remaining shreds of self-control and dignity and cleared his throat. "About what?"

"Why you're doing all this research into the Regency period."

"I'm not," he said. "You are."

"But you're publishing something on it, aren't you?"

"Unfortunately," he said honestly, "but it seems less painful now that you're here to do all my work for me."

She eyed him suspiciously. "And if I get it wrong?"

"You won't."

"You're very trusting."

"I'm going to force you to come sit in the front row when I deliver the paper. You'll have full credit, of course. I'm hoping the fear of being torn into by ancient female scholars bearing reticules will keep you on the straight and narrow."

She watched him for so long, he began to grow slightly uncomfortable. He finally put a bookmark in the text he was reading and gingerly closed it.

"Yes?"

She started to speak several times before she apparently cast caution to the wind. "I'm not sure I can do this."

"Do what?" he asked, feigning ignorance even though he knew exactly what she was talking about. Sitting in the same room with her was terrible. He wasn't sure if he wanted to pull her up out of her chair and kiss her senseless or bolt for the door. "Spend countless hours poring over musty old manuscripts?"

She looked at him evenly. "It's not the books that are bothering me."

He set his book aside, then leaned forward with his elbows on his knees. He clasped his hands and looked at her seriously. "Then what is it, Miss Alexander?"

She let out an uneven breath. "We've gotten off on the wrong foot," she said slowly.

"Today?"

"No, in general."

He looked at her, that beautiful, ethereal creature who had added a magical warmth to his office he'd never expected, and wondered how in the hell he was going to do anything but frighten her off. He took a deep breath. "Perhaps we should start afresh."

"And how do you propose we do that?"

"With introductions?"

She smiled and he thought he might have to sit down. He wasn't terribly surprised to find he was already sitting down. Peaches Alexander had that effect on him.

He stood up, then helped her out of her chair not because his mother expected that sort of thing but because Peaches deserved it. He held out his hand.

"Stephen Phillip Christopher de Piaget," he said inclining his head, "at your service."

"That's a mouthful," she said, putting her hand into his.

"My younger brother is similarly burdened, but his names are shorter," Stephen said with a smile.

Peaches only continued to watch him expectantly.

Stephen thought to ask her why, then it occurred to him that he already knew the answer. He tried not to sigh. "Must I recite the rest?"

"Yes, you must."

He had to sigh then. "Very well. I am the very fortunate possessor of the titles Viscount Haulton and Baron Etham, which means that I can get a decent seat at one or two restaurants in London. My father is the current Earl of Artane, which gets me decent seats at the theater. My PhD is in medieval studies with an emphasis in medieval languages and literature. Now, who are you?"

"Peaches Alexander," Peaches said, shaking his hand, then

pulling hers away. She sat back down and looked up at him. "That's it. You know the rest. School, closets, intentions, being one step away from a Dickensian level of destitution."

He sat down and resumed his position with his elbows on his knees. It put her almost within reach, which he thought was something of a boon.

He studied her by the light from his fire and the soft incandescent lights he refused to give up. She was, as could have been said about her sister, remarkably lovely. But he could safely say that he'd entertained the thought of having designs on Tess Alexander for less than five minutes before he realized she was just not the woman for him—and that had nothing to do with her looks, her personality, her passion for his passion, or the issuer of her passport. She had been destined to marry John de Piaget and he'd known that without knowing it.

Peaches, however, was a different story entirely.

"What led you to choose chemistry?" he asked, because he realized he'd been staring at her without speaking.

She sighed. "Because it was the hardest academic thing I could think of, and I was in a houseful of sisters—well, besides Cindi, of course—who were all trying to be as different from my parents as possible. I had originally thought that maybe med school would be the right path, but decided my first year of college that it wasn't what I wanted."

"What did you want?"

"I wanted to make a difference," she said. "Somehow."

"And you didn't think that would happen in a lab?"

She looked at him evenly. "Sorting socks isn't glamorous, but at least I saw the sunrise and sunset every day."

"I wasn't criticizing," he said mildly. "Just curious. What now?"

"I don't know," she said quietly. "Regency research, I suppose."

Which he was happy to let her get back to so he could digest what she'd said and plan his next move. He reached for his book, then stopped when he realized she wasn't finished with her questions.

"What do *you* want?" she asked.

You was almost out of his mouth before he had the good sense to engage the filter between his brain and his tongue. His mother had made certain he'd been born with it and his father had honed it from the time Stephen had said his first words, he was certain. He set his book back down and cleared his throat.

"What do you mean?"

"I mean, what do you want?" she asked. She made a circle with her pointer finger that encompassed his entire room. "This somehow doesn't jibe very well with the other you. The one that carries the sword. And then there's the nobility you that I don't even know, but I understand wears a tux and has a chauffeur and a Rolls. And a valet, as I've already seen."

"Humphreys is my social secretary."

She only laughed. "I think he's more your keeper."

Stephen might have—very well, he most definitely would have taken offense if anyone else had said the like. But somehow, coming from that astonishingly pretty woman sitting across from him—nay, she wasn't pretty. She was beautiful. But not in a hard, manufactured way. She was beautiful, true, but made even more so by an artless, almost vulnerable aura she projected that he hadn't had the chance to see until just that moment.

He realized with a start, that she was honestly interested in what he was thinking.

"I'm very content with my life," he said, because he wasn't about to say anything else.

"What part do you like the best?"

"Isn't your degree in chemistry, not psychology?" he asked lightly.

She only stared at him, a smile playing around her mouth, then she bent her head back to her book. "You need to go to Scotland soon."

"I went to medieval England recently. I think that will last me for a bit."

She didn't look up. "You're crabby."

That didn't begin to describe it. She had unerringly found his weakness and exploited it. He had difficulty, he could almost admit, trying to reconcile the different parts of himself: scholar, swordsman, and heir to a pile of stones that made him catch his breath every time he returned home.

He somehow wasn't surprised how unerringly Peaches had dissected him and left him lying there on the table.

He tried to get back to his reading, truly he did. But it was almost impossible. The longer he sat there, the more anxious he became.

"I never thanked you for the clothes."

He blinked. "What?"

She shot him a look. "I know you rescued me last weekend, and more than once. The gown was absolutely stunning."

He could only incline his head slightly. Words were beyond him.

"This is pretty snazzy, too," she said, fingering the sleeve of her sweater. "And the shoes fit."

"Humphreys has a good eye."

"And you have good taste."

"He does the work and I take the credit." He took a deep breath. "You looked lovely then, as now."

She studied him for a moment or two. "Why didn't you say anything?"

"About what?"

"About the clothes. You let me think they were from David Preston."

He shifted uncomfortably. In fact, he had to fight the urge to get up and pace. "You weren't—" He paused and tried again. "You didn't seem—" He set his book aside and rubbed his hands over his face. "Must we have this conversation?"

"I think you need a green drink."

What he needed was a cold shower and not just for the usual reasons. He desperately needed something to bring good sense back to its normal place of prominence in his life. He looked at Peaches seriously. "I didn't think you would accept them if you'd known they came from me."

She rubbed her hands over the knees of her trousers. "I'm sorry," she said quietly. "I misjudged you. I misjudged quite a few things."

"David Preston?" he asked, because he was too stupid to keep his mouth shut.

She opened her mouth, then shut it at the ringing of her phone. She sighed. "Sorry."

"No, go ahead."

She nodded, then picked up.

Stephen retrieved his book and dived right back into it. It was a fascinating treatise on marriage in the Middle Ages that he paid attention to for approximately ten seconds until he realized that Peaches was talking to none other than David Preston himself, that promiscuous, empty-headed, hard-hearted Duke of Kenneworth, who was missing one of his extremely valuable ceremonial swords.

Stephen wished he'd poached a handful of them.

"David, I really appreciate—"

David interrupted her. Stephen put on a neutral expression and waited for Peaches to sort things as she cared to. After all, he had no claim on her. He couldn't actually even claim her time as a researcher. He fully intended to pay her, though Tess had warned him the day before that Peaches wouldn't take any money from him. It was difficult to tell Peaches she couldn't date Kenneworth when he couldn't hold her job over her head.

Not that he would have anyway. If she wanted him, he wanted her to want him freely.

He listened to her protest that it really had been a lovely weekend and that she'd simply gotten lost and been rescued and taken home. She had left a message with his secretary to that effect. She protested further that dinner wasn't necessary and what a surprise it was to learn David was in Cambridge.

"Seven?" she asked. "Well, I might be—yes, that's true." She took a careful breath. "I'm doing research for the Viscount Haulton." She shot Stephen a quick look. "Yes, I suppose you could pick me up at his office if you like." She paused. "Yes, see you then."

Stephen buried his nose in his book, because it seemed safer that way.

Silence reigned supreme for several very long, very uncomfortable moments.

"That was David Preston."

Stephen looked up and smiled. "Was it?"

She was looking as neutral as he was trying to feel. "He wants to take me to dinner."

"Lovely of him, of course. Did he say how late he would be keeping you?"

She looked quite miserable, which he found very encouraging, actually. "I hope not late. I'll have to catch a train home—"

"Stay," he interrupted.

She blinked. "What?"

"I'll find you a spot within walking distance of the college," he said, reaching for his phone. "Then you won't have to travel back and forth to Sedgwick."

"But I didn't bring any clothes."

"Humphreys has excellent taste."

She looked at him seriously. "Stephen, you can't buy me a new wardrobe."

"Why not?" he asked lightly.

"Because I can't let your butler buy me knickers!"

"He's my social secretary."

She didn't smile. "It makes me uncomfortable. The idea of any of it makes me uncomfortable."

He felt his smile fading. "Does it?"

"Doesn't it seem a little strange that you're dressing me to go out with another man?" she asked, looking at him evenly.

"I'll have Humphreys buy something ugly for tonight."

She took a deep breath. That didn't seem to satisfy her, for she took a handful of others. She finally set aside her book and stood up. "I have to run."

"Run?"

"You know," she said, making a running motion with her fingers. "Run. As in, moving very quickly along a flat surface in tennis shoes."

"Trainers."

She glared at him. "Yes, those."

He set his book aside. "I'll go with you."

She looked at him in surprise. "Do you run?"

"Ian MacLeod suggested it."

She put her hands on her hips and scowled down at him. "Do you always do what he tells you to do?"

He banked his fire. "Only when he has a sword in his hands." He brushed off his hands and looked at her. "I started at Eton, actually. One does what one must, don't you know, to get along with one's responsibilities." Or get away from them, as the case had been on occasion. "Do you have gear?"

"I never go anywhere without it."

He waved her toward his loo. "Make yourself at home."

She looked at him briefly, then picked up a backpack and walked away. Stephen took the opportunity to make a quick call to Humphreys, who was more than willing to find something exceptionally lovely for Peaches to wear that night.

It was twenty minutes into a run in which Peaches wasn't even breathing hard that he realized he was perhaps dealing with something he hadn't expected.

"Enjoying yourself?" he asked.

She looked up at him. "Enormously. You?"

"Oh, yes," he panted. "It's brilliant."

"Should we go on, or are you finished?"

He leaned over and tried to catch his breath. "I'm fine."

"Did I tell you that I run the Seattle marathon every year?"

He almost sat down. "No, you did not, you vile wench."

She laughed. "You realize that wasn't English, my lord."

"I have an entire collection of things not English I could use on you."

She patted him on the back, which just about finished him off right there.

"You had probably better save your breath for them, hadn't you?"

He heaved himself upright and pursed his lips. "I don't suppose you'd want to carry me back to school, would you?"

She only smiled at him and ran away.

He watched her go. The only benefit he could see to doing something that restored her good humor so thoroughly was that at least he would be nursing sore muscles whilst she was out to dinner with a man who wasn't him.

And then he, poor fool that he was, followed after her.

Chapter 19

Peaches looked at herself in the bathroom mirror of a bed-and-breakfast room so luxurious, she didn't dare speculate about the nightly cost of it. Just the fact that it was within walking distance of Stephen's college sent shivers down her financial spine. She could only hope that Stephen was getting a break with a weekly rate. And if not, she would just have to trade him out her work for the accommodations. She wouldn't make any money—in fact she would probably end up owing him money—but she wouldn't feel like she was bankrupting him. Or being the recipient of his charity.

Not that he would have termed it such. Tess had often commented on his generosity, both with time and means, but Peaches had never expected to be the beneficiary of either.

Life was strange.

She jumped a little at the sound of her phone ringing. She wondered if it would be impolite to just let it ring through to her voice mail. The last person she wanted to talk to was David Preston. He had been charming the night before, attentive, said all the right, flattering things. If she had gone out to dinner with him a month earlier, she would have been absolutely giddy with delight. He was, as she had noted several times before, just right.

But last night instead of finding him flattering and charming, she had found him conceited and unpleasant. His interests were seemingly limited to complimenting himself and disparaging anyone from Artane. She had actually been rather surprised by the viciousness of his attacks on Stephen.

And rather ashamed of herself that she had, at one point, probably been all too willing to agree with them.

The only saving grace of the evening had been that Stephen had been waiting with his office door open when David had dropped her off, which had allowed her to avoid any unwanted advances. David had been quite obvious about his irritation that she'd offered a friendly handshake instead of a passionate embrace, but she'd found herself surprisingly unconcerned about what he thought.

It was odd how a few days in the company of a certain de Piaget lad had completely changed her perspective on quite a few things.

She blinked and pulled herself back to the present when she realized her phone was still ringing in her hand. She looked down, fully expecting to see David's number only to see Stephen's instead. She answered it, surprised he would call her when he knew she was going to be in his office in less than half an hour.

"Yes?"

"Change of plans," he said briskly.

Her heart stopped—and not in a good way. Maybe he'd decided that feeding, housing, and clothing her while she was dating however reluctantly another man just wasn't something he cared to do. "A change of plans?" she echoed.

"On-site research," he said, "in Bath. Would you object to that?"

She sat down on her bed because the relief that rushed through her gave her no choice. "I thought you were going to fire me."

He was silent for a long minute. "That thought hadn't crossed my mind, actually."

"Well, there is that."

"There is," he agreed. "So, are you amenable to a journey?"

She considered. A day spent closed up in an office with Stephen reading books, or a day spent partially cooped up in a car with Stephen but the rest of the time wandering through one of her favorite cities in England.

"Are you really going to make me work," she asked, "or is this just for fun?"

"A day off?" he asked, sounding faintly horrified. "Certainly not. I have note-taking supplies for you as well as a flask full of tasteless gruel for your lunch."

She let out her breath slowly, because the thought of notes and gruel and Stephen de Piaget all in the same place for an entire day was almost too good to be true. "I think I can live with that."

"Then hurry yourself into comfortable clothes, and let's be off."

She realized he was not only speaking French, he was speaking a rather vintage version of it. Obviously that little trip to medieval England had affected him adversely. She frowned. "I think we should use modern French today, my lord. People will look at us strangely otherwise."

"Do you think we could discuss that later so I don't freeze my arse off out here on your front stoop?"

"Is the tweed not keeping you warm?" she asked sweetly.

He made a noise of exasperation. "I'm wearing jeans, Peaches."

She smiled in spite of herself at the sound of his saying her name. And if just that had her going, she imagined she was going to be in big trouble for the rest of the day.

"I have jeans, too," she managed. And she did, and they weren't the ones she'd brought with her from Seattle with the smiley face patch over the rip on the bum. These were jeans that Humphreys had bought her that went with very lovely, stylish boots and yet another sweater in Stephen's favorite fabric.

"Then put them on and hurry."

"Be right there."

She hung up, flung herself into clothes, dragged a pick through her hair, and grabbed her backpack on her way out of her room. She thought it might be prudent to have breakfast to tide her over until she could have her gruel, so she poached a couple of scones from a sideboard and hurried for the front door.

She came to a skidding halt on the porch.

If she hadn't known better, she would have—well, she wouldn't have suspected she was looking at the future Earl of Artane. She struggled not to drop her scones, then considered the man standing twenty feet away from her. If there was one thing John de Piaget knew how to do, it was look like a very suave, very bad boy. Leather jacket, fast car, smoldering looks.

Maybe it ran in the family.

Peaches managed to get herself down the steps, down the walkway, and to a stop in front of a black-leather-jacket clad, jeans-wearing, boot-sporting man who didn't look like anyone they would let into Cambridge without a thorough background check. She would have put her hand over her racing heart, but she was holding on to scones.

"I'll bet Granny doesn't approve of this look," she wheezed. "Are you in disguise?"

One side of his mouth quirked up, finishing what was left of her knees and her good sense. "I own casual clothing."

"I can see that."

He opened the door. "You'd better sit down before you fall there."

"I'm weak because I haven't had breakfast yet," she said archly. She started to get in, then hesitated. "I don't think I should eat in your car. Not after everything else I've done to it."

He removed one of the scones from her hand. "It's just a car. There's tea waiting inside for you."

She looked at him seriously. "You are a very nice man."

He opened his mouth to say something, then apparently thought better of it. He settled for a hint of a smile and a nod toward the empty seat.

Peaches sat, supposing that since she'd already destroyed the inside of his car with her soggy self the weekend before, a few scone crumbs weren't going to make things worse. The inside of the car, however, didn't seem to be as trashed as she'd remembered it being. Humphreys at his usual work of busily making things right, apparently.

She waited until they were well out of Cambridge and Stephen had finished breakfast before she attempted any conversation. "The clothes are lovely. Thank you."

"You're welcome," he said, negotiating the rather heavy traffic. "Humphreys has good taste in ladies' wear." He shot her a brief look. "And you won't be giving me money for them."

"I wasn't planning on it," she said, finding herself slightly satisfied at his subsequent twitch of surprise. "I'll work it off researching."

"No, you won't."

"Yes, I will."

"Nay, lady, you will not."

"Don't think you're going to intimidate me with that medieval French," she said, trying to sound stern. "I understand you."

"Do you understand the swear words?"

"Tess needed someone to practice with and Aunt Edna's rigorous Gallic conversation had prepared us both for further study."

Stephen smiled briefly. "I think I would appreciate your aunt Edna."

"She's still tormenting morning glory in her garden," Peaches said, "and I'm sure she would find that your French meets her exacting standards." She looked out the window as the scenery crawled by. "I've thought about going and begging my garret back—"

"Don't."

She looked at him in surprise. "What?"

He shot her a look. "I have several things for you to research still."

She wished she had something witty and pithy to say in return, but all she could do was look at him and try to keep breathing normally. The truth was, while she was a good researcher, he could probably find a better one at the university. And she hadn't been born yesterday. He hadn't given her something to do just to keep her busy, or because he was taking pity on her.

She just couldn't bring herself to think about what in the world he was possibly thinking because it was too ridiculous to contemplate.

She spent the rest of the trip south—and it was a rather long trip south—making polite chitchat with him. She was fairly sure they had discussed everything from the unfortunate state of cuisine to be found in London to how much money her parents had socked away thanks to buying stock in cotton and hemp, but she couldn't have said for sure. All she knew was that she was in very great danger of undoing all the work she'd put into disliking Stephen de Piaget.

Fortunately for her heart, by the time they reached Bath, she had managed to make a rather depressing but accurate list as to why their relationship, such as it was, had no future.

She was the research assistant. He was the future Earl of Artane. She was a Yank. He was, again, the future Earl of Artane. She loved puttering in a garden, watching things grow, making small improvements to lives and closets. He was the bloody future Earl of bloody Artane, he wore tweed, and he would spend the rest of his life managing enormous estates and trying not to let his family be bankrupted by excessive taxes.

Besides, when it came right down to it—and she had to tell herself this several times before she could put the appropriate amount of enthusiasm behind the thought—she didn't really like him all that much. He was serious and studious and did lots of things she was really bored by such as filling young minds with tradition and history and glorious ideals of chivalry and nobility. She would be very happy when she had done all the research for him he needed and could get back to having him out of her life.

By the time he had parked his excessively expensive automobile and come around to open her door for her, she was beginning to think she might need a run. She grabbed her backpack and crawled out of the car, looking for the closest escape route. She realized she wasn't going to manage it only because Stephen was in her way. He still had hold of her door and his hand on the roof of his car, effectively boxing her in.

Or keeping her safe, depending on how one looked at it.

She was suddenly having a hard time catching her breath. "We can't do this," she blurted out, because she had to say something.

He looked at her in surprise. "What? Come to Bath?"

She realized she was on the verge of making a colossal ass of herself because she was obviously the only one who was thinking thoughts beyond picking up a few Regency tidbits for him to use in his next paper. She looked around quickly for something intelligent to say. "I mean, we can't go around town today without, ah, some water. To drink. In case we get thirsty."

He looked at her as if she had lost her mind.

She was beginning to think that might be the case.

He backed up, pulled her out of the way of the door so he could close it, then took her by the hand.

"We'll find some at our first opportunity. Until then, why don't we talk about sheepdogs." He glanced at her. "Or shepherds."

She blinked. "Why in the world would we want to do that?"

"Humor me."

She supposed it was better than slugging him. She settled for rolling her eyes. "The only thing I know about sheepdogs and shepherds is that they probably drive the sheep crazy with all their fussing."

He started up the street, towing her along with him. "Actually, it's my understanding that they do everything possible to keep their sheep safe."

"And herded," she muttered.

"Fussed over," he said, glancing at her. "There's a difference."

"Do you de Piaget men understand the difference?" she asked pointedly.

He stopped and looked at her. If she had been a more fanciful type, she would have thought he was considering pulling her into his arms and kissing her. She wondered if he noticed that she had lifted her hair off the back of her neck with her free hand. Just to get a little draft going, of course.

He brought her hand to his mouth and kissed the back of it. Peaches gaped at him.

"Better shut that," he advised. "People will think I'm saying appalling things to you."

"You are."

"I haven't said anything yet."

"You're looking at me."

He looked at her a bit more. "Why don't you reserve judgment for the day," he said with a small smile, "and we'll see how I do."

"With the herding thing?"

"That, too."

She closed her eyes briefly. "This isn't going to work."

"Are you sure?"

She looked at him, into his very lovely gray eyes, and had to take a deep breath. "I'm pretty sure."

He ran his thumb over the back of her hand. She wasn't sure he knew he was doing it, but maybe he was trying to soothe them both.

"Why don't you give me one day," he said very quietly. "Just one day of allowing me to herd you exactly the way I want to."

She swallowed, barely. A tall, extremely handsome, profoundly chivalrous man was asking her to give him an entire day to treat her like a fairy-tale princess, and she was kicking up a fuss?

"Okay," she breathed.

He looked at her closely. "Feel like running?"

"It would be the wisest thing to do," she said honestly, "but I think my shoes would give me blisters."

He smiled, that small little smile she was becoming hopelessly addicted to, then pulled her along with him down the street. "Don't expect me to buy you another pair."

"Don't you care about my blisters?" she managed.

"I care very much, which is why I think running would be a very unwise activity for you today. Being fussed over is much less hard on your feet. And given the fact that you almost ran me into the ground yesterday, I'm all for easy on the feet today."

"You know, Stephen," she said, "you can be very charming when you want to be."

He shot her another smile. "I want to be."

She walked with him for another few minutes, then looked up at him. "Why?"

"Why not?"

She looked at him seriously. "Is that the answer?"

He looked at her with a glance that was definitely better suited to a black leather jacket than a tweed sport coat, then pulled her out of pedestrian traffic. She wondered if he was going to give her another lecture on sheepdogs, or just a very long list of reasons why hanging out with a Yank was a good change from his trio of debutantes—well, minus the one who had tossed a valuable book into the fire.

But he didn't.

He took her face in his hands, bent his head, and kissed her.

Peaches was so surprised, her knees buckled. He caught her around the waist, slipped his free hand under her hair, and kissed her again. She clutched his arms because she had to in order to keep herself still on her feet.

He lifted his head and looked at her from stormy gray eyes. "That's why."

"I'm not sure I understand," she managed.

"Let me herd you for the day, then you tell me if you want further clarification."

She shivered. "Stephen—"

He kissed her again and did a proper job of it. Peaches put her arms around his neck because that seemed a very sensible thing to do. Well, that and in spite of the respectable number of men she had kissed over the course of her life, she had never before kissed one who made her want to hold on and never let go.

She came back to herself only because she heard a very loud complaint right next to her ear.

"Cheeky yobs," said a weathered voice in disgust. "Kissing out in the open!"

Stephen lifted his head and looked at a gray-haired granny. "I apologize, miss."

"Missus," said the woman sharply. "Mrs. Yeats."

"Mrs. Yeats," Stephen repeated dutifully. "My most abject apologies, Mrs. Yeats."

Mrs. Yeats scowled fiercely at him, then continued on her way. Peaches would have gaped at her, but she was too busy trying not to gape at Stephen. He only smiled at her, which finished what was left of her good sense.

"Regency delights?" he asked politely.

"Is that what that was?" she asked.

He laughed and took her hand to lead her off to who knew where. She didn't suppose she dared ask.

The whole thing was impossible. She was a nobody and he had three given names. She was a lowly clarifier of intentions; he was heir to the most magnificent castle on the north coast of England. She was a vegan; he probably had entire cows wrapped and put into his freezer for use at a moment's notice.

"I think I need a drink," she said thickly.

"There's a juice bar across the street."

"Thank heavens," she said with feeling. "Let's hope they have something green."

"Let's hope they have something drinkable," he muttered under his breath.

But he smiled as he said it and walked with her to the light, good citizen that he was, so they could cross the street without jaywalking. He bought her a green drink, had one himself with extra fruit to mask any hint of springlike taste, then burped discreetly on his way out the door.

"I fear for my digestion," he said honestly.

She feared for her heart, but she didn't say as much. She simply pulled her sunglasses down and followed him incognito to wherever it was he was taking her.

The day was magical and indeed very hard on her heart. They walked the streets, took in an exhibit on Jane Austen, nipped into a National Trust property on the Royal Crescent, and avoided the shopping district like the plague. Peaches was actually quite happy, as the afternoon began to wane, to walk into the most organic-looking pub Stephen could apparently find and have a plate of potatoes and veg. Stephen joined her, adding only a rather decent-smelling bowl of stew to go along with it. They were sitting on opposite sides of a table, which apparently gave him ample opportunity to herd her feet between his and keep them there.

"So?" he asked, toying with a cup of tea. "Herding or fussing?"

"Fussing?" she echoed in mock disgust. "You had me working all day memorizing trivia."

"I fed you," he reminded her. "Green things."

She looked at him seriously. "Yes, you did."

"And?" he asked. "What's the verdict?"

"The jury says you are a terribly charming man who can't help but herd," she said solemnly. "I think it's in your genes."

"Eight hundred years' worth," he agreed. "It seems to have worked for my relations."

She shook her head with a smile. "How odd it must be to know several of the sons of the man who built your family home."

"I'm not sure *odd* describes it," he said with a wry smile. "It does tend to put a little pressure on me to see that the place doesn't fall to the ground under my watch."

Peaches winced before she could stop herself because that

reminded her of all the things she had tried to avoid thinking about on the way to Bath, all the reasons she and Stephen could never be anything at all, all the things that had been driven right out of her empty head when he'd kissed her. But there was no denying the truth. She tried to pull her feet away, but he looked at her first in surprise, then with a frown.

"Where are you going?"

"Back to the sensible side of the table."

"Peaches—"

"Oh, David, look who we have here!" said a voice brightly.

Peaches looked to her left and blinked. It took her a moment to realize she was looking up at David and Irene Preston. She didn't look up at either of them for very long because they both immediately slid onto the benches, David next to her and Irene next to Stephen, leaving her with the opportunity to gaze on their wonderfulness at eye-level.

"Isn't this cozy?" Irene purred, looking at Stephen as if he were a tasty chocolate she intended to ingest at her earliest opportunity.

Peaches could think of many things to call the current arrangements, but cozy wasn't one of them. She found she was paying far more attention to how Irene was fawning over Stephen than she was to the fact that David had put his arm around her and was groping her shoulder. She pulled away and frowned at him, but he didn't seem to notice.

"Well, that's settled, Peachy," David said with the same sort of brightness Irene had used. "I'll pick you up at noon."

It took her a moment to understand what he was saying. "Noon?"

"Tomorrow," he said, then leaned closer and gave her a conspiratorial smile. "For lunch, if we can't think of something more interesting. Of course, Irene will be at loose ends, so Stephen will no doubt step up and be a gentleman. Won't you, Haulton?"

"Of course," Stephen said with absolutely no expression on his face. "Wherever you want to go, Irene."

"How fortunate we're all in Bath today," Irene said smoothly, "and that we have enjoyed the coincidence of running into each other." She slid Stephen a look. "Perhaps Miss Alexander would prefer to ride back to Sedgwick with David."

Stephen opened his mouth to respond, but Peaches kicked

him quite firmly on some part of his lower leg that made him flinch—on the off chance he thought he was going to dump her with a man who couldn't seem to keep his hands off her.

"A pity that isn't possible," he said, "given that she's in Cambridge this week." He looked at David blandly. "Wouldn't want to make you fight traffic, old man."

"But we're in Cambridge as well," Irene said. "David has business there, and I thought I should accompany him. How convenient for us all to be in close quarters. This also leaves us with no reason why we can't switch passengers."

Peaches would have chosen a different word than *convenient*, but she wasn't the one doing the choosing.

"Perhaps another time," Stephen said in a tone that said very clearly that the discussion was over, at least for him. "We have research to discuss, I'm afraid. Sheep lore, I believe, and other things that are vital to my current interests." He looked at her. "Isn't that right, Miss Alexander?"

Peaches nodded, then kept her mouth shut and focused on Stephen's tapping the side of her boot gently. She wasn't even sure he knew he was doing it, though a surreptitious glance his way during Irene's very lengthy extolling of the virtues of the shopping to be found in Bath told her differently.

The subsequent hour was miserable enough that she did her best to forget it. David couldn't seem to stop touching her, and she couldn't seem to convince him politely that he should. She wasn't sure if that was more or less unpleasant than watching Irene hang on Stephen.

She was vastly relieved when she finally found herself sitting in Stephen's car, heading back to Cambridge, though she wasn't at all sure why. Stephen was absolutely silent. She didn't want to know what he was thinking.

And then he held out his hand for hers. She looked at him quickly, but he was watching the road. She studied his hand for a moment or two, then reached out and put her hand in his. He laid her hand palm down on his thigh, then covered it with his own. That lasted until they hit the M25 and he had to negotiate London ring-road traffic. He brought her hand to his mouth, kissed it, then returned it to her lap.

She was happy for the chance to catch her breath and simply watch him as he watched traffic. It gave her the chance to study his face in a way she hadn't been able to until then. He had perhaps a handful of freckles sprinkled across his nose and very faint lines near his eyes. She would have, if someone had asked her a week ago where those lines had come from, said they were from scowling. Now, she supposed they were from a combination of smiling and many, many hours spent in Scotland, squinting at some crazed, sword-wielding Highlander.

"What?" he asked, after he'd glanced at her and realized she was watching him.

It took her a bit to be able to say what she wanted to. "I don't remember saying yes to David."

He chewed on that for a bit. "For lunch, or something else?"

"Either." She clasped her hands together in her lap. "I didn't realize I'd said yes to lunch tomorrow, but I couldn't think of a good way out of it. Not that there's any reason to get out of it, I suppose," she added.

"Hmmm," was all he said.

Peaches wasn't sure she could be any more uncomfortable. The urge to bolt was strong, but she was unfortunately buckled in and the weather had turned nasty. All she could do was sit in absolute luxury, listen to the BBC station Stephen turned on after he'd smothered one too many yawns, and wish that she were anywhere else. She wasn't sure where the kiss he'd given her earlier had come from, or where the herding had gone.

Maybe seeing the Duke of Kenneworth had reminded Stephen of his own obligations to get himself involved with a woman of a certain sort.

Like Irene Preston, for example.

Stephen wended his way through Cambridge until he pulled up in front of Holly's row house. He parked, fetched her out of the car, then walked her to the door. She turned to thank him and found herself in his arms. And once she was there, there was no point in not hugging him back. Which she did. She closed her eyes and tried not to frighten him with how hard she wanted to hold on to him.

"I'll see you in the morning," he said quietly.

She nodded, then pulled out of his arms. That he didn't stop her told her something. She wasn't sure what, but it was something. If he had wanted to discuss herding or kisses or plans for the future, he was certainly missing out on the opportunity.

She decided there was no point in waiting for him to speak. She walked up to the porch, let herself in, then looked at him once before she shut the door. His face was in shadows, but she could see he was wearing his customary politely serious expression.

She walked back to her room, not sure if she were more unhappy with David for intruding or Stephen for being so quiet.

The one thing she was sure of was that she was starting to seriously doubt that fairy tales even happened any longer.

Chapter 20

S tephen walked quickly back to his office. He had to admit the one thing he truly loathed about the profession of academia was the meetings. There was nothing worse than sitting in a room full of thinkers who had nothing more pressing to do than endlessly chew on details he couldn't have cared less about.

Well, he might have cared at a different time, only now he'd recently had a brief taste of history, he had continual access to living fountains of authentic details, and at present he had a woman sitting in one of his chairs that he wanted to see more of before she dashed off to lunch with a man he was truly beginning to loathe.

It wasn't that he hadn't disliked David Preston before. Sitting with the man on a pair of charity boards had given him ample opportunity to observe the depths of the good duke's lack of principles. Distaste had blossomed into a healthy disgust after a particularly egregious display of dishonesty at a gala put on for the benefit of a hospital. The true dislike hadn't actually begun until a recent weekend party at Payneswick where David had turned his roving eye on Peaches. Perhaps she hadn't noticed, but Stephen had. Kenneworth had been ridiculously indiscreet about broadcasting his interest in a new potential conquest. Stephen supposed the only reason Peaches hadn't paid for that socially was that she was the sister of the Countess of Sedgwick, a fact that he had nosed about quite loudly. He hadn't heard anyone say anything to Kenneworth, but there were few who crossed that unscrupulous duke who didn't come away scarred.

Stephen could safely say he had never found himself in that group, but that was likely because he had no skeletons in his past. He could thank his mother that he'd never done anything so stupid morally that it could be used against him in the court of public opinion and his father that he had been scrupulously honest in his business dealings. David might loudly call him a bastard, but he wouldn't be the first to do so. They were just words, and Stephen didn't pay heed to foolish words.

He reached his office to find the door locked. That alarmed him until he got the door open and realized Peaches was halfway out of her chair. He walked inside and shut the door behind him, sighing in relief. She looked at him solemnly.

"You're dressed for success."

He managed to nod.

"I thought you didn't have any classes today."

He shrugged out of his overcoat and set his portfolio on the chair by the door. "I don't."

"Then what's your hurry to get here, Mr. Verbose?"

He smiled in spite of himself as he cast himself down in the chair opposite her. "I was eager to see if you had found any Regency-era delights to share with me."

She studied him in silence for a long moment, long enough that he had to remind himself that he never squirmed. She was just so lovely, sitting there with the light from his fire caressing her flawless skin and—

He frowned. "You put your hair up."

"It matched the conservative skirt and sweater." She smiled, then her smile faded. "I have to go soon."

"Lunch with the charming and debonair Duke of Kenneworth?" Stephen asked with a lightness he most certainly didn't feel.

"It would seem so."

"You'll have a lovely time. No need to rush. It will all be here when you get back."

She smoothed her hands down her skirt. "I'm a little embarrassed."

He maintained a neutral expression. "Do the clothes not suit you?"

"Well, of course they suit me," she said crossly. "But I still think it's a little impolite to go out to lunch with one man while wearing the clothes another man bought for you."

"I wouldn't know," he murmured.

She glared at him, then rose and went to fetch her purse—a very lovely thing Humphreys had done a fine job selecting. Stephen rose only to find himself standing nose to nose with her.

"You can't possibly . . ." She took a deep breath. "Well, you know."

He clasped his hands behind his back. It was the only thing—the *only* thing—that kept him from clasping them around her instead. He took a very careful breath.

"I bought you a thing or two because I didn't want you to go back to Sedgwick," he said honestly.

"Because you needed me to work for you?"

"That, too."

She looked up at him miserably. "Aren't you taking Irene to lunch?"

"Cad that I am, I'm not," he said mildly. "Too much to do here."

She closed her eyes briefly, then turned and fled.

He watched the door close behind her, then sat down in his chair and swore. He swore for quite a while, actually, and the Duke of Kenneworth figured prominently in his slander. It made him feel warm and happy inside to eviscerate the man so thoroughly, but that didn't change the fact that David was enjoying Peaches's company for lunch whilst he was not.

He rose and began to pace. Perhaps Peaches was right and he needed a brief trip to Scotland. Perhaps she would come with him, so he might enjoy the pleasure of her company in one of his favorite places.

He didn't admit that to many, that he loved Scotland. His father would have been appalled that anything north of Hadrian's Wall held any fascination for him at all. But he loved the lochs and the mountains and the feeling of having stepped back centuries in time . . .

It was a perfect waste of an afternoon. He tried to work on half a dozen things that didn't hold his interest for more than a moment or two, considered a run, then finally found himself at the nearest juice bar, drinking sludge and beginning to acquire a taste for it. That necessitated a nip into a shop on the way back to school for a steak-and-kidney pie to counteract the adverse effects of too many greens. All those diversions enjoyed, he returned to his office and tried to work.

He looked up as the door opened suddenly. Peaches came in quietly, then shut the door behind her. She looked very serious.

He was on his feet before he knew what he was doing, then across the room before he thought better of it. He had pulled her into his arms before his good sense could scream he was moving too fast with her. After all, he'd already moved too quickly in Bath, hadn't he? And his lack of patience had driven her into David Preston's arms for lunch.

He started to pull away when he realized her arms were around him and she wasn't letting go.

"Did he hurt you?" He realized as the words were hanging there in the air that he'd said them with an anger he hadn't realized he was feeling.

She pulled back and looked up at him in surprise. "Of course not. It was a public place, after all. And I know self-defense."

"I would feel better about that if you spent a few days with Patrick MacLeod," he said grimly. "Was he unkind to you?"

She looked at him evenly. "This is shaping up to be a very weird conversation."

"And no hope of anything else anytime soon. And whilst I suppose I should worry about your physical state, I was more concerned about your heart."

She pulled away fully. "David Preston? Are you kidding? The guy's a total jerk. I never thought he was anything else."

He caught her before she walked away and gently turned her to him. He searched her face and saw that she had perhaps indeed entertained thoughts that she now found rather less than sensible.

"I have been deceived before as well," he offered.

"Were you in love with the ones who deceived you?"

He ignored the question. "Are you in love with David Preston?"

"That's pretty touchy-feely of you, Lord Haulton," she said sternly. "And appallingly personal."

He rubbed his hands over his face. "I think I need to run."

"I'll just bet you do. Put on your trainers, and let's go."

"And have you leave me unable to get out of bed tomorrow?" he asked with a snort. "I think not."

"Let's go do the track. I'll get bored after a few miles." She started to turn away, then looked at him. "The question still stands."

"You first."

She hesitated, then sighed deeply. "I was initially flattered by the attention and thought that it might result in the whole fairy tale." She shrugged, though he could tell she was feeling less than casual about the whole affair. "That's the absolute truth of it, and I can't believe I'm being that honest with you. It must be the stockings cutting off the circulation to my brain."

He smiled. "No, it's the thought of running me into the ground. A little pity beforehand is not uncalled for."

She folded her arms over her chest. "I believe, Lord Haulton, that you owe me an answer to my question."

"Run it out of me, wench."

"Don't think I can't."

He had absolutely no doubt of it. And she proved it to him quite handily not an hour later on the track where apparently she was indeed determined to run him into the ground. He finally begged her to stop, then walked until he had to lean over with his hands on his thighs and catch his breath.

"You're going to be the death of me," he wheezed.

"You don't have to run with me."

"That would leave me chasing you, which would be much worse, I assure you." He straightened, promised himself more time in trainers in the future, then looked at her. He pursed his lips. At least she was breathing hard for a change. "Once."

She blinked. "Once, what?"

"Love," he said succinctly. "Once."

She put her hands on her hips. "How did it turn out?"

He dragged his forearm across his forehead and prayed for good sense to return. He looked at her, finally. "Let's go."

Her mouth fell open. "That's all I get?"

"That's all you get."

"You—you—" She spluttered for a minute, then glared at him. "I bared my soul to you and *this* is what I get?"

He shrugged. "I'm a man."

"If we weren't in a public place, I would punch you right now."

He smiled, because he doubted it. "What would you like to do tonight?"

"Are you asking me out on a *date*, you perfidious rat?"

He laughed, because she was within reach, she didn't care for David Preston, and she was interested enough in his heart to call him names.

He was absolutely lost.

"Yes," he said happily. "I am."

"Well, I don't want to go," she grumbled. "Unless your offer is very good."

"Supper?" he ventured. "The symphony? A film?"

"Dinner at your house and the rest of the evening listening to you read the *Canterbury Tales*," she countered. "In the original vernacular."

He blinked. "Are you in earnest?"

"I think I can more easily wring details out of you when you have that little pucker between your eyes you get when you're concentrating."

"I don't have details—"

She walked away. "Let's go, sport."

S_{everal} hours later, he was sitting in front of his fire in his own study, wending his way through Chaucer's finest, acutely aware of the stunning woman sitting next to him on the sofa with her legs curled up underneath her. He finally could bear it no longer. He set the book down on his lap, turned, leaned forward, and kissed her.

He pulled back slightly to see how she was reacting. She wasn't plowing her fist into his nose or grimacing, so he slipped his hand under her hair and made a proper job of it.

"Details," she murmured at one point.

"About what?"

"About you know what."

"Once," he said, kissing her again.

"How did it turn out?"

"It hasn't turned out yet."

She opened her eyes and looked at him with a frown. "It hasn't?"

He shook his head. "Not yet."

She leaned her head back against his arm and looked at him seriously. "So, you're in love with this girl," she said carefully, "you don't know how it's going to turn out, and yet you're here with me?"

"Reading Chaucer, yes," he agreed.

"And a few other things, buster. And I wasn't talking about books." She looked at him in the vicinity of his chin. He might have thought she was near to bolting, but she had her fingers linked with his that rested on her knee and she wasn't pulling away. She considered for a bit longer, then met his gaze. "You are many things, Stephen, but you aren't a cad."

"Thank you."

"I don't think."

"Thank you," he said dryly.

"So, since you aren't a cad, why are you here with me?"

"I imagine," he said, bending his head and making further inroads into the indulgence of kissing her, "that you'll figure it out eventually."

"Are you patronizing me?" she asked sternly.

"Kissing you, rather."

"Why?"

He thought of half a dozen easy things he could have said, but could manage none of them, so he merely pulled back and looked at her. She was, as he had noted before, a terribly intelligent woman. And whilst he generally made a habit of schooling his features, he didn't do so at present. He simply looked at her and hoped exactly what he was feeling was showing clearly on his face.

And he saw in her eyes the precise moment that realization dawned.

Her mouth fell open. She pushed away from him and jumped to her feet. He was pleased to see that she wasn't all that steady on them, but she held him off and stepped a pace or two away. She wrapped her arms around herself and looked down at him in shock.

"You can't be serious."

It was obvious she was appalled, but he wasn't sure exactly why. Either she wanted nothing to do with him—which he feared—or she couldn't believe he wanted anything to do with her—which he couldn't imagine.

"Can't I?" he asked seriously.

She pointed at him with a trembling finger. "You're the bloody future Earl of Artane!"

He set Chaucer aside. "Is that it?"

She lifted her chin. "I am keenly aware, my lord, of our disparate stations."

His mouth had fallen open. He knew that because it took him a moment to close it. "What absolute bollocks."

"It isn't," she said, lifting her chin a bit more. "I am not willing to be a dalliance. And yes, I'm well aware that is what David Preston had in mind for me."

"I am not David Preston."

"No, you're the bloody future Earl of Artane."

"You said that already. And you shouldn't swear."

"Go to hell!"

He looked at her for a moment in silence, then he bowed his head and laughed.

"Besides, *bloody* isn't a swear word in the States," she said crisply. "And neither is *crap*."

He pursed his lips to keep from laughing again and looked up at her. "I suppose not."

She stepped back another pace and wrapped her arms around herself. "I need to run."

The look on her face did it. She looked positively shattered and that had about the same effect as having a trough of freezing cold water poured on him. Only the buckets at Artane were heated, because he and his father valued their horseflesh.

He realized he was rambling, but honestly, Peaches Alexander had him so off balance, he could hardly think straight. He rose and walked over to pull her gently into his arms. She was trembling, but he imagined that wasn't from the cold. She did, after all, have on a lovely cashmere sweater that Humphreys had so capably picked out for her.

And once she had stopped shivering as much, he was able to face what he hadn't wanted to before: that she didn't care for him.

"Do you think," he asked, when he thought he could, "that you might learn to overcome your dislike for me?"

Her arms were suddenly around his waist. "I never disliked you."

"So, are you telling me that it had descended to sheer loathing?"

The sound she made was muffled against his shoulder. It might have been a laugh, but he couldn't have said for sure. It was enough that she didn't sound as if she were weeping. She stood there in his arms for several minutes without speaking, then pulled away slightly and looked up at him.

"I don't think this will work, my lord."

He shrugged. "I'm not a bloody prince of the realm, darling. I can choose my own path."

"Stephen, you are, as I seem to have to keep reminding you, the future Earl of Artane. You can't date a Yank."

"I wasn't talking about dating you, Peaches."

She looked at him carefully. "Then what are you talking about?"

"A very medieval sort of wooing, then an incredibly public and overdone wedding."

Her mouth fell open. "You're asking me to *marry* you?"

"Well, I thought I would work on the wooing first."

She pushed out of his arms and backed away. She gaped at him for a moment or two in silence, then turned away and walked to the door. She paused with her hand on the wood, then turned and looked at him.

Tears were running down her cheeks.

He wondered when it would be—if ever—that the woman didn't leave him almost constantly winded. He took his pride in his hand and walked over to her. He hesitated, then reached out and drew her into his arms. That she came willingly was, he had to admit, something of a relief. He closed his eyes and rested his cheek against her hair.

"Are you sure you're not mistaking me for my sister?" she asked hoarsely. "She's the one with all the degrees and the title."

"No, Peaches," he said quietly. "I'm not mistaking you for your sister."

He held her in silence for several more very long, very pleasant minutes, then lifted her face up and brushed away the two stray tears that were still on her cheeks.

"Shall I tell you when it was I first loved you?" he asked quietly.

"Stephen—"

"It was when I found myself standing in Sedgwick's great hall," he continued, trying not to enjoy the sound of his name from her lips more than he should have, "wondering just where your sister Pippa had gotten to, and you walked in the door. Of course, Tess had been telling me stories of you for years, but I always held in the back of my mind that you couldn't possibly be that perfect."

"She exaggerates," Peaches managed.

"In your case, she certainly didn't."

"No one falls in love at first sight," she said quietly.

"Don't they?" he asked seriously.

"I think it takes about a week, actually."

He looked at her for a moment, then realized just what she was getting at. He blinked. "A week?"

She nodded. "About a week."

"Would you care to elaborate on that particular week?"

She smiled faintly. "Fishing, my lord Haulton?"

"Absolutely."

She sighed and tension seemed to go out of her. "You were our rock," she said. "*My* rock, actually, when Pippa left. You made me laugh, brought me tea, made me hike over those bloody dunes of yours to the beach and walk for hours. Of course, I didn't want to like you—or anything more, for that matter—because I knew nothing could come of it." She met his eyes. "You being who you are, after all."

"Rubbish—"

"It isn't," she insisted, "and that you take it seriously is part of your charm, actually." She shrugged lightly. "There you were, the handsome lord from the fairy-tale castle who got on his white horse to rescue me from the grief of losing a sister. Pretty potent stuff." She looked at him again. "I will say that you were a pretty quiet rescuer, though."

"That's because you left me breathless," he said honestly. "And I was afraid of making an arse of myself—which I did. I've been trying ever since to figure out how to get back into your good graces."

She looked at him seriously. "Stephen, this can't—" Her

phone rang from across the room. She looked at it, then at him. "That's probably Tess. She's the only one who calls this late."

"By all means, answer it." He looked at her seriously. "I'll be here."

Actually, he thought he would be better off sitting whilst he had the chance, so he retreated to the sofa. He sat with a sigh, leaned back against the couch, and contented himself with watching her. He had told her that it was stories of her that had first left him half in love with her, but that was simply a part of it. He had looked at her as she stood in the middle of Sedgwick's great hall and felt something in his soul shift, then settle. It had nothing to do with her beauty, or figure, or the way she had of putting her shoulders back and marching off into the fray. He had watched her smile and just known she was the one for him.

"It's David," she said.

Stephen found himself brought back to the present without mercy. He waved her on without comment because he could do nothing else. She frowned at him, then answered her phone. Stephen tried not to listen, but unfortunately his house was very quiet and he had very good hearing. The only thing that eased him any was that she didn't sound too terribly thrilled by her conversation.

"Tomorrow night?" Peaches said slowly. "Well, I'm not sure where Chattam Hall is— Oh, London. I see."

Stephen dragged his hand through his hair. Damn it. Chattam Hall belonged to his maternal grandmother who held court there each Saturday. He'd completely forgotten the upcoming weekend spectacle of supper and entertainment, though in his defense, he had been slightly preoccupied during the past few days. In the past, those Saturday parties had included his hobnobbing with politicians and his grandmother's steely eye looking over the women he danced with. At least he didn't have to worry about Victoria vying for his attentions at present. Unfortunately even with her out of the picture, it wasn't exactly the ideal situation in which to introduce Peaches to his grandmother.

But it was for damned sure he wasn't going to let her go with David Preston if he could prevent it.

He looked at Peaches and shook his head firmly.

She shot him a look he couldn't quite interpret. "Lord Haulton's grandmother? No, I didn't understand the connection. I have no idea if he'll be there or not."

Stephen pointed at her, then at himself, then he nodded pointedly.

Peaches ignored him. "I'm not sure what my plans are for the weekend. Let me call you back, all right?"

Stephen held up his hands as she rang off. "Honestly, it had completely slipped my mind. It isn't exactly anything I look forward to."

"Standing dates with the Terrible Trio?" she asked lightly.

He took a deep breath. "I have no idea, but it wouldn't surprise me. My grandmother's guest list is always extensive, so I'm sure they'll be there. Well, perhaps not Victoria, who has never, ever spent the night at my house. If you were curious."

"I wasn't."

"You're a terrible liar."

She sighed as she walked across the room and collapsed onto the couch next to him. "Then I probably shouldn't go."

"Of course you should," he said. "With me."

"Stephen," she said seriously, "I can't date you."

"Actually, you can do quite a bit more than that with me, but I am willing to concede that there needs to be some carefully premeditated maneuvering with my grandmother if we're to keep her from thinking too long on the fact that she hasn't had a hand in our relationship." That was perhaps understating the potential for his grandmother's ire, but there was no point in worrying over it beforehand. As he had told Peaches before, he was capable of choosing his own path. Whether others would agree with that path or not was something he couldn't control. He sighed. "I suppose you could allow Kenneworth to take you there if you think you can stomach him. I'll see that John and Tess are invited so they can take you home." He shot her a look. "First and last time, though, Peaches."

She considered, then picked up her phone and texted her change of mind. Then she set her phone down and looked at him seriously.

"Even if this were possible," she said slowly, "I'm not sure how this would work."

"One step at a time," he said easily.

She took a deep breath. "What's the first step?"

"We get through the evening tomorrow after you've spent the day in London being pampered."

"More things to work off," she said with a sigh.

"More herding," he corrected, then he paused. "Peaches, if I'm pushing you too fast, or pushing you in a direction you're not interested in . . ."

"What?" she asked politely. "You'll stop?"

He was tempted to match her tone, but he couldn't. "I might," he said simply.

She studied him in silence for a moment or two. "Would you?"

"I would change tactics," he amended, "but unless you gave me a very serious shove . . . well, no."

"This is insane." She blew a stray strand of hair out of her eyes. "You can't marry a Yank."

"It worked for my brother."

"He's not the heir."

He looked at her seriously. "We'll see if my father has any objections, which he won't. Then, if you're still unsure, we'll use that bloody gate near my father's hall, march up to either Rhys or Robin de Piaget, and get their blessing. Then will you be satisfied?"

She shrugged. "I'm only thinking of you."

"Stop being so bloody altruistic."

She smiled. "You shouldn't swear so much."

He rolled his eyes, but he also happily took advantage of the fact that she was willing to come a bit closer and allow him to do something more constructive than swear.

At least it would leave him with a few happy memories to think on whilst he was watching David Preston clumsily attempt to pursue her in a place where he couldn't simply take the man out in the back and shoot him.

Chapter 21

Peaches yawned as she waited for David to get in his side of the car and drive her to Chattam Hall, which apparently housed the most illustrious hostess in London who just happened to be Stephen's grandmother.

Louise Heydon-Brooke was, Peaches had learned, Stephen's maternal grandmother, which meant her connection to Artane was simply through her daughter's marriage. She was a baroness in her own right, which Peaches realized meant that Stephen would eventually have yet another title to add to his collection.

David got into the car with a whiff of cologne and arrogance, sighed gustily, and fired up his rather gaudy and ostentatious red Ferrari. He made revving noises and grinned at her.

She was not impressed.

She was thrilled when his phone rang and he could make all kinds of important conversation on speaker whilst he drove through nightmarish London traffic. It gave her ample opportunity to think about happier things, most notably that her day thus far hadn't included him.

She'd taken the train into London early and embarked on a

list of things to do that Stephen had insisted he pay for. She had ignored him, of course. She supposed that was stupid in a long-term sort of way, but she hadn't been able to bring herself to let him pay for more than he had already. She'd simply handed off her credit card for a facial and manicure, then taken a cab to go pick up her gown.

She had to admit that at that point, she had given up and given in. That might have had something to do with the note the salesgirl had handed her as she'd walked in a shop that only had a handful of things on display. Alarms had gone off in her head—the fewer items out, the more expensive they were—but she couldn't bring herself to turn around and run away. So she'd taken the note, opened it, then smiled in spite of herself.

I can only imagine what you've put on your card so far this morning that you shouldn't have. Please allow me this one small contribution to tonight's success.

SdP

Peaches had stood calmly through the fitting of a gorgeous pale-blue gown, then found herself escorted out to the curb only to find Humphreys waiting there with a black Rolls-Royce. She had managed to keep herself from gaping long enough to allow him to open her door for her. She had stopped, however, just before she'd gotten in.

"Where now, or do I dare ask?"

"The Ritz, I believe, miss."

"He's not good at moderation, is he?"

Humphreys had only smiled and shut her into the back of luxury.

She had indeed been expected at the Ritz, or so it seemed. She had been escorted upstairs by a very solicitous hotel employee, then opened the door to her room to find none other than Edwina there, marshaling her forces.

Peaches had showered, relaxed, and sipped green drink as her hair and makeup had been attended to. She had then been dressed, shod, and bedecked with things she couldn't believe hadn't come from some safe-deposit box somewhere. After she'd been examined for flaws and pronounced fairly lovely—it had been Edwina doing the pronouncing, after all—she had been wrapped up and sent off when called for.

All of which led to where she was at present, sitting in a very low-slung sports car that was far too flashy for her taste, and listening to a man she couldn't stand carry on a conversation she couldn't have cared less about. The only thing being in close quarters with him allowed her was the opportunity to think about a few things that had begun to nag at the edges of her thoughts.

It was odd, wasn't it, how vocal David always was about his dislike of Stephen. Actually, it was less dislike than it was a sort of a conceited disdain, as if he could mock Stephen de Piaget as often and as loudly as he liked yet suffer no repercussions for it. She wondered if that was part of the reason she'd been invited to Kenneworth House for the ball. Perhaps David had thought Stephen was fond of her and inviting her where he could so visibly pursue her had seemed yet another opportunity to provoke his nemesis.

She was rather sorry she had had any part in that, even unwittingly.

Chattam Hall, she noted as they pulled to a stop in the short circular driveway, was not Kensington Palace, but certainly bigger than she had expected. It was no wonder Stephen's grandmother watched him like a hawk. She probably loved the place dearly and just wanted to make sure it was taken care of after her death by Stephen's wife.

That didn't bode well for her, actually, but then again even thinking about being anything to Stephen de Piaget besides someone he would eventually come to his senses about and forget was fairly ridiculous—

"Off we go," David said, interrupting her thoughts by leaning over toward her with his lips puckered.

She almost knocked herself out reeling back to stay out of his way. He recovered admirably by pretending to check his hair in the mirror. She was thrilled to have her door opened for her and a gloved hand extended to help her out of the car. She smiled when she realized it was Humphreys.

"You're everywhere today," she whispered.

"Guarding the precious jewels, miss," he said solemnly, "and those wouldn't be the ones you're wearing."

Peaches blushed in spite of herself. "Thank you, Humphreys. You're very kind."

"It is an honor, Miss Alexander, to keep watch over you."

Peaches found herself unfortunately soon handed over to David, who entered loudly and drew so much attention to himself that it was all she could do not to look for a bathroom she could duck into. Then again, that hadn't worked out so well for her the last time she'd been in his company, so she pressed on as best she could.

Or so she thought until she saw Stephen standing next to a woman she could only assume was his grandmother, Lady Chattam. He was watching her with that grave smile he often wore.

Perhaps doubting her doubts might be a good strategy.

She looked at Stephen's grandmother and wasn't at all surprised by what she saw: a white-haired matriarch dressed in silks and dripping with jewels. She was also sharp as a tack, something Peaches discovered as she was presented to her.

"Ah, Miss Peaches Alexander," Lady Chattam said, looking Peaches over from head to toe in a brutally quick assessment. "You are, I believe, the Countess of Sedgwick's sister, are you not?"

"Yes, my lady," Peaches said, suppressing the urge to drop a curtsey.

"I believe you have met my grandson," Lady Chattam said, gesturing elegantly to Stephen. "The Viscount Haulton."

"We've been introduced," Peaches conceded. She didn't dare look Stephen in the eye, but she couldn't help noticing his hand reaching out for hers.

"Yes, well, that's all to the good," Lady Chattam said, stepping between them smoothly. "Kenneworth is, as usual, the last to arrive. We'll all go in to dinner now. Stephen, your arm."

Peaches took a deep breath and smiled politely. She hadn't expected a particularly warm welcome, standing there as she was without a title or buckets of money to keep her warm, and she hadn't been disappointed. She found herself stuck going down the hallway with David Preston, who deserted her after a few feet to apparently duck into the library for a little something before dinner. Peaches stood, abandoned in the middle of a crowd, until she felt a touch on her elbow. She turned and found John and Tess de Piaget standing there. She had never been more grateful for the sight of any two people before in her life.

"Thank heavens, the cavalry."

Tess was looking at her as if she'd never seen her before. "You look amazing. Did Kenneworth buy you that?"

Peaches suppressed the urge to squirm. "No," she said slowly. "He didn't."

Tess frowned for a moment, the wheels obviously working overtime, then her mouth fell open. *"Stephen?"*

Peaches managed a weak smile. "We haven't talked in a while, have we?"

"No," Tess said faintly, "but I think we need to." She paused. "Two of his girlfriends are here, you know. And Irene Preston, sharpening her fangs. I'm not sure her cousin Andrea isn't on the prowl as well."

"Can't blame them," Peaches said, touching the diamonds at her throat. "He has excellent taste."

"Yes," Tess said with a smile, "he does. In both jewels and women."

"Which we should discuss later," John said in a low voice. "His Grace is approaching."

Peaches allowed herself a heavy sigh before she pasted on her best company smile and turned to face David again. It was, she feared, going to be a very long evening.

The only thing that salvaged dinner was finding out, to her enormous surprise, that she was sitting not next to the Duke of Kenneworth, but Lady Chattam's grandson. Her chair was held out for her, she was seated, then she spent the next few seconds trying to breathe normally.

"Like the seating arrangements?" Stephen murmured.

"Love them," she murmured in return as her napkin was placed on her lap. She was even more grateful than usual for Aunt Edna's insistence she learn which fork was which on the off chance she ever found herself to tea somewhere fancy.

Stephen picked up his water glass. "You look stunning," he said, using it as cover.

"Thank you."

"Is that lipstick temporary or permanent?"

"Why do you ask?"

"Why do you think I'm asking?"

She smiled in spite of herself and declined to answer. Fortunately supper began before she could truly get herself into any trouble. The meal seemed interminable only because she was torn between being distracted by the deliciousness that was the Viscount Haulton in a tux and knowing that his grandmother was watching them both while pretending to be deeply interested in the conversations going on around her. It didn't help at all that Stephen tried to hold her hand under the table.

"I believe, my lord Haulton," she murmured, "that you are about to get yourself busted."

"Granny won't know," he said under his breath.

"The footmen will."

"They won't blame me."

"But your girlfriends might. One of them already has suspicions." Peaches smiled politely at him. "The blonde has been glaring daggers at me all evening. And let's not forget Irene Preston."

"Shall I look at you superciliously to throw them all off the scent?"

"You could try that, but you might want to first stop looking at my mouth."

He smiled gravely, that polite smile she'd seen so much of before she'd wound up in medieval England with him and her world had been turned completely upside down. Only now, she realized it didn't mean what she thought it had.

It meant he loved her.

"A waltz later?" he asked.

"If you like."

"Will I suit, do you think?" he asked, suddenly serious. "Aunt Edna, I mean."

Peaches was taken aback by the question only because it seemed odd that he should worry about passing muster with an obscure woman of such little consequence in the world. That he should care said something about his character.

And his feelings for her.

"Does it matter to you?" she asked.

"Very much," he said frankly.

"You know, you're going to have to stop this kind of thing in public places," she said, blinking a time or two in spite of herself. "You're going to get us both in trouble. And if you really want to know, yes, I think she'll approve."

The smile he gave her made her very relieved she was already seated. She suspected the only reason it hadn't brought his granny to her feet was that she had missed it. Peaches made sure Lady Louise was still engaged in overseeing her guests, then succumbed to the conversational demands of a rather robust man on her left who turned out to be a very keen gardener. She managed to make polite conversation with him in spite of Stephen's continually brushing her elbow with his, or pressing his foot against hers, or otherwise distracting her from ignoring him as she knew she should have.

There was mingling after supper, which was just as painful as she'd feared it might be. David kept her next to him the entire time, though she managed to avoid having his hands on all the various parts of her person that were polite to grab in public. She was rather relieved to hear the orchestra warming up, though she supposed she shouldn't have been. David would probably try to monopolize her for the entire night—and not because he had any feelings for her, but for his own perverse reasons.

The only thing that saved her was that Lady Louise's balls seemed to include only music for traditional dancing, which left David stumbling through several songs—something she hadn't noticed at Kenneworth House—before he steered her over to the punch bowl and helped himself.

"I say," drawled a voice suddenly in the poshest of tones from behind her, "Preston, old thing, don't you feel it's time to let someone else have a turn?"

Peaches turned to see none other than John de Piaget standing there, looking terrifyingly lethal in spite of his elegant evening clothes.

"Who?" David asked with a snort. "You?"

John lifted an eyebrow. "Family privilege and all that."

"Your keep doesn't even have a roof."

"No, but my wife's does and I'm happy to laze about as a kept man, so release my sister-in-law and go vex someone else with your troublesome self."

"How dare you," David said, drawing himself up and puffing importantly.

John took Peaches's hand and tucked it under his arm. "Spare us the dramatics."

"You won't dare talk to me this way," David said in a low but quite audible voice. "Not for long."

Peaches wasn't one to be unduly alarmed, but she couldn't deny that the tone of his voice had made her very uncomfortable. She walked with John out into the middle of the ballroom, then stopped and looked at him.

"What do you think?" she asked him in the vintage French she was fairly sure the bulk of the company wouldn't understand.

"I think I'm very happy my grandmother forced me to pay attention to a dancing master along with a master lutenist," he said pleasantly. "And your accent is excellent, you know. You'll make a certain lad who values that very happy over the course of his life."

She pursed her lips as he swept her into a waltz. "I wasn't asking that, though yes, you do dance divinely."

"Better than my nephew?"

She laughed a little and was grateful for a brief distraction. "I believe on that subject I will remain discreetly silent. You will, I'm sure, be relieved to know that Stephen's granny is watching you closely, but she isn't scowling."

"She's still trying to work out why I look so much like her grandson."

"What have you told her?"

"I haven't come within ten paces of the old harridan," John said with a mock shiver. "I don't dare, of course. We'll let her think what she wants for the time being." He looked over her head for a moment, then back at her. "As for our good duke, I think he's trouble. What kind, I don't know yet. But I'm watching him."

"I'm sure Stephen is enormously relieved."

"Actually, he is, though he told me to leave my blades in the car."

"And did you?"

He only smiled. Peaches smiled in return, because she had the feeling that John and Stephen were both prepared to wield more than their good looks if necessary.

"And there is the good Viscount Haulton, watching me with a frown whilst a number of his lesser cousins are looking at you with great interest. Where shall I deliver you first?"

"Cousins," she said faintly. "I'm not tangling with granny quite yet. I'm definitely not going to put myself between his girlfriends and their prey."

"I think that might be wise. I'll turn you over to the Chattam lads, then, until Stephen's tormentors tire of the chase."

Peaches didn't want to tell him that she suspected Stephen would give out long before his would-be brides would, but he had already deposited her with one of Lady Louise's lesser grandsons, who was astonishingly handsome, an excellent dancer, and content to limit his conversation to her health and the weather.

She was fairly sure it was Stephen's diamonds overwhelming him so.

*I*t was pushing midnight when she found herself standing with Tess and John, sipping punch. David had disappeared an hour earlier, which had pleased her. She'd had a remarkably lovely evening mostly dancing with Stephen's cousins and once with his brother Gideon, who had treated her as if everything concerning her future as part of the family were already settled. She'd had a delightful conversation with Gideon's wife, Megan, and spent enough time with Tess to help her keep her equilibrium. Life was, in spite of trying to pretend she had no feelings for Stephen, very good—

"Oh, my," Tess said faintly.

Peaches would have asked her sister what the matter was, but she shut her mouth around the question she hadn't managed to ask.

Stephen was walking toward her.

"Steady," Tess murmured.

"Shut up," Peaches suggested. "His grandmother isn't going to like this."

"I'm not sure he cares," Tess said honestly. "Enjoy your fairy-tale midnight moment."

"If he kisses me, I'll kill him."

Tess only laughed and allowed her husband to sweep her into his arms and out onto the floor. Peaches tried not to squirm as Stephen came to a stop in front of her, then made her a slight bow.

"My lady," he said gravely.

"You're mistaking me for my sister the countess."

"I don't think so," he said, with a grave smile. He held out his hand. "Will you?"

She put her hand into his. "Are you sure?"

"Absolutely."

"Your grandmother will have a fit."

"She'll recover." He led her out onto the floor, then gathered her into his arms. He sighed happily. "I think this might be worth the misery of the rest of the evening."

"Thank you," she said with a smile. "Though I will admit your cousins were charming and very polite."

"Transferring your affections to the other side of the family, love?"

She shook her head. "They don't have calluses."

He frowned slightly. "Calluses?"

She squeezed his right hand. "Calluses from swordplay. A girl has to have her standards."

"You know," he said, "I think no one would notice when the clock strikes midnight if I were to properly reward you for that comment."

She laughed a little, because she was in his arms and at the moment, everything seemed perfect.

Then the clock began to strike midnight.

And things took a turn she hadn't expected.

Chapter 22

S *tephen* stood in his grandmother's library at a quarter past midnight with Peaches at his side and felt something curling in his gut that certainly wasn't fear but felt too damned close to it for his taste.

He supposed that was an improvement from the intense irritation he'd felt fifteen minutes earlier when he'd been interrupted in the very act of pulling Peaches into his arms for a midnight kiss by one of his grandmother's footmen summoning him to the library. He'd arrived fully prepared to tell his grandmother to remember that he didn't need her permission to wed where it suited him only to find that there was something going on that seemingly had nothing to do with his amorous adventures.

His grandmother had been there, standing in the middle of her library looking thoroughly peeved. His brother Gideon had been off to one side with Megan, both of them wearing identical looks of, well, nothing. Then again, they had both seen enough over the years to have mastered the art of hearing the most appalling things without reacting. Tess and John had rounded out the group. He had been rather relieved to see that John hadn't brought his sword.

Though he half wished he had brought his own.

He now stood looking at the illustrious Duke of Kenneworth, who seemed to believe he was holding court, and folded his arms over his chest. "You've dragged us all away from a lovely party," he said briskly, "and we've humored you because we have decent manners. Please do us the favor of enlightening us as to the nature of your business so we can return to our familial entertainments."

David looked at him with a cold smile. "I was just waiting to make sure you in particular were here, Haulton, before I began. It's a pity your mother and father couldn't join us, but we'll make do with what we have."

"What in the hell are you talking about?" Stephen snapped. He didn't often lose his temper, but he could safely say that David Preston was approximately ten words from seeing it in full. It was one thing to be tormented by the fool and his viper of a sister Irene in public; being irritated by them in a family home was just too much.

"Yes, I'm finding the drama a bit much as well," Lady Louise said shortly. "Perhaps, young man, you forget who issued the invitation tonight and what bad behavior means for your social standing in the future."

"I wouldn't worry about me," David said smoothly. "I would be more inclined to worry about you."

Stephen watched his grandmother bristle. "Why should I worry about myself?"

"Because after you hear what I have to say," David said coolly, "you'll find you have quite a bit less sterling to use in splashing out for these affairs of yours."

"Don't be ridiculous," Lady Louise said.

"I'm not sure David knows how to be anything but ridiculous, Grandmother," Stephen said, "but perhaps he has some amusing anecdote with which to entertain us." He shot David a look. "It had best be very entertaining to have interrupted such a lovely evening."

David motioned toward the door. Stephen looked over his shoulder and realized that Irene and Andrea were standing there. They seemed, however, less eager to become part of the group than he would have thought them. He exchanged a look with John, who reached for Peaches and pulled her over to stand next to him. John then stepped in front of his wife and his sister-in-law and folded his arms over his chest. Stephen didn't suppose David Preston was intelligent enough to realize he'd just put himself in a room with men who wouldn't actually think very long before they tore him to pieces. He turned back to the problem at hand.

"Do you need yet a larger audience, David?" he asked shortly.

"If you'll shut your ever-running mouth," David said, his eyes full of something that wasn't at all pleasant, "I'll be brief. I am here to offer you the chance to save not only all your assets but your family name as well."

Lady Louise rolled her eyes with as much enthusiasm as she ever permitted herself. "You're mad." She caught the eye of her head butler standing just inside the doorway. "Hollingsworth, call the authorities."

"Hollingsworth, stay where you are," David said sharply. He looked at Lady Louise. "You'll listen to me, old woman, and you'll listen well."

Stephen hadn't realized his grandmother had come to stand next to him until he felt her fingers pinching the back of his arm hard enough that he flinched.

"I am holding on to my temper by the most tenuous of grasps," Lady Louise said in a voice that sent shivers down Stephen's spine. "Pray take a different tone, Your Grace, before I have you blacklisted by everyone worth knowing."

"Yes, spew it out," Stephen drawled with deliberate disdain, "before we all perish from the suspense."

David's mask slipped fully. "I shall," he said, looking at Stephen with undisguised hate, "and I'll direct my remarks at you. I have no idea why, but my cousin Andrea wants you."

Stephen blinked, because that was the last thing he'd expected David to say. "What?" he managed.

Lady Louise made a noise of impatience. "He absolutely will *not* marry a girl from some obscure village in the south. I don't care what she thinks she wants."

David shoved his hands in his pockets and rocked back on his heels. "You'll soon realize that Andrea will most assuredly have what she wants." He looked over his shoulder. "Andrea, come tell everyone what you found."

Stephen watched Irene give Andrea a shove that sent her sprawling—or it would have if Stephen hadn't leapt forward and caught her in his arms. He set her on her feet, then frowned at her.

"Why are you mixed up in this?"

She pulled away from him, then went to stand next to David. She lifted her chin, but wouldn't look at him. Stephen stepped back to stand next to his grandmother, more because it bought him a moment to think than anything else, though he supposed preventing his grandmother from stabbing David with the first thing she could lay her hands on could only be a good thing.

He was surprised at how thoroughly he had misjudged David's cousin—unless she had become caught up in something she hadn't been able to control.

He found himself less than eager to find out what that something was.

"I was going through my father's papers," Andrea said, her voice trembling, "when I found something in a sealed envelope. He was, of course, a great collector of antiquities, so there were many things of a particular age." She looked at David nervously. "I think—"

"Which you shouldn't," David said, patting her on the head. "I'll finish for you, Andrea, lest it prove too taxing. You see, what our little Andrea found in her father's papers was actually something that belonged to one of my ancestors." He looked at Stephen. "Aren't you curious as to what it was?"

Stephen didn't like the look in David's eye. He wasn't sure if the duke was strung out on drugs or if he were just mad, but he supposed it didn't matter. He didn't answer David, but he nodded.

"It was the winnings of a game of chance—"

"Unsurprising," Lady Louise said curtly. "The only thing that is surprising is that you have a hall left with all the gambling your father did."

David's expression hardened. "Yes, well, he was a reckless man."

"So are you," Lady Louise shot back, "for you spend just as much time at the sport as he."

"Fortunately for me," David said coolly, "I am far better at it than he was, and I have the wit to do my own research instead of relying on the work of others." He shot Stephen a look. "I believe that is your area of expertise, Haulton."

"And I believe you're an idiot," Stephen returned, "but that is beside the point."

"And you didn't find the deed," Andrea said in a low voice. "I did."

"Shut up, Andrea," David snarled.

Stephen blew out his breath. "Very well," he said impatiently, "someone did the work, David read about this game of chance, then decided it meant something to him."

"And I couldn't possibly be less interested in what that something was," Lady Louise said briskly. "Come, children, back to the party—"

"Just one moment," David said sharply, "if you please. I'm not finished." He looked at Stephen. "In that stack of Andrea's father's papers, I found an envelope with an unbroken seal."

"*I* found it," Andrea put in.

David whirled on her. "If you don't shut up—"

"If you touch her, you'll leave clapped in irons," Stephen said coldly.

"Clapped in irons," David echoed, turning back to him with a laugh. "What a quaint turn of phrase. But you always were one for history, weren't you? With any luck, you'll be limited to reading about it."

Stephen pursed his lips. "Why you would care I can't imagine, but go on. What was the deed to?"

"Yes, do tell," Gideon drawled. "A gold mine in Africa?"

"No," David said, not taking his eyes off Stephen, "it is a quitclaim deed to Artane and everything entailed on it."

Stephen blinked, then he laughed. "A valiant effort, David, but a futile one."

David smiled. "You don't think I'm that stupid, do you, Stephen?"

"Actually, I do think you're that stupid," Stephen said. "None of my ancestors would ever have been so foolish as to wager our hall on a game of chance."

"I had the paper authenticated, dated, and my lawyers very busy researching all possible legal challenges to my claim," David continued. "And to save you time wondering, there are none. It's solid."

"Let me see the deed," Stephen said, making certain he sounded utterly bored. "For the amusement of it, if nothing else."

"No," David said simply.

"Let me understand this," Lady Louise said, elbowing Stephen aside. "Do you have the cheek to tell me that someone from Kenneworth at some point swindled my son-in-law's hall away from him?"

David shrugged. "I have no reason to believe it wasn't a fair game of chance. And yes, Artane was put up as collateral and lost."

"Proof," Stephen said, reaching out his hand to keep his brother from launching himself forward. "We're not interested in your delusions of grandeur."

"I saw the deed," Andrea said. She shot David a look that sent chills down Stephen's spine. "And you keep up your end of the bargain or I'll take it back."

David turned on her. "I don't care about your ridiculous bargain—"

"You cheat!" she gasped.

"Well," he said with a shrug, "yes, I do."

"I'm curious," Stephen said, because he thought having a bit of infighting in the Kenneworth ranks could only be a good thing for the rest of them. "What was the bargain?"

Andrea turned on him. "I told David that he could have the deed if he delivered you to me in return."

Stephen clasped his hands behind his back. "What an interesting agreement, Andrea. Was I to be tied and gagged, or was David going to use his vast amounts of charm to convince me to arrive bearing jewels and silks?"

Andrea shot Peaches a look. "At least *I* have a pedigree. Your whore over there—"

"Stop it immediately," Lady Louise said. "There will be no foul language in my library, for it is still *my* library." She looked at David. "Before I throw you out, tell me what you want and let us have this over with."

David smiled. "What I want, Granny, is for your grandson to sell everything he has and buy my silence. If you find yourselves unwilling to part with your belongings, I'll have Artane. And once the scandal of your gambling ancestors hits the press, then *you*, Lady Louise, will not have the courage to throw these sorts of lavish parties any longer. My sister will take her rightful place as London's premiere hostess."

"And you'll find yourself with a bit more to toss away at cards, is that it?" Stephen said, suppressing a yawn. "Perhaps you should see a professional, Kenneworth, and address your addiction."

David's fury was impressive. "I'll give you seventy-two hours, because it will take you that long to begin to liquidate everything you have. Send me proof you've begun the process, or I'll go to the press."

"Send me the proof," Stephen shot back, "or I'll have you charged with slander."

"You don't want to make an enemy of me, Haulton, I guarantee it."

"Proof," Stephen said curtly, "or *I* go to the press. And you needn't worry about seeing Miss Alexander home."

"I hadn't," David said blandly. "I just assumed she would walk the streets, which is, I'm sure her habit."

Stephen realized that his grandmother was holding on to one arm and his brother the other only because he found he couldn't move.

"Hollingsworth, see the Duke of Kenneworth and his female relations out the front door," Lady Louise said briskly. "And make certain nothing inadvertently falls into their pockets as they leave."

David pulled something out of his jacket pocket, and tossed it at Stephen's feet. He smiled pleasantly, then left the room. Stephen watched Andrea and Irene follow after him and could hardly believe what he'd just heard. He pulled his arms away from his grandmother and brother, then looked at Gideon.

"Wake Geoff Segrave," he said shortly.

Gideon was already on his mobile, which Stephen appreciated. He could scarce wait to see what their attorney would have to say about the present disaster.

"I need a drink," Lady Louise said, her voice quavering just the slightest bit. "Megan, darling, come fix me a scotch and soda. Make it very light on the soda."

Stephen helped his grandmother into a chair, then went to pick up the envelope David had left behind. He walked over to lean against a sturdy bookcase, snagging Peaches's hand on his way by her. He looked at her briefly, then opened the envelope and pulled out a photograph of something written in a vintage hand.

An IOU for a gambling debt.

Using Artane as collateral.

He felt the blood drain from his face, immediately followed by the sensation of Peaches taking the piece of paper out of his hand.

"Oh, Stephen," she said in a very low voice, "this can't be legitimate."

"If it isn't, it's a bloody good forgery."

"The signature's covered up," she said looking at it closely, "and the date, as well."

"It wouldn't do for us to have too many details, would it?" Stephen said. He turned to her and put his arms around her.

"Stephen—"

"I don't care what anyone says," he said. "Just keep me from landing on my arse for the next five minutes."

"You could marry Andrea—"

"No."

She sighed and put her arms around him. He rested his cheek against her hair, careful not to muss the coiffure he hadn't yet had a chance to compliment her on, and closed his eyes.

"Let's go back home," he murmured, "and this time you can read Chaucer to me."

"I don't speak Old English."

"Then pick something you love," he said with a sigh, lifting his head and looking down at her. "Humphreys keeps Wodehouse in the pantry. And time-travel romances, I think."

"Either would do," she agreed.

Stephen sighed deeply. He was going to speak to Geoffrey Segrave first, then find some bloody historian—and he knew several—with no propensity for gossiping to have a look at the photocopy to give an opinion on its authenticity, then he was going to go for a run until he could face the fact that the paper Peaches was currently handing to John was the very image of something even he could see was genuine.

His home, gambled away by some fool. And the only way to have it back was likely to sell everything inside it and pay for David Preston's silence. The only way to avoid that would be—

His thoughts ground to a halt.

The only way to avoid that would be providing the funds he would need without having to sell every damned thing he owned and bankrupt his father as well. Perhaps by selling a few antiquities that had been set aside for that very purpose.

Things set aside by someone in the past who might have an interest in preserving Artane for future generations.

It was absolute pants, that idea, but he had already been to medieval England once and survived. Why not another trip?

Yes, he would definitely need a bit of familial help to keep Artane from falling into the hands of a family that had, he recalled from his encounter with that first lord of Kenneworth, never had any love for his own. And he suspected he knew exactly where to find that sort of man.

And when.

Chapter 23

Peaches would have preferred not to remember the remainder of her first foray into polite London society. Guests had been ushered out of Chattam Hall without delay and without an explanation for the absence of their hostess. Peaches hadn't been able to blame her. Lady Louise had disappeared to points unknown with Stephen when a messenger from Kenneworth had arrived, a briefcase full of proof in his hand. Neither of them had returned.

The rest of the company was still in the library in various states of distress. Peaches had helped Megan distribute beverages of all kinds, tried to make innocuous conversation with her sister, then decided that just sitting was going to drive her nuts.

She didn't understand how it was possible for a man to gamble away an entire estate on a single hand of cards. She also wasn't sure how Andrea's father had wound up with something that should have been in the possession of the heirs of Kenneworth.

What she could understand, however, was that Andrea wanted Stephen. Blackmailing him to marry her was original, though. It was obvious Andrea didn't know him at all if she'd thought that was going to work.

Or so Peaches hoped.

She paced along the hallway, trying to keep herself awake. Chattam Hall was absolutely gorgeous, full of all kinds of Victorian and pre-Victorian antiques. Peaches admired for a bit, then continued on down the hallway.

She shouldn't have stopped by the half-open door, indeed she told herself quite specifically that she was an idiot to stop in front of a half-open door, but her feet seemed to be acting of their own accord. She heard the voices and knew she should have continued on, but something wouldn't let her. She leaned against the wall just outside the door and eavesdropped shamelessly.

"There is no hope for the thing," Lady Louise was saying grimly. "It is as he says."

"Impossible," Stephen said firmly. "He's a—"

"Yes, yes, I know what he is, but in this, he has a case."

Peaches shook her head in silent admiration. The world might have been lying in ruins around her, but Lady Louise Heydon-Brooke would soldier on in spite of it. Stephen sounded less determined than furious, but Peaches couldn't blame him. She didn't want to believe that David had any claim to Artane, but it was difficult to deny what she had seen with her own eyes.

"I'll find a way to fund this," Stephen said.

"Yes, indeed you will," Lady Louise said briskly, "and you will do this by marrying."

There was a conspicuous silence, and then Stephen cleared his throat.

"I believe, Grandmother, that I am far past the age when—"

"You are inclined to give into foolish dalliances? Yes, I should hope so. You will wed, sir, and you will wed the girl I choose for you. She will possess not only a title but vast resources. It is the only way."

"No—"

"It is your duty, Haulton," Lady Louise said with a crispness that made Peaches flinch. "It is a duty, I add unnecessarily, which you have been shirking for at least a decade and which you will shirk no longer."

"Ridiculous," Stephen said shortly. "Grandmother, with all due respect, I will not be told whom to marry. Not even by you."

"You will," Lady Louise said icily, "or you will never see a bloody penny of my money."

"Do you actually believe I care for any of that?"

"You will, my boy, when you are the Earl of Artane and need to repair your roof." She made a noise of disbelief. "Is this how you were raised, Stephen? To throw away everything your ancestors fought and bled for, guarded, shepherded through countless wars and intrigues, simply because you continue to entertain a preposterously romantic notion of marital love?"

Peaches listened to a silence that went on for several minutes.

"Have you a list, Grandmother?" Stephen said finally.

"I do," Lady Louise said shortly, "and I will choose someone suitable from it. I absolutely refuse to see that pile of stones that is your father's heart and soul be sold off to silence that damned fool from Kenneworth. Worse still that it should fall into his hands."

More silence ensued.

"Keep her for your mistress if you like, for she is very lovely. But you will not wed her."

"Is that all, Grandmother?"

"That is all, Stephen."

Peaches tried to run away before the door opened fully, but she couldn't. Stephen looked as if he'd just finished a marathon and thought throwing up might be a good thing to do next. He took her hand and pulled her along with him.

"You shouldn't," she said, pulling her hand away.

He stopped and looked at her. His eyes were a dark, stormy gray. "I suppose you heard all that."

"I didn't mean to."

"Well, she damn well meant you to," he said angrily. He took her hand again and pulled her with him. "We're going home."

"I can ride with Tess and John—"

"You will most definitely not ride home with them. You will come home with me."

"Listen, buster, I'm not going to be your mistress."

He stopped so suddenly she almost tripped. He steadied her with his hands on her arms, then looked at her seriously.

"Do you think for one minute I would ask you to be?"

She shook her head, because she knew if she spoke, she would weep. And she never wept. She pointedly ignored the fact that she had suffered from a brief bout of the sniffles in Stephen's library the evening before.

"I'll see to this the old-fashioned way."

"Are you going to shoot him?" she asked in surprise. "Or your grandmother?"

He blinked, then he smiled very briefly. "She is a matriarch in the grand tradition, but she will see reason eventually. As for the other?" He put his arm around her shoulders and walked with her down the long hallway. "No, I won't shoot him, though I'm tempted. It will take money and vast amounts of it."

"And where will you get that?"

"I'm working on it."

"Do you believe him?"

He sighed deeply. "I have no reason not to."

She paused with him as he bid a very short good-bye to her family and his brother and sister-in-law, then allowed him to bundle her up and help her into his car. The drive back to Cambridge was accomplished in silence, though he did put her hand palm down on his leg and hold it rather tightly.

They were pulling into his driveway before she thought she could speak casually.

"You can change your mind, you know."

He glanced at her. "Peaches, darling, it would take much more than this for me to change my mind."

"This is pretty big."

"So is my affection for you."

"Affection?" she asked, and she smiled because she couldn't help herself.

"I'm trying not to frighten you off."

She smiled truly then, because he was so utterly charming.

He turned the car off, then simply sat there in silence for a bit. "You could change your mind, you know," he said finally.

"Why would I?" she asked. "I don't have any money. If you don't have any money, then we'll both not have any money together. Though I'll tell you now that I think I would be much more suited to a life of poverty than you would be."

He shot her a look. "Do you, indeed?"

"Yes," she said easily. "You with your *very* soft life, never pitting your considerable brainpower against obscure and obsolete languages, never getting off your fetching backside to do anything but trot from your soft office chair to an equally climate-controlled lecture hall."

He laughed. "Climate-controlled, my arse."

"Oh, is it chilly inside those ancient halls where you ply your dastardly trade? What deprivation you already suffer."

He shifted in his seat to look at her. "Let's leave that for a moment and discuss my fetching backside."

"You, my lord, are a lecher."

"And you, my love, looked absolutely breathtaking tonight."

She smoothed her hands over the skirts of her gown. "I pulled the—well, I was going to say I pulled the tags off the gown so we can't return it, but it didn't have any tags which was very frightening. I'm not sure I could get your money back anyway, though. There's sherbet on the hem."

"When did you spill sherbet on the hem?"

"*I* didn't spill it," she said pointedly, "*you* did. While you were trying to grope me during dinner."

He smiled and lifted her hand to kiss it. "I was trying to be discreet. Unfortunately."

"You were taking liberties."

"Darling, you have no idea the liberties—well, never mind. I wouldn't have taken liberties, even if I'd had you to myself. A chaste kiss, perhaps, at the appropriate moment." He unlocked the car and reached for the door. "Let's go inside and see if that moment arrives."

She waited for him to open her door for her, then chewed on her words until they were standing just outside his house. He put the key in the lock, then looked at her.

"What?" he asked quietly.

"What would you do if you lost it all?"

He shrugged. "Sell the car, move to France." He glanced at her briefly. "We might grow grapes."

"I don't drink."

"Neither do I. Apples, then, or olives."

"We'd have to move to Italy for olives."

"My Italian is terrible," he admitted. "How is yours?"

"I could get us to the loo and onto a train, but that's about it."

He let her into his house, shut and locked the door behind them, then pulled her into his arms. "Thank you," he said with feeling. "I needed a little levity."

"Levity?" she echoed. "I have to be honest with you, Stephen, I'd much rather know you as poor and insignificant. Your titles and wealth are not assets."

He looked at her gravely. "Can you live with them?"

"Your grandmother doesn't think I should."

"My grandmother talks too much."

"I don't think she'll be the only one talking."

"Do you care?"

"Do you?"

He shot her a look. "I absolutely do not."

She only lifted her eyebrows briefly. She didn't care what anyone said about her, but that was because she knew who she was, how she treated others, and where she was going. Comments on her choice of road or destination didn't bother her.

But she imagined they would bother her plenty if her road lay alongside Stephen's.

He took her hand and led her into his library. Humphreys rose from tending the fire and brushed off his hands. He made Stephen a bow, then nodded to her.

"My lord," he said, "Miss Alexander. Can I bring you anything?"

Stephen shrugged out of his coat and tossed it over a chair. "I'm fine. Peaches?"

She shook her head, then allowed Stephen to take her wrap and hand it to Humphreys.

"I think we're well off for the moment," Stephen said. "We'll raid the kitchen later if we need something."

"Then I'll be on my way, my lord. I'll return first thing."

Peaches watched him leave, watched the library door close, then found herself turned around and drawn into Stephen's arms. She looked up at him and smiled.

"What is it?"

He put his hand along her cheek. "I missed the activity I'd planned to engage in at midnight. I thought I'd make up for it now."

She laughed a little in spite of herself. "After all that's gone on tonight, you're thinking about kissing me?"

"Thinking about it, dreaming about it, planning on doing a thorough job of it," he said, bending his head toward hers.

She put her arms around his neck and enjoyed his very thorough job of what he was doing. He finally lifted his head and looked at her.

"Well, at least that won't change if we're both broke."
She laughed and pulled his head back to hers.

She woke up, disoriented, then realized she had fallen asleep on the couch in Stephen's library and that out of self-defense while he was trolling through books she'd been too sleepy to ask the names of. Stephen was gone, though the fire was still burning in a useful fashion. She sat up, pulled the blanket that had been draped over her around her shoulders, then went to look for the master of the house. She only found Humphreys, but she supposed he was a good second best.

"Where is Viscount Haulton?" she asked, smothering a yawn behind her hand.

"He went out, miss."

"To school?"

Humphreys hesitated. "A bit farther than that, I suspect."

Peaches froze, then felt her way down into a chair at the kitchen table. "In what farther direction did he go, do you suppose?"

"North, miss."

She was somehow not at all surprised, though she was surprisingly panicked. "Which car did he take?"

"The Range Rover, miss."

She felt something slither down her spine. It was dread, pure and simple. "Did he say what he was planning to do?"

"If I remember correctly, miss, he said he had some investigating to do at the family seat. He left you a note, if you care to read it over breakfast."

She wasn't sure she could stomach any breakfast, but Humphreys was already pulling green things out of the fridge and firing up a juicer she hadn't noticed before. She might have smiled over that, but she was too busy opening the card and reading what was scrawled in Stephen's bold hand.

Don't follow me, and I mean that. I'll be back before Kenneworth's deadline, solution in hand. Be a good girl, sit in front of the fire, and let Humphreys feed you.

I love you,
Stephen

Well, obviously he was off to do something ill-advised. It occurred to her, with that same feeling of dread, that she knew just what that something was going to be. He was going to use that great big X near Artane to get back to the past and do . . . what? Wander around and look for buried treasure?

Unless he'd found something during the night that he hadn't shared with her.

She looked at Humphreys, who was concentrating on his mixture.

"Humphreys, do you have any idea what Lord Haulton was reading last night?"

"He came out of the library very early this morning, miss, but without any books. I daresay he left them in the library."

She considered. "Do we have any costumes?"

"What sort of costumes are we looking for?" he asked, glancing over his shoulder.

"Oh, you know," she said, waving her hand negligently, "Renaissance-faire-type things. Medieval gowns. Shoes. A dagger to slip into a belt." She looked at him innocently. "That sort of thing."

"In the wardrobe, in the spare room, miss."

"Would you drive me to the station in a bit?"

He looked faintly horrified. "The station? Why would you take the train, Miss Alexander, when you could travel in comfort and style?"

"Do you have the keys to the Mercedes?" she asked in surprise.

He patted the pocket of his suit coat. "I like to keep them close, on the off chance they're needed in a hurry."

Of course. She considered, then looked at Stephen's valet. "He wants me to stay here."

"No doubt, miss." Humphreys turned back to pouring her juice. "I'll have the car ready for travel whenever it suits you."

Peaches smiled to herself as she thanked him for the juice he handed her, then walked back into the library. She considered the books she hadn't noticed before lying on a table in front of the fire and decided that before she rushed off, she might as well know what Stephen was thinking.

She could only hope she wouldn't miss anything.

Chapter 24

Stephen stood on a stop just outside his father's walls, looked up at the modern-day castle rising into the air in front of him, and took a deep breath. It was the same view he had looked at for the whole of his life, but somehow it was as if he were seeing it for the last time.

Obviously lack of sleep had made him maudlin.

He rubbed his hands over his face and reviewed his morning so far. He had arrived at Artane before dawn, parked in the car park, then gone inside his father's hall. He had written his mother a note and asked her to move his car inside for him, giving her the excuse that he was going hiking for the next few days with friends and would be having a lift from them. He'd left his keys with the note, retrieved his shorter sword from where he'd left it near the front gate, and gone out into the darkness.

The honest truth was, he'd initially looked at the time travelers he'd met with a very jaundiced eye. While he had never been one to mock others openly, he had certainly indulged in his own private, silent snorts of disbelief.

That was until he'd met Kendrick de Piaget, his uncle, who wasn't precisely a time traveler but had most assuredly had a most interesting journey to the present day. Kendrick looked very much like Gideon, but that could possibly have been coincidence. Stephen couldn't say he'd spent all that much time with Kendrick initially, so his exposure to those of a different vintage had been light.

And then he'd had the pleasure of meeting both Zachary Smith and John de Piaget within a year of each other. If listening to Zachary's tales hadn't made the hair on the back of his neck stand up, listening to Zachary's wife Mary—Stephen's auntie, as it happened—babble on in perfect Norman French had been. Her husband's command of it had been equally impressive.

And he and John de Piaget could have passed for twins if it hadn't been for the age difference.

He'd already spoken to Zachary whilst about the happy work of rescuing Peaches from the past, so he'd had nothing further to ask him. Now that he'd had his own experience with time gates, he thought he might know what to expect.

It wasn't the traveling through time that gave him pause. It was what he would find on the other side of that stretch of centuries that left him almost frozen in place.

On one side of the gate, his current side, lay a situation that was absolute pants. He could hardly wrap his mind around it, but there was no denying that David Preston, the wastrel Duke of Kenneworth, held the deeds to Artane, Haulton, Blythewood, and Etham. His attorney, the very canny Geoffrey Segrave, didn't think that included the private property inside, but that hardly mattered. Artane was priceless, and not just for the history and the memories it held. Stephen imagined they could liquidate every personal item possessed by the entire family yet still not have enough to meet an appraised price. The situation was absolutely impossible.

It had occurred to him, as he'd watched Peaches sleep on the couch in his library, that he would be wise to set aside something in trust for their children—assuming he was able to earn enough to have anything to set aside for children he could only hope to have with her—something apart from his lands and titles that was untouchable. It was a pity his father hadn't had a better lawyer to do the same for him.

It was then that he'd begun to consider with deadly seriousness the germ of the idea he'd had at Chattam Hall. What if he could convince one of the early lords of Artane to set aside something for future generations?

Or, rather, for him?

He had left Peaches sleeping peacefully, driven like a fiend north, and arrived at his ancestral home well before dawn. He'd written the aforementioned notes, then slipped out of the castle before dawn and retreated to where he was now, the appropriate spot near his father's keep, to consider possible destinations in time. He'd known where the gate lay partly because he'd seen Pippa step through it to the past, and partly because he could see it there, shimmering in the morning sun.

He'd wondered how many souls had stepped on that unassuming patch of ground and found themselves in a place they hadn't intended to go? Or perhaps it only worked at certain times and for certain people.

He sincerely hoped the time and the person was right at the moment.

He hoped for either Rhys de Piaget or Mary's father, Robin. He didn't know either of them himself, but he knew from very brief and uncomfortable conversations—the discomfort coming from his side, of course, thanks to his inability to believe the things he was hearing—with both Mary and John that either man was reasonable, fair, and shrewd. Robin was the more unreasonable swordsman, spending innumerable hours in the lists torturing his guardsmen, but both had loved Artane. Stephen supposed he could have chosen any number of men through the ages to visit, but for some reason, he was drawn to the past.

The artifacts were worth more, actually.

He looked up at his father's keep in front of him, closed his eyes, then stepped forward.

The sense of vertigo was so strong, he stumbled forward until he finally found his footing in a layer of crusty snow that hadn't been there a heartbeat before. He looked up, almost dreading what he would see.

The floodlights were gone, but it was Artane, thankfully. He had no idea what the year was, but he would find that out soon enough. Perhaps things would go very well, and he would meet Robin just a month after John had left him—

He shook his head. That would mean that Nicholas should have been in his early thirties at their last encounter, which he certainly wasn't. And those sons of his, the blond twins who had bought them a meal at the inn when he had gone back to rescue Peaches, those lads had been perhaps twenty, possibly younger. If the gates worked according to the wishes of the person using them, then perhaps he would arrive in the past soon after the last time he'd been there.

The thought of it gave him a sharp pain between his eyes, actually, so he turned his thoughts to something else. The sun was beginning to rise over the sea. He watched it, then sighed. Some things never changed, thankfully.

He kept a careful eye on the guards he could see standing on the walls, then made his way up to the gates. He was stopped, which he expected, and his business demanded, which he also expected.

His announcement that he had a message for the lord of the keep from his brother was apparently enough to earn him a trip inside the gates. He could only hope the journey wouldn't end inside Artane's dungeon. He knew what that place felt like in the twenty-first century. He had no desire to experience it in all its medieval glory.

He held it together quite well, to his mind, until the moment he found himself standing in front of one of the hearths in the great hall. There was something profoundly strange about standing in his own home, the home he had lived in from the moment of his birth, yet knowing he was standing in the same spot eight hundred years before he'd been born. He was surrounded by guardsmen, which didn't surprise him. What he hadn't expected was to be facing the lord of Artane and feeling as though he were looking into a mirror.

That de Piaget ancestor was older than he was, substantially, but he carried himself like a young man. He was roughly the same age as Nicholas had been, so Stephen wondered if it might be Robin himself.

"Lord Robin," one of the guards said sternly, "this man here presented himself at the gates and said he had a message for you. Said he needed to deliver it himself." He handed over Stephen's sword. "He was carrying this."

Stephen watched Robin pull the sword halfway from the sheath, freeze briefly, then resheath the sword. Very well, so it couldn't be mistaken for anything but a modern sword. He'd had it made to his specifications by a man Ian MacLeod had recommended without reservation. Robin looked at it again, then handed it back to Stephen.

"Nice sword."

"Thank you, my lord Artane."

Robin lifted an eyebrow briefly. "I believe, lad, that you should follow me."

"But, my lord," said the guardsman, aghast.

"I believe, William," Robin drawled, "that I can handle this dangerous lad here for as long as it takes to cut his business from him. You may follow us to my solar and stand without. If I need aid, I'll call for you."

Stephen glanced at the guard and found himself the recipient of a lingering dark look. He doubted anything he could say would improve matters, so he kept his mouth shut, his hood close around his head, and followed Robin across the great hall.

It was, he had to admit, very, very strange.

Once they had reached Robin's solar, which was actually still the lord's solar in Stephen's time, and Robin had shut the door and bolted it, Stephen began to breathe a bit easier. He wasn't any less weary, though, and it took a fair amount of control not to simply sit down across from Robin when he cast himself down into a chair and looked up at Stephen casually. But he waited, because that was his grandfather, the usual number of generations removed sitting there, and he had been taught decent manners.

"Take off your cloak, lad, and let me have a look at you."

Stephen pulled his hood back, then took off his cloak completely. He watched Robin as he did so, wondering what the man's reaction would be.

Robin would have made an amazing poker player.

"Who are you?" Robin asked politely.

"Stephen, my lord."

Robin studied him. "And your father?"

"Edward, my lord," Stephen said. "The twenty-fourth Earl of Artane."

Robin rubbed his finger over his mouth, as if he strove not to smile. "Interesting. I assume you have a particular reason for presenting yourself at my hearth at such an early hour."

"For aid."

"Did your sire tear my poor hall to ruins?"

"Nay, some fool somewhere along the way gambled it away to the bastards from Kenneworth and the current duke has decided he'll call in the marker."

Or words to that effect.

Robin shook his head. "That Hubert of Kenneworth is a terrible pain in the arse. He's never been fond of us, but recently his ire has become unreasonable. Do you know he claims that one of my, ah . . . er—"

"Natural sons?" Stephen supplied gingerly.

Robin looked at him darkly. "Aye, one of those—the number of which is ridiculously inflated, I'll have you know. He claims that one of those lads gave him a right proper thrashing. He's vowed retribution."

Stephen cleared his throat. "I believe, my lord, that I might need to assume responsibility for that brief encounter."

Robin pursed his lips, but his eyes were twinkling. "I'm unsurprised. And not unhappy to know that one of my lads was behind the fray." He waved Stephen down into a seat. "Tell me of these troubles you're having."

Stephen sat, accepted a wonderful rich ale that he hoped would leave him sober, then told in as few words as possible what had happened with David.

"And have you seen proof of this . . . marker?" Robin asked.

"Yes," Stephen said, "a copy of it. My attorney agrees it is binding." He paused. "My lawyer, I mean."

"We have them, too," Robin said in disgust, "and I'm certain they cost just as much gold now as they do in your day." He studied Stephen. "You look like you haven't slept."

"I haven't," Stephen said. "I've been in a fair bit of haste."

"I'll find you a bed in a minute, but first satisfy my curiosity. Who do you know there in that Future of yours?"

Stephen sipped. "Zachary Smith and his wife, your daughter, who is expecting a child."

Robin almost dropped his ale. "Damnation, but I'll never accustom myself to this. Who else?"

"Your son Kendrick, his wife, and their six children." He looked at Robin. "Five are lads, just like him."

"And Nick's wife, Jennifer, is your brother Gideon's wife's sister," Robin said easily. "Is that right?"

Stephen blinked, then laughed a little. "Aye, my lord, that is right."

"You'll have to tell me the names of my grandsons," Robin said, "and the wee granddaughter. But later. Let's find you food first. I'll join you, for I have a full day's work still before me and need something strengthening."

Stephen followed Robin out of his solar, then happily helped himself to a substantial breakfast in Artane's kitchens, accompanied by Artane's lord who apparently wasn't above eating at the worktable whilst his staff went about the work of the day.

Stephen did his best to ignore the surreptitious looks he got.

"Are my clothes so poorly chosen?" Stephen asked finally.

"I daresay they think you're a relation," Robin said, looking amused. "And no doubt admiring your cheek to show yourself at my hall. I'll leave it to you to speculate on just who they think you might be."

Stephen felt his mouth fall open. "How awkward."

Robin snorted. "Not for you, I'd imagine, but 'tis damned awkward for me. Let's go find Anne and get introductions out of the way. I'll find you a bed and let you sleep for a pair of hours whilst I give your tangle a bit of thought." He slid Stephen a look. "Unless you had a solution already."

"I was thinking a hefty bag of gold stuffed behind a rock in a fireplace."

"Stephen, my lad, it would take more than one, I imagine." He rose with the ease of a man in his prime and picked up his sword. "We'll speak on it later, perhaps in the lists. You do know how to wield that sword, don't you?"

"Barely."

"Well, that's something we'll work on right away," Robin said with a grin that sent chills down Stephen's spine. "No sense in coming all this way and just putting your feet up, is there?"

"Nay, my lord," Stephen said. "There isn't."

The rest of the early morning was something of a blur. He met the lady of the house, slurred out a few details for her about her children who were living in a time not their own, then cast himself down on a bed before his eyes closed of their own accord.

It would take more than one, I imagine.

Robin had said those words and Stephen had to admit he agreed. He wasn't one to act precipitously, but he had perhaps been a bit hasty in his research the night before. He had looked through a list of heirs of Artane to see which one might have been stupid enough to put up the place as collateral for a game of chance. Finding none, he had fallen back on his original idea, which had been to seek out one of the first lords of Artane and convince them to set aside even a small bit of gold that Stephen might sell in the future and pay David Preston off.

It was obvious he was going to have to think of something else, though he honestly had no idea what that something might be.

Chapter 25

"I do believe there is something amiss, miss."

"Are they open for tourists today, do you think?"

Humphreys considered. "Not on a Sunday, Miss Alexander. And this has the feeling of something perhaps less than ideal."

Peaches agreed with Humphreys's assessment of the situation. Artane was, in her experience, a fairly busy place even with just those who came to staff it, but there was something odd about the way the cars in the car park were situated. She jumped out of the car the moment she could and left Humphreys to deal with the parking of Stephen's Mercedes. She ran up to the castle gates, which were wide open. For some reason that struck her as very unsettling somehow. Mrs. Gladstone was not manning her booth, of course, because it was Sunday, but for some reason the emptiness there only added to Peaches's unease.

She ran up the way toward the keep, then slowed to a stop as she came into the courtyard. She stared in horror at the emergency vehicles still there. The door of the ambulance was being shut there in front of her.

Her first thought was that something had happened to Stephen. She rushed over to stop one of the attendants and find out for sure. That wasn't difficult considering he was walking without haste to get back inside his truck.

"What happened?"

"His Lordship," the man said, then shook his head slowly.

Peaches felt her mouth fall open. "Lord *Edward*?"

The man ducked his head, as if he feared he'd said too much. He only looked at her briefly before he sidled by and escaped inside the cab of the ambulance.

Peaches ran past him and up the steps to the front door. She didn't knock, she simply opened it and walked inside. The first person she saw was Megan de Piaget chasing after her little girl. Megan caught sight of her, scooped up her daughter, and crossed the hall to her.

"Peaches," she said with feeling. "Where's Stephen?"

"I thought he was here," Peaches said. "What happened?"

Megan took a deep breath. "Lord Edward had a heart attack—"

"Did they already take him to the hospital?" Peaches asked in surprise. "Was that a second ambulance outside?"

Megan looked very pale. "But he's dead, Peaches. It was too much for him—oh, I thought you knew." She put her arm around Peaches and pulled her with her across the floor. "David Preston sent a lawyer this morning with a letter full of exactly what he told us last night. Apparently Lord Edward was so shocked, it—well, it was too much for him."

"I can't believe it," Peaches said hollowly. "How is Gideon—no, how is Lady Helen holding up?"

"Devastated, the both of them," Megan said. "Stephen was here sometime last night and left a note that he was going hiking and would be out of range for a bit. He doesn't know, and we can't figure out how to get hold of him."

Peaches sank down weakly into a chair in front of the hearth. She had had her suspicions before, of course, but held on to the hope that perhaps Stephen wouldn't actually do something crazy. Now, though, she was sure she knew where he'd gone. She looked at Megan and saw realization dawn in her eyes.

"You don't think," she began slowly. "Would he?"

"He would, and he did," Peaches said. "I'm sure of it."

"But why?" Megan asked in surprise. She let her little girl go and sat down in the chair next to Peaches. "What was he thinking?"

"He was looking for a way to save his father's hall." She paused. "His hall now, isn't it?" She looked at Megan. "That's difficult to think about, isn't it?"

Megan reached out and put her hand on Peaches's arm briefly. "I wouldn't think about it, if I were you. I think you're going to have your hands full just waiting for him to get back."

"Waiting?" Peaches said with a snort. "I'm not waiting."

"Peaches," Megan said in a low voice, "you can't mean to try to follow him."

"I'm not going to follow him. I'm going to go off and do my own thing."

"I don't think you should."

Peaches had to admit that same thought had occurred to her, but then again, she was in love with the heir to Artane. If she could help him, she would.

"I'm actually not quite sure where he went," she admitted. "Or when, rather. I looked through Stephen's library this morning to try to figure out what went on at the time Artane was gambled away. That was made much easier by the books Stephen had obviously looked through the night before."

"What did you find out?"

"That I need to look harder."

"And then what do you think you're going to do?" Megan asked in surprise. "Go back and change history? James Mac-Leod says it's catastrophic."

"I'm not changing," Peaches said. "I'm nudging. And I'm not doing anything until I figure out just where to nudge." She looked at Megan seriously. "Will they mind, do you think, if I go nose around in their library?"

"Of course not," Megan said, then she smiled gravely. "You should come say hello to Lady Helen first. She likes you a lot, and it would mean quite a bit to her."

Peaches considered. "She won't ask me any prying questions about Stephen's whereabouts, will she?"

"Peaches, my friend, if you're going to be married to a man who thinks nothing of hopping through time, you're going to have to learn to lie now and then. You might as well start now."

Peaches pursed her lips. "I don't suppose you're speaking from experience."

"Oh, no, not me," Megan said with a half laugh. "I just deal with ghosts. Gideon and I leave the time traveling to everyone else. Let's go find the current lady of the house."

Peaches sat for a couple of hours with Helen de Piaget, trying to offer what service and compassion she could. When Stephen's mother finally went to lie down, she slipped off and headed for Artane's library.

She had already spent her share of time looking through Stephen's offerings that morning, but he'd had no pre-Victorian or Victorian-era books out.

And for some reason, she just had a feeling that was the era she should be looking in.

After all, if a man was going to be a gambler and gamble away an entire estate, he would have to have buddies who were willing to put up the same sort of collateral. She thought perhaps it would have been possible at the turn of the twentieth century to find enough landed gents to play cards with, but to her mind it seemed more like something that might have been done during either the Victorian or Regency period.

She had wondered, now and again, if she might have had an unhealthy fascination with Jane Austen's world.

She hadn't been looking for very long, actually, before she stumbled upon a situation that was so perfectly matched to what she was looking for, she could hardly believe what she was reading. Lord Reginald de Piaget, Earl of Artane during the beginning of the nineteenth century, had been, from very brief and sketchy reports, a man interested in wagers.

That was one way to put it, she supposed. She reached for a book on the Kenneworths she had found after a good hunt and opened it to the same time period. The Duke of Kenneworth during the same time period, Lionel, had been as famous for a spectacular string of wins as he had been for the number of very exclusive mistresses he had kept.

Typical.

She supposed Lionel wasn't her man given that he was in the direct line, though he certainly would have been the easiest suspect. She sighed, then started to shut that book when she caught sight of his death date. Lionel had died fairly young, though Peaches found no indication of cause. Perhaps it was nothing more than the usual problem of bad water, bad hygiene, and a duel at dawn.

She shut the book slowly, then stared off unseeing into the fire. If Lionel had been the one to win the title to Artane in a card game, why hadn't he claimed it immediately? Or had he intended to just torment Reginald de Piaget for a bit before demanding Artane and the other properties entailed on the estate?

She frowned, because something didn't fit. If Lionel had died before he could claim his winnings, why hadn't his brother Piers trotted out the IOU? She supposed it was possible after the heir's death that Piers had been too busy running things to rifle through his brother's papers. Perhaps he had simply tossed everything that wasn't cash into a box and forgotten about it. But that didn't explain why Andrea Preston's father had had the deed and not David's father.

She opened the book back up, retraced her steps, then followed the line down from Lionel's grandfather—

And found that Lionel had had an infant son living when he'd died, which mean that Piers hadn't inherited the title, he'd simply held things together until the little lad had come of age and claimed his father's title.

Apparently, that son hadn't claimed all his father's papers. It was the only way Andrea Preston could have found the IOU in her father's things.

She memorized dates, names, and places, then shut the books. "Bingo," she murmured.

"Bingo?"

She almost fell off her chair. She recovered with difficulty, then turned around to see who was standing at the door.

It was, unfortunately, Zachary Smith, inveterate time-traveler, leaning casually against the doorjamb with his arms folded over his chest.

"Well, hello, my lord," she said with a bright smile. "How is Wyckham?"

"Almost finished," he said, "a fact for which I am profoundly grateful. How is the library?"

"Interesting, but I'm always interested in a good book." She rose and stood in front of her books on the off chance Zachary got any ideas about borrowing them. "It's nice to see you, Zach, but I gotta go."

"Do you gotta?" he asked, not moving. "Where?"

"Oh, just back to my room."

"Megan says you don't have a room yet."

Megan talks too much, Peaches thought, but she didn't say as much. She only restacked her books behind her back, then rubbed her hands together as she walked over to the door.

"I'm off to get one," she said. *In another century.* "How's Mary?"

"Feeling better, and you're changing the subject."

Peaches had been herded enough by de Piaget men and de Piaget men-by-marriage to know if she didn't push right on through Zachary Smith, she wouldn't get out the front door.

"It's not a very interesting subject and considering all the Regency delights I've been researching for Stephen, I know interesting. Now, if you'll excuse me, I'll go see if I can be useful." *Somewhere.*

Zachary didn't move. "I know where he went."

Peaches stuck her finger in her ear. "I'm not at all sure I know what you're talking about, but I do know I'm in a bit of a hurry. So, if you'll excuse me—"

"I would have done the same thing in his place," Zachary continued relentlessly, "and told the woman I loved, the woman I was leaving behind, to *stay* behind. I can't believe Stephen didn't do the same thing."

"Oh, he left me a little love note," Peaches said, wondering if it would be rude to just give Stephen's uncle a good shove. "Why don't you let me by and I'll go get it? You and Mary can reread it with me, and we'll all enjoy it again."

Zachary wasn't smiling. "I don't suppose it would do me any good to list for you all the perils associated with what you're contemplating."

"What?" she asked with the best laugh she could muster. "A trip downstairs to the kitchen?"

He wasn't laughing with her. "Peaches, this is nothing like a trip downstairs to the kitchen. The dangers are real and quite often fatal."

She put her shoulders back. "I know."

Zachary pursed his lips, then he reached down behind him and pulled up a very rustic-looking pack. "You should take this," he said. "You know, on that adventure you know all about."

She would have smiled, but she was too terrified to. "Are there snacks inside?" she managed.

"Beef jerky and pork rinds."

"You know, you aren't very funny."

"That's what your would-be lover says to me as well," Zachary said mildly, "but he blames it on too many adventures having warped me."

"Have they?"

He looked at her seriously. "The gate here is . . . turbulent, which is why I would hazard a guess Stephen told you very explicitly to stay behind and knit—"

"Read."

"Whatever." He blew out his breath. "You know, it's very difficult to know where he went, *and* the odds of you landing in the same place are very slim."

Peaches slung the pack over her shoulder and held the strap because she thought it might hide her trembling hands a bit better. "But it isn't impossible."

"Not entirely."

"That's enough," she said.

He shook his head slowly, smiling faintly. "Peaches Alexander, you are a formidable woman."

"No," she said, her mouth suddenly very dry. "I'm terrified."

"Good," he said without hesitation. "You should be. Do you have a knife?"

"Knife?"

He nodded at her shoulder. "In the pack. Stow it somewhere on your person where it can't be seen but can be reached. And be prepared to use it." He rolled his eyes. "I can't believe I'm saying any of this. You're absolutely crazy to go without at least some sort of training." He looked at her, hard. "Could you kill someone if you had to?"

She couldn't even nod.

"That's what I thought."

"He needs to know his father is gone," she managed, "and he needs to know what I just found out."

"You can tell him both when he gets back."

"It will be too late then," she said, starting to feel a little panicked. "David gave us seventy-two hours. We're already through almost twenty-four and look what that jerk has done.

Stephen needs to be looking in a different direction instead of—"

"Talking Robin de Piaget into hiding things in the wall?"

She blinked in surprise. "Why would you think that?"

"It's a long story," Zachary said with a smile, "having to do with some enterprising souls in James MacLeod's family. Keep going with what you were telling me. Stephen will think he's taking care of things, but then what?"

"He won't be looking in the right place."

"And you know the right place?"

"I know the right place," Peaches said, "and I think I'm close to the right person."

Zachary shifted. There was now room enough to escape if she'd wanted it, but now she had him listening and not lecturing, she supposed she could ask him for help.

"I need Regency-era clothes for both of us," she said. "I'll wear the medieval ones Humphreys dug up for me in Stephen's house for the first leg of the trip."

"You can't go today," Zachary said firmly. "It's too late."

"If I can get clothes together and be gone in an hour, I'll have plenty of time to get there before dark."

"Get where?" he asked politely. "I'm not sure you were clear about that before."

"Medieval Artane. Then Stephen and I will head to Regency-land and change history."

Zachary sighed, then rubbed his face. "It goes against my grain to send a woman through time unprotected."

"And just who am I going to take with me?" Peaches asked reasonably. "You, a father-to-be? John, a new husband? Kendrick, who might give his father a heart—" She shut her mouth before she finished the rest of that sentence. "I'll be fine. Just a little step in and a little step out and there I am at Artane."

"And if it's the wrong year?"

"I'll deal with it."

He looked at her seriously. "And if you can't?"

"Then I can't," she said.

He sighed. "I'll go look for costumes."

"Thank you, Zach."

"Thank me when you get back safely with that crazy man you're in love with."

"How do you know I'm in love with him?" she asked lightly.

"You wouldn't be contemplating this trip if you weren't."

Peaches smiled, though she thought it might have been a less successful smile than she would have wanted. She watched Zachary go, then made her way to Megan's room where her accomplice was waiting for her.

She would pack in a hurry, then be on her way.

And hopefully catch Stephen before he made decisions they both might come to regret.

Chapter 26

Stephen stood in the mud, shaking with weariness, and wondered what in the hell he'd been thinking to come anywhere near medieval Artane. Scotland was rugged, Ian MacLeod was fierce, and Claymores were heavy. But facing a grinning Robin of Artane—his grandfather several generations removed—and realizing that said grandfather was likely pushing sixty but had the energy of a twenty-year-old with no qualms about putting it constantly on display was terrifying.

He suspected he shouldn't admit how much he was enjoying it.

Indeed, the entire trip had been less unsettling than it should have been—no, actually, it was worse than that. He had relished every moment of it. It was everything he'd fascinated by for the entirety of his life on display in front of him, happening in real time. He had toyed with the idea of regretting not having brought even his phone to record what he was seeing, but decided almost immediately that there was something too magical about what he was experiencing to record it anywhere but in his memory.

Though he was, he had to admit, taking furious mental notes.

He did, however, regret having slept so long. He'd woken

from his nap to find it well into the afternoon and Robin still apparently mulling his alternatives. He'd eaten a decent meal, then been invited to bring his sword out to the lists and engage in a little diversion whilst Robin continued with his thinking. He had been somehow unsurprised to hear that Robin had already spent the bulk of his day there, exercising his garrison.

"So, tell me what sort of care you've taken of my hall there in that future of yours," Robin said, suddenly, looking far too energetic for Stephen's taste.

Stephen tried not to notice that Robin wasn't even breathing hard, damn him anyway. He would have tried to humor the man with tales of modern Artane, but found himself preoccupied by the task of remaining something besides a repository for Robin's very sharp sword.

The afternoon wore on slowly. Stephen was tremendously grateful when Robin paused in his attentions and looked to his left.

"That's a remarkably beautiful woman there," he said, again not sounding in the slightest bit out of breath.

Stephen cursed silently at his own inability to catch his breath, looked, then realized that looking was bad for two reasons. One, the split second he shifted his attention away from Robin, Robin caught the hilt of his sword with the tip of his own and flicked it out of Stephen's hands. It went arse over teakettle several times, flashing brightly in the late-afternoon sun an embarrassing number of times, before it landed point down in the mud. It quivered until Robin casually reached out and put his hand on it to still it.

Second, just looking over to his right and finding none other than Peaches Alexander standing at the edge of the lists in a cloak he certainly hadn't provided for her had caused him to lose what was left of his breath in a particularly abrupt way.

Robin came to stand next to him.

"She bears a strong resemblance to Persephone, my youngest brother's wife."

"That is likely because she's Persephone's older sister," Stephen wheezed.

"She's very different from her sister."

Stephen looked into gray eyes that were the mirror of his own. "You can tell that from a single look?"

Robin tapped the spot between his eyes. "My superior ability to judge a body with just a glance coming yet again to the fore. Henry's courtiers live in fear."

"I imagine they do."

Robin studied Peaches a bit longer. "What does she do?"

Stephen thought about all the things he could have said about that remarkable woman standing there looking slightly defiant. He was sure Robin would have managed to wrap his superior intellect around any and all of them, but to limit Peaches to what she could do was to sadly understate her gifts. She could organize, and change lives, and alchemy, and leave him unsettled and off-balance. But she could also see through all the noise and the trappings, find the dreams lying there, and help nurture them into reality. He had listened to Tess tell him stories of that for years, then seen the same thing for himself. He looked at her for another moment in silence, smiled briefly at her, then looked at his grandfather.

"She loves," he said simply.

Robin shot him a look of amusement. "Even a loser like you?"

Stephen smiled wryly. "You, my lord Artane, have spent far too much time learning a rather inappropriate amount of modern slang. And whilst I would certainly wish it, I hardly dare hope that she does."

"Perhaps you had best work on that whilst you have my glorious hall and superior larder at your disposal. I would give you my thoughts on wooing a woman of obviously very fine breeding and heart, but they would, I fear, be lost on you."

"You know," Stephen said thoughtfully, "I'm fairly certain John said almost the same thing to me several days ago."

"And where do you think John learned anything useful?" Robin asked archly. "From me, of course. I'm pleased to know that very soft life in the Future hasn't ruined his wits." He nodded toward Peaches. "Perhaps you'd best go welcome your lady properly before she decides someone else might be more to her liking than you."

Stephen thought that very good advice, so he fetched his sword, resheathed it, then made Robin a low bow before he walked off the field and over to where Peaches was standing in the company of several lads Stephen imagined were Robin's nephews. He started to speak to her, then froze.

There were two fair-haired young men there, twins, who were looking at him—or, rather, *not* looking at him with a purposefulness that for some reason struck him as very suspicious. They also looked a great deal like Nicholas of Wyckham, which made him even more suspicious.

He wondered, accompanied by a frown he couldn't help, if those had been the sons Nicholas had been traveling to that inn to meet. But that would have meant . . .

The thought of what that said about other members of his extended family traveling through time was just too much to consider at present. He promised himself a good grilling of the two later, then looked at Peaches and folded his arms over his chest.

"I am surprised to see you here," he said in his best medieval Norman French. Well, he lied it in his best medieval Norman French, because he wasn't at all surprised to see her there. But he supposed it was better to sound annoyed than accepting, on the off chance she ever thought to try another time gate on her own. "Surely you didn't think I needed a rescue."

She looked at him as if he'd lost his mind. "Of course not."

"Well," he said, feeling slightly more medieval than was likely good for him. "That's as it should be."

"Though I would have if you had needed it."

He blinked, then looked at that stunning, intelligent, courageous woman who could have just as easily stayed where he'd put her and waited for him to be about his business, and actually saw her. She wouldn't have, he was positive, risked her life and potentially his as well by coming to find him unless she'd had a very good reason.

He didn't, as he had said to Robin before, dare hope it was because she loved him.

He hardly dared touch her in his current condition, but one of the benefits of training like a fiend in the Middle Ages was it was so cold, the sweat was converted quite quickly to solid form. He pulled her into his arms and held her tightly.

"Forgive me," he whispered.

She was holding on to him as though she were rather happy to see him, all things considered. "For what? The medieval barbarian response?"

He laughed a little and pulled back only far enough to look her in the eye. "That, too."

She leaned up and kissed him briefly. "Forgiven."

Stephen would have thanked her properly for that, but he was distracted by the conversation that had started up next to Peaches.

"Oh, so that's how it is," a voice said knowingly.

"What a surprise," another voice said dryly.

Stephen looked over Peaches's head at the twins, then singled out the one on the right for further scrutiny. "Have we met?"

"Theophilus de Piaget," the blond said, grinning. "And this is my less handsome, less intelligent but far more mischievous brother, Samuel."

Samuel made Stephen a low bow. "At your service, always. Now, who are you again?"

"Stephen," Stephen said, imagining the less he said, the better.

"Stephen of where?" Samuel asked innocently. "Somewhere near here, perhaps? Are you a relative? You look so much like Phillip, I daresay you could be bro—"

Theophilus slapped the back of his brother's head sharply. "He looks like no one," he finished, shooting his brother a warning look. "No one we would know, surely." He looked at Stephen and made his own low bow. "My lord, I believe your lady looks cold. Why don't I escort her inside and leave you to your torture—I mean, *exercises* out here with Uncle Robin?"

Stephen looked at Peaches and studied her for a moment or two. Whilst she seemed happy to see him, surely that wouldn't have been enough to induce her to risk traveling through time. There was something else afoot, something that he could see in her face was rather more serious than he might have wished it to be. He glanced at Theophilus. "Why don't you retreat a safe distance away from my sword and let me have speech with my lady first?"

"'Tis probably just as well, Theo," said Samuel with a look thrown his twin's way that Stephen couldn't quite decipher. "Undue scrutiny and all."

"From Uncle Robin, of course," Theophilus said, returning his brother's look.

"Who else?" Samuel asked politely.

Who, indeed? Stephen didn't know, didn't want to know, and didn't bother to ask. He simply waited until the twins had retreated a discreet distance before he looked at Peaches again.

"What happened?" he asked in a low voice. "Did you find something?"

She nodded. "I read what you had left open in your library in Cambridge, but I couldn't get over thinking that there had to be more to it than met the eye."

"And what did you discover?" he asked warily.

"That one of your more recent ancestors was a keen gambler and his contemporary at Kenneworth was, it would seem, a very skilled cheat." She smiled faintly. "It's a good thing I've been researching all that Regency history."

Stephen groaned. "Why do I think this means I'm going to be going somewhere else and mincing about in heels?"

"Because we're having this discussion in medieval England, in the freezing cold, and neither of us thinks it's weird. I left a suitcase full of Regency gear hidden behind a rock."

He smiled. "You're a wonder."

She wasn't smiling, though. He found that her seriousness had quickly become his.

"There's something else," he said, looking at her in surprise. "Isn't there?"

She started to speak, then looked to his right. Robin had come to stand next to him. Stephen introduced them to each other, then watched Peaches's face as she and Robin chatted very briefly. The chill that ran down his spine when she turned to look at him was very unpleasant.

"What is it?" he asked hoarsely.

She put her hands on his arms he hadn't realized he'd crossed over his chest again. "It's your father."

He blinked. That surprised him, for his father had been in perfectly good health when he'd seen him the week before. "Did he have an accident?"

She shook her head slowly. "He had a heart attack."

"Well, what have they done for him?" Stephen demanded. "Is he in hospital . . . or . . ." He stopped speaking because he saw the answer in her face. He knew he had swayed only because Robin's hand was suddenly on his shoulder, grasping him with such strength that he winced. He took a deep breath and looked at Peaches. "He's gone, isn't he?"

Her eyes were full of tears. "Stephen, I'm so sorry."

Stephen shook his head, because he couldn't imagine it. "But he was fine last weekend. I talked to him yesterday morning and he was well." He looked at her bleakly. "I don't understand."

She hesitated.

"Was it an accident, or . . ."

"He had a letter from the Duke of Kenneworth."

Stephen felt as if he'd run into a brick wall. "I'm going to kill him." He shook off Robin's restraining hand. "I am going to kill David Preston with my bare hands—"

"Nay, you are not," Robin said firmly. "Hand your sword to your lady, lad, and we'll have a run. And you'll come back to your senses before you do something stupid to whichever whoreson this David Preston happens to be."

"His mother is a very lovely woman," Stephen managed.

"I'm sure his father's mother wasn't," Robin said shortly. "Hand over your sword, boy, and let's start before Anne sends out torches to light the way."

Stephen fumbled with the buckle but his hands were shaking too badly to be of any use. Peaches unbuckled the leather belt for him, then put her arms around his neck and held him tightly for a brief moment. She kissed his cheek quickly, then stepped back and took his sword from him. Then she simply looked at him, her eyes full of the anguish he supposed she was seeing on his face. He took a deep breath, then looked at Robin, who had propped his sword up against a stone seat. Robin only nodded at the twins.

"See Mistress Peaches inside, lads, and introduce her to the lady Anne. Remember that she's Persephone's sister, though I'm not sure how you could forget. We'll join you in my solar in a bit."

The lads made polite conversation with Peaches as they started to lead her off. She looked over her shoulder only once. Stephen looked at her, because he simply couldn't manage anything more than that. He waited until he couldn't see her any longer before he turned to Robin.

"I'm ready."

"Do you do this in your day?"

"Actually, I do."

"You probably get the urge from me," Robin said seriously. "Don't let yourself go to fat, lad, there in that soft life of yours. Running will keep your wits sharp and your body strong. And it is very useful in stopping yourself from doing something stupid until your head has cleared."

Stephen had to agree that was very good advice, but he did so silently. He also ran with Robin around the perimeter of the lists until he thought he would either pass out from exhaustion or manage to speak without weeping. It was at that precise moment that Robin stopped, leaned over with his hands on his thighs for a moment until he caught his breath, then straightened and looked at Stephen.

"I used to be able to run farther," he said with a grimace.

"Well, you've run me into the ground."

"You're soft," Robin said, clapping him on the shoulder. He looked at him gravely. "And you're now lord of Artane, my lad. All the more reason to save it for your sons, wouldn't you agree?"

Stephen nodded wearily. "I do agree."

"I take it your lady has brought you tidings pertinent to your business?"

"She has," Stephen said, "in spite of the fact that I told her to stay home."

Robin patted him on the back and smiled pleasantly. "That's the sort of wench to have, if you ask me. But never let them forget who is lord." He paused. "I will admit after all these years that that is slightly more difficult than I anticipated it would be."

Stephen didn't doubt it. He walked with Robin back to the house, contemplating the absolute improbability that he was now on equal if not rather uncomfortable footing with the man next to him. It was a pity that had to come at the expense of his father's life.

He had a wash, then found himself escorted to the lord's solar where the door opened for him. He went inside, not exactly sure what he would find.

Peaches was sitting there next to the hearth with the firelight playing against her dark hair. She looked up at him.

And she smiled gravely.

He shut the door with his foot, then strode over to her and pulled her up and into his arms. He found that it was quite some time before he even dared attempt speech. He wasn't one to weep, indeed he couldn't remember the last time he'd indulged in tears, but he was damned close to it at present. But since grief was nothing more than a distraction from the task before him, he settled for a handful of careful breaths before he finally loosened his embrace and looked at Peaches.

"Where are the lord and lady of the house?" he asked, ignoring the hoarseness he could hear in his own voice.

"Off seeing to supper," Peaches said, "though I imagine that was just an excuse to give us privacy." She looked up at him. "They're very kind to loan us their solar."

"It beats the bloody hell out of the dungeon," Stephen said with feeling.

She smiled a half smile. "I imagine it does." She pulled away but kept hold of his hand. "Come sit by the fire, my lord. Your hands are cold."

He made himself at home in a chair he wasn't sure didn't currently find itself in a glass case on the second floor in modern Artane, then pulled Peaches down onto his lap. He held her in front of that roaring fire for several minutes in silence except for the crackling and popping of the wood in the hearth. When he thought he could manage it, he sighed deeply.

"What a day," he managed.

She lifted her head from his shoulder and looked at him. "Stephen, I'm sorry about your father."

He smoothed his hand over her hair, carefully avoiding any tangles. "How is my mother?"

"Devastated, as you might expect." She shrugged slightly. "Gideon and Megan are there, along with Zachary and Mary. Of course they knew where you had gone, and Zachary sent me along after you."

"I'll kill him."

"He gave me a very long lecture beforehand, which I think he thought would deter me," she continued, shooting him a chiding look. "I told your mother I was going to look for you, that I was fairly sure where you'd gone." She paused. "She would, I'm sure, prefer to see you sooner rather than later."

"I'd rather it be sooner, to tell the truth." He took a deep breath. "Tell me why I shouldn't go back home and kill Preston right now."

"Because they'll throw you in jail for murder," Peaches said reasonably.

"I could lure him back to another century, then kill him," Stephen muttered, half under his breath.

She smiled very faintly. "James MacLeod most definitely wouldn't approve."

"I wouldn't tell him."

"He would know."

He dragged his free hand through his hair. "Unfortunately, I imagine he likely would. So, what did you discover? I take it you read what I'd read."

"That, and I spent some time in your father's library. The nineteenth Earl of Artane, Reginald, was a bit of a gambler."

"Wonderful," Stephen said heavily. "So, you think he might have bet the farm and lost it?"

She shrugged helplessly. "It's only a guess, but the situation with the Prestons makes me wonder if Reggie might be our man. His contemporary, Lionel, died while his son was a baby, leaving his brother in charge for some time. The son eventually grew up and took the title, but it makes me wonder if with all that time with the keys to the cabinet, as it were, Uncle Piers managed to appropriate a few things he thought might not be missed. He died shortly after turning over things to his nephew, leaving his heirs perhaps not knowing what they had hidden in his effects."

"Which would explain why Andrea's father had the deed," Stephen said with a deep sigh.

"That's what I was thinking." She paused. "It's just a hunch."

Stephen imagined it was a very good hunch, one that he would willingly follow, even if it meant wearing heels and short pants.

"And I'm not sure how we can change things," she continued, "without changing too much."

"Perhaps we could just change the outcome of the game and leave everything else alone," he said thoughtfully.

She nodded. "I suppose so."

"Was it cards or swords?"

"Cards," she said, "I think."

"Thank heavens," he said with feeling. "At least it wasn't pistols at dawn."

Peaches frowned at him. "Have you ever *played* poker, Stephen?"

"How do you think I began my collection of first editions whilst at Eton?" he asked archly.

She smiled. "With ill-gotten gains?"

"They were very well gotten, darling, though I never thought the skill would come in handy after school." He rubbed his hands over his face. "I should have brought something on the history of card games and betting during the early nineteenth century."

He looked up to find her holding out a book to him. He took it, read the title, then looked at her and smiled.

"Thank you."

"You're welcome."

"I'm still going to shout at you for coming back here."

"No, you're not," she said, sounding not at all intimidated. "Well, I suppose you can try, but I won't be standing there to listen."

He imagined she wouldn't be. He sighed. "I want you to go home."

"I'm sure you do."

He smoothed her hair back from her face. "I truly do not want you coming with me, love," he said quietly, "though I suppose that is safer than trying to send you home by yourself."

"I think so," she agreed. "And for all you know, you might need me there."

"I certainly hope not," he said, "and that isn't because I don't want you near me." He shook his head and swore briefly. "This is the very last time we do this. The stress is about to do me in."

"Don't let it," she said very quietly.

He gathered her close again and simply held her until he felt his heart begin to beat less fiercely and the tension had left her. He rubbed his hand over her back absently.

"Thank you," he said quietly. "For coming to tell me. I know that isn't the only reason, but if it had to be told, I would rather have heard it from you." He paused. "I'm sorry not to be there for my mother."

"You couldn't have known, which she understands. Kendrick was on his way when I left, so I imagine he and Gideon will keep her busy enough until you get home."

He considered for a moment or two. "Should I tell her the truth?"

"That you traipsed through time to save your hall?" she asked, lifting her head to look at him. "It might make her feel better, and I don't think it will surprise her. When I told her I was going off to find you, she gave me a look."

"What sort of look?"

"The look a woman gives another woman when she knows the second woman is lying. She also promised me she would hold it together until you were home and told me to tell you as much."

He smiled in spite of himself. "Then we'll hurry."

"Do you think it's possible to land in the right time?"

"If we're going to be wearing Regency gear, we had better hope so." He leaned forward and kissed her softly. "You look tired. Beautiful, but tired. Let me feed you and we'll at least sleep for a few hours before we press on. I think I would like an hour or so to beat some details out of those blond-headed twins."

She smiled. "Think they bought us lunch?"

"I know they bought us lunch, which means they gave us that map, which means they've been poking around in their father's things and learning all kinds of un-medieval details. I believe I should tell them that following in their uncle John's footsteps would be ill-advised."

"Because he's unhappy?" she asked gravely.

"Because the thought of two medieval teenagers on the road in modern-day England is terrifying," he said with a snort. "John is tremendously happy which would only add to the allure of a century those brats don't belong in. As for us, let's go find our hosts and see if we can beg dinner."

She rose, then looked at him gravely. "I'm so sorry, Stephen, about it all."

He sighed deeply and pulled her close again. "I won't commit murder, but if I can find a way to humiliate that—" He had to take a deep breath. "The illustrious Duke of Kenneworth will think twice about opening his bloody big mouth again."

"One could hope," she said quietly.

He kissed her forehead, because it was safer that way, then put his arm around her shoulders and pulled her with him to go find the current lord and ask for something to eat.

Chapter 27

Peaches sat at the lord's table in the great hall of Artane and looked up at the ceiling. It was the same hall she'd walked through a dozen times when she'd been mourning over her sister, then when she'd come to Artane to look for Stephen. That she should be sitting in the medieval incarnation of it, next to its future lord, should not have been all that strange.

Though she had to admit it was.

She looked at Stephen, who was sitting next to her simply leaning back in his chair and watching her with a small smile.

"What?" she asked.

He only shook his head. "I'm just happy to have you here."

"Are you?"

"In spite of everything, yes, I am."

Robin leaned around his wife and looked at them. "And I'm happy to have you both here."

Peaches looked at him, feeling slightly puzzled over that. She could imagine why he would want to see Stephen, but she had no claim on anything that belonged to either the keep or him. He was looking at her, however, with a serious twinkle in his eye. She had heard from Mary in casual conversation one long afternoon spent walking on the beach that her father had been a terrible tease. Peaches couldn't imagine what he had to tease either her or Stephen about, but judging by the look in his eye, he'd found something.

"We appreciate your hospitality," Stephen said, looking at Robin with an expression Peaches understood completely. "How lovely of you to entertain us."

"Entertainment," Robin said, snapping his fingers as if he'd just remembered something he'd forgotten. "Or, even more interesting, nuptials."

"Robin," Anne warned.

He ignored his wife and smiled brightly. "You know, it's been a bit since we had a wedding, and I don't think you two should be traveling together unwed or unchaperoned."

Peaches felt her mouth fall open. "A wedding?"

"Don't like him, eh?" Robin asked with a knowing wink.

"Robin," Anne said with a long-suffering sigh, "stop poking at them."

"I'm not poking at them, I'm looking out for their future safety and welfare. Besides, I was robbed of two weddings that I can think of and others I will be too dead to know about. This is the least they can do to soothe my injured pride."

Peaches felt Stephen grope for her hand under the table.

"My lord," he began slowly, "I haven't even begun to woo her—"

"No time like after the wedding to begin." He handed Stephen something. "There's a start for you. No need to thank me."

Peaches looked at the very lovely, very medieval looking gold band lying on Stephen's open palm, then she looked at him. He looked at Robin for a moment or two in silence, then turned to her. He smiled at her, that gravely polite smile she loved.

"Well?" he asked quietly.

"Oh, by the saints," Robin exclaimed. "Is that the best you can do?" He looked at his wife. "I fear for the continuation of my line, truly I do."

Peaches watched Stephen shoot him a dark look, which she thought was rather brave, given the circumstances. She'd seen Robin in the lists. Then Stephen looked at her.

"You know this isn't exactly how I planned on seeing this happen."

She couldn't help herself; she laughed. The last thing she had thought she would be doing in medieval Artane was getting married, but somehow it seemed fitting. She smiled at her yet-to-be-made fiancé. "Well, I don't require all that much wooing."

"That's fortunate, because you'll have about fifteen minutes of it," he said dryly. "But I could remedy that over the course of the rest of our lives."

She looked at him seriously. "You know that your grandmother wouldn't approve, don't you?"

"Granny isn't around to offer an opinion. And she's my mother's mother." He nodded toward Robin. "He likes you, and he has a sword to use in expressing potential disapproval."

Peaches felt her smile fade. "And when your grandmother finds out?"

He leaned close and put his mouth against her ear. "I am the Earl of Artane, my love," he murmured, "and I don't give a damn what my grandmother says. If she could remove her nose from her guest lists long enough to see the truth of it, she would see that Artane could not have a finer mistress." He pulled back and looked at her. "Well?"

She saw Robin watching her with a smile and thought that maybe Stephen's grandmother could perhaps learn to deal with things. She looked at Stephen. "I believe I would consider listening to a proposal of marriage."

Stephen pursed his lips. "My lord Artane has been a bad influence on you."

"I'm afraid so."

She watched as he pushed his chair back, stood, then made Robin and Anne a low bow. "My lady's father is unavailable," he said seriously. "So, if you wouldn't mind—"

"Of course I wouldn't mind," Robin said. "I'll happily stand in for her sire. I'll dower her properly, of course, but what of you, little lad? What do you bring to this union? A little hut on the shore? A silver coin or two?"

Peaches laughed in spite of herself at the look Stephen gave Robin. Robin only returned that look blandly.

"Very well, I can divine that on my own." Robin waved expansively. "Go ahead and ask her, lad. If she says you aye, I'll have the priest fetched."

Peaches watched Stephen go down on one knee in front of

her right there at the supper table and found that what had seemed like a potentially amusing story to tell her sister had suddenly become all too real. She found that she was shaking, badly. Stephen looked up at her, his own expression very serious.

"I know what you're thinking."

She nodded. "I imagine you do."

He looked at her hands, then met her eyes. "And if it were instead in a little vineyard on a hill in Tuscany, what would you say?"

"Yes."

"Could you just pretend, then?"

Peaches looked around her at a hall that was nothing short of magnificent, a hall that had stood for eight hundred years, protected and defended by generations of de Piaget men and women who had been completely committed to preserving their family's heritage. She looked at Robin and Anne, who were sitting close together behind Stephen. Robin's arms were around his wife, his cheek against her silvery blonde hair, his expression grave. Anne was watching her with a look that said she understood exactly what Peaches was thinking.

Peaches looked at Stephen again. "I don't think any of your other girlfriends would appreciate your hall."

"But you would."

"I would," she agreed, finding it necessary all of the sudden to blink a time or two to keep her tears where they belonged. "Is it midnight?"

He smiled. "Somewhere."

She took a deep breath. "Then yes. And yes again." She paused. "In case we need to do this at a different time."

He stood up, then pulled her up and into his arms. And then he exercised his lordly prerogative and kissed her thoroughly.

"Ring!"

Peaches heard Robin bellow the word, but it took a moment or two before what he'd said registered. She smiled at Stephen as he put the ring on her finger, then pulled her back into his arms.

"Oh, there'll be none of that yet," Robin said, shoving back his chair and rubbing his hands together. "We need to fetch the priest and tromp out to the chapel. You don't think I'm going to allow you to wed her right here at the table, do you? And you, my lad, should probably go have a wash."

Stephen looked at Robin in surprise. "I already did."

"Go have another."

Stephen opened his mouth, considered, then shut it. "As you will, my lord."

"Ah, deference," Robin said, sounding supremely satisfied. "Let's go find candles and torches. And have a very short ceremony."

Two hours later, Peaches sat in front of a fire in a guest chamber that had been filled with candles, delicate edibles, and her newly made husband.

She was, she had to admit, very glad to be sitting down.

Stephen had locked the door, settled her comfortably in front of the fire, then paced until he finally came to a stop in front of her.

"This is my room."

She looked up at him in surprise. "In the twenty-first century?"

He nodded, then rubbed his hands over his face. "I wish I drank."

"No, you don't." She smiled up at him. "Are you flipped out?"

He looked at her suddenly, then smiled. "I probably should be, but somehow I'm not." He walked over to her, pulled up a stool, and sat down in front of her. He took her hands and looked at her seriously. "This isn't exactly how I envisioned our wedding proceeding."

"Well, the chapel was lovely," she said philosophically. "And the guests were still family, in a manner of speaking."

"The chapel is still lovely eight hundred years from now," he said, "but we would have had more age-appropriate family surrounding us. Though I'm not sure the lighting would have been any better."

"I think candlelight is very romantic," she said.

"Which is fortunate," he said, "given that since none of my forbearers has dared install electricity, we would have enjoyed the same in our day."

"Then what's the difference?" she asked with a shrug. "Great food, family, a fire in the fireplace—"

"A wedding gown befitting your beauty, photographers, my mother and brother, your sister and her husband?" He brought her hands to his mouth and kissed them. "A carriage drawn by horses to drive us to a Rolls waiting to whisk us to the airport for a flight to Paris for a honeymoon?"

"Nah," she said with a smile, "I'd rather rough it here in medieval England."

He smiled, apparently in spite of himself. "You realize we'll have to do it all again for everyone else when we return home."

"Do you mind?" she asked wistfully. "If this time is just for us?"

"Peaches, darling, I wouldn't mind if the rest of our lives were just for us," he said seriously. "But given that they won't be, no, I don't mind. I wouldn't have it any other way." He smiled that brief, grave smile that she had come to love. "You, here with me, in this fairy-tale castle on the shore. And a honeymoon in Regency England to look forward to. I can perfectly understand why you're thrilled with the entire scheme."

She laughed and reached out to put her arms around his neck. "You can keep Paris in the back of your mind for the next honeymoon if you want to."

"I believe I shall. And whilst I would never admit this to anyone but you, I would be thoroughly delighted to have you and an endless supply of decently prepared French cuisine in the same locale for an extended period of time."

She sighed. "Salads with exquisite dressings."

"Filet mignon and foie gras."

Well, there were obviously just some things they would have to agree to disagree on. But before she could start a list of those sorts of things for him, he kissed her, which left her unable to think about anything but the man who had pulled her up and into his arms who had gone to unbelievable lengths already to rescue her, their home, and their future.

And for the rest of the night, she supposed that was enough.

Chapter 28

Stephen stood in the hallway of Artane's upper floor in a time definitely not his own and wondered just how in the hell it was he was going to rid himself of the body he was holding under the arms. He looked at Peaches and nodded at the door she was standing in front of.

"We'll put him in there."

She nodded and opened the bedroom door—his bedroom door, as it happened, which was just as unsettling as it had been six hundred years earlier in Robin de Piaget's time—then held it open whilst he dragged an unconscious Regency wastrel inside. That wastrel happened to be his grandfather a few generations removed, which was the only reason Stephen hadn't already dropped him on his fool head. Peaches shut the door, then lit a lamp with the help of a match. She turned and looked at him.

"I suppose that was one way to do it," she said cheerfully.

He had to admit it had been. They had arrived in Regency Artane just as the sun was setting and managed to blend into the crowd that was making its way up the path to the great hall. Stephen would have thought he'd stumbled onto a period piece

set if it hadn't been for the all-too-real smell from the stables
and the guests alike.

Things had gone fairly well until he'd come face-to-face with
Reginald de Piaget, current earl of Artane, and realized that he
probably should have aimed for a party where the guests had
been wearing masks. Reginald goggled, gurgled, then patted
himself to look for something Stephen decided abruptly
wouldn't be in their best interests for him to find. His and Peaches's best interests, that was. He had grasped Reginald firmly by
the arm and smiled pleasantly.

"I wouldn't," he had advised.

Reginald had ripped his arm away. "I'll have your name, sir,
or you will face me over pistols at dawn!"

"Oh, let's avoid that," Stephen had demurred. "Why don't
you instead divulge a few details about the current lord of Kenneworth you're about to face over cards with nothing left to wager but your ancestral hall and all its entailed properties?"

Reginald de Piaget, that very keen gambler, had blanched,
then opened his mouth with what Stephen had seen was the intention to call for aid. That had resulted in a trip upstairs,
Peaches creating a diversion by getting something in her eye,
and Stephen using Patrick MacLeod's favorite heel-of-hand-
under-chin technique to render the other man blissfully unconscious.

All of which left him now looking at his hapless progenitor
lying on the floor, drooling prodigiously.

"What an idiot," he muttered.

"You really want to just tie him up?"

Stephen shrugged. "I am at a loss for any other solution."

"Oh, I fully agree with it," she said, studying Reginald de
Piaget, who was lying unconscious at her feet. "I'm just wondering where we'll put him once we've got him swaddled."

"We'll gag him and shove him under the bed. But I'll need
his cravat first. He seems to favor that truly revolting color of
green."

Peaches looked at him, then came to put her arms around
him. "Stephen . . ." She shook her head and held him tightly. "If
any of your students could see you now, they would be impressed."

"Because I managed to clunk my hapless grandfather from

the past on the head and drag him down the hallway? Into my own room again, which I will tell you this time is causing me a rather substantial bit of discomfort. Though at least I know my way around, if you know what I'm getting at."

She considered, then glanced at Reginald. "How hard did you hit him?"

"Very."

"Then we'd better take advantage of that—and no, not for anything more than removing his cravat and jacket."

"I thought you wanted to honeymoon in Regency England."

She laughed and pulled away. "I did but that was before we got here and I started not being able to breathe normally. Let's hurry before we're stuck here permanently."

He had to agree that was something he had no stomach for, so he set to the task of compromising part of his grandfather's modesty. He removed Reginald's coat, shirt, and cravat, then put them on. He stood still whilst Peaches adjusted the bile-green cravat, then looked at her.

"What do you think?"

"I think you're gorgeous," she said. "Even in that color, which is truly disgusting. I don't think anyone will be able to tell the difference between you and your drooling grandfather there. Now, let go of me. You should be using your time to review your gambling strategies."

"I reviewed them last night," he said, drawing her back into his arms. "The time change and all that." He looked at her solemnly. "It kept me awake."

"That wasn't all that kept you awake."

"Now that you mention it, no, it wasn't—"

She laughed, sounding a little breathless. "Stephen de Piaget, you're a rake."

"It's the bilious cravat," he said, praying he wasn't going to bring home lice thanks to putting it on. "It's making me reckless."

She pursed her lips. "Yes, I'm sure that's it." She looked at him, then shivered. "Please let's have this over with, really. I'm ready to go home."

He sighed deeply, then held her close for several minutes in silence.

"Thank you for marrying me," he said finally.

"Really?"

He nodded. "Yes, really." He held her for another very long moment, then stepped back reluctantly. "Let's go see to this so I have a home to take you to. Though I will tell you I'm finding it very difficult to concentrate on the task at hand." He smiled at her. "You're very distracting in your Regency garb."

"Shall I tell you tales about David Preston to inspire you?" she asked lightly.

He pursed his lips. "I think that might have done it right there, darling. Let's see to Reggie, then I'll go put the game into motion."

"I'll go mingle."

He looked at her seriously. "Be ready to run, Peaches."

"Do you think we'll need to?"

"At this point, love, I wouldn't be surprised by anything."

She leaned up on her toes and kissed him briefly. "Play well."

"Stay within reach."

She looked up at him seriously. "That is the place I would like to be for the rest of my life."

He hugged her quickly, then let her go before he either sobbed like a babe or told her he'd changed his mind about trying to save his hall and they would just have to move to Italy and work on growing olives. He exchanged one last look with her before she slipped out the door and he turned to the first task of the night, which was to get his ancestor out of sight.

He only hoped the rest of the night's activities would be so easily accomplished.

It was sunrise when he stumbled with Peaches up toward Artane's gates. Modern Artane's gates, his father's gates—

Only they weren't his father's gates any longer. They were his gates.

"Are you okay?"

He looked at his wife of eight hundred years and smiled wearily. She was wearing her Regency clothes with a backpack over her shoulders, looking as if she'd spent the night rolling in the mud. He was also wearing Regency clothes, but instead of a backpack, he was carrying a sword. But he suspected he also looked like he'd spent the night rolling in the mud.

Which was exactly what they'd been doing.

"I'm numb," he admitted, "from cold, terror, and lack of food." He shook his head slowly. "If we'd had to eat any more of that slop Reggie was serving, I would have lain down right there at the card table and surrendered."

She smiled up at him, a bit of dirt on her cheek flaking off as she did so. "I would say indigestion was what turned the tide in that very dodgy game—Lionel of Kenneworth suddenly coming down with food poisoning, I mean—but I think he would have feigned stomach trouble just the same to get out with his pride intact simply because you'd outcheated him."

"I didn't cheat," Stephen said archly.

"Liar."

He looked at her, then smiled in spite of himself. "Very well, I didn't see any reason not to use his own ploys against him. But I'll have you know and want it remembered for future generations that all the sterling I won at cards during my Eton years was won fairly."

"Just Eton?" she asked politely. "Not at Cambridge?"

"I have an extensive collection of first editions," he admitted. "You don't think I would spend *my* money on them, do you?"

She smiled, then her smile faded. "You didn't answer the question I was really asking." She nodded toward the castle. "Are you okay?"

He took a deep breath, then nodded. "I will be."

"Do you want me to catch a train—"

He started to make an offhand comment, then realized she was serious. "Of course not," he said in surprise.

"But, Stephen, this is a really personal—"

"Peaches, darling, we've spent the past two days being really personal. And I spent days and days and days before then wishing that there was some way I could convince you to become very personal with me." He stopped and looked down at her seriously. "I will hold my mother because I am her son, and I love her. But I want you there as well. Unless, of course," he added slowly, "it would make you uncomfortable."

She shook her head. "No, it won't. I'll stay, if you like."

He studied her for a moment or two. "How long do you think it will take, my lady, before we don't tiptoe around each other anymore?"

"I think you'll need to date me a few times," she said solemnly. "And scare up some of that wooing you keep promising me."

He drew her into his arms, held her for a moment in silence, then pulled back and kissed her briefly. "We'll attend to what we must here first, then I'll see if we can't indulge in a bit of the other. Will that suit?"

She turned to look at Artane sitting there in front of them, waiting. She took a deep breath, then nodded. He took her hand, then walked with her through his gates.

He nodded as they passed Mrs. Gladstone, who was at her post very early, wearing black. He almost continued on, then he stopped and poked his head into her booth.

"Good morning, Mrs. Gladstone," he said politely.

"Good morning, Lord Stephen," she said seriously. "I'm very sorry about your father."

"Thank you," he said simply, because he'd had two days to reconcile himself to the reality of what he would face when he returned home. "I am extremely grieved that I wasn't here."

She seemed to consider her next words carefully. "There've been those from Kenneworth nosing about," she said with a frown. "Don't much care for them."

"Well, I'll see to that for us."

"I hope you will, my lord."

Stephen nodded, then took Peaches's hand again and started up the long path toward his father's—

He had to take another deep breath. No, it wasn't his father's hall any longer. It was his hall. He looked at Peaches.

"They haven't had the funeral yet," he said, intending that it come out as a statement of fact.

"They wouldn't have," she said in a low voice. "Too many people know where you went to allow it."

He nodded. "We might have to tell my mother."

"Probably."

"But not your parents."

She smiled. "They would just congratulate us on a good trip and go back to their cannabis-laced brownies. I'm not sure it's worth the phone call."

He looked at her seriously. "I won't be that sort of father."

"It's one of the reasons I married you, my lord."

He stopped and started to turn her toward him when he caught a movement out of the corner of his eye.

He uttered an obscenity.

It was his grandmother, striding toward him with a purpose. His first instinct was to pull Peaches behind him, but he chalked that up to too much time spent in the past. Instead, he kept hold of Peaches's hand in spite of her efforts to pull it away.

Lady Louise Heydon-Brooke of Chattam Hall came to an abrupt halt in front of him and looked at him down her aristocratic nose—which was no mean feat considering she was a foot shorter than he was.

"Where," she said crisply, "in the bloody hell have you been, Stephen? Camping? With this *girl*?" She wrinkled her nose. "You smell terrible."

"Thank you, Grandmother," Stephen said politely. "Now, if you'll excuse us, my lady and I are on our way to the hall where we will make ourselves presentable and take up the duties awaiting us there."

"Let go of her, Stephen."

Stephen felt Peaches's eyes on him. He definitely felt his grandmother boring a hole into his head with her gaze. He looked at his wife, lifted a single eyebrow, then turned to his grandmother.

"I was hoping to ease you into this, Grandmother," he said evenly, "because I love you dearly. You have been a constant in my life, guiding me through the sometimes thorny paths I've trod thanks to my station in life."

His grandmother paled. "Don't tell me."

Stephen looked at Peaches again, but she was only watching him solemnly, as if she were silently telling him to do whatever he thought best. Actually, he knew that's what she was thinking because they'd had long conversations about many things whilst hiding in the beach grass, trying to avoid being killed by not only lads from Kenneworth but Reginald de Piaget's footmen. He took a calm, measured breath, then looked back at his grandmother.

"I won't spread this about. In fact, in order to show you the place that you have had in my life and will continue to have in my life and the lives of my wife and children, I will share a detail that only you will know."

"I need a brandy."

"Later," Stephen said, offering her his arm. "You see, Grandmother—yes, take my arm and let's walk back to the hall—I decided that what I was missing in my life was someone who would have married me if I'd had nothing."

"But Irene," Lady Louise said faintly. "Lady Zoe, or even that vapid Brittani—"

"Were terribly fond of my trappings, but they didn't particularly care for me. And as you know, I can be difficult."

"Don't be polite, Stephen," his grandmother said with a heavy sigh. "You can be an unmitigated ass when it suits you."

"Then aren't you happy I found an exceptionally beautiful, well-mannered, intelligent girl who was willing to take me on and love me in spite of my flaws?"

He watched his grandmother look around him and size Peaches up. She looked up at him, then.

"That lovely girl there?"

"That lovely girl there."

"You eloped?" she asked, sounding as if she most definitely needed something strengthening.

"We did," Stephen said cheerfully, "but I'm sure a wedding in a fortnight's time will put that all to rights in your mind, won't it?"

"A fortnight? Don't be ridiculous. I'll need a month to send out proper invitations. Six weeks would be more suitable." She shot him a warning look. "And you'll put this elopement behind you until then, sir, or you'll deal with me."

Stephen pursed his lips, then began to curse when he heard Peaches laugh. He looked at her, not quite understanding why she found the thought of casting him from her bed so amusing, then at his grandmother, who he was quite sure found the thought of Peaches casting him from her bed *extremely* amusing.

"Have you two been plotting behind my back?" he asked sourly.

His grandmother abandoned him and went to link arms with Peaches, who he had to admit smelled much better than he did.

"Forgive an old woman her prejudices," Lady Louise said bluntly. "He is my favorite grandson, you know, and I have many to choose from. But I'm the first to admit he has flaws, not the least of which are those rather fetching gray eyes of his."

"They are lovely," Peaches agreed.

"I've heard rumors that you went through a time where you didn't care for him much."

"I had my prejudices as well," Peaches admitted. "But your grandson is hard to resist."

Stephen found his grandmother looking around Peaches to catch his eye.

"A month."

"A fortnight," he insisted.

"Don't be daft," she said. "I'll never manage that." She considered, then pursed her lips. "I suppose you could have adjoining rooms until then. If you were discreet."

"Thank you, Grandmother," he said dryly.

"Of course Peaches will need to come stay with me whilst we see to her trousseau, leaving you here to see to your father's affairs. I think that will take at least a month."

Stephen promised himself that he would put his foot down very soon. But his grandmother was on her best behavior and Peaches was still holding his hand, so perhaps he would just herd his grandmother toward the cooking sherry and his wife upstairs and see if he couldn't have his way after all.

It had been, he conceded as the sun was setting many long hours later, an eternal day. He stood on the roof of the castle, leaning against the parapet as had been his habit for as long as he could remember, and looked out over the darkening sea. He had made up interesting tales for his grandmother and the servants about his recent activities, comforted his mother with promises of more interesting stories another day, then seen to the details of his father's funeral.

And he hadn't seen nearly as much of his wife as he would have liked.

He felt arms go around his waist, but he didn't jump. He merely turned, leaned his hip against the wall, and gathered his companion against him, wrapping his arms securely around her.

"I hate heights," Peaches said, her words muffled against his jacket.

"I won't let you fall."

"You haven't yet."

He smiled and held her tightly. "I won't in the yet to come, either."

She stood with him in silence for quite some time, turning her face so she could look out over the sea as well. She finally pulled back far enough to look up at him.

"How are you?" she asked seriously.

He sighed. "Grieved," he admitted, "though there is something about the timing of this that strikes me as being fated. I would never tell my mother that, but there it is."

"I think she feels it, too," Peaches said quietly. "She said she is very fond of the wee house at Etham."

The house at Etham was anything but wee, but it was in the south and the gardens were spectacular. Stephen sighed deeply.

"That doesn't surprise me," he said. "I'm not sure she's ever loved the north, or the sea." He looked down at her. "What do you love, my lady?"

"You," she said simply. "And the sea. And the walls of your keep that whisper with wind and history and ghosts that don't do anything but bow when I walk past them."

He laughed uneasily. "Do they, now. How fortuitous that they seem to know already who and what you are to me."

"I have the feeling that entry we made in the big book of de Piaget genealogy under Lord Robin's watchful eye has been looked up before." She smiled at him. "Not many Peaches in the past, I don't imagine. Maybe we should have used aliases."

He shook his head. "We'll let our children puzzle it out."

"And your relations, all of whom have been giving me knowing looks all afternoon," she said with a shiver. "Megan already asked me if we were staying in your room or if she should make up one for me just for appearances."

"And what did you tell her?"

"I told her that your grandmother said we could have adjoining rooms."

"We don't have any adjoining rooms at Artane."

"Well," she said looking up at him, "so you don't, which solved that problem fairly well."

He smiled dryly. "Did you tell Tess?"

"Yes. She said it wasn't nice to inflict payback that way, though she did remind me that I had been a witness at the local clerk's office when they were married, well, you know."

"We'll send her an invitation to our other, well, you know."

She laughed at him, then leaned up to kiss him quickly. "I'm going to leave you up here to brood for a bit."

He smiled seriously. "How did you know?"

"That you needed it?" she finished. She pulled out of his arms. "Robin told me that the lords of Artane, those who truly have it in their blood, need a fair amount of time alone on the roof." She smiled. "I told him I would make sure you had enough."

Stephen had to take a deep breath. "I love you."

"I know," she said simply. "Come find me later and I'll tell you what I think about you."

He laughed a little, because he thought that he would be cutting his roof time rather short over the subsequent few months if Peaches de Piaget was waiting for him somewhere below.

He watched her go, returned her wave as she walked through the guard tower doorway, then turned back to his contemplation of the sea. He supposed he would need to make an early start with Peaches in the morning to make London before David's two o'clock deadline, though he was slightly surprised to find out how little he cared what happened.

Because he already knew.

David would enjoy the flashing cameras of the paparazzi, the reporters breathlessly awaiting his announcement, his lawyers straining at their bits. And then he would open his safe-deposit box and draw out two envelopes. One would contain the IOU, which David had already handled and Stephen had forged whilst pretending to be Reginald in the past—rendering it quite useless. The other would contain, so David would think, the quit-claim deed to Artane.

Only it wouldn't quite contain what David expected it to.

Stephen turned back to his contemplation of the sea and smiled.

Chapter 29

Peaches leaned her head back against the headrest of the passenger seat of Stephen's Mercedes and closed her eyes. As usual, that only made her dizzy, so she turned and looked at her husband.

He was wearing a very lovely dark gray suit that almost matched his eyes, a discreet burgundy tie, and sunglasses. He was frowning slightly, but she couldn't blame him. London traffic was, as usual, terrible.

"Well?" she asked. "Are you relieved?"

He pushed his sunglasses up on his head and looked at her. "Must I be honest?"

"Yes, my lord Artane, you must be honest."

"Then I'll tell you that I am thoroughly, profoundly, bloody relieved," he said with a gusty sigh. He shot her a quick smile. "There was a moment or two when David was making a production of pulling out the quitclaim deed and the cameras were flashing in our faces that I wondered if we were on the brink of a humiliating slide into ignomy and destitution."

"Having David take another look at the IOU and realizing it had magically been changed from his getting Artane to his having to give up Kenneworth was a nice touch," she noted. "I'm not sure, though, that he appreciated all the thought that had gone into it."

"Or how quickly I'd made Lionel witness it," Stephen said dryly. "I think the poor lad might have questioned the finish of the game if he hadn't started puking his poor guts out at the right moment."

"I suppose that piece of cake I offered him might have had something to do with that," she said modestly.

He looked at her and his mouth fell open. "You didn't."

"My parents are herbalists," she said. "I think I can safely say they've dried and smoked just about every herb out there. But never lobelia. It's hard on the tummy."

He reached for her hand. "Remind me to thank you properly for the help. I didn't realize."

"I thought you had enough on your mind already and wouldn't refuse a bit of extra help." She let out a long, slow breath. "I have to admit I was pretty nervous there in the bank, but I wasn't about to miss the show." She studied him thoughtfully. "It's a good thing you have quick reflexes. David might have broken your nose otherwise."

"All thanks to Patrick MacLeod," he said cheerfully, "who I'm not sure *hasn't* broken my nose a time or two."

"Irene's not going to be happy with how she looks in the morning."

"That's what she deserves for standing behind me, muttering nasty things about my family," he said, "though I am sorry her nose will never be the same."

Peaches watched him kiss the back of her hand, then put her hand on his leg and cover it with his. He watched the road, but he did glance her way now and again.

"Are you relieved?" he asked.

She sighed lightly. "I'm happy it's over. I feel sorry for Raphaela, though. She didn't deserve any of this."

"I wouldn't worry about her," Stephen said with a faint smile. "She'll move to her family's villa in France and grow grapes for wine. She's already issued an invitation for us to come stay for a bit this summer."

"What will happen to Kenneworth House?" Peaches asked. "Will they have to sell it?"

"To the National Trust, no doubt. David's gambling was much more extensive than he admitted to anyone. I don't imagine they have the funds to keep the place up. As for what he'll do?" He shrugged. "Continue to fritter away his legacy until he has none left, I suppose. But I'm not sure any of his line has ever possessed much sense."

"Well, we know about that first lord Hubert," she said.

Stephen shivered. "I think I can safely put away any thoughts of trotting through any more gates in the grass to view anyone's ancestors. I'm not even sure I'm interested in getting to know any more of mine."

"Robin and Anne were lovely."

"Ha," he said with a snort. "You didn't have Robin of Artane running you into the mud in the dead of winter so he could have himself a bit of a think."

She patted his leg. "It was a good thing I'd prepared you the week before, wasn't it?"

He squeezed her hand. "Yes, darling, it was. And don't think I didn't appreciate it."

"Want to run this afternoon?"

"No," he said with a surprised laugh. "Do you?"

"I wouldn't mind," she said honestly.

"And then what? Supper? A film?"

"Chaucer in your library."

He shot her a brief look. "Are you humoring me?"

She only shook her head and smiled. "Loving you, rather."

He took a deep breath. "A run, Chaucer, then you can tell me all about the other."

"You forgot the green drink."

He blew his hair out of his eyes, then pulled his sunglasses back down and concentrated on the road.

But he was smiling.

And so was she.

She was still smiling not quite a month later when she stood with him in a little chapel inside the walls of a glorious medieval castle that stood on a bluff overlooking the sea and married him.

Again.

They were surrounded by family and friends and, she was

quite sure, several other souls she couldn't quite see. It was a
perfect day that had capped a perfect handful of weeks full of all
sorts of things she hadn't expected.

The first was how fond she would become of his grandmother. The woman was a prodigious shopper, and her taste was
flawless and her ability to wring concessions out of snooty cou-
turiers a wonder to behold. And when she wasn't spending Stephen's money or haranguing hapless shop owners, she was
relentlessly teaching Peaches the ropes of proper British society.
She did so in a way, though, that had left Peaches feeling as if it
had been her place all along, not just something she had fallen
into by chance.

Peaches had managed to sneak a few days in with Tess and
John, taking long walks with her sister as she waited for Stephen
to finish up class and drive south. They had discussed endlessly
the karmic ramifications of three sisters marrying three men
from the same family, but come to no useful conclusions except
that she and Tess were happy and they hoped Pippa was happy
as well.

She had also strolled arm in arm with Stephen's mother along
the shore with Artane watching over them like a dragon perched
on the bluff, ready to defend them at a moment's notice. She had
answered all of Helen's very pointed questions about everything
from how it was John de Piaget could look so much like Stephen
to just exactly where she and Stephen had gotten married the
first time.

Peaches had to admit Stephen's mother had a strong stomach.

The rest of the time, she'd simply been with Stephen himself,
pretending to read while he was working, puttering around in his
kitchen, discussing housekeeping at Artane with Humphreys,
and trying to decide what she was going to do with the rest of
her life. It took her almost a month to decide exactly what that
something was going to be, and her inspiration came from a
relatively unlikely source.

Anne of Artane.

Peaches had considered at length what Anne would have
done if she had been in the twenty-first century with everything
and anything she could have possibly wanted at her fingertips,
hers just for the asking.

And she knew, because Anne had pulled her aside for a simple but heartfelt discussion of the role Peaches would be taking on in another time. Anne had told her quite bluntly in an endearing mix of modern English and medieval French that if she had had everything she could only imagine Peaches would have, she would have lived her life the same way. She would have loved her husband, loved her children, and loved those who had come within her scope of influence.

Because in the end, nothing else mattered.

Peaches considered that during her wedding day, as she danced with her husband—twice-wed now—and supped with her family, and relished the company of those who had come to wish them well.

She thought about it as she rested in her husband's arms.

And when she woke to find him gone, she looked over on his pillow to find a note there.

Meet me on the roof—SdP

She put on warm clothes and climbed the stairs of her fairy-tale castle, and walked out onto the roof and into the arms of her handsome prince. And after he'd spent a sufficient amount of time warming her up, she smiled into his lovely eyes.

"Happy, my lord?" she asked.

"Very, my lady," he said.

She paused, then considered. "Aren't you freezing?"

"I'm freezing my arse off up here," he said with an exasperated laugh. "I thought you would rescue me half an hour ago."

"Is that my job," she asked. "To rescue you?"

He pulled her closer, made serious inroads into expressions of affection that apparently required no words, then lifted his head and looked down at her.

"We'll take turns."

"Well, we have so far."

He put his arm around her shoulders. "Let's go discuss that a bit more, shall we?"

She looked up at him seriously. "Have you had enough time on the roof today, Stephen?"

He smiled. "Yes, and I'll let you know if I need more. But for the moment, I would rather retreat to a comfortable spot in front of a hot fire with you."

"In your room."

"Yes, Peaches my love, in my room," he said quietly. He paused. "Foolish as it might seem not to take the master's bedroom, this seems fitting somehow, don't you think?"

She thought many things, not the least of which was that Robin of Artane would thoroughly approve of the man standing in front of her. He was still trying to juggle a graceful exit from his university responsibilities while taking on the entire burden of managing Artane, but everywhere he went, he left people feeling as though they mattered to him. She knew this, because she had gone with him to meet his tenants, watch his students, and bring smelling salts to Dr. Trotter-Smythe when he'd seen her and Tess walking out of Stephen's office together. Without fail, those who had been the beneficiaries of his interest and time had pulled her aside to tell her how grateful they were to him. Even Irene Preston had written him a very brief note thanking him for not pressing charges against her brother for defamation of character.

She had written Irene a note, thanking her for all her kindnesses at David's house party those many weeks earlier. She supposed Irene would think it yet another fist to the nose, but Peaches had meant it sincerely. If she hadn't been trapped in that terrible hovel of a room at Irene's direction, driven out into the night by Irene's words . . . well, she didn't like to think about where she would be at the moment.

"What are you thinking about?" Stephen asked, his voice rumbling in his chest. "How lovely that hot fire is I left you in our bedroom?"

"Actually," she said, resting her head against his shoulder and smiling, "I was thinking about that Kenneworth house party."

"Heaven forbid," he said with an uncomfortable laugh. "You aren't."

She lifted her head and looked at him. "I was. If it hadn't been for Irene getting you there and making my life miserable, I might still be waiting to fall in love with you."

"I'll tell you a secret," he admitted. "I had no intentions of going—though in my defense I had no idea you would be there—until a trio of very vocal shades appeared in my office and told me I should reconsider."

"Did they?"

He pursed his lips. "Very well, they promised they would haunt me endlessly if I didn't march manfully into the fray. But once I found you at Kenneworth House, I found myself thinking about them with quite a bit more fondness."

"And then you rescued me."

"At least once," he agreed. He bent his head and kissed her softly. "And I would do it again a thousand times."

"Even to medieval England with all its trappings?"

"All its trappings," he said seriously. "All of it, my love, all for you, as many times as required, and I would never count the cost."

"But you would rather stay here."

He laughed a little. "Darling, we have a hot fire in the bedroom and an Aga in the kitchen. Yes, I would rather stay here. Wouldn't you?"

She looked up at him, lord of the keep under her feet, keeper of her heart, a man who left her breathless every time he kissed her, every time he touched her, every time he looked at her, a man who loved her not in spite of who she was but because of it . . .

"Yes," she said, pulling out of his arms, "I would rather stay here. But not on the roof any longer tonight, aye?"

He laughed and turned her toward the guard tower.

Chapter 30

Stephen de Piaget, Earl of Artane, the former Viscount Haulton, and still-current Baron Etham, stood on the edge of a party in full swing and found himself quite grateful that his hall hadn't needed the repairs he'd watched Zachary Smith make to Wyckham.

The place was stunning now, what with its second-floor gallery, spectacular Norman arch stretching from one side of the great hall to the other, and authentic-looking tapestries that stretched from floor to ceiling—

He paused and squinted. The tapestries looked like they were moving, but that could have been his imagination. He was, he would be the first to admit, slightly sleep deprived.

That's what happened when one had a small son who found life too exciting to spend much time asleep.

He looked for his wife and son who were off socializing with souls of various vintages. Mary de Piaget Smith, Countess of Wyckham, had spent the past half hour dancing with her husband, but had now reclaimed her nine-month-old daughter and was talking to one Peaches Alexander de Piaget, Countess of

Artane, who held on to her four-month-old son, the Viscount Haulton and future Earl of Artane.

It was altogether humbling to think that for all he knew, Robin of Artane was standing in the shadows somewhere, watching his daughter talk to the woman who was responsible for providing yet another lad to keep Artane's legacy close to his heart.

The tapestry moved. Stephen wasn't altogether certain he hadn't seen the shadow of two heads peeking out from behind it.

"I have a feeling about something."

Stephen looked next to him to find Zachary Smith standing there, frowning thoughtfully at the tapestry in question.

"Do you?" he mused. "What sort of feeling?"

"A disquietish, paranormally sort of feeling."

"I believe I'm experiencing that, as well."

Zachary looked at him. "Didn't you tell me that Nicholas's twins—those would be your nephews by marriage, you know—had just happened to arrive at a particular inn at precisely the right moment to feed you and Peaches in the past?"

Stephen nodded slowly. "They did."

"And didn't you find it strange that they left you a bag of gold and something else to interest you?"

"A map," Stephen said dryly, "which I told you about quite some time ago."

"Interesting that they knew *when* to find you, don't you think?"

"Coincidental," Stephen blustered.

The look Zachary shot him left Stephen pursing his lips.

"Very well, *too* coincidental for comfort. What are you suggesting?"

"That teenagers are trouble."

"Especially twins."

"Your wife could attest to that, I'm sure. I try not to imagine what Kendrick faces with those three boys of his." Zachary shuddered. "Sometimes it keeps me up at night."

Stephen thought about pointing out that the child who should be worrying Zachary was his own daughter given the character of her extremely independent and fearless mother, but he refrained.

And then he exchanged a brief look with the Earl of Wyckham before they both strode across the dance floor.

Two blond lads bolted for the kitchens.

It took several minutes to corner them, partly because there were two of them and partly because they seemed to have a more than passing familiarity with Wyckham's inner workings. Stephen looked around the kitchen to find every exit blocked by men in the family including Zachary, Kendrick, Gideon, and Zachary's father whose eyes were absolutely enormous. Stephen lifted his arm as Peaches ducked under, holding young Robin. She looked at the boys who were standing back-to-back in the middle of the kitchen, swords in their hands.

"Interesting."

One of the lads looked at Stephen, his mouth fell open, then his sword fell from his fingers.

"'Tis Uncle Robin. And Auntie Persephone—"

"Don't be an idiot," the other lad said, elbowing him sharply in the back. "It isn't, and that isn't Aunt Pippa, though she looks a bloody sight like her, doesn't she? I daresay that's Kendrick over there." He paused. "He's looking passing old, don't you think?"

"I do," said the other lad, blanching.

His brother backed up a bit harder against him. "I think we did it."

Kendrick rolled his eyes and strode forward. "Samuel and Theophilus de Piaget, you are a pair of silly arses."

The lads threw their arms around Kendrick and hugged him. Stephen leaned against the door and put his arm around Peaches as he listened to the boys babble about their trip and wonder when it was they could get pizza and crisps.

Stephen soon found himself being introduced to and carrying on a fairly decent conversation with the two lads who would save his and Peaches's stomachs, if not their lives, quite some time earlier. Or later, in their future, which was his past. It depended, he supposed, on one's perspective.

"Your English is very good," he remarked at one point.

"We're bilingual," Theophilus said proudly. "Aren't we, Sam?"

"We are," Samuel said, puffing out his chest. "And a bloody dodgy business it was learning all we have." He looked at Kendrick. "Where's the fridge?"

Kendrick only pointed to Zachary. "Ask Mary's husband. Surely you remember him, lads."

Theophilus and Samuel gulped as one, then inched their way over to Zachary to offer all sorts of deferential, positive chitchat no doubt intended to leave him offering to put them up indefinitely. Stephen exchanged a look with Zachary, then left the kitchen. Things would go how they went, he would invite the boys to Artane and make sure they knew when they were supposed to be buying him lunch in a few years, then he would happily stand with Zachary and give them both the boot back to where they belonged.

It was for damned sure he wasn't going to let them near his car keys.

He paused on the way to the great hall and looked at his wife, that lovely, loving woman who had thrown herself into her role as Countess of Artane with an energy and enthusiasm that left him slightly exhausted, actually. Or that could have been the runs along the beach she'd dragged him on until she'd realized right after their second wedding that she was pregnant.

Which he suspected had happened right after their first wedding.

If anyone thought it unusual that she had given birth to a full-term baby eight months after their pictures had been in the papers, they'd been too discreet to say anything to her face and too intimidated to mention it to him.

They would tell their son the truth, someday. After all, Stephen couldn't guarantee that he wouldn't find out there was more to Artane than just thick walls that kept the weather and the world at bay.

But until that time, he would be the keeper of its secrets, the defender of its inhabitants, and the man who passed every day of his life profoundly grateful for the woman who had been willing to plot her path alongside his.

He had truly been blessed far beyond what he deserved.

family lineage in the books of
LYNN KURLAND

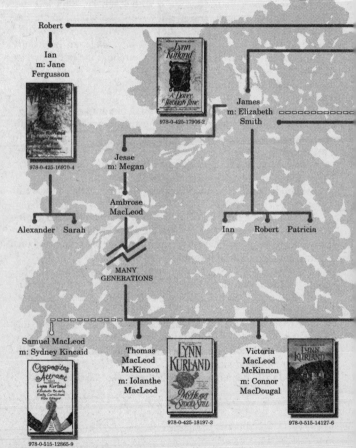

Robert

Ian
m: Jane
Fergusson

978-0-425-16970-4

James
m: Elizabeth
Smith

978-9-425-17906-2

Jesse
m: Megan

Ambrose
MacLeod

Alexander   Sarah

Ian   Robert   Patricia

MANY
GENERATIONS

Samuel MacLeod
m: Sydney Kincaid

978-0-515-12865-9

Thomas
MacLeod
McKinnon
m: Iolanthe
MacLeod

978-0-425-18197-3

Victoria
MacLeod
McKinnon
m: Connor
MacDougal

978-0-515-14127-6

MACLEOD

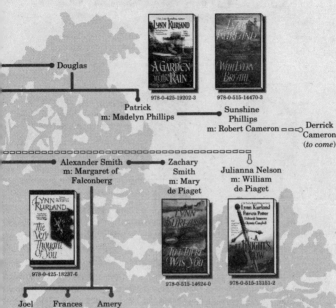

Douglas

Patrick
m: Madelyn Phillips

Sunshine
Phillips
m: Robert Cameron --- Derrick
Cameron
(to come)

978-0-425-19202-3

978-0-515-14470-3

Alexander Smith
m: Margaret of
Falconberg

Zachary
Smith
m: Mary
de Piaget

Julianna Nelson
m: William
de Piaget

978-0-425-18237-6

978-0-515-14624-0

978-0-515-13151-2

Joel   Frances   Amery

Megan MacLeod
McKinnon
m: Gideon de Piaget

978-0-515-12174-2

Jennifer MacLeod
McKinnon
m: Nicholas
de Piaget

978-0-515-14296-9

PA-4860

LYNN KURLAND

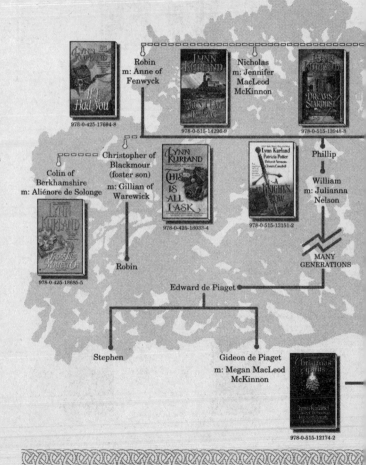

Robin
m: Anne of Fenwyck

If I Had You
978-0-425-17694-8

Nicholas
m: Jennifer MacLeod McKinnon

978-0-515-14296-9

Dreams of Stardust
978-0-515-13948-8

Phillip

Christopher of Blackmour (foster son)
m: Gillian of Warewick

Colin of Berkhamshire
m: Aliénore de Solonge

978-0-425-18685-5

This Is All I Ask
978-0-425-18033-4

A Knight's Vow
Patricia Potter, Deborah Simmons, Glynnis Campbell
978-0-515-13151-2

William
m: Julianna Nelson

MANY GENERATIONS

Robin

Edward de Piaget

Stephen

Gideon de Piaget
m: Megan MacLeod McKinnon

Christmas Spirits
978-0-515-12174-2

DE PIAGET

Rhys de Piaget
m: Gwennelyn
of Segrave

Another Chance to Dream — 978-0-425-16514-0
The More I See You — *(This Mans Moment)* 978-0-515-14951-7
One Enchanted Evening — 978-0-515-14791-9
978-0-515-15065-0

Amanda
m: Jake
Kilchurn

Christmas C·A·T — 978-0-425-15542-4

Miles
m: Abigail
Garrett

Isabelle

John
m: Tess
Alexander

Montgomery
m: Pippa
Alexander

Peaches
Alexander
m: Stephen
de Piaget

Kendrick
m: Genevieve
Buchanan

Stardust of Yesterday — 978-0-425-18238-3

Mary
m: Zachary
Smith

Till There Was You — 978-0-515-14624-0

Jason
m: Lianna
of Grasleigh

Tapestry — 978-0-515-13362-2

The More I See You — 978-0-425-17107-3

Richard of
Burwyck-
on-the-Sea
(foster son)
m: Jessica
Blakely

Robin   Phillip   Jason   Richard   Christopher   Adelaide Anne

Thomas
MacLeod
McKinnon
m: Iolanthe
MacLeod

My Heart Stood Still — 978-0-425-18197-3

Victoria
MacLeod
McKinnon
m: Connor
MacDougal

978-0-515-14127-6

PA-7468

There's no time like the present . . .
if you're running from the past.

From *New York Times* bestselling author
LYNN KURLAND

ONE MAGIC MOMENT

Medieval studies scholar Tess Alexander is thrilled for the chance to live in a medieval castle. But then a trip to the village brings her face-to-face with the owner of the local garage, who looks a great deal like the man who married her sister . . . eight hundred years in the past. She's determined to remain objective about magic and destiny, yet she can't help but wonder about that mysterious, sword-wielding mechanic who tugs at her heart . . .

"[Kurland] consistently delivers the kind
of stories readers dream about."
—*The Oakland Press*

"Kurland is a skilled enchantress."
—*Night Owl Romance*

penguin.com

M1022T1211

From *New York Times* bestselling author
LYNN KURLAND

ONE ENCHANTED EVENING

PAST...

Montgomery de Piaget has the task of rebuilding the most dilapidated castle in all of England. A bit of magic might aid him—if only he still believed in that sort of thing.

PRESENT...

When Pippa Alexander is invited to England to provide costumes for an upscale party, she jumps at the chance to showcase her own line of fairy-tale-inspired designs. Not that she believes in fairy tales, or magic that whispers along the hallways of an honest-to-goodness medieval castle . . .

AND FUTURE...

But the castle is full of more than cobwebs, and danger lurks in unexpected places. And only time will tell if Montgomery and Pippa can overcome these obstacles to find their own happily every after . . .

Praise for Lynn Kurland

"Clearly one of romance's finest writers."
—*The Oakland Press*

penguin.com

M800T1110